"[The] rousing fourth adventure for kick-ass werecoyote auto mechanic Mercedes Thompson." —*Publishers Weekly*

"Mercy is not just another cookie-cutter tough-chick urban fantasy heroine; she's got a lot of style and substance and an intriguing backstory. Series fans will appreciate the resolution of some ongoing plotlines, and the romantic tension is strong." —*Library Journal*

"[Mercy is] one of the best of the kick-ass heroine crop." —*Locus*

IRON KISSED

"An increasingly excellent series . . . *Iron Kissed* has all the elements I've come to expect in a Patricia Briggs novel: sharp, perceptive characterization, nonstop action, and a levelheaded attention to detail and location. I love these books." —Charlaine Harris, #1 *New York Times* bestselling author

BLOOD BOUND

"Once again, Briggs has written a full-bore action adventure with heart . . . Be prepared to read [it] in one sitting, because once you get going, there is no good place to stop until tomorrow." —*SFRevu*

"Plenty of action and intriguing characters keep this fun. In the increasingly crowded field of kick-ass supernatural heroines, Mercy stands out as one of the best." —*Locus*

MOON CALLED

"An excellent read with plenty of twists and turns. Her strong and complex characters kept me entertained from its deceptively innocent beginning to its can't-put-it-down end. Thoroughly satisfying, it left me wanting more."

—Kim Harrison, *New York Times* bestselling author

"Patricia Briggs always enchants her readers. With *Moon Called* she weaves her magic on every page to take us into a new and dazzling world of werewolves, shapeshifters, witches, and vampires. Expect to be spellbound."

—Lynn Viehl, *New York Times* bestselling author

Praise for the other novels of Patricia Briggs

DRAGON BLOOD

"It goes without saying, I suppose, that I'm looking forward to seeing what else Patricia Briggs does. If *Dragon Blood* is any indication, then she is an inventive, engaging writer whose talent for combining magic of all kinds—from spells to love— with fantastic characters should certainly win her a huge following and a place on many bookshelves."   —*SF Site*

DRAGON BONES

"I enjoyed *Dragon Bones* . . . This is an enjoyable, well-written book, with enough plot twists and turns to keep the reader's attention. This book is sure to appeal to lovers of fantasy."

—*The Green Man Review*

"[Briggs] possesses the all-too-rare ability to make you fall hopelessly in love with her characters . . . It's good stuff all the way . . . You find yourself carried away by the charm of the story and the way Briggs tells it."   —*Crescent Blues*

THE HOB'S BARGAIN

"This is a 'Beauty and the Beast' story but unlike any I've ever read. Ms. Briggs blends adventure, romance, and innovative fantasy with a deft hand. [I] highly recommend this one to all my readers."   —S. L. Viehl, national bestselling author

"[A] fun fantasy romance . . . There's plenty of action, with battles against raiders and magical creatures, a bard who isn't what he appears, and an evil mage—but there's also plenty of humor and some sweet moments of mischief and romance."   —*Locus*

"Briggs has a good ear for dialogue and pace, and a marked talent for drawing complex characterizations . . . If you're looking to while away some time with a good story full of magic and wonder, you might find it worthwhile to accept *The Hob's Bargain*."   —Rambles.net

"It is easy to like Patricia Briggs's novels. Her books are perfect for a Friday evening or a late Saturday afternoon when you don't want to have to work to enjoy your reading. Her books are clever, engaging, fast-moving, and with plots that manage to be thought-provoking without being heavy-handed. A warning, however—make sure you don't start the dinner cooking or the lawn watering before you curl up with one of her books, because you'll end up with a burnt dinner and a soggy lawn and an enjoyable few hours lost in another world."
                    —*Romantic Science Fiction & Fantasy*

WHEN DEMONS WALK

"An interesting cross between a murder mystery, romance, and fantasy . . . There are enough twists and turns in the plot to keep most readers' interest."   —*VOYA*

"Patricia Briggs proves herself a rare talent as she devises a clever mystery with appealing characters in a fantasy setting . . . top-notch reading fare."   —*Romantic Times*

WOLFSBANE

PATRICIA BRIGGS

ACE BOOKS, NEW YORK

THE BERKLEY PUBLISHING GROUP
Published by the Penguin Group
Penguin Group (USA) Inc.
375 Hudson Street, New York, New York 10014, USA
Penguin Group (Canada), 90 Eglinton Avenue East, Suite 700, Toronto, Ontario M4P 2Y3, Canada
(a division of Pearson Penguin Canada Inc.)
Penguin Books Ltd., 80 Strand, London WC2R 0RL, England
Penguin Group Ireland, 25 St. Stephen's Green, Dublin 2, Ireland (a division of Penguin Books Ltd.)
Penguin Group (Australia), 250 Camberwell Road, Camberwell, Victoria 3124, Australia
(a division of Pearson Australia Group Pty. Ltd.)
Penguin Books India Pvt. Ltd., 11 Community Centre, Panchsheel Park, New Delhi—110 017, India
Penguin Group (NZ), 67 Apollo Drive, Rosedale, North Shore 0632, New Zealand
(a division of Pearson New Zealand Ltd.)
Penguin Books (South Africa) (Pty.) Ltd., 24 Sturdee Avenue, Rosebank, Johannesburg 2196,
South Africa

Penguin Books Ltd., Registered Offices: 80 Strand, London WC2R 0RL, England

This is a work of fiction. Names, characters, places, and incidents either are the product of the author's imagination or are used fictitiously, and any resemblance to actual persons, living or dead, business establishments, events, or locales is entirely coincidental. The publisher does not have any control over and does not assume any responsibility for author or third-party websites or their content.

WOLFSBANE

An Ace Book / published by arrangement with Hurog, Inc.

PRINTING HISTORY
Ace mass-market edition / November 2010

Copyright © 2010 by Hurog, Inc.
Map by Michael Enzweiler.
Cover art by Mélanie Delon.
Cover design by Annette Fiore DeFex.
Interior text design by Laura K. Corless.

ISBN: 978-0-441-01954-0

ACE
Ace Books are published by The Berkley Publishing Group,
a division of Penguin Group (USA) Inc.,
375 Hudson Street, New York, New York 10014.
ACE and the "A" design are trademarks of Penguin Group (USA) Inc.

PRINTED IN THE UNITED STATES OF AMERICA

10 9 8 7 6 5 4 3 2 1

AUTHOR'S NOTE

Which, not being a part of the story, may be skipped

I wrote *Wolfsbane* in between *When Demons Walk* and *The Hob's Bargain*.

Careerwise, it was a dumb thing to do, and I knew it. *Masques* had been out of print for a couple of years by that point, and I was aware that its sales figures were abysmal and no one in his right mind would reprint it. My editor, Laura Anne Gilman, had left Ace for Roc (which at the time was owned by a different publishing company). After she left, Ace politely declined publishing *When Demons Walk*, for several very good reasons. First, the editor who had liked my work was gone. Second, my sales record was not good. *Masques* had failed. *Steal the Dragon* had done all right, but it'd had a terrific cover by Royo. I was pretty sure that, at least for the time being, my career as a writer was over. So I wrote the book I wanted to write.

I had lived with Wolf in my head since I was in fifth or sixth grade . . . maybe since I first read *The Black Stallion* by Walter Farley and recognized the pull of the powerful, dangerous creature who loves only one person. By the time

I'd written three books, I knew that I had a lot to learn—and that I had learned a lot about writing since I wrote *Masques*. I still consider *The Hob's Bargain* my first professional work. It was the first book I wrote that turned out exactly as I'd envisioned it, the first one that I wrote from craft rather than instinct. I wanted to take those new skills and turn my hand to giving Wolf and Aralorn a story more worthy of them.

Wolfsbane was the result. Eventually, somewhat to our mutual surprise, Ace bought *When Demons Walk*, *The Hob's Bargain*, and the first book that really sold well for us, *Dragon Bones*. *Wolfsbane* stayed on my shelves, and every once in a while I thought a little wistfully about it. I admit, believing that this day of publication would never come, I borrowed things from *Wolfsbane* for other stories—you might see them. You might even pick up on a few that I haven't noticed.

So here, for your enjoyment, is a book from early in my career that has never seen the light of day—and without you, dear readers, would still be moldering on a floppy disk somewhere. I hope you have as much fun with it as I have.

BEST WISHES,
PATRICIA BRIGGS
SOMEWHERE IN THE DESERT OF EASTERN WASHINGTON

ONE

A winterwill cried out twice.

There was nothing untoward about that. The winterwill—a smallish, gray-gold lark—was one of the few birds that did not migrate south in the winter.

Aralorn didn't shift her gaze from the snow-laden trail before her, but she watched her mount's ears flicker as he broke through a drift of snow.

Winterwills were both common and loud . . . but it had called out just at the moment when she took the left-hand fork in the path she followed. The snow thinned for a bit, so she nudged Sheen off the trail on the uphill side. Sure enough, a winterwill called out three times and twice more when she returned to the trail again. Sheen snorted and shook his head, jangling his bit.

"Plague it," muttered Aralorn.

The path broke through the trees and leveled a little as the trees cleared away on either side. She shifted her weight, and her horses stopped. On a lead line, the roan, her secondary mount, stood docilely, but Sheen threw up his head and pitched his ears forward.

"Good lords of the forest," called Aralorn, "I have urgent business to attend. I beg leave to pay toll that I might pass unmolested through here."

She could almost feel the chagrin that descended upon the brigands still under the cover of the trees around her. At long last, a man stepped out. His clothing was neatly patched, and Aralorn was reminded in some indefinable way of the carefully mended cottage where she'd purchased her cheese not a half-hour ride from here. The hood of his undyed cloak was pulled up, and his face was further disguised by a winter scarf wound about his chin and nose.

"You don't have the appearance of a Trader," commented the man gruffly. "How is it you presume to take advantage of their pact with us?"

Before she'd seen the man, she'd had a story ready. Aralorn always had a story ready. But the man's appearance changed her plans.

Though his clothes were worn, his boots were good-quality royal issue, and there was confidence in the manner in which he rested his hand on his short sword. He'd been an army man at some time. If he'd been in the Rethian army, he'd know her father. Truth would have a better chance with him than any falsehood.

"I have several close friends among the Traders," she said. "But as you say, there is no treaty between you and me; you have no reason to grant me passage."

"The treaty's existence is a closely guarded secret," he said. "One that many would kill to protect."

She smiled at him gently, ignoring his threat. "I've passed for Trader before, and I could have this time as well. But when I saw you for an army man, I thought the truth would work as well—I only lie when I have to."

She surprised a laugh out of him though his hand didn't

move from his sword hilt. "All right then, Mistress, tell me this *truth* of yours."

"I am Aralorn, mercenary of Sianim. My father is dead," she said. Her voice wobbled unexpectedly—disconcerting her momentarily. She wasn't used to its doing anything she hadn't intended. "The Lyon of Lambshold. If you delay me more than a few hours, I will miss his funeral."

"I haven't heard any such news. I know the Lyon," stated the bandit with suspicion. "You don't look like him."

Aralorn rolled her eyes. "I *know* that. I am his eldest daughter by a peasant woman." At the growing tension in her voice, Sheen began fretting.

His attention drawn to the horse, the bandit leader stiffened and drew in his breath, holding up a hand to silence her. He walked slowly around him, then nodded abruptly. "I believe you. Your stallion could be the double of the one cut down under the Lyon at the battle of Valner Pass."

"His sire died at Valner Pass," agreed Aralorn, "fourteen years ago."

The bandit produced a faded strip of green ribbon and caught Sheen's bit, tying the thin cloth to the shank of the curb. "This will get you past my men. Don't remove it until you come to the Wayfarer's Inn—do you know it?"

Aralorn nodded, started to turn her horses, and then stopped. "Tell your wife she makes excellent cheese—and take my advice: Don't let her patch your thieving clothes with the same cloth as her apron. I might not be the only one to notice it."

Startled, the bandit looked at the yellow-and-green weave that covered his right knee.

Softly, Aralorn continued. "It is a hard thing for a woman alone to raise children to adulthood."

She could tell that he was reconsidering his decision not to kill her, something he wouldn't have done if she'd kept her mouth closed; but she could clearly remember the walnut brown eyes of the toddler who held on to his mother's brightly colored apron. He wouldn't fare well in the world without a father to protect him from harm, and Aralorn had a weakness for children.

"You are a smart man, sir," she said. "If I had wanted to have you caught, it would have made more sense for me to go to Lord Larmouth, whose province this is, and tell him what I saw—than for me to warn you."

Slowly, his hand moved away from the small sword, but Aralorn could hear a nearby creaking that told her that someone held a nocked bow. "I will tell her."

She nudged Sheen with her knees and left the bandit behind.

———

She crossed the first mountain pass late that night, and the second and last pass before Lambshold the following afternoon.

The snow was heavier as she traveled northward. Aralorn switched horses often, but Sheen still took the brunt of the work since he was better suited for breaking through the crusted, knee-deep drifts. Gradually, as new light dawned over the edge of the pass, the mountain trail began to move downward, and the snow lessened. Aralorn swayed wearily in the saddle. It was less than a two-hour ride to Lambshold, but she and the horses were going to need rest before then.

The road passed by another small village with an inn. Aralorn dismounted and led her exhausted horses to the stableyard.

If the hostler was surprised at the arrival of a guest in the morning, he gave no sign of it. Nor did he argue when Aralorn gave him the lead to the roan and began the task of grooming Sheen on her own. The warhorse was not so fierce that a stableboy could not have groomed him, but it was her habit to perform the task herself when she was troubled. Before she stored her tack, she untied the scrap of ribbon from Sheen's bit. She left the horses dozing comfortably and entered the inn through the stable door.

The innkeeper, whom she found in the kitchen, was a different man from the one she remembered, but the room he led her to was familiar and clean. She closed the door behind him, stripped off her boots and breeches, then climbed between the sweet-smelling sheets. Too tired, too numb, to dread sleeping as she'd learned to do in the past few weeks, she let oblivion take her.

The dream, when it came, started gently. Aralorn found herself wandering through a corridor in the ae'Magi's castle. It looked much the same as the last time she had seen it, the night the ae'Magi died.

———————

The forbidding stairway loomed out of the darkness. Aralorn set her hand to the wall and took the downward steps, though it was so dark that she could barely see where to put her feet. Dread coated the back of her throat like sour honey, and she knew that something terrible awaited her. She took another step down and found herself unexpectedly in a small stone room that smelled of offal and ammonia.

A woman lay on a wooden table, her face frozen in death. Despite the pallor that clung to her skin and the fine lines of suffering, she was beautiful; her fiery hair seemed out of place in the presence of death. Arcanely etched iron manacles, thicker than the pale wrists they enclosed, had left scars testifying to the years they'd remained in place.

At the foot of the table stood a raven-haired boy regarding the dead woman. He paid no attention to Aralorn or anything else. His face still had that unformed look of childhood. His yellow eyes were oddly remote as he looked at the body, ancient eyes that revealed his identity to Aralorn.

Wolf, thought Aralorn. *This was her Wolf as a child.*

"She was my mother?" the boy who would be Wolf said at last.

His voice was unexpected, soft rather than the hoarse rasp that she associated with Wolf.

"Yes."

Aralorn looked for the owner of the second voice, but she couldn't see him. Only his words echoed in her ears, without inflection or tone. It could have been anyone who spoke. "I thought you might like to see her before I disposed of her."

The boy shrugged. "I cannot imagine why you thought that. May I return to my studies now, Father?"

The vision faded, and Aralorn found herself taking another step down.

"Even as a child he was cold. Impersonal. Unnatural. Evil," whispered something out of the darkness of the stairwell.

Aralorn shook her head, denying the words. She knew better than anyone the emotions Wolf could conceal equally well behind a blank face or the silver mask he usually wore. If anything, he was more emotional than most people. She opened her mouth to argue, when a scream distracted her. She stepped down, toward the sound, into blackness that swallowed her.

She came to herself naked and cold; her breath rose above her in a puff of mist. She tried to move to conserve her warmth, but iron chains bound her where she was. Cool metal touched her throat, and Wolf pressed the blade down until her flesh parted.

He smiled sweetly as the knife cut slowly deeper. "Hush now, this won't hurt."

She screamed, and his smile widened incongruously, catching her attention.

It wasn't Wolf's smile. She knew his smile: It was as rare as green diamonds, not practiced as this was. Fiercely, she denied what she saw.

*Under her hot stare, her tormentor's yellow eyes dark-
ened to blue. When he spoke a second time, it was in the
ae'Magi's dulcet tones. "Come, my son, it is time for you
to learn more."*

"No."

*Something shifted painfully in Aralorn's head with rude
suddenness and jerked her from the table to somewhere
behind the ae'Magi, whose knife pressed against the neck
of a pale woman who was too frightened even to moan.*

Truth, thought Aralorn, feeling the rightness in this dream.

*The boy stood apart from his father, no longer so young
as her earlier vision of him. Already, his face had begun to
show signs of matching the Archmage's, feature for feature—
except for his eyes.*

*"Come," repeated the ae'Magi. "The death you deal
her will be much easier than the one I will give her. It will
also be easier for you, Cain, if you do as I ask."*

*"No." The boy who had been Cain before he was her
Wolf spoke softly, without defiance or deference.*

*The ae'Magi smiled and walked to his son, caress-
ing his face with the hand that still held the bloody knife.
Some part of Aralorn tensed as she saw the Archmage's
caressing hand. Bits and pieces of things Wolf had told
her coalesced with the sexuality of the ae'Magi's gesture.*

*"As you will," said the sorcerer softly. "I, at least, will
enjoy it more."*

*Rage suffused her with hatred of a man she knew to
be dead. She stepped forward, as if she could alter events
long past, and the scene changed again.*

*The boy stood on the tower parapet; a violent storm
raged overhead. He was older now, with a man's height,
though his shoulders were still narrow with youth. Cold
rain poured down, and Wolf shivered.*

"It's power, Cain. Don't you want it?"

Slowly, the boy lifted his arms to embrace the storm.

But that taint of wrongness had returned, and Aralorn

called upon her magic, girded in the truth of natural order, to pull it right. She had no more magic than the average hedgewitch, but it seemed to be enough for the job. Once more, the scene shifted subtly, as if a farseeing glass were twisted into focus.

"It's power, Cain. Don't you want it?"

"It comes too fast, Father. I can't control it." Wolf spoke the words without the inflection that would have added urgency to them.

"I will control the magic." When Wolf appeared unmoved, the ae'Magi's voice softened to an ugly whisper. "I can assure you, you won't like the alternative."

Even in the storm-darkened night, Aralorn could see Wolf's face blanch, though his expression never altered. "Very well, then." There was something quiet and purposeful in his voice that Aralorn wondered at. Something that only someone who knew him well would have heard.

Wolf bent his head, and Aralorn was aware of the currents of magic he drew. The Archmage closed his hands on his son's shoulders; Wolf flinched slightly at the touch, then resumed passing his power on to his father. Lightning flashed, and the magic he held doubled, then trebled, in an instant. Slowly, Wolf lifted his arms, and lightning flashed a second time, hitting him squarely in the chest.

He called it to him on purpose, thought Aralorn, stunned. If he had been wholly human, he would have died there, and his father with him. For a green mage, whose blood comes from an older race, lightning contains magic rather than death—but he would have had no way of knowing that. He didn't know what his mother had been, not then.

For an instant, the two stood utterly still, except for the soundless, formless force Wolf had assembled; then a stone exploded into rubble, followed by another and another. The broken bits of granite began to glow with the heat of wild magic released without control. Aralorn couldn't tell if Wolf was trying to control the magic at all, though the ae'Magi had stepped back and was gesturing wildly in an attempt to stem the tide. Shadow was banished by the heat of the flames. Aralorn saw Wolf smile . . .

"No!" cried the ae'Magi, as molten rock splattered across Wolf's face, from a stone that burst in front of him. Wolf screamed, a sound lost in the crack of shattering stone.

The ae'Magi cast a spell, drawing on the very magic that wreaked such havoc.

A warding, thought Aralorn, as a rock fell from a parapet and bounced off an invisible barrier that surrounded the ae'Magi as he knelt over his unconscious son.

"I will not lose the power. You shall not escape me today."

The scene faded, and Aralorn found herself back in the corridor, but she was not alone.

The ae'Magi stepped to her, frowning. "How did you . . ." His voice trailed off, and his face twisted in a spasm of an emotion so strong she wasn't able to tell what it was. "You love him?"

Though his voice wasn't loud, it cracked and twisted until it was no longer the ae'Magi's voice. It was familiar, though; Aralorn struggled to remember to whom it belonged. "Who are you?" she asked.

The figure of the ae'Magi melted away, as did the corridor, fading into an ancient darkness that began to reach for her. She screamed and . . .

———

Awake, Aralorn listened to the muffled sounds of the inn. Hearing no urgent footsteps, she decided that she must not have screamed out loud. This was not the kind of place where such a sound would have been dismissed. She sat up to shake off the effects of the nightmare, but the terror of the eerie, hungry emptiness lingered. She might as well get up.

She'd begun having nightmares when Wolf disappeared

a few weeks ago. Nightmares weren't an unexpected part of being a mercenary, but these had been relentless. Dreams of being trapped in the ae'Magi's dungeon, unable to escape the pain or the voice that asked over and over again, "Where is Cain? Where is my son?" But this dream had been different . . . it had been more than a dream.

She pulled on her clothes. Her acceptance of what she had seen had been born of the peculiar acceptance that was the gift of a dreamer. Awake now, she wondered.

It had felt like truth. If the ae'Magi were still alive, she would have cheerfully attributed it to an attack by him—a little nasty designed to make her doubt Wolf and make his life a little more miserable. An attack that had failed only because she had a little magic of her own to call upon.

But the ae'Magi was dead, and she could think of no one else who would know the intimate details of Wolf's childhood—things that even she had not known for certain.

It was a dream, she decided as she headed out to the stables. Only a dream.

TWO

The path to Lambshold was all but obscured by the snow, but Aralorn could have followed it blindfolded even though she hadn't been here in ten years.

As Sheen crested the final rise, Aralorn sat back in the saddle. Responsively, the stallion tucked his convex nose and slid to a halt. The roan gelding threw up his head indignantly as his lead line pulled him to an equally abrupt stop.

From the top of the keep, the yellow banner emblazoned with her father's red lion, which signaled the presence of the lord at the keep, flew at half mast, with a smaller, red flag above.

Aralorn swallowed and patted Sheen's thick gray neck. "You're getting old, love. Maybe I should leave you here for breeding and see if I can talk someone out of a replacement."

Sheen's ear swiveled back to listen to her, and she smiled absently.

"There's the tree I found you tied to down there, near the wall."

She'd thought she was so clever, sneaking out in the dead

of night when no one would stop her. She'd just made it safely over the wall—no mean feat—and there was Sheen, her father's pride and joy, tied to a tree. She still had the note she'd found in the saddlebags with travel rations and some coins. In her father's narrow handwriting the short note had informed her that a decent mount was sometimes useful, and that if she didn't find what she was looking for, she would always be welcome in her father's home.

The dark evergreen trees blurred in her sight as Aralorn thought about the last night she'd lived at Lambshold. She swallowed, the grief she'd suppressed through the journey home making itself felt.

"Father." She whispered her plea to the quiet woods, but no one answered.

At last, she urged Sheen forward again, and they walked the perimeter of the wall until they reached the gate.

"Hullo the gate," she called briskly.

"Who?" called a half-familiar voice from the top.

Aralorn squinted, but the man stood with his back to the sun, throwing his face into shadow.

"Aralorn, daughter to Henrick, the Lyon of Lambshold," she answered.

He gestured, and the gates groaned and protested as they opened, and the iron portcullis was raised. Sheen snorted and started forward without urging, the roan following behind. She glanced around the courtyard, noting the differences a decade had made. The "new" storage sheds were weathered and had multiplied in her absence. Several old buildings were no longer standing. She remembered Lambshold bustling with busy people, but the courtyard was mostly empty of activity.

"May I take your horses, Lady?"

The stableman, wise to the ways of warhorses, had approached cautiously.

Aralorn swung off and removed her saddlebags, throwing

them over one shoulder before she turned over the reins for both horses to the groom. "The roan's a bit skittish."

"Thanks, Lady."

Not by word or expression did the stableman seem taken aback at a "Lady" dressed in ragged clothes chosen more for their warmth than their looks. By then, both the clothes and Aralorn had acquired a distinct aroma from the journey.

Knowing the animals would be well cared for, she started toward the keep.

"Hold a moment, Aralorn."

It was the man from the wall. She turned and got a clear look at his face.

The years had filled out his height and breadth until he was even bigger than their father. His voice had deepened and hoarsened like a man who commanded others in battle, changed just enough that she hadn't recognized it immediately. Falhart was several years older than she was, the Lyon's only other illegitimate offspring. It was he who had begun her weapons training—because, as he'd told her at the time, his little sister was a good practice target.

"Falhart," she said, her vision blurring as she took a quick step forward.

Falhart grunted and folded his arms across his chest.

Hurt, Aralorn stopped and adopted his pose, waiting for him to speak.

"Ten years is a long time, Aralorn. Is Sianim so far that you could not visit?"

Aralorn met his eyes. "I wrote nearly every month." She stopped to clear the defensiveness out of her voice. "I don't belong here, Hart. Not anymore."

His black eyebrows rose to meet his brick red hair. "This is your home—of course you belong here. Irrenna has kept your room just the way you left it, hoping you'd visit. Allyn's toadflax, you'd think we were Darranians the way you—" He stopped abruptly, having been watching her face closely. His jaw dropped for a moment, then he said in a completely different voice, "That is it, isn't it? Nevyn got to you. Father said he thought it was something of the sort, but I thought you knew better than to listen to the half-crazed prejudices of a Darranian lordling."

Aralorn smiled ruefully, hurt assuaged by the realization that it was anger, not rejection, that had caused his restraint. "It was more complicated than that, but Nevyn is certainly the main reason I haven't been back."

"You'd think that a wizard would be more tolerant," growled Hart, "and that you would show a little more intelligence."

That turned her smile into a grin. "He's not all that happy about being a wizard—he just didn't have any choice in the matter."

"You could have won him over if you had wanted to, Aralorn." He had not yet decided to forgive her. "The man's not as stupid as he acts sometimes."

"Maybe," she conceded. "But, as I said, he wasn't the only reason I left. I was never cut out to be a Rethian noblewoman, any more than Nevyn could have lived in Darran as a wizard. Sianim is my home now."

"Do they know you're a shapeshifter?" he inquired coolly.

"No." She grinned at him. "You know that the only people who would believe such a story are barbarians of the Rethian mountains. Besides, it's much more useful being a shapeshifter if no one knows about it but me."

"Home is where they know all of your secrets, Featherweight, and love you anyway."

Aralorn laughed, and the tears that had been threatening since she heard about her father fell at last. When Falhart opened his arms, she took two steps forward and hugged him, kissing his cheek when he bent down. "I missed you, Fuzzhead."

He picked her up and hugged her, stiffening when he looked over her shoulder. He set her down carefully, his eyes trained on whatever he had seen behind her. "That wolf have something to do with you?"

She turned to see a large, very black wolf crouched several paces behind her. The hair along his spine and the ruff around his neck was raised, his muzzle fixed in an ivory-fanged snarl directed at Falhart.

"Wolf!" Aralorn exclaimed, surprise making her voice louder than she meant it to be.

"*Wolf!*" echoed an archer on the walls, whose gaze was drawn by Aralorn's unfortunate exclamation. The astonishment in his voice didn't slow his speed in drawing his bow.

Lambshold had acquired its name from the fine sheep raised here, making wolves highly unpopular in her father's keep.

Aralorn threw herself on top of him, keeping herself between him and the archer, knocking Wolf off his feet in the process.

"Aralorn!" called Falhart behind her. "Get out of the way."

She envisioned the large knife her brother had tucked in his belt sheath.

"Hart, don't let them . . . *ooff*—Damn it, Wolf, stop it, that hurt—don't let them shoot him."

"Hold your arrows! He's my sister's pet." Falhart bellowed. In a much quieter voice, he added, "I think."

"Do you hear that, Wolf?" said Aralorn, an involuntary grin pulling at the corners of her mouth. "You're my pet. Now, don't forget it."

With a lithe twist, Wolf managed to get all four legs under him and threw her to one side, flat on her back. Placing one heavy paw on her shoulder to hold her in place, he began to industriously clean her face.

"All right, all right, I surrender—ish . . . Wolf, stop it." She covered her face with her arms. Sometimes he took too much joy in fulfilling his role as a wolf.

"Aralorn?"

"*Irrenna.*" Aralorn turned to look up at the woman who

approached. Wolf stepped aside, letting Aralorn get to her feet to greet her father's wife.

Irrenna was elegant more than beautiful, but it would take a keen eye to tell the difference. There was more gray in her hair than there had been when Aralorn left. If Irrenna wasn't as tall as her children, she was still a full head taller than Aralorn. Her laughing blue eyes and glorious smile were dulled by grief, but her welcome was warm, and her arms closed tightly around Aralorn. "Welcome home, daughter. Peace be with you."

"And you," replied Aralorn, hugging her back. "I could wish it were happier news that brought me here."

"As do I. Come up now. I ordered a bath to be prepared in your room. Hart, carry your sister's bags."

Futilely, Aralorn tried to keep her saddlebags on her shoulder, but Falhart twisted them out of her hands as he said in prissy tones, "A Lady never carries her own baggage."

She rolled her eyes at him before starting up the stairs into the keep.

"Dogs stay out of the keep," reminded Irrenna firmly when Wolf followed close on Aralorn's heels.

"He's not a dog, Irrenna," replied Aralorn. "He's a wolf. If he stays out, someone's going to shoot him."

Irrenna stopped and took a better look at the animal at Aralorn's side. He gazed mutely back, wagging his tail gently and trying to look harmless. He didn't quite make it in Aralorn's estimation, but apparently Irrenna wasn't so discerning because she hesitated.

"If you shut him out now, he'll only find a way in later." Aralorn let a note of apology creep into her voice.

Irrenna shook her head. "You get to explain to your brothers why your pet gets to come in while theirs have to stay in the kennels."

Aralorn smiled. "I'll tell them he eats people when I'm not around to stop him."

Irrenna looked at Wolf, who tilted his head winsomely

and wagged his tail. "You might have to come up with a better story than that," Irrenna said.

Hart frowned; but then, her brother had seen Wolf when he wasn't acting like a lapdog.

Having heard the acceptance in Irrenna's voice, Wolf ignored Hart and leapt silently up the stairs to wait for them at the door to the keep.

Aralorn stepped into the great hall and closed her eyes, taking a deep breath. She could pick out the earthy smell impregnating the old stone walls that no amount of cleaning could eradicate entirely, wood smoke from the fires, rushes sweetened with dried herbs and flowers, and some ineffable smell that no place else had.

"Aralorn?" asked her brother softly.

She opened her eyes and smiled at him, shaking her head. "Sorry. I'm just a bit tired."

Falhart frowned, but followed Irrenna through the main hall, leaving Aralorn to fall in behind.

The cream-colored stone walls were hung with tapestries to keep out the chill. Most of the hangings were generations old, but several new ones hung in prominent places. Someone, she noticed, had a fine hand at the loom—she wondered if it was one of her sisters.

She tried to ignore the red carnations strewn through the hall: spots of bright color like drops of fresh blood. Red and black ribbons and drapes were hung carefully from hooks set in the walls, silently reminding her of the reason she had returned to Lambshold. The joy of seeing Hart and Irrenna again faded.

This was not her home. Her big, laughing, cunning, larger-than-life father was dead, and she had no place here anymore. Wolf's mouth closed gently around her palm. A gesture of affection on the part of the wolf, he said, when she asked him about it once. She closed her fingers on his lower jaw, comforted by the familiar pressure of his teeth on her hand.

The hall, like the courtyard, was subdued, with only a minimal number of servants scurrying about. On the far end of the room, the black curtains were drawn across the alcove where her father's body would be lying. Wolf's teeth briefly applied heavier pressure, and she relaxed her hand, realizing she'd tightened her grip too much.

At the bottom of the stairs, Irrenna stopped. "You go on up. I'll let the rest of the family know that you're here. Your old dresses are still in good condition, but if they don't fit, send a maid to me, and I'll see what can be done. Falhart, when you have taken Aralorn's bags up, please attend me in the mourning room."

"Of course, thank you." Aralorn continued up the stairs as if she had never refused to wear the dresses fashion dictated a Rethian lady confine herself to—but she couldn't resist adding dryly, "Close your mouth, Hart. You look like a fish out of water."

He laughed and caught her easily, ruffling her hair as he passed. He drew his hand back quickly. "Ish, Aralorn, you need to wash your hair while you're at it."

"What?" she exclaimed, opening the door to her old room. "And kill off all the lice I've been growing for so long?"

Hart handed her bags to her with a grin. "Still smart-mouthed, I see." When Aralorn tossed her bags into a heap on the floor, he added, "And tidy as well."

She bowed, as if accepting his praise.

He laughed softly. "Irrenna will probably be sending something up for lunch, in case you don't want to eat with the crowd that will be gathering shortly in the great hall. I'll see that someone carries hot water up here as well."

"Falhart," said Aralorn, as he started to turn away. "Thank you."

He grinned and flipped her a studied gesture of acknowledgment (general to sublieutenant or lower), then strode lightly down the hall.

Aralorn stepped into the room and, with a grand sweep

of her arm, invited Wolf to follow. As she closed the door, she glanced around the bedchamber and saw that Falhart was closer to the mark than she'd expected. Her room wasn't exactly as she'd left it—the coverlet was drawn neatly across the bed, and the hearth rug was new—but it was obvious that it had been left largely as it had been the last time she'd slept here. Given the size of Lambshold and the number of people in her family, it was quite a statement.

"So," commented the distinctive gravel-on-velvet voice that was Wolf's legacy from the night he destroyed a tower of the ae'Magi's keep, "tell me. Why haven't you come here in ten years?"

Aralorn turned to find that Wolf had assumed his human shape. He was taller than average, though not as tall as Falhart. There was some of the wolf's leanness to his natural form, but his identity was more apparent in the balanced power of his movements. He was dressed in black silk and linen, a color he affected because it was one his father had not worn. His yellow eyes were a startling contrast to the silver player's mask he wore over his scarred face.

It wasn't actually a player's mask, of course: No acting troupe would have used a material as costly as silver. The finely wrought lips on its exaggerated, elegant features were curled into a grimace of rage. She frowned; the mask was a bad sign.

Aralorn wasn't certain if he'd chosen the mask out of irony or if there was a deeper meaning behind it, and she hadn't thought it important enough to ask. He used the mask to hide the scars he'd gotten when he'd damaged his voice—and to put a barrier between himself and the real world.

It was her vexation with his mask rather than a reluctance to answer his question that prompted her to ignore his query and ask one of her own. "Why did you leave me again?"

She knew why; she just wondered if he did. Ever since

he'd first come to stay with her, even back when she'd thought he really was a wolf, whenever they grew too close, he would leave. Sometimes it was for a day or two, sometimes for a month or a season. But this time it had hurt more, because she thought they had worked past all of that—until she awoke alone one morning in the bed she'd shared with him.

She might not need him to tell her why he'd left, but she did intend to discuss it with him. She needed to tell him, if he didn't already know, that the change in their relationship meant that some other things would also have to change. No more disappearing without a word. Anger would distract her from the bleak knowledge that her father was gone, so she waited for Wolf to explain himself. *Then* she would yell at him.

He caught up her bags in a graceful motion and took them to the wardrobe without speaking. He closed the door, and, with his back to her, said softly, "I—"

He was interrupted by a brisk knock at the door.

"Later," he said, then with a subtle flare of shape and color, he flowed into his lupine form. She thought he sounded relieved.

Aralorn opened the door to four sturdy men bringing in steaming buckets of water and a woman bearing a tray laden with food.

Watching them pour water into her old copper tub in the corner of the room, she rethought the wisdom of pushing Wolf. He was a secretive person, and she didn't want to push him away or make him feel that there was a price to pay for staying. She didn't want to lose him just because she needed to yell at someone before she collapsed in a puddle of grief. She stuffed both anger and grief down to pull out later. She wasn't entirely successful, judging by the lump in the pit of her stomach—but the tub offered an opportunity to find another way to relieve her emotions.

When the heavy screen had been placed in front of the tub to reduce the cold drafts, she dismissed the servants.

She stepped behind the screen and began stripping rapidly out of her travel-stained clothing. Perhaps it would be best if she answered his question; it would give him a graceful way out of answering hers. Now, what had he asked?

"It seemed best," she said with playful obscurity, stepping into the tub.

"What seemed best?" From the sound of his voice, Wolf had moved from where she'd last seen him, curled before the fire with his eyes closed—a pose that seemed to reassure the servants, who had eyed him uneasily.

"That I leave here and not come back."

"Best for whom?" *He is closer now,* she thought, smiling to herself.

Sinking farther down in the luxuriously large bathing tub, she rested her head on the wide rim. Should she give him the short answer or the long one? She laughed soundlessly, then schooled her voice to a bland tone. "Let me tell you a story."

"Of course," he replied dryly.

This time Aralorn laughed aloud, a great deal of her usual equanimity restored by the hot water and the macabre voice of her love. She chose to forget, if only for a while, the reason that she was here, in her old bedchamber. "Once," she began in her best storyteller manner, "and not so long ago, there was a lord's son who, for all that he was still but a young man, had already won a reputation for unusual cunning in war. Additional notoriety came to him from a source no one had reckoned upon."

She waited.

At last, with a bare touch of amusement, he said, "Which was?"

"'Twas a night in midwinter with a full moon in the air

when a servant heard a thunderous knocking on the keep door. A man clothed in a close-woven wool cloak stood before him, carrying a covered basket. 'Take this to the lord's son,' he said, thrusting the basket at the servant. As the servant closed his hand on the handle, the man in the cloak stepped away from the door and leapt into the air, shaping himself into a hawk." She splashed her toes, enjoying the feeling of the water washing away dried sweat. Bathing in a tub wasn't quite as good as the Sianim bathhouses, but it was a lot more private. "The servant took it to the lord's son and described the unusual messenger who had delivered it. The young man removed the cover from the basket, revealing a girl-child with the peculiar gray-green eyes common to the race of shapeshifters. Next to her, tucked between a blanket and the rough weave of the basket, was a note. He read it, then threw it into the fire.

"Taking the baby into his own hands, he held her up until she was at a height with him. 'This,' he announced, 'is my daughter.'

"He introduced the baby to her three-year-old brother and her grandfather. Her grandfather was not pleased to find out his son had been meeting a woman in the woods; but then, her grandfather was not best pleased with anything and, as it happened, died of apoplexy when he was served watered wine at a neighbor's banquet only a few months later, and so had little influence in his granddaughter's life.

"The young man, now lord, decided he needed a wife to care for his children and to bear heirs for the estate. Presently, he found one, several years younger than himself. She looked at the trembling waifs and promptly took them under her wing. The children were delighted, and so was the lord—so much so that in due time there were twelve additional siblings to play with."

Aralorn ignored Wolf's choked-off laugh and explained blandly, "In most households, the life of a bastard child is miserable at best. I can't remember not knowing that I was illegitimate, but I never minded it much. As for being half shapeshifter . . . I've already told you that my father did his best to make sure that I was aware of my mother's people. Other than that, it was no more than an unusual talent I had. The people in the Rethian mountains are used to magic—most of them can work at least some of the simpler spells. Since the Wizard Wars, seven ae'Magi have come from these mountains. If anyone had ever felt I was odd, they'd grown used to it by the time I was grown. The worst problem I had was convincing Irrenna that I didn't want to be a Lady. Falhart taught me swordplay and riding, real riding, and by the time my parents found out, it was too late. Father said I might as well know what I was about and had the weaponsmaster teach me, too."

"Idiot," commented Wolf, sounding much more like his normal sardonic self. "He should have beaten you and sent you to bed without supper. Ten years in Sianim, and you still can't use a sword."

"Not his fault," replied Aralorn easily. "A sword never felt right in my hands, not even Ambris, and she's an enchanted blade. Hmm . . . now that's a thought."

"What?"

"I wonder if it has to do with the iron in the steel. Green magic doesn't work well with iron, while it has an affinity for wooden things . . . Maybe that's why I'm so good with the staff. But it doesn't seem to affect my ability with knives."

"I have always found modesty becoming in a woman."

"Best staffsman or -woman in Sianim," she said, unruffled. "Including longstaff, quarterstaff, or double staves. Now hush, you've interrupted."

"I shall sit quietly and contemplate my misconduct," he replied.

"That should take a while." Aralorn sank down until the warm water touched her chin. A benefit of having large people in one's family was that all of the tubs were big enough to stretch out in. "I guess I can wait that long—but the water will get cold."

There was a long pause. Aralorn stifled a giggle.

"Your story?"

"Finished so soon? I would have thought such a grave task would have taken longer."

"Aralorn," he said gently, "please continue. You were telling me of your wonderful childhood and why that meant that you had to stay away from your family for so long."

"My story," she continued grandly. "Where was I? It doesn't matter. When I was eighteen, my oldest legitimate sister, Freya—mind you she's still younger than I am—was betrothed in one of those complex treaties Reth and Darran spend months drawing up every few years or so and break within hours of the signing. It seems that a rather powerful Darranian noble had a mageborn second son who needed a bride."

Aralorn took a moment to rub soap into her mouse brown hair, hoping to evict the fleas that had taken up residence during her travels. Despite her joking with Falhart, she didn't think she had lice. "So Nevyn came to live at Lambshold. He was shy at first, but he and Freya turned out to be soul mates and fell quietly in love several months after they were married."

She ducked under the water to rinse the soap out of her hair. She didn't particularly want to continue, but some things would become obvious—and it generally wasn't a good thing to take Wolf by surprise. As soon as she was above water again, she continued. "I liked him, too. He was quiet and willing to listen to my stories. He had this air of . . . sadness, I suppose, that made us all treat him gently. He was the only one who defied Irrenna's edict about animals in the castle. He didn't keep pets, but anyone who found a hurt animal brought it to him. At times his suite looked more like a barnyard than the barnyard did." Aralorn hesitated, and said in a considering tone, "At the time, I was afraid I liked him too much. In retrospect, being older and wiser now, I think I wanted what Freya and Nevyn had together rather than Nevyn himself."

She soaped a cloth and began scrubbing at the ingrained dirt in her hands. "Now, I had long since gotten out of the habit of using my shapeshifting abilities at Lambshold. Father was very good at spotting little mice where they didn't belong. Irrenna was very clear on what was polite and impolite: Turning into animals in public wasn't polite. It never occurred to me that Nevyn didn't know what I was."

She examined her hands and decided they were as good as they were going to get. "I did know that he wouldn't think it proper for a Lady to fight, so I talked Falhart into practicing with me in the woods. It wasn't too difficult because he was starting to get teased when I beat him."

Her hair still felt soapy, so she dipped her head underwater again. She cleared her face with her hands and continued. "Nevyn didn't like girls who ran around in boys' clothing and would have been horrified to know that his wife's sister could best him in a fair fight—even with a sword. If you think I'm bad . . ." She let her voice trail off suggestively.

"Swordsman or not, I thought Nevyn was the epitome of what a young hero ought to be." She smiled to herself. "I admired his manner of seeing things in black and white—which was very different than the way my father saw things."

Aralorn paused. "About half a year after Nevyn came, Father drew me aside and told me that Freya was concerned with the amount of time her husband spent with me. When you see Freya, you'll understand why I didn't take that warning too seriously. Even if I had a crush on Nevyn, I knew he couldn't possibly look at me when he had Freya. But my younger sister is a wise woman."

Aralorn waved her hand in the top of the cooling water and watched the swell dash against her knee. "It seems that Freya was not mistaken in her apprehension. Nevyn had been flattered by my worship-from-afar, something that Freya was too pragmatic ever to do. I think he was a little intimidated by Freya, too."

"He attempted you?"

Aralorn snorted. "You make it sound like I'm a horse. But that's the general idea. He was teaching me to speak Darranian in Father's library. I was too stupid—"

"Young," corrected Wolf softly.

"—young *and* stupid to read his earlier manner correctly. It wasn't until I examined the incident later that I realized he could have misinterpreted my response to several things he said. He could very well have thought that I was eager for him."

Wolf growled, and she hurried on. "At any rate, he tried to kiss me. I stepped on his foot and elbowed him in the stomach. About that time, I heard my sister's voice in the corridor. Knowing that no good could come from Freya's finding me with Nevyn—even though nothing happened—I turned into a mouse and escaped out the window and into the gardens."

"And how did your Darranian take that?" asked Wolf.

"Not very well," admitted Aralorn, smiling wryly. "Obviously, I wasn't there for the initial shock, but when I came in to dinner, Nevyn left the table. Freya apologized to me for his behavior—all of it. From what she said, I understand that he confessed all to her, which is admirable. He also claimed that it was my evil nature that caused his 'anomalous' behavior. She didn't believe that—although Nevyn probably did—but Freya wasn't too happy with me anyway." She smiled wryly. "But Freya wasn't why I left. I'd seen Nevyn's face when he saw me: He was afraid of me."

Wolf walked around the screen. He wore his human

form, but the mask was gone, and his scars with it. It could have been illusion—human magic—but Aralorn sometimes thought that it was the green magic that he drew upon when he chose to look as he had before he'd burned himself. Surely a mere illusion would not seem so real; but then, maybe she was prejudiced in favor of green magic.

The unscarred face he wore was almost too beautiful for a man, without being unmasculine in the least. High cheekbones, square jaw, night-dark hair: His father had left his mark upon his son's face as surely as he had his soul.

She would never let him see the touch of revulsion that she felt for that face, so close to the one his father wore. She knew that he wore it now in an attempt to be vulnerable before her, so that she could read his emotions better, for the scars that usually covered his face were too extensive to allow for much expression.

"It hurt you," he said. "I am sorry."

Aralorn shook her head. "I've grown up since then and learned a thing or two along the way. I've stayed away from Lambshold for my sister's sake, and, I think, for my father's as well. He loves—loved—Nevyn like another son. My presence could only have divided this family. And Nevyn . . . Nevyn came to us broken. One of us had to leave, and it was easier for me." She thought a moment. "Actually, looking back, it's rather amusing to think that someone thought I was an evil seductress. It's not a role often taken by folks who look like I do."

Although his lips never moved, his smile warmed his habitually cold eyes. "Evil, no," he commented, his gaze drifting from her face.

"Are you implying something?" she asked archly, not at all displeased. She knew she was plain, and her feminine attractions were not enhanced by the muscles and scars of mercenary life—but it didn't seem to bother Wolf.

"Who, me?" he murmured, kneeling beside the bath. He

pressed a soft kiss on her forehead, then allowed his lips to trail a path along her eyebrow and over her cheekbone. Pausing at the corner of her mouth, he nibbled gently.

"You could seduce a glacier," commented Aralorn, somewhat unsteadily. She shivered when the puff of air released by his hushed laugh brushed her passion-sensitive lips.

"Why, thank you," he replied. "But I've never tried that."

"I missed you," she said softly.

He touched her forehead with his own and closed his eyes. Under her hand, his neck knotted with tension that had nothing, she thought, to do with the passion of a moment before.

"Help me here, love," she said, scooting up in the tub until she was sitting upright. "What's wrong?"

He pulled back, his eyes twin golden jewels that sparkled with the lights of the candles that lit the room. She couldn't read the emotion that roiled behind the glittering amber, and she doubted Wolf could tell her what it was if he wanted to. He reacted to the unknown the same way a wild animal would—safety lay in knowledge and control; the unknown held only destruction. Falling in love had been much harder on him than it had been on her.

"I wasn't going to ask you again," she said. "But I think I had better. Why did you leave?"

Wolf drew in a breath and looked at the privacy screen as if it were a detailed work of art rather than the mundane piece of furniture it was. One of his hands was still on Aralorn's shoulder, but he seemed to have forgotten about it.

"It's all right," said Aralorn finally, sitting up and pulling her legs until she could link her arms around them. "You don't—"

"It is not *all right*," he bit out hoarsely, tightening his grip on her shoulder with bruising force. He twisted back to face her, and his kneeling posture became the crouch of a cornered beast. "I . . . *Plague it!*"

Aralorn scarcely had time to realize that her cooling

bathwater had become scalding hot before Wolf pulled her out dripping like a fish onto the cold stone floor. She took the time to snatch the bath sheet and wrap it around her twice before joining Wolf near the tub, watching as the water erupted into clouds of billowing steam. After a moment, she opened the window shutters to disperse the fog in the room.

"I could have burned you," he said, looking away from the empty tub, his voice too quiet.

"So you could have." Aralorn pursed her lips, and wondered how to handle this new twist in their relationship.

She knew him well enough to know that heating the water hadn't been a bizarre practical joke: He had a sense of humor, but it didn't lend itself to endangering people. It meant that his magic was acting without his knowledge— sternly, she repressed the tingle of fear that trickled over her. Unlike Aralorn, his magic, human or green, was *much* better than the average hedgewitch's: But her fear would hurt him more surely than a knife in his throat.

"I should have told you before," he said without looking at her. "I thought it was just my imagination when things first started happening around me. They were little things. A vase falling off a table or a candle lighting itself." He stopped speaking and drew in his breath.

When he spoke again, his ruined voice crackled with the effort of his suppressed emotion. "I wish I had never discovered I could work green magic as well as the human variety. It was bad enough before, when I was some sort of freak who couldn't control the power of the magic I could summon. At least then it only came when I called. Ever since I started using green magic, I've been losing control. It tugs me around as if I were a dog, and it held my leash. It would be better for you if I left and never came back."

As he spoke the last words, he made a swift gesture, and the steam clouds disappeared from the room. Aralorn stepped in front of him, so he had to look at her.

Smiling sweetly, she reached up to touch his face with both hands. "You leave, and I'll follow you to Deathsgate and back," she said pleasantly. "Don't think I can't."

His hands covered hers rather fiercely.

"Gods," he said, closing his eyes. Aralorn couldn't tell if it was a curse or a prayer.

"Green magic has a personality of its own," she said softly. "One of the elders who taught me likened it to a willful child. It responds better to coaxing than force."

Yellow eyes slitted open. "Do you not have to call your magic? Just as any human mage would do?"

"Yes," agreed Aralorn, though reluctantly. She hated it when he shot down her attempts to make him feel better.

Wolf grunted. "A human mage is limited by the amount of pure, unformed magic he can summon and the time he can hold it to his spell. The magic you call is already a part of the pattern of the world, so you have to respect that limit. I tell you that this *magic*"—he spat the word out—"comes when it wills. If you are not frightened by that, you should be. Remember that *my* magic is not limited except by my will. This does not heed my will at all. I cannot control it, I cannot stop it."

Aralorn thought about that for a moment before a cat-in-the-milk-barn smile crossed her face. "I do *so* hate being bored. You always manage to have the most *interesting* problems."

She caught him off guard and surprised a rusty laugh out of him.

"Come," she said briskly, "help me dry off, and we'll eat. My mother's people live near here—maybe they can help. We'll stop there before we go back to Sianim."

THREE

Aralorn walked to the great hall, with Wolf ghosting beside her, once more in lupine form. When she'd told him he didn't have to accompany her, he had merely given her a look and waited for her to open the door. When he wanted to, the man could say more with a look than most people managed with a whole speech.

She'd searched through the clothing still in her closet, trying to find a long-sleeved dress that would cover the scars on her arms. The dresses were all in beautiful condition (many having never been worn), but the fashions of ten years ago had tight sleeves that she could no longer fit into thanks to a decade of weapons drills. She'd settled for a narrow-skirted, short-sleeved dress and ignored the scars.

The room was crowded, and for a moment she didn't recognize anyone there. Ten years had made changes. Some of the crowd were tenant farmers and gentry who held their manors in fief to her father; but from the number of very tall, blond people in the room, Aralorn thought most of them were her family, grown up now from the rag-tag bunch of children she remembered.

Wolf received some odd looks, but no one asked about him. It seemed that mercenaries would be allowed their eccentricities.

She smiled and nodded as she waded through the crowd, knowing from experience that the names would sort them-selves out eventually. Usually, she was better at mingling and chatting, but this wasn't just work, and the black cur-tain that hung in the far corner of the room held too much of her attention.

In the alcove behind the curtain, her father's body was laid out in state—awaiting the customary solitary visits of his mourners. Visits where the departed spirit could be wished peacefully on his way, old quarrels could be put aside, and daughters could greet their fathers for the first time in a decade.

She'd seen him now and again, the last time at the coro-nation of the new Rethian king. *But I was working, and he never recognized me under the guises I wore.*

"Aralorn!" exclaimed a man's voice somewhere behind her.

Aralorn gave herself an instant to collect her scattered thoughts before she turned.

The young man slipping rapidly through the crowd wasn't immediately identifiable, though his height and his golden hair proclaimed him one of her brothers. She hesitated for a moment, but realized from his age and the walnut-stained color of his eyes who he had to be—the only other boy near his age had blue eyes. When she searched his features she could see the twelve-year-old boy she'd known.

"Correy," she said warmly, as he came up to her.

Wordlessly, he opened his arms. She wrapped her arms around him and returned his hug. The top of her head was well short of his shoulders in spite of the torturously high heels on her shoes.

"You shrank," he commented, pulling away to reveal a twinkle in his dark brown eyes.

She stepped back so she wouldn't strain her neck looking at him. "Back less than a day, and already I've been insulted twice for my size. You should have more respect for your elders, boy."

"Correy—" A female voice broke into the conversation from somewhere over Aralorn's left shoulder. "Mother's looking for you. She says you forgot to get something that she needed for something else, I forget what. I can't believe that you are wearing a sword; Mother will pitch a fit when she sees that you're wearing a weapon to Father's wake." A tall, exquisitely groomed woman of somewhere around thirteen or so tripped past Aralorn without so much as a glance and stopped at Correy's side.

Correy rolled his eyes, looking for a moment much more like a boy of twelve than a grown man. With a smile for Aralorn, he reached out a brotherly arm and snagged the immaculately clad girl around the neck and pulled her to his side. "You won't recognize this one, Aralorn, as she was only four when you left. Lin has set herself up as the mistress of propriety at Lambshold. She wants to go to court and meet the king. I think she envisions him falling desperately in love with her."

The girl, only inches shorter than her brother, struggled out of his hold and glared at him. "You think you're so smart, Correy—but you don't even know that you shouldn't wear swords at a formal gathering. Mother's going to skin you alive."

Correy smiled, ignoring her wrath. "I meant to tell you that black looks exceptionally well with your hair."

"You really think so?" Lin asked anxiously, suddenly willing to listen to her brother's previously dismissed judgment.

"I wouldn't say so else, Lin," he said with obvious affection.

She kissed his cheek and drifted off, taking little notice of her long-lost sister.

"I apologize for her rudeness . . ." began Correy, but Aralorn smiled and shook her head.

"I was fourteen once, myself."

He smiled and glanced down casually at Wolf, but when he met the solemn yellow gaze, he started. "*Allyn's toad-flax*, Aralorn, Mother said you'd brought your pet, but she didn't say he was a wolf."

He knelt to get a better view, careful not to crowd too close. "I haven't seen many black wolves."

"I found him in the Northlands," said Aralorn. "He was caught in an old trap. By the time he was healed, he'd gotten used to me. He still comes and goes as he pleases. I didn't know he'd accompanied me here until he showed up in the courtyard."

"Hey, lad," crooned Correy, cautiously extending his hand until he touched the thick ruff around the wolf's throat.

"You don't have to be quite so careful. He's never bitten anyone yet . . . at least not for petting him."

There were too many people in the room for her to worry about the purposeful steps that approached her from behind, but she did anyway. Hostility always had that effect on her.

The man striding toward them was dark-haired and dark-eyed, the epitome of a Darranian lord. Not as handsome as Wolf—who was half Darranian and looked it—and less dangerous-looking, though he had something of Wolf's grace when he moved. *Nevyn,* she thought with a touch of resignation accompanying her nervousness.

He stopped in front of her, close enough that he was looking down, forcing her to look up to meet his eyes. "You profane this gathering by your presence, shapeshifter."

"Nevyn," she greeted him courteously.

From the corner of her eye, she noticed Wolf pull away

from Correy and slink toward Nevyn, his lips curled back from his fangs.

"Wolf, *no*," she said firmly, hoping he would listen.

Yellow eyes gleamed at her, but the snarl disappeared as he trotted back to her side.

When she was certain Wolf was not going to do anything rash, Aralorn turned her attention back to Nevyn; but the distraction had done her good—and that might have been Wolf's intention all along. He was a subtle beast. Prepared now, she examined the Darranian sorcerer. The years had been kind to him, broadening his shoulders and softening his mouth. The shy anxiety that had plagued him had faded, leaving behind an intense, handsome man who looked prepared to defend his family from her.

"I am truly sorry you feel that way," she said. "But the Lyon is my father, and I will stay for his burial. For his sake, I bid you peace. If you feel it necessary, perhaps we could discuss this in a less public forum."

"She's right, husband," said a firm voice, and a woman, slightly taller than Nevyn, materialized to Aralorn's left. In Freya, Lin's promise of beauty was fulfilled. Thick red-gold hair hung in glorious splendor to her slender hips. Her belly was gently rounded with pregnancy, but that robbed her figure of none of its grace. The dark blue eyes that glanced a quick apology at Aralorn were large and tilted. "This is neither the time nor the place for this conversation."

"Freya," said Aralorn, smiling, "it's good to see you again."

Mischievousness lit the younger woman's smile as she patted her husband's arm before she left him to hug Aralorn. "Don't stay away so long next time, Featherweight. I missed you."

Aralorn laughed, grateful for the change of topic. "I missed you, too, Puff."

Correy gave a crack of laughter. "I'd forgotten that name. None of the youngsters got nicknames once you'd gone."

"Maybe," said Freya, her eyes twinkling as she folded her arms and puffed out her cheeks in the manner that had given her the once-hated appellation, "I didn't miss everything about your absence."

"If I remember Irrenna's letters correctly, your child is due this spring, right?" asked Aralorn.

Freya nodded and started to say more, but Irrenna, emerging from whatever social emergency had been keeping her at a distant corner of the room, called Aralorn's name.

Hurrying forward, Irrenna pressed a kiss on Aralorn's cheek. "Come, dear, the alcove is empty, so you can pay your respects to your father."

Although she knew the smile on her face didn't change, Aralorn felt a cold chill of grief. "Yes, Irrenna. Thank you."

She followed her stepmother's graceful form through the crowd. They paused here and there for introductions—Irrenna had taken refuge from her grief in the social amenities called for at any large gathering.

Wolf ventured ahead and found a corner near the black curtain where he was unlikely to be stepped on and settled quietly. Aralorn murmured something polite, squeezed Irrenna's hand, and continued to the curtained alcove on her own.

The black velvet was heavy, and it shut out a great deal of the sound from the outer room. Incense burned from plates set at the head and foot of the bier, leaving the room smelling incongruously exotic. She let the curtain settle behind her before stepping farther into the little chamber.

It was unadorned except for three torches that were ensconced on the stone walls, sending flickering light to touch all but the narrowest shadows. On the opposite side of the round room was a thick wooden door that was used to take the body to the burial grounds outside the keep. It was a small chamber, with space for only eight or ten mourners to cluster around the gray stone bier that held sway here, a private place.

The man on the stone slab didn't look like her father, though he wore the same state robes she had seen him in at the Rethian king's coronation. Aralorn's lips twitched when she remembered he'd been thieving sweet cakes out of the kitchens. *Green and brown velvet embroidered with gold.* She touched the rich cloth lightly with her fingertips. He had been an earthy man; it was fitting that his burial clothing reflected that.

"You should have died in battle, Father," she whispered. "Sickness is such an inglorious way to die. The minstrels are already singing ballads of your ferocity and cunning in battle, did you know that? They'll make up a suitably nasty foe to have dealt your mortal wound just to satisfy their artistic souls."

The stone of the raised bier was cold on her hips, surprising her because she hadn't realized she had stepped closer. "I should have come sooner—or stopped you at court when I saw you there. I'm a spy, did you know that? What would you have done if the scullery maid, or the groom who held your horse, shifted into me? Would you have had me tried as a traitor to Reth? Sianim's mercenaries aren't Reth's enemies until they are paid to be. You know I would never betray Reth's interests for my adopted home."

To Aralorn, touch was as much a part of talking as the words themselves. Almost without conscious thought, she bent forward, cupping her hand on his flaccid cheek . . . and stilled.

She had touched dead people before—a lot of them. She had even touched a Uriah or two, who were dead-but-alive. Her shapeshifter blood did more than allow her to change shape and light fires; it made her sensitive to the patterns of life and death, decay and rebirth.

Beneath her fingertips, the pulse of life was still present— and it didn't have the fragility of someone near death.

Despite his appearance, her father seemed to be merely sleeping, though he did so without breath or color in his face.

"Father?" she said softly, her pulse beginning to race with possibilities. "What is this that you have gotten yourself into?"

She searched for sorcery, human or green, but her magic found nothing. She began to sing softly in her mother's tongue. Singing allowed her to focus her magic, letting her see more than just the Lyon's still form.

She had never been hungry for the power that magic could bring, so she'd never done much besides learn how to reshape her face, change into a few animal forms, and open locked doors. This was entirely different, but she had to try something.

She struggled for a while before she was able to discern the pulses and rhythms of his life; more difficult still was finding the underlying organization that was at the heart of all life. Just as she thought she found the Lyon's pattern, something dark bled through. She sought it, but it faded before her searching, as if it had never been. Deciding it might have been a fluke of her inexperience, Aralorn returned to her original search. As soon as her concentration was elsewhere, the darkness returned.

This time it caught at her magic as if it were a living thing. Startled but not alarmed, Aralorn stopped singing. But the connection between her magic and the shadow didn't dissolve. Creeping up through her magic, the darkness touched her. As it did, pain swept through her, raking her with acid claws.

"Wolf," she croaked, meaning to call out, but her voice was only a hoarse whisper as she fell to her knees.

———

Lying just outside the curtained alcove, Wolf listened to Aralorn's singing and wished he couldn't feel the stirring of green magic at her call. He didn't know what she was doing, but he sent a thread of silence around the curtain, hiding the sound of her music from everyone except him.

No one needed to know that she called magic, not when so many here disapproved of her. He'd seen the looks that Aralorn had ignored. She chose to believe that they did not hurt her, but he knew better.

The pads of his feet tingled, and the air thickened with the sharp, clear presence of Aralorn's magic. He shifted irritably but stilled when the singing stopped. Abruptly, Wolf surged to his feet, trying to put a name to the change he sensed. Then, faintly, he heard her call his name.

He bolted under the curtain to find Aralorn curled on her side, and the magic in the air so strong it almost choked him—not Aralorn's magic; hers never stank of evil.

"Eavakin nua Sovanish ven," he spat, straddling Aralorn as if his physical presence could ward off the attack of magic. At the end of his speaking, the dark magic reluctantly faded back from Aralorn. He shaped himself into his human form: He could work magic whatever shape he took, but there were some spells that he needed his hands for.

"Kevribeh von!" he commanded as he gestured. Rage twisted his voice as it could not touch his fire-scored face. "She is mine. You will not have her."

As suddenly as it had come, all trace of the magic that had attacked her disappeared. The chamber should have retained a residue of it—he could detect the traces of his own spellwork—but the shadow magic was gone as if it had never been.

Wolf moved aside as Aralorn began to push herself up.

"Wolf," she said urgently, "look at him. Look at my father and tell me what you see."

"Are you all right?" he asked, crouching down beside her.

"Fine," she said dismissively, though at the moment

she seemed to be having trouble sitting up. He helped her. "Please, Wolf. Look at my father."

With a curt nod, Wolf turned and approached the bier.

———

Aralorn wrapped her arms around herself and waited for his answer. When Wolf stiffened in surprise, she clenched her hands into fists. He set his right hand over the Lyon's chest as he made a delicate motion with his left.

Remembering what had happened to her when she had used magic, Aralorn said, "Careful."

It was too late. Even without her magic, she saw the unnatural shadow slipping from under the Lyon's still form to touch Wolf's hand.

"Plague it!" Wolf exclaimed, using Aralorn's favorite oath as he stumbled back from the bier, shaking his hand as if it hurt.

The shadow vanished from sight as quickly as it had come.

"Are you all right?" asked Aralorn, staggering to her feet. "What is it?"

Wolf walked slowly around the stone pedestal, careful not to touch it. He frowned in frustration. "I don't know. I can see it, though, when it moves. It seems to have a limited range."

"Is it a spell of some sort?"

Almost reluctantly, Wolf shook his head.

"It's alive then," said Aralorn. "I thought it might be." The hope she'd been clinging to left her. The life that she'd sensed had been the shadow-creature and not her father at all.

Of course the Lyon was dead. She sucked in a deep breath as if air could assuage the hurt of departing hope.

The sound brought Wolf's gaze to her, his amber eyes glittering oddly in the flickering light. "So is your father."

"Wolf?" she whispered.

The rattle of the brass rings that held the heavy curtain over the door gave brief warning before both Correy and Irrenna burst in. Wolf dropped his human form for the wolf more swiftly than thought. If one of the intruders had looked sharp, they would have caught the final touches of his transformation, but their attention was on Aralorn, still sitting on the floor.

"Are you all right?" asked Irrenna anxiously, surveying the dust on Aralorn's dress and the dazed expression on her face.

"Actually, yes," replied Aralorn, still absorbing the certainty that Wolf had given her. "Much better than I was." Then she smiled, accepting the improbable. She might have been mistaken, but Wolf would not have been.

"I apologize then," said Correy, clearly taken aback at her cheerfulness. "I saw your wolf scramble under the drapery, and I thought something might be wrong. That door"—he gestured to the oaken door that led to a small courtyard—"is usually kept barred, but I could have sworn I just heard a man's voice." Though his words were an explanation for the discourtesy of interrupting a mourner, his voice held a dozen questions.

Aralorn shook her head. "No one came in from the courtyard. I have noticed this room can distort sound—it might be the high ceiling and the narrowness of the room."

Wolf gave her a glance filled with amusement at her storytelling. She patted him on the head and climbed laboriously to her feet.

"You look as if your visit with Henrick did you some good," commented Irrenna after a moment. "I'm glad you are more at peace."

Aralorn smiled even wider at that. Trust Irrenna to be too polite for bluntness.

"Well"—Aralorn paused, almost bouncing with excitement—"I'm not certain 'peace' is quite the right word. I would say joyous, exuberant, and maybe exultant—though that might be pushing it a bit. I wouldn't be too hasty about burying Father tomorrow—he might not be best pleased."

Her brother stiffened, drawing himself up indignantly, but Irrenna, who knew her better, caught his arm before he could say anything.

"What do you know?" Irrena's voice was hushed but taut with eagerness for all that.

Aralorn spread her arms wide. "He's not dead."

"What?" said Correy, his voice betraying his shock.

Irrenna took a step forward and peered closely into Aralorn's face. "What magic have you wrought?" she asked hoarsely.

At the same time, Correy shook his head with obvious anger. "Father is dead. His flesh is cold, and there is no pulse. I don't remember that your humor lent you toward cruelty."

The smile dropped from Aralorn's face as if it had never been. "You've been listening to Nevyn."

Irrenna stepped between them, shaking her head. "Don't be absurd, Correy. If Aralorn says that he lives, then he lives. She wouldn't make up a story about this." She drew in a tremulous breath and turned back to Aralorn. "If he is not dead, why does he lie so still?"

Aralorn shook her head. "I'm not certain exactly, except that there's magic involved. Has Father annoyed any wizards lately?"

Irrenna looked thoughtful for a moment. "None that I know of."

"You think Father's ensorcelled? Who do you think did it? Nevyn?" asked Correy. "I know death when I see it, Aralorn. Father is dead."

Aralorn looked at him, but she couldn't read his face. "I don't know Nevyn anymore. But the man I knew would never have put everyone through all of this."

"You are certain it was a human mage?" asked Irrenna. She'd reached out to touch the Lyon's hand.

"Have you been having difficulty with the shapeshift-ers?" asked Aralorn.

"Father's been working with them to improve the live-stock." Correy was still stiff with distrust. "But last month, something burned out a crofter's farms on the northern bor-ders of the estate, one of the places where they'd been con-ducting their experiments. All that's left are the stone walls of the cottage, not even the timbers of the barn. Father said he didn't think it was the shapeshifters, but I know that they've been nervous about dealing with humans."

Aralorn nodded her understanding. "I haven't had time to look very closely at the spell holding the Lyon. I can check if it was a shapeshifter's doing or a human mage's."

She took a step forward to do just that, but Wolf placed himself foursquare before her.

"I can do it without using magic," Aralorn said, exasper-ated. She'd momentarily forgotten, in her excitement, that her family would think it odd that she explained herself to her wolf. Ah well, she could hope that they would chalk it up to the stress of the moment. She needed to see the Lyon. "All I want to do is *look*. The shadow-thing only came out before when magic was being patterned."

"What shadow-thing?" asked Correy.

"I don't know," Aralorn said. "Something odd happened when I was using magic."

Reluctantly, Wolf stepped aside. Aralorn managed an-other half step before Wolf again stepped between her and the bier; this time his attention was all for the shad-ows under the silent form laid out on the stone table. He growled a soft warning.

"What is it?" asked Irrenna.

Aralorn narrowed her eyes, catching a flicker of move-ment in the shadow under the Lyon's still form. She moved around Wolf and reached out, watching the shadow stretch away from her father's fingertips and slide toward hers.

Wolf took a mouthful of the hem of her dress and jerked his head. If she'd been wearing her normal clothes, Aralorn would have caught her balance. As it was, the narrow skirt kept her legs too close together, and she fell backward on the cold floor again. This time she bruised her elbow.

"Plague it, Wolf—" she started, then she heard Correy's exclamation.

"What *is* that?"

Irrenna gasped soundlessly, and Aralorn turned to look. The shadow was back, rising over the top of the bier as if it had form and substance. Wolf crouched between her and the thing, his muzzle curled in a soundless snarl.

Aralorn pushed herself away from the shadow to give him more room. As she distanced herself, the shadow shrank, until it was nothing more than a small area under her father where the torchlight could not reach.

"I think," said Aralorn thoughtfully, getting to her feet, "that we need to seal this room so no one comes in. There must be some plausible explanation we can give them. It's a little late to start talking about quarantine for an unknown disease, but . . ."

"Why didn't that happen before?" asked Correy. "There have been any number of people who have been around Father's . . ." He hesitated a moment, staring at the bier, then he smiled, a great joyous smile. ". . . around Father after he was ensorcelled."

"That's a good question," said Aralorn briskly, with a nod that acknowledged his capitulation without gloating over it. "It was dormant until I worked some magic when I first noticed Father wasn't as dead as he appeared. The magic might have triggered it. Regardless of what it is and why it didn't act sooner, it certainly seems to be active now."

"I propose that we tell everyone as much as we know," suggested Correy in a reasonable tone of voice. "We're not

Darranians to be frightened of a little magic—but wariness comes with the territory."

Aralorn was nonplussed for an instant, then a slow smile lit her face. "I've gotten used to fabricating stories for everything—I'd forgotten that sometimes it is possible to tell everyone what's really going on—it *is* good to be home."

———

The activity around the bier room had attracted the attention of several people in the great hall. When Correy drew back the curtain, Aralorn saw that Falhart was standing near the opening with a slender woman who could only be his wife, Jenna. Nevyn and Freya were there, too.

Correy glanced around the room with an assessing eye. Impatiently, he grabbed a pewter pitcher from a surprised servant and dumped the liquid it contained onto the floor. With a boyish grin, he took the empty vessel and flung it against a nearby stone pillar. The resultant clamor had the effect of silencing the room momentarily.

"Good people," bellowed Correy, though the effect was somewhat marred by the silly grin on his face. "I am here to announce that my father's interment has been indefinitely postponed because of a slight misconception on our part. It seems that the Lyon lives." He had to wait a moment before the noise level dropped to where he could be heard. "My sister, Aralorn, has determined that it is some ensorcellment that holds Father in thrall. I will send to the ae'Magi at once for his aid. Until he arrives, I would ask that no one enter the chamber."

"You say the shapeshifter wishes no one to enter?" Nevyn's face was pale. Freya touched his arm, but he shook himself free of her hand.

"*I* say no one enters," snapped Correy.

"There is a trap of some sort," said Aralorn before matters

between the two men worsened. "I have neither the skill nor the knowledge to deal with it. I fear that anyone without safeguards would be in danger of ending up in the same state as my father." She bowed her head formally at Nevyn. "As you are far better trained than I, you are free to enter or not as you wish."

Nevyn gave a shallow nod but didn't move his eyes from Correy. "I would like to verify her opinion."

"Fine," said Correy.

"Have a care," murmured Aralorn, as Nevyn brushed past her to enter the smaller room.

Aralorn looked at Wolf and gestured after Nevyn. He sighed loudly and ducked through the curtain behind the human mage.

While Irrenna dealt with the questions thrown at her, Falhart picked up the dented pitcher and handed it to Correy with a brotherly grin. "Never thought to see the day that my courtly brother dumped good ale on the floor in a formal gathering."

Correy took the pitcher with a sheepish smile and shrugged. "It seemed . . . appropriate."

Falhart turned to Aralorn. "Well, Featherweight, you did it again."

She raised her brows. "Did what?"

"Managed to put the whole household in an uproar. You even turned Correy into a barbarian like ourselves. Look at all the work you caused the servants: This room will smell like a brewery for a se'night."

Aralorn drew in her breath and puffed out her chest and prepared to defend herself. Before she could open her mouth, she was engulfed in Falhart's arms.

"Thanks," he said.

When Falhart set her down, Correy picked her up in a similar fashion, then gave her to an older man she recognized as one of the Lyon's fighting comrades—and she wasn't the only woman passed from one embrace to the next. From there the gathering took on the festiveness of Springfair.

Out of the corner of her eye, Aralorn saw Wolf find a place under one of the food-laden tables. Knowing from his actions that Nevyn was safely out of the curtained alcove, she relaxed and enjoyed herself.

———

Nevyn had no intention of working magic while under the watchful eye of Aralorn's companion, who had inexplicably followed him.

He usually loved four-footed beasts of all kinds, but the cold yellow eyes of the wolf gave him chills. Would it have followed him if it were only a pet wolf as she claimed? Was it some relative of hers? He couldn't tell the shapeshifters from any of the other creatures of the forest.

After completing a brief inspection of the room, Nevyn rejoined the guests. He would return to the Lyon when everyone was gone.

The tenor of the evening had changed during the short time he'd been gone. The quiet, hushed crowd had grown boisterous and loud, forgetting, in their joy at Aralorn's news, that the Lyon still was in danger.

Nevyn watched his wife dance with Correy for a moment, but he was uncomfortable with the noisy crowd. He disliked strangers and gatherings of people. Not even eleven years in Lambshold had managed to change that. Without so much as a touch of envy, he watched the others celebrate: He liked knowing that so many people cared for the man who'd been a much better father to him than his own.

Smiling faintly, he turned and left the room, taking care to leave unseen. If Freya knew he'd gone, she would follow him—not understanding that he wanted her to enjoy herself. He loved her more because they were different, and had no desire to change her.

The smile grew more comfortable on his face as he took the servants' stairs to reach the suite he shared with his wife. He felt better than he had for a long time. Aralorn's discovery took a large portion of the weight of responsibility off his shoulders. He'd dreaded the thought that he would have to stop the burial himself despite the assurances he'd received to the contrary.

He felt guilty for what had been done to the man he loved as a father. But that would soon be over as well. He also hadn't wanted to hurt Aralorn, and she would be hurt when she realized that she was responsible for her father's condition: She was too smart not to make the connection. At least she wasn't in any danger, not now.

He truly believed that she was something unnatural—even evil—but part of him still had a tender spot for the funny, teasing girl who had welcomed him to Lambshold. For that child's sake, he hoped this would soon be over. He'd hurt her tonight. He hadn't meant to, but he had to remind himself what she was lest he begin to forget the terrible things that magic could do no matter how good the man wielding it.

He entered his bedroom with a sigh of relief. One of his cats jumped down from the chair it had been sitting on to strop itself against his leg.

Nevyn stripped off his formal dress, leaving it where it fell. The cat mewed imperatively, and he picked it up before lying down in the bed he shared with Freya.

"Problems, Nevyn?" whispered an accentless voice in Darranian from the shadow-laden window alcove.

Nevyn jumped, still unused to the way the mage could appear out of nowhere. "My lord," he greeted him. "I was just thinking. It happened as you said it would. Aralorn discovered the spell, though she managed to stay out of the trap as you feared she might." He was glad of it, he thought with unusual defiance.

The sorcerer emerged from the alcove and stood in the light of the single candle Nevyn had left burning. He was taller than Nevyn and moved like a warrior despite the wizard's robes he wore. His hair was the same color as the black cat that rested on Nevyn's lap. His eyes were cobalt blue.

"Don't fret," he said, his voice matching the perfection of his face. "She could only escape because *he* was there."

Nevyn shook his head. "I saw no one enter the room but Aralorn, Irrenna, and Correy."

"Nonetheless," said the other man again, "it was *his* magic that stopped the *banishan* from completing its work. That you did not see him enter is hardly surprising. My son is capable of great magics. There is a door into the bier room—a lock would be no barrier to a mage of his caliber." He paused, then snapped his fingers. "Of course," he said softly. "I should have thought . . . The girl, Aralorn, has been known to travel quite often with a large black wolf. Was he there?"

"Yes," answered Nevyn. "What does that have to do with her escape from the trap, my lord ae'Magi?"

The other man looked thoughtfully at Nevyn. Then he smiled. "Since my son's attempt on my life, I no longer hold that title—it belongs to Lord Kisrah, who holds the Master Spells. You may address me as Geoffrey, if you like."

"Thank you," said Nevyn.

"My son is the wolf," said Geoffrey. "It is some effect of the combination of my magic and his mother's that allows him to take that shape as if it were his own. Be careful when he is about."

Nevyn nodded. "I'll do that."

"Thank you." Geoffrey smiled. "You look tired now. Why don't you sleep. Nothing more will happen tonight."

Nevyn found that he was more tired than he remembered. He was asleep before Geoffrey left the room.

———

In her bedchamber, Aralorn stepped behind the screen to remove the torn dress and the shoes as well. Pulling her toes up to stretch her protesting calf muscles, she listened to the sounds of Wolf stirring the coals in the grate.

"Did you get a good enough feel for the spelling to tell if it was a human mage who attacked my father?" she asked, pulling a bedrobe off the screen and examining it, curious. It was the shade of old gold embroidered with red, and the needlework was far finer than any she had ever done. "I couldn't get close enough to tell."

"I don't know," replied Wolf after a moment. "The magic in that room didn't feel like human magic—at least not always. Nor did it feel the way green magic does." There was a pause, then he continued in a softer voice. "There's black magic aplenty, though. It might be some effect of the corruption that makes it difficult to say whether it is a human or one of your kinsmen responsible."

"Most everyone here is a kinsman of mine," she said, and wrapped the robe around herself.

She sighed. The robe was unfamiliar because it quite obviously belonged to one of her sisters. The sleeves drooped several inches past her hands, and the silk pooled untidily at her feet. She felt like a child playing dress-up.

"If it is human magic, Nevyn is the most obvious culprit."

Reading her tone, Wolf said, "You find that so far-fetched?"

"Let's just say that I'd suspect the shapeshifters—I'd suspect *myself*—before I'd believe that Nevyn harmed my father," she said, standing on her toes without appreciably affecting the length of fabric left on the ground. "Me, yes— but not my father. When Nevyn came here . . . something in him was broken. My father accepted him as one of us. He bellowed at him and hugged him, and Nevyn didn't

know what to make of him." Aralorn smiled, remembering
the bewildered young man who'd waited to be rejected by
the Lyon as he'd been rejected by everyone else. "Nevyn
wouldn't hurt my father."

"So what are we going to do?"

"Tomorrow," she said, "I'd like to find my mother's
brother and see what he has to say. If he did this, he'll tell
me so—my uncle is like that. If not, I'd like him to take a
look at the shadow-thing. He's familiar with most of the
uncanny things that live here in the mountains."

She tried rolling up the sleeves. "By the way, did you
ward the alcove to keep curiosity seekers out, or are we
relying on Irrenna's guards?" The soft fabric slid out of the
roll as easily as water flowed down a hillside.

"I set wards."

Deciding there was nothing to be done about the robe,
Aralorn stepped around the screen. Unmasked and scarred,
Wolf set the poker aside and turned to face her. He stopped
and raised an eyebrow at her, his eyes glinting with unholy
amusement.

"You look about ten years old," he said, then paused and
looked at her chest. "Except, of course, for certain attributes seldom found in ten-year-olds."

"Very funny," replied Aralorn with all the dignity she
could muster. "Some of us can't magically zap our clothing
from wherever we put it last. Some of us have to make do
with what clothing is offered us."

"Some of us can do nothing but complain," added Wolf,
waving his hand at her.

Aralorn felt the familiar tingle of human magic, and her
robe shrank to manageable size. "Thanks, Wolf. I knew
there was a good reason to keep you around."

He bowed with a courtier's flair, his teeth white in the
dim light of the room. "Proper lady's maid."

Aralorn snorted. "Somehow," she said dryly, "I don't
think you convey the right air. Any Lady worthy of her title

would not let you close enough to tie her laces . . . untie perhaps, but not tie."

Wolf walked by her on the way to the bed and ruffled her hair. "I prefer mercenaries."

She nodded seriously. "I've heard that about you wizards."

She was drifting contentedly off to sleep snuggled against Wolf's side when he said, "I've been assuming this was a spell, but it could be something the shadow-creature is doing to him."

She moaned. "Sleep."

He didn't say anything more, but she could all but feel him thinking.

"All right, all right," she groused, and rolled over onto her back with a flop. "Why do you think it is the shadow-thing holding my father?"

"I didn't say that," he corrected. "But we know nothing about it, or about the spell holding your father. You're the story collector. Have you heard any stories about a creature who holds its victims in an imitation of death?"

"Spiders," she answered promptly. She was very awake now. For some reason she'd assumed that since the Lyon was still alive, he'd stay that way until she and Wolf figured out how to rescue him.

"You know what I mean," Wolf said. "Is there something that uses magic to bind prey as large as a human?"

"No," she said, then continued reluctantly, "not explicitly—but there are a lot of strange creatures I don't know much about. The North Rethian mountains were one of the last places settled. Many of the old things were driven here from other places as humans moved in. Supposedly, the Wizard Wars destroyed most of the really dangerous ones—but if the dragon survived, other things might have made it as well. That leaves a lot of candidates, from monsters to gods."

"Gods?" he asked.

She tapped his chest in objection to the sneer in his voice. Wolf, she had long ago realized, was a hopeless cynic. "If the Smith built weapons to kill the gods, there must have been gods to kill. I'll have you know that this very keep was cursed once. Family legend has it that one of the Great Masters who began the Wizard Wars razed a temple dedicated to Ridane, the goddess of death, before erecting his own keep here." She lowered her voice and continued in a whisper. "It is said that *Her* laughter when he died was so terrible that all who heard it perished."

"Then how did anyone know that *She* laughed?" Wolf asked.

She poked him harder. "Don't ruin the mood."

His shoulder shook suspiciously, but he was quiet. She settled back against him, slipping her hand under his arm.

"My uncle," she said, "told me that the shapeshifters lived in these mountains before humans ever came this far north. They were driven into hiding here by a creature they called the *safarent*—which translates into something like big, yellow, magic perverter." She waited for his reaction.

"Big, yellow, magic perverter?" he said, his voice very steady, making the name even more ridiculous.

"Sort of the way your name, in several Anthran dialects, would translate into hairy wild carnivore which howls," she replied. "Would you prefer the Great Golden Tainter of Magic?"

"No," he said dryly.

"Anyway," she said, happy to have her attempt to amuse him succeed, "the shapeshifters were already hiding when humans came. It's probably why they survived here and nowhere else."

"So what happened to the . . . *safarent*?" asked Wolf, when Aralorn didn't continue.

"Probably the Wizard Wars," she said. "But the stories are pretty vague." She closed her eyes and hugged his arm to still her fears. "I'll get my uncle to look at the Lyon tomorrow."

Wolf grunted and began nibbling at the soft place behind her ear, but she was too worried about her father to follow his mood.

"Wolf," she said, "do you think I should try my sword? It might be able to rid us of that shadowy thing, or even break the spell that holds my father."

Carrying an enchanted sword wasn't the most comforting thing to do. It intimidated her to the point where she tried to ignore it most of the time. Since she'd used it on Wolf's father, she hadn't even practiced with it—though she carried it with her always so that no one else picked it up.

Wolf nipped her ear sharply and rolled her on top of him, shifting her until he could see her face.

"Ambris, once called the *Atryx Iblis*," he said thoughtfully.

"Magic eater," she translated.

"Devourer sounds much more impressive," he said, "if we're still debating translations. That name is the only thing we really know about it, right?"

"What do you mean? There are lots of stories, not about the sword, I grant you, but the Smith's weapons—"

"—cannot be used against humankind," he broke in. "They were built to defeat the gods themselves: the black mace, the bronze lance, and the rose sword. 'Only a human hand dare wield them—'"

"'—against the monsters of the night,'" she said completing the quotation. "I know that." Then she thought about what he'd said. "Oh, I see what you mean. You think the stories might be wrong."

"My father was a monster, but he was a human monster. You, my sweet, are not human."

"Half," she corrected absently, "and I'm not so certain

about your father. Other than your Geoffrey and a few Uriah, I don't think I've ever actually ever so much as wounded anyone with it. I seldom use it except for training, where the idea is *not* to cut up your opponent. For real fighting, I use weapons I'm more competent with. Wolf, if your father was human, Ambris shouldn't have worked against him."

Wolf tapped his fingers absently on her rump with the rhythms of his thoughts. "Perhaps the Smith's interpretation of human was broader than ours. He might have included half-breed shapeshifters as human. My father was trying to become immortal like the gods—maybe he succeeded far enough that the sword could be used against him."

"For the spell holding my father, it doesn't matter what its capabilities, does it? I'm not going to try and kill anyone with it—just break a spell. It did break through the ae'Magi's wards—"

"No, it didn't."

She sat up then so she could look at him. "What do you mean?"

"Ah," he said. "You wouldn't know. My father's wards protected him by preventing any weapon from doing physical damage. Magical damage is more difficult to guard against by warding, and he believed that he was more than capable of protecting himself from magical attack. Your sword never did draw blood. The wards stayed there until his magic died."

He threw back the covers, set her off him, and arose. "There's an easy way to see if it can break spells as well."

He pulled a small bench to a clear spot in the room and made a few signs in the air over it. Stepping back, he shook his head. "We might as well test it against a more powerful spell, since that is what we will be facing." He made a few more gestures. "Now nothing should be able to touch this bench."

Still tucked warmly under the covers, Aralorn snickered. "The Bench No Axe Could Touch Nor Rump Rest Upon," she intoned, as if it were the title of some minstrel's song.

"At least not until the magic wears off in a week or two," said Wolf. "I've worked a series of spells on this bench. Do you want to try your sword on it?"

Aralorn left the warmth of her bed and found Ambris where she'd tucked it under the mattress before attending the gathering. Unsheathing it, she watched the reflected glow from the fire shine on the rose-colored blade.

It was small for a sword, made for a young boy or woman rather than a full-grown man. Except for the metal hilt, it could have been newly forged—but no one made swords with metal grips anymore. After the Wizard Wars, when most of the mages were dead, metal hilts hadn't been much of a problem. Being connected to a dying magician by metal was a *very* bad idea. Now hilts were made of wood or bone, and had been for the past few centuries as the mageborn slowly became more numerous again.

The metal hilt hadn't worried Aralorn when she'd chosen it from the armory before she'd left Lambshold. She'd always been able to tell mageborn from mundane. The sword had been the right size and well balanced, so she'd taken it. For years, she'd carried it, never realizing that she held anything other than an odd-colored, undersized sword fit for an undersized fighter.

She approached the bench and examined it thoughtfully.

"It won't attack back," said Wolf, apparently amused at her caution. "You can just hit it."

She gave him a nasty look. She always felt awkward with the blasted weapon even though years of practice had made her almost competent. The recent change in their relationship had made her, to her surprise, a bit shy around him. She wanted to impress him, not remind him just how poor a swordswoman she was.

Experimentally, she swung the sword at the bench. It bounced off as if propelled, the force of it almost making Aralorn lose her grip. Shifting her stance, Aralorn tried simply setting the sword against the warding. The repelling force was still there, but by locking her forearms and leaning into the sword, she managed to keep it touching the spell. She held it there for a while, before she gave up and let the sword fall away.

"You need to follow through better," said Wolf with such earnestness that she knew he was teasing.

Aralorn turned and braced both hands on her hips and glared at him, but not seriously. "If I required your opinion, I'd give you over to my father's Questioner and be done with it."

He raised his eyebrows innocently. "I was only trying to help."

She snorted and spun, delivering a blow to the bench that should have reduced it to kindling, but it did no damage at all.

"I don't think it works this way," she said. "It's not heating up at all, and when I used it on the ae'Magi, it was so hot I couldn't hold it."

"All right," said Wolf. "Let's try this. I'll try to work a spell on you while you hold the sword up between us."

Aralorn frowned. "Correct me if I'm wrong, but aren't you being a little rash? If that's why it killed your father, then it could do the same to you."

He didn't say anything.

She had a sudden remembrance of the look on his face as he'd called lightning down upon himself in her dream. *It was only a dream,* she told herself fiercely.

"Plague take you, Wolf," she said as mildly as she could. "It's not important enough to risk your life over. If it won't work on the spells, it can't help us here."

"It might work against the shadow-thing we both saw,"

he said. "Then perhaps you and I could examine the spells holding your father more closely."

"Fine," she said. "Then we'll try it on that. Do you want to go down now?

Wolf shook his head. "Wait until morning. There are a lot of creatures who are weakened by the rising of the sun—and I'm tired."

Aralorn nodded and slid Ambris back into the sheath before storing her in the wardrobe. She watched Wolf release the spells he'd laid on the bench, creating quite a light show in the process. Reaching out with the sixth sense that allowed her to find and work magic, she could feel the shifting forces but not touch them—what he was using was wholly human in origin.

Later, when the banked fire was the only light in the room, Aralorn snuggled deeper into Wolf's arms.

It will be all right, she thought fiercely.

————

Late in the night, long after the inhabitants of the castle had gone to sleep, a man emerged from the shadows of the mourning room and stepped to the curtained alcove that contained the slumbering Lyon, his path lit by a few torches left burning in their wall sconces. He pulled back the curtains and started to step into the room but found himself unable to do so.

He placed a hand on the barrier of air and earth that Wolf had erected.

"Yes," he said softly, "he is here."

The warding would keep out human visitors, but he was something more. The tall, robed figure dissolved into the darkness and reappeared inside the room. Before he materialized completely, a shadow slipped from the side of the man on the bier.

"Ah, my beauty," crooned the intruder. "It's all right. I know, you were never meant to face *his* powers. I forget things now. I had forgotten that he could take the form of a wolf, or we would have been ready for him." The shadow stroked against his legs like a cat, emitting squeaks and hisses as it did so. "Hold the Lyon fast, little one. We will force them to come to us."

FOUR

The chill wind weaved its way through Aralorn's heavy woolen cloak with the ease of a skilled lover, and she shivered in spite of the layers of clothing she wore. Although the keep was barely out of sight, the bones of her hands ached from the bitter chill. It always took weeks for her to acclimate to the cold northern winter.

Wolf, warm under his thick pelt, observed her attempts to tame her cloak, and asked, "Why did you decide to walk? Sheen would be much faster, not to mention warmer."

"The shapeshifters' village is difficult to reach by horse—sometimes impossible—and that area of Lambshold is too dangerous to leave him tied for any length of time." Aralorn winced at the sharpness of her voice. His question had been reasonable; there was no need to give him the edge of her tongue because she was disappointed.

Before first light, they had visited the bier room and attempted to use the sword to slay the creature. Neither she nor Wolf, who, plague take the man, was a much better swordsman, had been able to even touch the shadow-thing with Ambris. The shadow had melted away from the sword with laughable ease.

Wolf hadn't been able to tell anything more about the spells that held her father than he had before. Black magic had been used, but the pattern of the spelling was too complex to decipher while distracted by the creature who lurked in the bier room.

The only good thing to come out of the visit was that, as far as Wolf could determine, her father was no worse off this morning than he'd been last night. Scant comfort when his condition was so close to death that most people could not tell he was alive.

Wolf gave the clear skies a skeptical glance. "No clouds—I suspect it will be colder than sin. Why don't you shapechange? Your mouse and goose aren't much good here, but the icelynx is adapted for this area."

The wind gusted, blowing snow into Aralorn's face.

"Good idea" said Aralorn. "Then the shepherds will attack me, too." She took a deep breath and reined in her temper. Snapping at Wolf was not going to free her father any faster, and for all that Wolf appeared so impassive, she knew better than most how easy it was to wound him. "Sorry. It's all right. I'll warm up as we walk."

"I would not fret much about a bunch of sheepherders."

Aralorn slanted a glance at him, unable to tell if he was serious or teasing. "They are my father's men. No use stirring them up unduly if we don't have to—besides, I'd just as soon talk to anyone we see. You never know what kernels of information might prove useful."

They followed one of the main paths for several miles; this close to the keep, it was usually well traveled even in the dead of winter. They didn't meet anyone, but it surprised her how much livestock had been left in the high pastures. Usually, they'd have been brought down to the lower, warmer valleys before any snow fell.

The first few herds they passed were distant, but she

could tell they were not sheep from their color. When she
had lived in Lambshold, there had been few herds of cattle;
they were better suited for more temperate climates.

By chance, they came upon a herd unexpectedly close,
and she caught a good look at the short, stout animals with
long red hair that would have done credit to one of the
mountain bears.

She stopped where she was and frowned at them a
moment. Softly, so the animals wouldn't be alarmed and
charge, she said, "Ryefox."

"Crossbred, by those horns," Wolf replied. "I saw a
ryefox drive away a bear once. Good eating, though."

"If they're only half as nasty as their full-blooded relatives, I'd rather face a half dozen Uriah," commented Aralorn. "Naked," she added, as one of the animals took a step
toward them.

"They're almost as sweet-tempered as you are this
morning," observed Wolf.

"Hah," she said, forgetting that she'd been trying to
keep quiet so as not to arouse the ryefox crossbreeds.
"Look who's talking, old gloom and doom."

Wolf wagged his tail to acknowledge the justice of her
comment, but only said, "I wonder that he found a cow or
bull willing to go near enough to a ryefox to breed."

"This must be the livestock experiment that Correy was
talking about last night. The one my uncle was helping my
father with."

She kept a wary eye on the herd as they walked, but the
ryefox appeared to be satisfied that their territory wasn't
being threatened and stayed where they were.

A chest-high rock wall marked the boundary where the
grazing ended and the northern croplands began. Aralorn
caught the top of the wooden gate barring the path and
swung over without bothering to open it. Wolf bounded
lightly over the fence a few feet away and landed chest deep

in a drift of snow. He eyed her narrowly as he climbed back onto the path. Aralorn kept her face scrupulously blank.

She cleared her throat. "Yes, uhm, I was just going to advise you that this area gets windy from time to time—the mountains, you see. And . . . uh, you might want to watch out for drifts."

"Thank you." replied Wolf gravely, then he shook, taking great care to get as much of the snow on Aralorn as he could.

As they continued their journey, the path began to branch off, and the one that they followed got narrower and less well-defined with each division.

"Why farm this?" asked Wolf, eyeing the rough terrain. "The land we just traveled through is better farmland."

"Father doesn't do anything with this land. His farms are along the southern border, several thousand feet lower in altitude, where the climate is milder. But there is good fertile soil here in the small valleys between the ridges—the largest maybe twenty acres or so. The crofters farm it and pay Father a tithe of their produce for the use of the land and protection from bandits. He could get more gold by running animals here instead—but this makes good defensive sense. The lower fields are easily burned and trampled by armies, but up here it's too much trouble."

"Speaking of burning," said Wolf, "something has burned here recently. Can you smell it?"

She tried, but her nose caught nothing more than the dry-sweet smell of winter. "No, but Correy said that one of the crofts had been burned. Can you tell where the smell is coming from?"

"Somewhere a mile or so in that direction." He motioned vaguely south of the trail they were following.

"Let's head that way then," she said. "I'd like to take a look."

They broke with the main path to follow a trail that twisted here and there, up and down, through the stone ridges. It had been well traveled lately, more so than the other such trails they had passed, although a thin layer of snow covered even the most recent tracks. As they neared the farm, Aralorn could smell the sourness of old char, but it didn't prepare her for the sight that met her eyes.

Scorched earth followed the shape of the fields exactly, stopping just inside the fence line. The wooden fence itself was unmarked by the blaze, which had burned the house so thoroughly that only the base stones allowed Aralorn to see where the house had been. All around the croft, the fields lay pristine under the snow.

Wolf slipped through the fence and examined the narrow line that marked the end of the burn.

"Magic," he said. He hesitated briefly, his nostrils flaring as he tested the air. "Black magic with the same odd flavor of the spells holding the Lyon. Look here, on the stone by the corner of the fence."

She stepped over the fence and knelt on the blackened ground. Just inside the corner post, there was a fist-sized gray rock smudged with a rust-colored substance.

"Is it human blood?" she asked.

Wolf shook his head. "I can't tell. Someone used this fire and the deaths here to gather power."

"Enough power to set a spell on my father?"

Before he could answer, the wind shifted a little, and he stiffened and twisted until he could look back down their path.

Aralorn followed his gaze to see a man coming up the trail they had taken here. By his gray beard, she judged him to be an older man, though his steps were quick and firm. In ten years a child might become a man, but a man only grayed a bit more: She matched his features with a memory and smiled a welcome.

"Whatcha be doing there, missy?" he asked as soon as he was near enough to speak, oblivious to Aralorn's smile.

"I'm trying to discover what kind of magic has been at

work, Kurmun. What are you doing here? I thought your farm was some distance away."

He frowned at her, then a smile broke over his face, breaking the craggy planes as if it were not something he did often. "Aralorn, as I live and breathe. I'd not thought to see tha face again. I told old Jervon that I'd have a look at his place, he's still that shook. Commet tha then for tha father's passing?"

She smiled. "Yes, I did. But as it turns out, Father's not dead—only ensorcelled."

Kurmun grunted, showing no hint of surprise. "Is what happens when tha lives in a place consecrated to the Lady. Bad thing, that."

She shook her head. "Now, that was taken care of long since. You know the family's not been cursed by the Lady since the new temple was built. This is something quite different, and it may take a few days to discover what. I thought the burning of the farm might have something to do with it."

The old man nodded slowly. "Hadn't thought there was a connection, but there might, there might at that. Have a care here, then. Tha father, he took ill here."

"I didn't know that." But she could have guessed.

Black magic had long carried a death penalty. A mage would avoid it as much as possible. It only made sense that the black magic Wolf felt here would belong to the spell on the Lyon.

"Aye, he come here tha day after it burned. Walked the fence line, he did. Got to the twisted pole over there and collapsed."

"Now, that's interesting," said Aralorn thoughtfully. "Why didn't anyone at the hold mention it?"

"Well," replied Kurmun, though she hadn't expected him to answer her question, "reckon they didn't know. Just he and I here, and I tossed him on his horse and took him to the hold. They was in such a state that no one asked where it'd happened. Only asked what, so that's all I told they. This is some young men's mischief, thought I then." He made a sweeping gesture that encompassed the burnt farm. "Tha father was felled by magic. Didn't rightly think one had much to do with t'other myself. But if tha thinks it so, then so think I now."

"I think it does," she said. "Thank you. Did we lose any people?"

He shook his head. "Nary a one. Jervon's oldest daughter come into her time. The missus and Jervon gathered they children and went up to attend the birth. Lost a brace of oxen, but they sheep was in lower pastures."

"Lucky," said Aralorn. "Or someone knew that they were gone."

Kurmun grunted and scratched his nose. "The Lady's new temple ha' been cleaned and set to rights. Word is that there's a priestess there now; I be thinking tha might want to be stopping in and talking to her. Happens she may help tha father. Happens not." He shrugged.

"Ridane's temple is being used?" There had been a lot more activity in the gods' temples lately. She didn't see how that could have any bearing on the Lyon's condition, but she intended to check out anything unusual that had happened recently. "I'll make certain to visit."

"I'll be on my way then," he said, tipping his head. "Told my son's wife I'd find a bit of salt for her out of the hold stores." As he turned to go, his gaze met Wolf's eyes. "By the Lady," he exclaimed. "Tha beast's a wolf."

"Yes," agreed Aralorn, adding hastily, "He doesn't eat sheep."

"Well," said the old man, frowning, "see that he don't. I'd keep him near tha so some shepherd doesn't get too quick with his sling afore he has a chance to garner that tha wolf doesna eat sheep."

"I intend to."

"Right." Kurmun nodded, and, with a last suspicious look at Wolf, he was on his way.

As soon as he was out of sight, Wolf said, "He called the death goddess the Lady?"

Aralorn smiled briefly. "Lest speaking her name call her attention to him, yes. The new temple is nearly five centuries old. 'New,' you understand, differentiates it from the 'old' temple that my long-dead ancestor had razed to build a hold. There wasn't much left of the new temple when I last saw it; it's been deserted for centuries. I wouldn't think it would be possible to resurrect anything from the piles of stones. In any case, the temple is on the other side of the estate, so we'll have to go there another day."

She tapped her finger on a fence post. "This burned down before my father came here. Wouldn't it have to happen at the same time?"

"There are ways to store power or even set spells to complete when certain conditions are met—like having your father come to this place."

"It was a trap," said Aralorn, "set for my father. The burning of the croft served both as bait and bane. Anyone who knew my father would know that he'd investigate if one of his people's houses burned." She shuffled snow around. "This farm is not too far from the shapeshifters' territory. Other than knowing that it is possible for them to use blood magic, I don't know what they would do with it or how. My uncle will know."

"It could be a human mage," said Wolf. "But any mage who came by here could tell that there was black magic done here. Why would they risk that? My father's reign excepted, the ae'Magi's job is to keep things like this from happening. They kill black mages, Aralorn. Only my father's assurances and his power kept them from killing me—and they had no proof such as this. When we discover who did this, he will die. Why risk that merely to imprison the Lyon when killing would have been easier? What did he accomplish that was worth that?"

Silence gathered as Aralorn stared at the blood-splattered rock.

"Nevyn could do this," said Wolf. "As long as no one knows I'm here, he will be the first one Kisrah ae'Magi will suspect. Nevyn first trained under old Santik."

Aralorn frowned. She'd forgotten that as the ae'Magi's son, Wolf would know a lot of the politics and doings of the mageborn. "Santik is someone Kisrah would associate with black magic?"

Wolf sighed. "His reputation wasn't much better than mine—it wouldn't surprise me or anyone else to find that he'd slipped into dark ways. Certainly, his library would have had the right books; nearly all the great mages have books they aren't supposed to."

"Nevyn's first master was a great mage, too? Was that because of his family's station?" Aralorn asked. "I thought the reason they married him off to my sister was that he wasn't good enough to be a wizard proper. I've never seen him use magic at all."

"He can work magic," Wolf said. "They'd never have wasted Kisrah—or Santik, for that matter—on just any apprentice. But between Santik and being a Darranian-born mage, Nevyn learned to hate being a wizard. When Kisrah was satisfied that Nevyn could control his magic, he let him choose his own path."

"You knew Nevyn," said Aralorn slowly. It wasn't in the details; those were something any wizard might know of another. It was the sympathy in Wolf's voice. "Why didn't you say something to me before?"

"We weren't friends," he said. "Not even acquaintances, really. Kisrah was a particular favorite of my father's—"

"Because your father enjoyed playing games with honorable men," muttered Aralorn.

"—*whatever* his reason," continued Wolf, "and Kisrah

brought Nevyn to the ae'Magi's castle several times. Nevyn was quiet, as I remember him, always trying to disappear into the background. He had plenty of courage, though. I think I frightened him to death, but he never gave ground."

"Ten years ago you were just a boy," said Aralorn. "Nevyn's a couple of years older than me—which makes him more than five years older than you."

"I frightened a lot of people, Aralorn," Wolf said.

She ruffled the fur behind his ears. "Not me. Come, let's go visit my uncle so you can frighten him, too."

As they climbed higher in the mountains, the area became heavily wooded, and they left behind all signs of cultivation. Here and there great boulders were scattered, some the size of an ox and others as big as a cottage. The narrow path they followed was obviously traveled by humans and game alike, and few enough of either. The dense growth, steep slopes, and snow made it difficult to find a place to leave the path. At last, Aralorn found a shallow, frozen creek to walk on.

"It must be uncomfortable to do this in the spring," commented Wolf, stepping onto the snow-covered ice.

"It's not easy anytime," replied Aralorn, momentarily busy keeping her footing. After a moment, she realized his comment had more to do with the streambed they followed than the difficulty of the trail. "You don't have to come this way exactly. All that's necessary is to find someplace in this part of Lambshold that is not often traveled. Then you can find the maze."

"The maze?" Wolf sounded intrigued.

She smiled, stopping to knock the snow that had packed itself around the short nails that kept the leather soles of her walking boots from slipping on the ice and snow. "You'll see when we find it. But if you'd care to help, keep your eye out for a bit of quartz. I need it to work some magic. There should be quite a bit of it in the steep areas, where there's no snow to cover it."

They came to a small clearing bordered on two sides by the sharp sides of a mountain. Aralorn crossed the clearing and began searching for rocks on the steep areas where the sun and wind had left large sections bare.

"It doesn't have to be quartz," she said finally. "Sandstone would work as well."

Wolf lifted his snow-covered nose from a promising nook under a clump of dead brush. "You could have said so earlier and saved yourself a case of frostbite. There is sandstone all over here."

Aralorn tucked her cold, wet hands underneath her sweaters and warmed them against her middle as Wolf searched back and forth over the area they'd just covered. She'd taken her gloves off to push aside the snow that the afternoon sun had begun to thaw. They had too far to travel to risk getting her gloves wet. When she could feel her fingers again, she pulled the gloves out of her belt and slipped them over her hands.

"You know," she said, as he seemed to be having no success finding the sandstone, "aren't the crystals on your staff quartz?"

"I ought to let you try casting a spell using one of them," said Wolf, not lifting his gaze from the ground, "but I find that I have become more squeamish of late. Ah, yes, here it is."

Aralorn bent to pick up the smooth yellowish brown stone Wolf had unearthed and polish it free of dirt on her cloak.

"Sandstone is for perseverance," she said, "quartz for luck. Which is why I started out looking for quartz: I suspect we'll be spending the night up here."

Wolf lowered his eyelids in amusement. "If you want luck, I have some opal you could use."

"Thanks, but I'll pass," Aralorn demurred. "Ill luck I don't need."

She held the stone in her closed hand and raised her arm to shoulder height. Closing her eyes, she began singing. The song she chose was a children's song in her mother's tongue—though the words didn't matter for the magic, just the pattern of the music, which would be their key to entering her mother's world.

Slowly, almost shyly, awareness of the forest crept upon her. She could feel the winter sleep encasing the plants: wary curiosity peering at them from a rotted-out cedar in the form of a martin; the brook waiting for spring to allow it to run to the ocean far away. Finally, she found what she had been searching for and brushed lightly against the current of magic threaded throughout the forest. When she was certain it had perceived her, she stopped singing and allowed the awareness to pass from her. She looked down at the rock in her hands and, just for a moment, could see an arrow.

"Now, why doesn't it surprise me that we have to travel up the side of the mountain?" she grumbled. She showed the arrow to Wolf, then tossed the stone back on the ground since it had served its purpose. "I should have brought some quartz from home. Irrenna won't have disturbed my stashes of spell starters."

"The maze would have been different?" asked Wolf, pacing beside her as she started up the mountain.

"It's always different," replied Aralorn. "The magic I worked to find the start of the maze will only work with sandstone or quartz—someone's idea of a joke, I suspect. You know—'Only with luck or persistence will you find the sanctuary hidden in the heart of the mountains.' The kinds of words storytellers are fond of. I prefer to start with luck."

The mountainside looked rougher from the bottom than it actually was, an unusual occurrence in Aralorn's experience. All the same, she almost missed the stone altogether, hidden in plain sight as it was in the midst of a dozen other large boulders.

"Good," she said, turning abruptly off her chosen path upward and taking a steep downward route that brought her skidding and sliding to the cluster of granite boulders. "The maze remembers me."

"Ah?"

Aralorn nodded, touching a stone half again as tall as she was and twice as wide. "This stone is the first. The identity stone—for me that has always been granite."

"Granite for compromise," rumbled Wolf, "or blending."

"Right," she smiled. "Blending—that's me. You'll have to touch it, too."

Wolf pawed it gently, drawing back quickly as if he had touched a candle flame. "That's not magic," he said, startled.

"No," agreed Aralorn, waiting.

"It's alive."

"That's the secret of the maze," she agreed.

She drew a simple rune on the granite boulder with a light touch of her finger. As with the sandstone, a directional arrow appeared, outlined in shimmering bits of mica. It pointed across the mountain.

As they started on the indicated route, Wolf was silent. Aralorn left him to his thoughts and concentrated on staying aware of their surroundings. The stones could be difficult to find. She was so busy peering under bushes that she almost missed the waist-high rock standing directly in her path, as out of place in its environment as a wolf in a fold.

"Obsidian," observed Aralorn soberly, touching the black, glasslike surface. The second stone would be Wolf's. The maze's choice surprised her at first; she'd half expected hematite, for war and anger. But the stones of the maze had read deeper than that, identifying Wolf's nature as clearly as they had seen hers. He wore the mask of anger on his face, but his heart was enclosed in sorrow.

"This one's yours," she told him, in case he'd missed its

significance. "Obsidian for sorrow. The rest we find will be something about both of us."

"Sorrow?" commented Wolf.

"Yes," said Aralorn. "Like the maze as a whole, the first stones can tell you more than that. They'll show you a bit about yourself and the pattern you're living now—if you interpret what they're saying correctly. I've always mostly ignored what the maze had to say about me, but you can try it if you'd like. Touch the stone for a minute or two, and it will tell you something."

He hesitated, then took a step sideways and leaned against it, saying as he did so, "I'm not certain this is wise. I've never been fond of prophecy."

"Mmm. Remember, it's not a prediction of things to come: It's an assessment of who you are now. And they're not infallible."

After a bit, he stepped away. He didn't say anything, so she didn't ask him what he'd seen. She drew the rune she'd used before, and the arrow appeared on the top of the stone, sending them at a shallow angle downward.

"The next stones are less personal and intended to help predict the near future—some of the time. The language of stones is pretty limited. Mostly it will just present attributes we have or will need."

"Not very helpful," said Wolf, and Aralorn grinned at him.

"Not that I've ever noticed."

During the next several hours, they wandered from stone to stone, finding serpentine for wit, quartz for luck, and malachite for lust (she snickered a bit at that one). They ate the salted meat and cheese Aralorn had brought with them. As the sun reached its zenith, they started down the path the malachite had chosen for them. The stone they found was amethyst, protection against evil. When they came to a second, then yet a third amethyst, Aralorn grew concerned.

"I wonder if the stones will let us through," she said, crouching in the snow beside the melon-sized crystal. "They might not if they think that harm will enter with us."

"Do you want me to wait here?" Wolf asked softly. "You might find this easier on your own."

Realizing he'd taken the message incorrectly, she raised her eyebrow. "Amethyst may be protection from evil, but the stones have already appraised you and have named you sorrowful. If they had judged you as harshly as you judge yourself, we would never have come this far."

"Then you took quite a chance not coming here alone."

She braced both hands on her hips. "I took no chances."

"Stubborn as a pack mule," he said.

Since she'd heard a number of people claim that, she couldn't disagree.

She drew another rune and saw that their path led upward, as it had for the past few stones.

"I hope this ends soon," she grumbled. "I really don't want to spend the night outside. It's cold, it's getting late, and we still have to make the trip back."

Waiting at the top of the climb was a wolf-sized chunk of white marble.

"Judgment," said Aralorn in satisfaction. She thought it would be the last one, but found another maze stone at the top of a twisting bramble-and-brush-filled gorge.

"Rose quartz," murmured Wolf. "It seems we are welcome here."

Even so, Aralorn was unsurprised when the stone pointed them down the gorge.

"I knew I should have held out for luck," she said. "Sometimes, there are ways around the gorge."

There was no trail. Aralorn tore the knee out of her pants and almost lost her cloak before they arrived safely at the bottom. Wolf, of course, had no difficulty at all.

They emerged from the deep undergrowth into a small grotto. From the cliffs overhead, a solidly frozen waterfall plunged into an ice-covered pool. The transformation from the dense gray vegetation to the pristine little valley was shockingly abrupt, as if they had stepped into someone's neatly kept castle garden. Even the snow that covered the ground was evenly dispersed, unmarred by footprints.

"This is it," announced Aralorn with satisfaction. After a moment, she nodded toward the waterfall. "I spent one summer trailing streams in this part of Lambshold, trying to find every stream anywhere near here, and never found one that came through this grotto. I even tried to back-track this one, but I never managed it. I'd look away for a moment, and the stream would be gone."

"I could do that with a variation of the *lost* spell." Wolf eyed the rushing water speculatively.

"If you say so." She heaved a theatrical sigh. " 'Frustrating' is what I called it."

He laughed. "I'll bet you did. Isn't there supposed to be someone here?"

"No, this is just the end of the maze. There's a trail over by the waterfall," Aralorn said, and began picking her way up the path that edged the pond.

A thin layer of snow turned to a sheet of ice as they approached the waterfall. Aralorn set her feet carefully and kept moving. Wolf drew to a halt and growled.

"I know," said Aralorn quietly, stepping behind the shimmering veil of the frozen waterfall. "Someone's watching us. I had expected them earlier."

The difference between the bright daylight and the shadow of the falls caused her to stop to allow her eyes to adjust. Wolf bumped into her, then slipped past, examining the stone surface of the cliff face behind the waterfall. Behind a thin sheet of ice over the rock where a few last trickles of water had frozen, there was a small tunnel in the rock.

"That goes in about ten feet and ends," said Aralorn. "I stayed there overnight once, but it was summer."

The far end of the narrow path behind the falls was frozen over, but a few hits with the haft of one of her knives broke a small hole, and her booted foot cleared a space large enough to climb through.

Once out from under the waterfall, their way twisted up the side of the mountain. The path was cobbled, and the smooth stones were slicker than the natural ground. Aralorn tried to walk beside the path as much as she could. The climb was thankfully short, only to the top of the falls.

Over the years, the stream that formed the waterfall had cut a deep channel between the two mountains that fed it with the runoff from the snowy peaks. The path was cut into the side of one mountain several feet above the stream, winding and twisting with the course of the water.

After walking a mile or so, the path turned abruptly away from the mountain, through a thicket of brush and into a wide valley.

Wolf could still feel the eyes watching them, though he couldn't tell where the spy was. It was not magic that told him so much, but the keen senses of the wolf. Not scent, nor sight, nor hearing, but faint impressions gathered from all three. It distracted him as he examined the place to which Aralorn had brought them.

The valley was surrounded by steep-sided hills that reminded him of the valley in the Northlands where he'd spent the past winter, although that had been far smaller. Someone had taken a lot of time to find a place this sheltered. The stone path, now half-buried in the snow, led up a slight incline to a pair of gateposts. Other than those, the valley appeared empty. Perhaps, he thought as he followed Aralorn, the village was located over the next rise.

Then, between one step and the next, magic rose over him from the ground, momentarily paralyzing him with its strength. Defensively, he analyzed it: a blending illusion that utilized the lay of the land to hide something in the valley.

Without conscious act, he found himself holding the magic to break the spell, magic that had nothing to do with the familiar, violent forces he normally worked. This was a surge of power that took its direction from the brief alarm he'd felt at the sudden wall of magic. It flared in an attempt to twist out of his fragile hold and attack the ensorcellment before him. The effort it took to restrain it challenged his training and power both.

"Wolf?"

Even wrapped as he was in the grip of his power, her voice reached him. Fear of what his magic would do to her gave him the strength to contain it, just barely.

————

"Wolf?" Aralorn said again, kneeling beside him.

She didn't dare touch him as he swayed and shook with rhythmic spasms. Gradually, the spasms slowed and stopped. He took a deep, shuddering breath and looked up at Aralorn.

"Problems?" she asked.

"Yes."

"Do you want to wait for me back by the waterfall?"

"No," he said. "It's all right now. It just took me by surprise."

She looked at him narrowly for a moment before deciding to accept his word on the matter.

"Fine, then. There is some kind of protective illusion over the village. I don't think we ought to tamper with it, but if we approach, I suspect we'll be met."

"Such an illusion is not the usual practice?" He sounded as controlled as he usually did, though he was so tense she could see the fine trembling of his muscles.

Aralorn shook her head in answer. "Not when I lived here."

Though the village was hidden, the gateposts that marked the entrance were still there. Wolf, the ruff on his neck still raised from his battle for control of his magic, ranged in random patterns to either side.

"Stay on the path," she warned him. "They wouldn't have left the gateposts here if they didn't have something nasty protecting the village from people who aren't polite enough to enter by the proper way."

When she tried to walk between the gateposts, a barrier of magic stopped her. It wasn't painful, just solid.

Aralorn drew the rune she'd used in the maze on the left-hand pillar, but the barrier remained. She frowned but didn't try to force her way through the gate.

Instead, she spoke to the watcher who'd accompanied them from the waterfall. "I have come to speak with Halven, my uncle." Her tongue fought her a little as she curled it around the shapeshifter language that she hadn't used since she'd last been here.

Beyond the posts, the wind stirred the snow into random swirls. The quiet was oppressive and uncomfortable.

Turning to Wolf, Aralorn said, "They may make us wait for a long time. Sometimes, the oddest things strike them as humorous."

Without reply, Wolf made himself comfortable though he fairly vibrated with tension. Aralorn shivered as a cold breeze ran under her cloak.

"It is cold here," said a man behind her in the same tongue she'd used. "You must want to talk to this uncle very badly."

Wolf came to his feet with a growl; he hadn't heard the man approach.

She put a hand on his head, then turned to face the stranger.

Shapeshifters were hard to identify: They could assume any features they chose. Nothing in the beautiful face and artfully swept-back bronze hair was familiar. Voices, though, were more difficult to change, and given a moment to recover, she knew who it was. She smiled.

"Badly," she agreed, switching to Rethian for Wolf's sake. "I would have waited a lot longer than this, Uncle Halven."

"You might have indeed," he replied without altering his language, "had I not seen you myself. I am not high in favor at this moment, and you never were."

"You flatter me," Aralorn replied. She continued to speak Rethian. If he was going to be rude, she'd follow his lead. "As I recall, I was too insignificant to warrant animosity."

Halven smiled like a cat—with fangs and cold eyes. "Aralorn the half-breed certainly was, but the Sianim spy is a different matter altogether."

She raised her eyebrows. "Spy? Who says I am a spy?"

"If you would talk," said Halven mildly, "it would best be done here."

"That's fine," she said. "I apologize in advance for keeping you out in the cold."

"Not at all." Halven was suddenly all gracious host, though he'd yet to switch to Rethian, which he would have if he'd really been in an accommodating mood. "What brings you and your dog here on this chilly morning?"

Wolf was sometimes mistaken for a dog by people who hadn't seen him move because he lacked the usual gray coat. It surprised her that Halven would mistake him, though, and she almost turned to look at Wolf. But she didn't want to draw her uncle's attention to him.

Assuming the shapeshifters were as resistant to the ae'Magi's magic as she had been, there was no reason they would be upset about his death; but she would rather they didn't know any more about Wolf than was necessary. Unlike the people at Lambshold, if Halven looked closely, he might be able to tell that Wolf was a shapeshifter—and a both green and human mage of great power. With that much information, it was only a step to identify him as

Cain ae'Magison, who killed the ae'Magi. The shapeshifters didn't talk much to people in the outside world, but that was one thing she would rather no one knew. The ae'Magi's spells ensured that almost everyone loved him—and if they knew where Cain was, they would try to kill him.

The maze stones knew what, and who, Wolf was already, but they seldom spoke anymore.

"Have you heard that my father's been taken ill?" she asked.

"I'd heard he was dead," replied Halven flatly.

"Yes, well these things do get exaggerated upon occasion, don't they?" Aralorn said. "I'm pleased to tell you that he's alive, but there is some sort of magic binding keeping him in a deathlike trance. I wondered if you might know something about it."

For a moment, her uncle's expression changed, too quickly for her to catch what it was he felt; she hoped he was glad the Lyon wasn't dead.

Seeing her face, Halven laughed with real humor that pierced the armor of his outward charm like a ray of sunlight through a stained-glass window. "You want to know if I did it, eh?"

"That was the general idea," she replied.

"No, child, I haven't done anything to him. As a matter of fact, we have begun to exchange favors." He shook his head in bemusement. "I never thought I would deal with a human, but the Lyon is nothing if not persistent—much like his daughter."

Relief swept through her. Halven prided himself on being truthful in all things. If he'd hurt her father, he'd have told her or found some clever way of not admitting one way or the other.

"Would you be willing to come and look at him? I've never seen anything like the spell that holds him—I can't even tell if it is green magic or human."

Halven was shaking his head before she finished speaking.

"No. Call down one of the human mages. My position in the quorum of elders is touchy enough without risking a visit to the human stronghold. They feel I have compromised our safety, though they agreed before I helped your father with his breeding project."

"The ryefox," said Aralorn thoughtfully. "That's the reason for the new glamour and protection for the village. Too many people know you're here. What did my father give you for your help?"

"The Lyon has deeded this section of Lambshold to me and my kindred by special dispensation of the new king. We also have a treaty calling for the protection of our land by the Lord of Lambshold in perpetuity."

"If the Lyon said it, it is true," said Aralorn. Then she raised an eyebrow. "*If* he had time to tell my brother Correy about it. You can't expect Correy to take *your* word on the matter, given the suspicion that you yourself might have caused my father's strange condition."

The Lyon wouldn't have left it to chance, she knew. He would have recorded it immediately—but Halven might not know that.

"Your manipulation is heavy-handed, Aralorn," he said.

She shrugged. "I only tell you what you have been telling yourself. The Lyon probably told my brother. *Probably* my brother will hold to my father's word—even with the suspicion that will be aimed toward the shapeshifters. But it would be better for you if the Lyon was returned to health. Irrenna has sent word to the ae'Magi, but the spells are black magic. Kisrah may be quite brilliant, but his reputation does not make him an expert in the dark arts."

"And I am?" he asked.

"How old are you?" asked Aralorn. "Kisrah is only a few years above forty. How many more centuries have you spent learning? Don't tell me that you have nothing more to offer us than a human mage."

"Persistent," he said chidingly. "I told you his affliction

was none of my doing, child. Making an agreement with the Lyon is one thing; going to the keep is an entirely different matter. I will not endanger my people further."

Aralorn met his gaze. "Come. Because I ask it of you. Because my mother would have done so if she had lived."

His eyelids fell to cover the expression in his eyes as he thought. She wasn't certain her appeal would be enough, especially because she had no idea if her mother cared enough for the Lyon to come to his aid.

It might just be possible that he would want to come. No one could resist the Lyon's charm when it was directed at them, not even, she hoped, Halven. If he liked her father enough . . .

———

Wolf watched Aralorn's uncle with sympathy—Aralorn could talk a cat into giving up its mouse. He could only understand her half of the conversation, but he could tell quite a bit from Halven's gestures and Aralorn's speech.

Wolf wondered, for a moment, why Aralorn had told him once that her uncle was indifferent to her. The poor man hadn't even taken his eyes off her long enough to notice that her pet was a wolf. The shapeshifters had few children—Halven, Wolf knew, had none at all.

———

"Leave the humans to their own trials, my dear," said a lark as it landed on Halven's shoulder. Her voice was light and high-pitched, making it difficult to understand her.

He shrugged irritably, sending the small bird to perch on top of a gatepost. "Does this concern you, Kessenih? Tend to your own business."

Aralorn could have cheered. Nothing was as likely to persuade her uncle to go to the hold as his wife's opposition.

"Very well, Aralorn," he said, "I'll accompany you to see your father. Is that silly goose still the only bird you do?" He stopped abruptly and frowned. "That dog"—he paused, frowning at Wolf—"wolf of yours is going to slow us down."

Halven had looked at Wolf but hadn't been able to detect his nature. Shapeshifters always knew their own—but Halven hadn't seen Wolf for what he was any more than Aralorn had at first.

"Why don't you meet me there?" she suggested. "I'll walk back with Wolf. Maybe the stones will aid our travel."

Halven frowned. "All right. I will ask the stones to speed you to Lambshold. Sometimes that helps." In a flutter of hawk feathers, he was gone.

FIVE

"So, you've grown up, halfling," observed the lark, having fluttered to one of the gateposts after Halven made his abrupt switch.

Aralorn bowed shallowly to the yellow-and-black-banded bird. Not certain how much Rethian her aunt understood, she switched back to the shapeshifters' tongue Kessenih had used. "As you see, Aunt."

"No good will come of this." The lark's beady eyes focused malevolently on Aralorn. "If it is known he is gone to the castle again, he will be cast out. They came close to doing it when he helped the Lyon with his cattle breeding. He was told not to contact the humans again without the approval of the quorum."

Aralorn looked at the snowy ground for a moment. She didn't know how far to trust Kessenih. Her aunt hated her husband almost as much as she despised Aralorn herself.

"It is his decision to make," Aralorn said at last, a little fiercely. "I have no choice but to ask him to make it."

"Selfish child," her aunt decreed.

"Perhaps so," agreed Aralorn, "but the fact remains that the shapeshifters benefit as much from my father's continued existence as I do, if not more. It is in your best interest to keep Halven's activities a secret, as you will share his fate if he is exiled."

"Then you'd best be gone from here before someone notices," snapped Kessenih as she exploded into flight.

Wolf waited until she was gone before speaking. "She said something that upset you?"

Aralorn nodded, switching back to Rethian. "My uncle is risking a lot to help us."

"He's going to help? I couldn't tell."

"He's meeting us at the castle." She shrugged, feeling discouraged as well as guilty for asking Halven to risk so much.

"He says he didn't have anything to do with Father's current problem. There appears to be opposition to the aid Halven gave Father in breeding the ryefox. Judging from my aunt Kessenih's attitude, I think that there could be enough opposition to having humans know of their presence that they might be willing to kill to stop the association with humans." Aralorn gave him her best smile. "It would be simpler if the shapeshifters didn't have a hand in this. If the people here are convinced that my father's affliction came at the hands of the shapeshifters, it would mean war."

"We'll have to see to it that doesn't happen." He paused. "If necessary, we could provide them with a villain."

She glanced at him, and said sharply, "Oh, no, you don't. You've been maligned quite enough as it is. Let the late ae'Magi's evil son disappear from view after his father's death."

She started hiking back toward the waterfall. "My uncle might be able to do something about the creature that is guarding the Lyon. He's a lot older than he looks—and powerful. If nothing else, he should be able to tell us what the shadow-thing is."

As they exited the waterfall, Wolf glanced over his shoulder, then froze, pricking his ears. Aralorn followed his gaze and saw that the smooth surface of snow behind them was unmarred by any sign of their passage.

"It's always that way," murmured Aralorn. "There are never any trails—not even of casual wildlife. I don't know why the stones extend the effort since no one can come here without first going through the maze. They are very old, though, and have their own ideas of what's important."

She headed for the place they'd entered the grotto, where the undergrowth was thinner. Ascending the gorge was worse than climbing down had been—at least while they'd been going downhill, when she slipped it was in the right direction. It didn't help that Wolf seemed to have no trouble at all and spent most of his time waiting for her to struggle through the underbrush.

They emerged finally into a level meadow, where frozen strands of grass poked gracefully through the snow at the bases of fifteen gray monoliths set in a circle, each one the height of a man. It looked nothing at all like the place that had been at the start of their descent earlier that day.

"The maze stones as they are from this side of the maze," said Aralorn. "Do you want to take a closer look?"

Without replying, Wolf stepped into the circle.

"The story is that each of the stones was once a shapeshifter. They gave their lives to protect the remnants of their people," she said.

High above them, a red-tailed hawk called out.

Aralorn looked up. "That's my uncle. We'd best be on our way."

"You know where we are?" asked Wolf, leaving the circle after a last thoughtful look.

She shook her head. "After we pass through the center

of the maze stones, there is a barrier to cross outside the circle—here it is, do you feel it?"

The wolf shivered briefly as he started through it. Quickly, Aralorn grabbed a handful of fur and followed.

"Sorry," she said, releasing his pelt. "If you cross separately, we'll end up in two different places."

"Ah?" Wolf turned to look behind him. There was no clearing, no monolithic stones, only dense forest. "A translocation spell? It didn't feel like it."

Aralorn frowned, smoothing the fur she'd ruffled on his back. "I don't know how like your translocation spell it is. With green magic it is possible to build . . . pathways from one area strong with magic to another. The stones direct the paths and work magic constantly to keep the valley safe." She smiled. "If they listened to Halven, it shouldn't take us long to get home."

The woods closed in upon them, and the path they trod became a knee-high growth of evergreens amid the older trees. Here and there, it became so choked with brush that they had to leave it altogether and look for a better way around. It was in the middle of one such detour that they came upon an old abandoned stone hut in a small clearing.

"The hermit's cottage," exclaimed Aralorn in surprise. She looked around the forest and shook her head. It was funny how familiar everything suddenly looked when she knew where she was. "I should have figured it out earlier: This is the only part of Lambshold that has so much forest. We're not as close to the keep as we could be, but if we head due south from here, we should make it before dinner."

As she turned to look at Wolf, something crashed through the trees half a dozen yards away. She turned to see an animal as tall as Sheen and even more massive emerge from the forest. It let out a hoarse moaning sound that started deep in its chest and rose to a high-pitched mewl.

The terrible cold of its breath touched her face though she shouldn't have been close enough to feel it. The animal was covered with a thick white coat that darkened to a dirty yellow in the heavy mane that ringed its neck. Its blunt-featured face was similar to a bear's, but the intelligence in the eyes above the yellow-fanged mouth made it much more threatening.

"Howlaa," murmured Aralorn in disbelief as she stumbled back.

The creatures were rare, even in the Northlands, where they hunted with the winter winds. She'd never heard of one this far south, but, she recalled abruptly, the trappers had been whispering about an increase in the magical creatures of the Northlands for the past few years. Frightening as the beast was, the storyteller in her captured images of the creature.

Her fascinated gaze traveled from the howlaa's fangs to its glittering diamond eyes and stopped. Awareness of anything but the howlaa faded to insignificance. Distantly, she felt an odd dizziness that rapidly increased to nausea. Though she knew she stood firmly planted on the ground, she could feel nothing solid under her feet. As she swayed, torn adrift from her moorings, the wind touched her—gently at first.

Sadness, despair. It is out of place here and dying from the warmth. Aralorn winced away from the alien deluge but could not escape the net the howlaa had caught her in.

———

There were some things a human mind was never meant to understand . . . the color of warmth and the voices that rode the winter winds. How to ride the blue currents of biting ice. The many textures of evil and its seductive, icy grip. Evil gave generously to those who knew ITS call . . . IT had sent this one to look for a shapechanger. IT wanted

*the wolf dead and promised a return to icy sheets that went
on forever in all directions.*

A pained whine added itself to the growing cacophony
surrounding her. Ice-colored eyes turned from her.

Without the grip of the colorless gaze, Aralorn fell to
her hands and knees, unable to feel the bite of the snow, for
she'd been touched by something even colder. The wind
blew past her. Gathering its chill thoughts and whispering
to her in a thousand thousand voices, voices that murmured
and shrieked of death, of evil and all its incarnates. She
couldn't pull any one thing out of the deluge, only flinch
from it and cower in terror.

A muffled grunt sounded from nearby, this time as human
as the howlaa's whine was not.

Wolf, she thought. The thought of him allowed her
to pull her hands to her ears, and the voices ceased with
blessed suddenness. Awareness returned, and she looked
up at Wolf in human guise, his back to her, confronting
the howlaa.

Despite the blood that dripped from his shirt to melt the
snow, Wolf wielded his black staff with cool grace. The
crystals that grew from one end of the staff glittered like
the eyes of the howlaa, while the finger-long, sharp metal
talons on the other end dripped blood.

The talons were a weapon of a sort. Against a human
opponent, they could be deadly—but against the howlaa's
thick hide and inner layer of fat, the short blades were virtually useless. It was unlike him to choose such an inept
method of attack—unless he hadn't known the things were
immune to magic. His education in such matters was a bit
haphazard—gleaned from books rather than teachers. His
magic would have been an excellent weapon against a natural creature like a bear or wild boar, but it would help him
not at all against the howlaa.

Stumbling to her feet without using her hands (as they
were covering her ears against a cacophony of voices that

couldn't possibly be there), Aralorn noticed there was something wrong with her vision as well. Some things were blurry, while others were incredibly detailed.

Focusing on the fight, she drew her hands away from her ears and frantically stripped away her hampering cloak before the voices could claim her again. She had left her sword at Lambshold, worried that such a powerful weapon would antagonize the shapeshifters; now she wished she'd brought it along.

Aralorn drew her knives, one in each hand, and watched the rhythm of the fight to see where she could best attack. *Come on, concentrate,* she thought. The effort of ignoring the muttering tones caused her to break out in a light sweat in spite of the ice and wind.

Wolf struck with the clawed end of his staff, and the howlaa turned away, bawling angrily as the sharp points scored its side. With a growl, it snapped at the staff and received another slash. Had the talons on Wolf's staff moved, or was it merely an effect of whatever the howlaa's gaze had done to her?

Aralorn shook her head in an attempt to drive away thoughts and voices alike. She needed to know where the battle would move, not what Wolf's staff was doing. It was hard to read the purpose of Wolf's pattern of attack. He wasn't looking for a possible fatal hit, just using his staff to poke and prod the creature in the sides. He wasn't trying to back away to the woods, where the howlaa's size would work against it. It was as if . . . of course, Wolf was trying to pull the howlaa away from her—just like one of the idiotic, plaguingly foolish heroes in a bard's tale. He probably could have backed off and conjured something more useful than his pox-eaten staff if he hadn't been worried about her.

Wolf's next attack should come *there*, and the howlaa would close from the right. Just as it had kept away pain, cold, and terror over the years, the taste of battle forced the voices into the background at last.

As silent as Wolf himself, Aralorn edged around the battle until she was behind the howlaa. When all of its attention was on Wolf, she ran and sprang into the air, leaping on the howlaa's back as if it were a horse and she a youngster trying to show off. She clamped her legs beneath its shoulder blades and plunged her sharp steel knives into either side of its neck, where the fat was not as thick.

Rising on its haunches, the howlaa sang, a high, piercing death-song that the wind answered and echoed. Aralorn clung to its back as it rose, her face against the coarse, musky-smelling fur while the creature's blood warmed her cold hands and made the hafts of her knives slick.

The howlaa jerked again as Wolf hit it in the throat with his staff, sinking the talons deep into flesh. He shifted his grip on the staff and braced his weight against it to force the dying animal sideways.

If not for Wolf's quick action, the howlaa would have fallen backward on top of Aralorn. As it was, she loosed her hold on her knives, jumped off the animal, and ran out of the reach of the powerful claws, which were flailing about wildly.

From opposite sides, she and Wolf watched the creature's death throes. It struggled for a moment more, then lay still. Aralorn shivered and retrieved her cloak from the snow where she'd tossed it.

"One of your relatives?" asked Wolf, cleaning the end of his staff in the snow.

Aralorn shook her head, pulling the enveloping folds of wool around her, trying to still the shudders of cold and battle fever. "No, it's a howlaa."

The fight done, the murmuring voices fought for her attention, though they were quieter than before. She knew she should do something, but she couldn't remember what.

Wolf finished cleaning the ends of his staff, then buried it in the snow so he could tuck his hands under his arms to warm them. He walked over to the dead animal and nudged it gently with a foot. "What is a howlaa doing so far south?"

"Hunting," replied Aralorn softly. She noticed that the wind was dying down.

Wolf left off examining the dead beast. "Aralorn?"

"It was sent to get you, I think. I . . ." The wind died down to nothing, taking the voices with it. Cautiously, she relaxed.

"Are you all right, Lady?"

She smiled at him, trying for reassurance. "Ask me tomorrow. What about your shoulder?"

He shook his head. "A scratch. It'll need cleaning when we get to the keep, but it's nothing to worry about."

She insisted on seeing it anyway, but he was right. She'd held on to the rush of battle until she was certain he was all right. Her worry satisfied, she relaxed.

Taking the edge of his black velvet cloak, Wolf wiped the smudges of tree sap and howlaa blood off her face. Finishing her nose, he pulled a few sticks out of her hair and pushed it back from her eyes.

"I don't know why you bother," said Aralorn. "Ten steps through the trees, and it will look just as bad."

Wolf's amber eyes glittered with amusement. He made a motion toward his mask as if he were going to take it off, when his gaze passed by her, and he stopped. Aralorn turned to see the red-tailed hawk perched on the dead howlaa.

"Where did you find a shapeshifter powerful enough that I could not tell he was anything other than a wolf who followed at your heels?" Her uncle spoke in his native tongue.

Without replying, Aralorn translated his speech into

Rethian for Wolf. She was too tired for verbal battles—
though translating wasn't much better.

"She found me, and I followed her home," said Wolf
dryly.

"So why do you need me, child?" Halven switched to
Rethian, though his tone lost none of its hostility. "I felt
the force of the magic he called when you were imperiled;
your shapeshifter is surely as capable as I."

"No," said Wolf.

"He only knows human magic," said Aralorn, when it
became obvious that Wolf had said all that he would on
the matter.

Her uncle let out a coughing sound and ruffled his feathers. "I am not stupid. No human mage could hold the shape
of a wolf for so long without being trapped in his own
spelling."

"His father, who raised him, was a human mage," she
said cautiously, not wanting to give too much away. "We
think his mother was a shapeshifter or some other kind of
green mage. His ability to work green magic . . . fluctuates."
She wouldn't tell her uncle how badly it fluctuated, not
now. Perhaps later, when he was in a better mood. "In
green magic, he has only the little training that I've been
able to give him, and you know how poorly trained I am."

"Your own fault," he snapped.

"Of course," she said, happy to have distracted him to
a more familiar frustration. "Wolf has already looked at
the spells holding Father. Perhaps you might be able to tell
how they were cast, but neither of us could figure it out.
There is this also: Father is guarded by some sort of creature that I have never even heard stories about. We thought
you might be able to identify it."

"Why didn't you tell me about all this before?" asked
Halven in a dangerously soft voice.

Tired as she was, Aralorn found the energy to grin.

"What?" she said. "And use my best ammunition first? I thought that you would be much harder to convince, and I'd have to pull out the shadow-thing to draw you to the keep out of curiosity. I wasn't counting on Kessenih doing half the work for me."

She couldn't be sure, but she thought she saw an answering amusement rising in her uncle's eyes.

"We think," said Wolf slowly, "that your people have nothing to do with this. If you can banish the creature who guards him, or tell us how to do it, then with luck we can unwork the spell and identify the caster."

Halven raised his eyebrows. "I hadn't heard that you could trace a black spell back to the wizard."

"If it is human cast, I can," said Wolf.

The shapeshifter cocked his head. "So if I can help you rid the Lyon of this creature, you can deal with the black magic binding him?"

"If it is black magic, worked by human hands—yes."

"I thought," said Halven with soft intent, "that human mages proscribed black magic. A mage caught using it is killed."

"Working black magic is," replied Wolf. "But unworking it usually requires no blood or death."

"You are very familiar with something that is supposed to have been forbidden for so long."

"Yes, and you are not the first to note it," agreed Wolf, without apparent worry, though Aralorn curled her hands into fists. He took such a risk. Her uncle would figure out who he was, and she no longer knew him well enough to predict what Halven would do. If he told any of the humans about it, Wolf would become a target for anyone. The Spymaster, Ren, liked to say that anyone could be killed, given enough time, money, and interest in accomplishing that person's death.

"If I am seen by a human mage," Wolf continued, "he will most certainly attempt to see that I am killed. It is to spare myself needless effort defending myself that I spend so much time as a wolf."

The wind had been teasing the treetops, but as the sun moved down and removed that slight source of warmth, it began to blow in earnest once more. Aralorn lost track of the conversation, unable to tell one voice among many. Keeping her face impassive, she slipped her hand onto the curve of Wolf's elbow and kept her mouth closed for fear of echoing the shrieks reverberating in her head.

Wolf glanced at her face, then said something to Halven.

The hawk cocked its head and gave a jerky nod. With a leap and a thrust of wings, it took flight.

Wolf waited until the hawk was out of sight before turning back to Aralorn. The wind howled through the trees, making Wolf's cloak snap and crackle around her as he drew her under its shelter.

"What is it, Lady?" he asked, the rough velvet of his voice penetrating the chaos that rang in her head.

"The wind," she whispered. "It's the wind. I can *hear* them."

" 'Them'?" He frowned at her. "Who do you hear?"

"Voices." She saw the worry in his eyes and tried to explain better. "An effect of the howlaa's gaze, I think."

He didn't speak again; she drew comfort from the warmth of his body and the strength of his arms. Her hands weren't sufficient to block out the noise, but they helped. She wasn't aware of time's passing, but when the wind finally died down, the sky was noticeably darker, and a light skiff of snow had begun to fall.

She pulled away slowly, meeting Wolf's worried gaze with one of her own. "In the Trader Clans, when a man goes insane, they say that he is listening to the wind. I have always wondered what the wind said."

Wolf nodded slowly. "I have heard that the Traders have another saying—may your road be clear, your belly full, and may you never get what you wish for."

Aralorn summoned a grin. "Just think of the legends I can spawn now . . . the woman who could hear the wind—it has a certain rhythm to it, don't you think?"

"More likely it would be the woman who died in the winter because she couldn't quit talking long enough to get out of the cold," replied Wolf repressively.

Her smile warmed into something more genuine. "By all means, let us avoid such an ignominious fate." She gestured grandly to the underbrush that covered the old trail. "Away, then, to the Lyon's keep."

He bowed low. "Allow me to retrieve your knives first?"

"Of course," she said, as if she hadn't forgotten them. She slipped the knives, cleaned by Wolf, back into their sheaths and strode into the woods.

Her heroic stride was shortened somewhat by the waist-high aspen seedlings and drifts of snow nearly as high, but her spirits lifted all the same—how many people could claim to have met a howlaa and survived? Her optimism was greatly helped by the wind's continued absence.

By the time they reached the keep, the snowfall was no longer so light, and Aralorn was grateful to have Wolf's eyes to depend upon rather than her own feebler senses—he had shifted back to lupine form as soon as the keep was in view. The sentries allowed her entrance through the gates without challenge.

She took the time to shake out her cloak and dust the worst of the snow off Wolf before she opened the door into the keep. As the warmth of the hall fire touched her cheek, a red-tailed hawk landed lightly on her shoulder. Ignoring the surprised expressions of the servants, she transferred the bird to one of her arms, which were protected by the layers of clothing she wore, and handed off her cloak. The hawk climbed her arm and perched once more on her shoulder. Her sweaters had slipped to one side, leaving only a single layer of clothing between her skin and the hawk's sharp talons.

"You be careful," she admonished her uncle. "I don't want any more scars. I look odd enough in an evening gown as it is."

Halven flexed his talons lightly without gripping hard enough to hurt.

"All right," she said.

The hawk unfurled his wings slightly to keep his balance as she strode through the keep. Wolf trailed silently behind. With the funeral preparations on indefinite hold, most of the visitors had left, and the servants were busy with dinner, so the back ways through the keep were empty—at least until they passed by a turret staircase near the mourning room.

"Why does Mother let you bring your pets into the keep when we can't even bring in our dogs? Is she frightened of you? Or do you have her bewitched like Nevyn says?" asked a young voice coolly.

Aralorn took two steps back until she could see the area under the stairs clearly. In her hurry, she hadn't seen the dim light cast by the oil lamp, but now that her attention had been drawn to it, she could see that a small study had been neatly tucked into the cramped space beneath the stairs. The keep was not overly large, and with a family the size of the Lyon's brood, it took cleverness to find a place unclaimed by anyone else.

The boy who'd spoken sat perched on a stool with a large book on his lap. He was on his way to gaining the height of the rest of the family—already he was taller than Aralorn—but he was painfully thin. His wrists were bare for several inches where he had outgrown his shirt, an oddly vulnerable touch for such a self-possessed young man. It took a moment for her to see the toddler she knew in the man he was becoming.

"No coercion," replied Aralorn lightly. "I doubt a . . .

howlaa could frighten Irrenna. I've seen her face down Father a time or two, and he's much more scary than I could ever be. Nor sorcery either—I don't have the kind of power that can influence people's thoughts." Once she would have said that no one did, but recent history had proven otherwise. "The wolf would worry the shepherds if he wandered freely about, Gerem. It's safer for everyone if he stays with me."

Gerem was a year younger than Lin. Aralorn remembered him as a quiet little person with an unexpected stubborn streak. The icy blue eyes that glittered with dislike and fear were something new. This kind of moment was why she'd left Lambshold. Bad enough that Nevyn felt that way about her; to have her family fear her was more than she could bear. She felt a sudden empathy with Wolf.

"And the hawk?"

"Hmm," said Aralorn, trying not to let his coldness hurt—she had, after all, left when he was a toddler; he couldn't know her. "Lady Irrenna doesn't know about the hawk yet."

"If the Lady Irrenna objects, I will shift back to human," said the hawk softly. "But I prefer to stay as I am."

"Shapeshifter," Gerem whispered, his eyes widening.

Aralorn nodded. "Yes. I told Irrenna . . ."

"Is he the one who did it?"

Aralorn gave him an assessing look. There was something in his voice that led her to think that he was attempting offense rather than speaking out of belief.

"You overstep yourself, accusing a guest of this house." She dropped the friendly tone she'd been using and replaced it with ice. "He did nothing but volunteer to look at the workings of the spell."

The hawk tilted its head to the side. "I will answer the boy, Aralorn Sister's Daughter. You need not come to my defense. I have not ensorcelled the Lyon at any time, Master Gerem. If I were inclined to use my magic in such a fashion, I would certainly have done it decades ago, when it might have done me some good. As it is, his incapacity has inconvenienced me greatly."

Gerem looked embarrassed. His rudeness, thought Aralorn, had been directed at her.

Recalled to his manners, the boy bowed graciously, if briefly. "My apologies, sir. My words were ill directed."

The hawk bent to preen his wing. Aralorn nodded formally and proceeded on her way.

"I think we just saw Nevyn's influence," commented Wolf, once they were out of earshot.

"Ah yes, Nevyn—the wizard who dislikes magic." Halven sounded amused.

Aralorn smiled without humor. "Something tells me I'm going to have a long talk with Nevyn before I leave. Speaking of people who do stupid things, why did you announce your presence to my brother? Kessenih informed me that you've taken a serious risk coming here."

"As if no one would have thought 'shapeshifter' when you came into the keep with a hawk on your shoulder," murmured Wolf. "A hawk like the one that brought you here as a baby."

"Plague take it," said Aralorn. "I didn't think of that. The howlaa must have stolen all that was left of my wits."

"Peace, child," replied the hawk with amusement. "Kessenih worries overmuch. I have dealt with the quorum before, and I will again. They need me more than I need them."

SIX

There was a guard seated just outside the entrance to the bier room. She'd told Irrenna the room was warded, but apparently someone thought that Aralorn's wards would be insufficient to keep people away. Since they might have been right—if *Aralorn* had set the wards—she was amused rather than offended.

The guard rose to his feet as they entered. "Lady Aralorn."

"It might be wise if you leave for a candlemark or two," she said. "My uncle has agreed to look at the Lyon, and he might work some magic. If anyone asks you, tell them it is on my authority."

He probably wouldn't be in any danger, but the shadow that guarded the Lyon worried her. There was no way to tell what it was capable of until they knew more about it. If Wolf and Halven were going to be prodding it with magic, she'd prefer to keep the defenseless away.

The guardsman glanced at the hawk riding her shoulders and blanched a bit, letting his gaze slide to the safety of her human face. "As you say, Lady. I'll report to the captain, then return in two candlemarks." So saying, he started off with suspiciously brisk steps.

But she must have been wrong about how much her uncle frightened him because he stopped abruptly and turned back. "The Lyon gave me my first sword and taught me to use it."

"Me, too," she said.

"Luck and the Lady be with you," he said, then executed an about-face and continued on his way.

As soon as the guard was out of sight, Wolf trotted to the entrance to the alcove where the Lyon lay in state. He sniffed at it suspiciously.

"What is it?" asked Aralorn.

Wolf shifted abruptly to human form, wearing his usual mask to hide his face from her uncle. He ran his fingers carefully over the edge of the entrance.

"Someone's attempted the warding," he said.

"What?" asked Aralorn. She touched the stone where he had, but she could only feel the power of his wards. The human magic was beyond her ability to decipher for subtleties.

"Someone started to unwork the wards I set this morning. He left off halfway, as if something interrupted him, or he decided not to go on with it."

"Maybe he couldn't get through," she suggested.

He shook his head. "No, he knew what he was doing—he could have dispelled it."

"Nevyn?" she suggested.

He shrugged, then touched the air just in front of the curtain, letting his hands rest on the surface of the warding. "I can't tell, but it must have been him. Unless there are other mages who live in Lambshold. I wonder if he recognized my work."

"Could he?"

"Maybe."

"Irrenna said she was calling on Kisrah for help—though

I wouldn't have thought she could get a message to him so soon," Aralorn said. "Nevyn is the more likely candidate. As far as I know, there are no other trained mages on my father's lands right now. I'll ask around, though." What if Nevyn figured out Wolf was here?

"If the wards were not breached, what does it matter?" asked Halven.

"Wolf is not very popular among the wizards right now," said Aralorn. Though Geoffrey ae'Magi had disappeared without a trace in a keep filled with hungry Uriah, rumor had attributed his death to his son Cain—who was also her Wolf.

"Oh Mistress of the Understatement," murmured Wolf, "I salute you."

Her uncle clacked his beak in an irritated fashion and launched off her shoulder, taking human shape as he landed.

"I know of a human mage that many of the mages are searching for," he said.

Aralorn raised her chin, and Halven laughed. "No need to look daggers at me, child. I can hold my tongue. What need have I to please a scruffy lot of bungling human mages?"

She stared at him, but Wolf, either easier to appease or not as worried, released the warding with a quick gesture of his left hand, saying, "Past time we attended to our immediate business." He threw back the curtain and exposed the Lyon's dark chamber to the light from lamps in the mourning room.

Aralorn's father lay unchanged upon the bier. Wolf reached into a shadowed area and pulled out his staff from wherever it had been since he left it in the woods. As he took it up, the crystals that grew out of the top flared brightly before settling into a blue-white glow that chased the darkness from the room where the Lyon rested.

Halven strode through the entrance and Aralorn followed him, leaving Wolf to close the curtains and hide their activities from prying eyes.

Halven looked closely at the bier for a moment before turning to Aralorn. "I thought you said there was a creature guarding him. I see—*by faith!*"

Aralorn twisted around to look toward Wolf also. Against the wall, where there should have been no shadows at all, there was a subtle dimness that oozed slowly down the stone. It was only a little darker than the room itself, almost as if it were her imagination painting monsters. She turned back to Halven and opened her mouth to speak, when her uncle's rough grip pulled her aside and behind him.

Wolf, too, had turned to see what caused Halven's exclamation. The shadow caught his eye just as it touched the floor and abruptly shot forward. It rippled swiftly over the stones, flowing around Wolf on both sides, like a stream of water around a rock—though no part of the shadow touched him. It drew to a halt in front of Halven, stopped by the barrier of the shapeshifter's magic.

———————

Shielding, thought Wolf, recognizing the patterning though the magic Halven used was different. Even as he thought it, the shadow-thing oozed through a hole in the shield spell that hadn't been there an instant before. Halven responded with another shield, but that obviously wouldn't answer for long.

The power of Halven's magic called answering force from Wolf. He could feel magic seeping in from the old stones that surrounded him, enticing him with its nearness, but he feared its ability to do more than its designated task. With an effort so fierce that it left him with a headache, he forced the green magic away.

Instead, he reached for the more familiar forces he had always worked with. Though outwardly more destructive than green magic, the raw magic that was the stuff human mages could weave responded to his control as a harp to an old bard.

With careful dispatch, he created an adaptation of the magelight spell, seeking to cancel shadow with light. His spell should have flared with white light as it touched the shadow, but nothing happened. The creature might have expanded a little, but he wasn't certain. It paused, then threw the light spell at Halven.

Wolf felt the surge of force Halven called upon to block both the light and the creature, felt it as if it were coming from his own hands. The brilliant light was swallowed by Halven's open palm, and once more, the creature was turned away.

Wolf knew the other mage had begun to tire; the flow of Halven's magic had become erratic though no less powerful. The shapeshifter was doing all he could to keep the creature back; it was up to Wolf to stop it from getting Aralorn. Oh, it might have been trying to get her uncle, but bone-deep instinct told him that was not true.

Something about the way the thing absorbed his spell reminded him of demons—which reminded him of a spell.

Before he started to gather magic, he found himself abruptly filled with more than he could use. Startled, he paused, and the magic began to form its own spell. It wasn't until that moment that he realized the magic he held was green magic.

He controlled his frustration and ruthlessly broke the weaving already begun, stripping the natural magic of its essence and turning it back to the chaotic energy of the wild, but less willful, magic human wizards used. This he wove and focused, ignoring the pain that backlashed through him from his struggles.

The spell he chose was only to be found among the books of the black mages, for it had one use: to hold demons safely when they were summoned unbound. However, the spell required neither death nor blood, so he patterned it— hoping anything that could hold a demon would hold the shadow-creature as well.

The spell finished, he threw it at the creature, careful that it did not touch Halven. To his relief, it fell as it should have, a glowing circle of light containing everything in the room between Halven and Wolf. He held his breath as the shadow touched the light and drew back from the binding, prowling restlessly within the circle's confines.

Wolf shrank the boundaries until the shadow was enclosed in a circle the size of a foot soldier's shield. The creature cowered in the small area in the center of the spell, where it shivered, small and dark, like a slug exposed to open air.

The green magic he had not used continued to fight him, struggling for the freedom to complete the pattern it had begun. He wasn't sure what he was going to do with it when he got it under control. Human mages were very careful to draw only as much power as they needed, since magic left unformed was dangerous. He had no idea what a similar situation with green magic would do.

The magic fought against his dominance like a wild stallion bridled for the first time, and he found himself losing his grip on it. Reaching for a firmer hold, he found that he was grasping nothing; the green magic had faded, dissipating like fog in the sun.

He would have felt more reassured if he thought it was gone rather than merely biding its time. Sweating beneath his mask, he turned his attention to his companions. As he did so, he realized he hadn't struggled with the magic for as long as he thought: Halven and Aralorn had just closed in on his prisoner, apparently unaware of the battle he'd just barely won. Grateful for the mask that hid his features, he turned his attention to the shadow-creature.

"Baneshade," said Halven, looking at the creature. "Interesting."

"What's a baneshade?" asked Aralorn.

Wolf stepped to the edge of the binding and examined the thing himself, saying, "I hadn't thought of that.

They used to be quite common, I understand. The wizards before the Wizard Wars used them. They were nasty little creatures who lived in dark places, usually where magic had been performed—deserted temples and the like. On their own, they're said to be harmless enough, but they can work like a sigil—keeping a human spell going for an indefinite length of time." He paused. "Or they can store power. They were supposed to have the ability to alter some spells a little, too. I had assumed they were long gone." He was pleased that his voice came out as controlled as it usually was.

"It didn't act like something that was harmless," said Aralorn.

"I saw another one once," commented Halven. "When I was younger, I sometimes wandered from place to place. There was a deserted building—not much larger than a hut, really. I was told it was haunted by the ghost of one of the great wizards from the time of the Wizard Wars. The building didn't feel that old to me, but it did have a bane-shade. It took me a while to find a name for the thing." He turned his attention to Wolf. "Why didn't you try capturing it that way before?"

"I didn't even think of it." It was black magic, and he tried not to use it. He didn't have to use blood to call enough power to build the spell, but most other human mages would have.

Halven raised his eyebrows but didn't comment. Instead, he turned to the bier. "Now that that's taken care of, I suppose I should look at this spell."

He laid his hand on the Lyon's head and began humming in a rich baritone. After a moment he pulled back and looked at Wolf. "I think it's human magic. But there is something else as well. Perhaps you ought to look."

Wolf looked at the shadow his magic held. "Hold a moment. I need to fix the spell so I can work other magic."

He drew a sign on the stone floor with his finger, then

touched the glowing circlet. The symbol he'd drawn flared orange before disappearing. "That should hold it."

He released the spell, knowing that the rune would maintain the spell for the time he needed. Stepping past it, he approached the bier. Like Halven, Wolf laid his palm on the Lyon's forehead. With his free hand, he gestured in a controlled motion as he closed his eyes.

"Black magic," he said finally, pulling away. "I still can't tell if it is human or not, but I'll take your assessment. I don't recognize the patterning, but it's been muddled enough it could be anyone—maybe the baneshade's work. It almost has the feel of a collective effort, but it is hard to tell. There is a second spell as well, but it doesn't seem to have been activated. Hopefully, Lord Kisrah can unravel it."

Halven nodded in satisfaction. "I thought it felt as if there was more than one hand involved."

"Can you break the spell that holds him?" asked Aralorn.

"Not this one," said Halven.

Wolf shook his head. "Lady, I could try. I would rather wait until I find out just what the spell is, though. I've never seen its like. It will be far less dangerous to your father if I know what I'm working with."

Halven tapped his finger idly on the stone bier. "Why didn't anyone else notice he wasn't dead? Surely someone should have noticed his body didn't behave properly?"

"He's not breathing, has no pulse, and is as cold as stone," answered Aralorn. "What was there to notice?"

Halven's brows rose. "His body didn't stiffen as a corpse would."

"Well," said Aralorn, looking for an explanation, "Kurmun rode here with Father from the croft—that would not have been long enough for a corpse to rigor. It is traditional to leave a body in the cellar for a full day before dressing it out—to give the spirit time to depart. There was no reason for anyone to notice."

"A useful tradition," observed Wolf. "It is so much easier to work with a pliable corpse."

Halven smiled grimly. "So if you had not come, he would have been buried?"

Aralorn nodded, but Wolf said, "There's no way to tell, is there? I think perhaps someone would have conveniently discovered it at the last moment—and would have seen to it that word was sent to Aralorn, as the family's own green mage. Perhaps it would have been suggested that shapeshifter magic had done this."

"You think this was set to draw me here?" asked Aralorn.

He shrugged. "I don't know. But it is significant that the Lyon is held by black magic when his daughter is"—he paused—"has a friend who has the reputation of being the last black mage—the rest being controlled by the ae'Magi's power over them. I think that it is further interesting that the baneshade was inactive until you walked in—and it has been after you ever since."

"What would it want with me?" asked Aralorn.

"I believe the spell that it attempted to place on you when we first discovered it is the same one that binds your father. Perhaps the person who engineered all of this decided he wanted more certain bait."

"Bait for you." She considered it.

"Someone would have to want you very badly to go to this much trouble," commented Halven.

"Yes," admitted Wolf. "Quite a few people do."

Despite the seriousness of the subject, Aralorn grinned. "Every woman wants to find herself a man who is desired by so many others."

"Why were they so careful to make certain the Lyon lives?" asked Halven, ignoring Aralorn. "It would have been just as easy to kill him. Aralorn would have come to pay her last respects."

"Perhaps the one who set the spell likes him," replied

Wolf, and Aralorn knew he was thinking of Nevyn. "Sometimes, Aralorn, the most obvious answer—"

His speech stopped as he felt the ripple of his hold spell dissolving. He shifted his gaze to see what had happened just in time to observe the last of the daylight fade and the shadow flow across the stone floor. Wolf didn't have a chance to gather magic, or even call out a warning—the baneshade was moving too fast . . .

A surge of green magic, his own magic, flared suddenly. There was so much of it that the whole room glowed with the unearthly midnight blue light that flowed down his staff like wax from a candle.

The room looked sinister and nightmarish, full of darkness and deep shadows. At Aralorn's feet, a bare handspan from her heel, the baneshade hissed, glowing ice blue— lighter by far than anything in the room—held in place by Wolf's magic.

Aralorn, quick acting and quicker witted, jumped away from it, stopping only when she touched the wall. Wolf began belatedly seeking dominion of the magic before it could do anything more. Although its initial action was beneficial, Wolf didn't want to chance harming Aralorn or Halven.

As he reached for it, he discovered it was already weaving itself into a pattern of destruction that allowed him no room to gain control. The light began to concentrate around the baneshade, flowing from the corners of the room until the cool white illumination from the staff dominated once more.

Glowing a deep indigo, his magic appeared viscous as it surrounded the creature, consolidating in a thick mass near the floor. There was a moment of stasis, then a fog began to rise from the blue-black base, a fog that had the odd effect of illumination and concealment at the same time.

By the curious radiance of the fog, the baneshade appeared

to have a solid form, but it didn't last long enough to be certain. Wolf caught a glimpse of fine downy fur before the outer surface began to bubble and dissolve with a terrible stench that reminded him of something long dead at the first touch of the fog. Flesh and bones were revealed in turn, each dissolving with a speed that testified to the power of the magic that consumed it. In the end, there was nothing left but the vaporous mist of darkness at Wolf's feet and a malodorous scent that permeated the room.

In that moment, when the destruction was complete, Wolf tried again to dominate his magic. Cold sweat ran down his back, and for a moment, all he could see were *flames melting stone, destructive magic only he could call tearing apart everything in its path.* He blinked and set the memory aside with the conviction that someone was about to die. His magic was good at killing. He needed coolness that fear would interfere with if he was going to keep everyone safe, keep Aralorn safe.

Frantically, he fought for control, barely aware of the pain when he fell to his knees. He had to stop it before it hurt Aralorn; he felt certain that if it touched—

Aralorn's firm hands locked on his shoulder as the cloud whipped violently out of his control, sweeping around the room. Aralorn dodged, but it touched her anyway, ruffling her hair.

Wolf cried out hoarsely, but the magic left her unharmed and came for him.

Yes, he thought, *let it be me.*

The swirling mist slid aside as it touched a barrier spell that Wolf had not called, and it turned the destructive force without ever quite meeting it. Again, Wolf grappled with it, fighting to bring it under control before it had another chance at Aralorn.

Words drifted by his ears, Halven's words. He ignored them.

"No, plague you, listen to me. *Wolf.*" Aralorn was less

easily disregarded. "My uncle says let it go. Don't hold it. Release it. It's done what you asked; if you release it, it will go."

Fear gnawed at his control, giving the magic more room to act, and the mist concentrated on the barrier the shapeshifter had set.

"I can't!" He gritted out the words. The damaged vocal cords made speech more difficult than usual. "Aralorn."

"It won't hurt her." Halven's voice was low and soft, as if he were soothing a wild beast. "Let it go."

At last, because he had no better plan, Wolf did as the shapeshifter suggested. For a long moment, he thought it had done no good. The magic continued to rage, pushing hard at a warding Halven had thrown up around them. Then it faded, until only a faint trace lingered in the air, evidence that magic had been worked there.

"Fluctuates," muttered Halven in a voice of great disgust. "As the gods gave us life, your control *fluctuates*, she said."

Wolf hung his head in exhaustion, sitting on the ground because he didn't have the energy to stand. With a gesture, he dissolved the mask, letting the cool air touch his scarred face.

Aralorn knelt behind him, her hands still on his shoulders. "It was attacking you, Wolf. What happened?"

———

He didn't reply to her question. Looking at him, she wasn't sure he'd heard her. Eyes closed, he was breathing in great gulps of air like a racehorse after the meet of its life. Without the mask, his face was pale and covered in sweat.

Halven examined the massive burn scars that covered Wolf's ruined face. Her uncle's eyes widened a bit as he took in the extent of the damage. He shared a thoughtful look with Aralorn.

Her uncle waited until a little color had returned to

Wolf's face and his breathing had settled before he spoke. "Has anyone ever told you it's unhealthy to work green magic when you have a death wish?"

Aralorn took in a breath so deep it hurt. Though Wolf's self-destructive tendencies were nothing new to her, she'd thought he was getting better, thought she'd been helping him to heal.

"If I had been a tad less powerful," Halven continued, "it would have killed you. If you don't ask anything of the magic you gather, it strives to do what your inmost self desires—regardless of your awareness of those desires. I would have thought that even a human-trained mage would know better than that."

"I didn't gather it." Wolf's voice was hoarser than usual, but he opened his eyes and managed a respectable glare.

"I have to disagree," replied Halven, not visibly intimidated, "though you certainly shouldn't have been able to. Usually, green magic only responds to the call of a mage who is in tune with the world around him—and from the demonstration we've just had, I would say that you are not even in tune with yourself."

Wolf reached up and gripped Aralorn's hand hard with his own. "I almost killed you—again," he said without taking his eyes from Halven. "The baneshade broke through the demon-imprisoning ring. I saw it come after you, and there was no time to do anything."

"In your moment of need, you were served," said Halven, sounding as if he were quoting something.

Aralorn glanced at her uncle and nodded. "I've heard of green magic doing that—but only in stories."

"That's because only an uneducated *human* mage wouldn't know how to control his magic."

Wolf came to his feet, swaying. Aralorn was hampered by his tight grip on her hand, but Halven grabbed his shoulder to steady him.

"Easy there," he said. "Give yourself a minute."

Wolf stepped away from the unaccustomed touch and looked at Aralorn. "Are you hurt?"

She shook her head. "Not at all." If she'd broken every bone she had, she would have said the same. But, as it happened, the thick flow of Wolf's magic had been a caress rather than a strike.

"You weren't attacking *her*," said Halven impatiently. "The only one who had anything to worry about in this room was you."

Wolf looked away from them both. He reached up to touch his mask, something he did when he was uncomfortable. But his mask wasn't there, and when his fingers touched the scars, he flinched. Aralorn wasn't the only one who saw it.

"When you want to be rid of that reminder," said Halven, "come to me, and I'll teach you how to heal yourself. You've the power, and I can teach you the skill." He looked at the floor, where the baneshade had been. "It was best to destroy the baneshade anyway. It seemed to be focused on Aralorn, and the things can be dangerous in a place as old as this."

"Plague it," said Aralorn softly, as a sudden thought occurred to her. "Kisrah is coming here. We might have a problem."

"What is it?" Wolf tightened like a predator scenting prey; even his body seemed to lose the fatigue that had made his moves less fluid than usual.

"The night your father died, when I came back after you, Lord Kisrah was there."

"He would know you?" asked Wolf intently. "As the daughter of the Lyon?"

"Although I have absented myself as much as possible from human affairs," broke in Halven mildly, "I do know that this has become a dangerous conversation. I wish to know nothing about Geoffrey ae'Magi's death." He hesitated. "If you survive all of this, *Wolf* . . . come to me, and we will talk about your recalcitrant magic. Good luck to you both." He heaved up the bar on the door to the outside and left by that way.

Aralorn shut the door behind him and settled the bar back in place. "Kisrah saw me quite clearly, as a matter of fact—I wasn't expecting to run into anyone at the time, so I was wearing my own face. I don't think he connected me with my father—we would have heard something. Kisrah was caught well and good by the last ae'Magi's spells. If he knew, he'd have come after me before this. But he can hardly miss me when he comes here."

"I can handle Kisrah if he becomes a problem," Wolf said mildly enough to frighten Aralorn.

"Thank you," she said. "But I don't think that we would survive killing a second ae'Magi."

"We could do it every year on the anniversary of my father's death," suggested Wolf. "Though technically Kisrah would be our first, as my father was killed by the Uriah after you stole his magic."

He was joking, she thought, though sometimes it was difficult to tell. He liked it that way.

"I saved Kisrah's life," she said, returning to the matter at hand. "The lady he was sleeping with had a tendency to eat her lovers. Sadly, he was unconscious, so he won't know he owes me." She ran her fingers over her father's hand. It was cool to the touch. She continued thoughtfully. "You know, he obviously didn't recognize me at the time, but he has the right contacts. If he wanted to find out badly enough who I was, he could. As ae'Magi, he would have access to all the knowledge of black magic he wished."

"Especially with most of my father's library at his disposal," agreed Wolf as he took a step back and leaned against the wall. Not to relax, noticed Aralorn worriedly, but to keep himself upright. His consonants softened with fatigue, leaving his voice difficult to understand. "It is true that he was very close to my father, certainly close enough to thirst for revenge. But I know Kisrah; he would never touch the black arts."

"Neither would Nevyn," said Aralorn somberly.

Wolf sighed. "I don't want it to be him. I like him, Aralorn." Wolf didn't like many people. Aralorn suspected that he could count them on the fingers of one hand, with fingers left over. "Shortly before I left, when I was at my most vicious, he cornered me. He told me he was concerned about rumors he'd been hearing. Things that might get a man killed if the wrong person heard about them. He suggested that the rumors might die down without more sparks to fuel them."

"What did you tell him?"

Wolf's scarred lips quirked in an attempt at a smile. "I invited him to meet me at the next full moon and find out if they were true."

"Not overly intelligent on your part, my love," observed Aralorn dryly. "If he'd gone to the council, they'd have been able to pull you in for questioning."

"I was young." He shrugged.

"It amazes me," she said thoughtfully, "how many people knew you were working black magic and never stopped to ask how you learned such things on your own—or wondered why the ae'Magi didn't stop you."

"Everyone knows that there are books if you know where to look for them." He sighed softly and returned to the original topic. "It could be Kisrah, I suppose. Hatred and vengeance are corrupting emotions. Perhaps they could have caused him to use black magic. I would hate to see him caught in a web spun by my father."

"It could be Nevyn," she offered. "He might have found the connections between you and me, and between us and the ae'Magi's death. He knows that I am a spy in Sianim, and he knows Kisrah. Kisrah could have told him about seeing me at the ae'Magi's castle the night he died, described me well enough that Nevyn identified me.

Nevyn loved your father—he used to tell me stories about him—and he certainly loves my father. Since he distrusts magic of any kind, black magic might not bother him as much as it would Kisrah."

Wolf thought a moment—or else he dozed; Aralorn couldn't tell which—then he shook his head. "The croft, perhaps, might have been possible for Nevyn. It wouldn't have called for much skill, but the spell binding your father was done with both power and craft. Poor Nevyn had more teaching than he wanted, but he fought it. I heard Kisrah fussing over him to my father—all that talent and too scared of magic to use it." He gave Aralorn a bleak look. "My father would pat him on the back and commiserate with him. Told him that a Darranian mage was bound to be a mess." Geoffrey ae'Magi, Wolf's father, had been Darranian. "They would laugh and then my father would tell his good friend how worried he was about me, about how I was fascinated by the darker magics." He closed his eyes for a deep breath. When he opened them again, he said, "My father was afraid to teach me, I think, for fear that the monster he created would be too powerful for him to control. Kisrah tried his best with Nevyn, but I doubt that he knows much more than I do."

He turned to her, a mockery of his usual graceful movements, and made a negating gesture. "He was given to Kisrah to apprentice partially because of Kisrah's easy nature but also because Kisrah had the power to control a rogue sorcerer. When he was first apprenticed to Santik, Nevyn had the potential to become a master, maybe even ae'Magi. By the time he went to Kisrah, he was capable of little more than lighting candles. Santik was brought up on charges of abuse and neglect, his powers sealed away from him by the ae'Magi. Ironic isn't it, that my father convicted another mage of abuse? Kisrah worked with Nevyn, but finally gave in to Nevyn's own wishes once he was certain that Nevyn knew enough for safety. So Nevyn is

much like me—a powerful mage who doesn't know what
he's doing. Which is why I don't think he's our villain. He
simply does not have the skill to create something like the
spell that holds your father. He's a good man, Aralorn. I
don't think he did this."

Aralorn looked at Wolf, surprised at his long speech.

It made her suspicious.

She thought about what had happened that night and
realized why Wolf was painting such a clear picture for
her. Poor Nevyn indeed. A decade of spying and influencing the thoughts of others without attracting their attention
had honed her instincts: She knew when someone was trying to manipulate her in return.

So Nevyn was a powerful mage, was he? Hurt by someone who should have protected him. A good man.

Wolf, on the other hand, was a devious man, her lover:
She had a weakness for devious men.

"I am certain," she said slowly, "that you believe Nevyn
had nothing to do with this." Or he wouldn't have offered
the man to her on a platter.

Sometimes, she thought, you had to tell someone that
you loved them; sometimes you had to beat them over the
head with it.

"I don't love you for your powers, Wolf. Nor for the
beauty of your body." His hand twitched toward his scarred
face. "I certainly don't love you because you were abused
by your father." Her voice began to take on the bite of her
anger, not all of which was feigned. "I *certainly* don't love
you because you are a powerful mage. Nevyn's powers
or lack of same may have made a half-grown child look
at him twice, where one look at you would have sent her
running—but I'm grown now and have been for some time.
So tell me"—she was snarling at him now—"*why* are you
trying to turn my attention to Nevyn with the skill of a
village matchmaker?" She changed her voice, giving it an
elderly quaver and a Lambshold crofter's accent. "'Look

at this wonderful man, wounded, yet noble—a powerful mage in need of tender care. So he's married to tha sister, so he hates shapeshifters—what's a little challenge?' "

She needed him to talk about what was bothering him in order to address it. She needed to goad him; perhaps a shift to gentleness would work—he hadn't experienced enough to be entirely comfortable with it. "I don't need Nevyn, dear heart. I have you."

"Of course," he snapped. She was glad to see anger because sadness in his eyes tore her soul. "Oh, *I* am any maiden's dream. A master wizard—except the only magic I know, other than a few basic spells, is black magic, and it will, at some future time, ensure my death at the hands of any mage who can back me into a corner. Without my conscious will, green magic randomly chooses to use me to call itself into being and do whatever the"—he paused and drew in a deep breath and deliberately relaxed his shoulders—"and do whatever seems fit at the time. You are better off without me."

The prudent thing, Aralorn considered, would be to allow him to work it out on his own. *She* knew he'd never hurt her, not even with magic he couldn't control; she was even fairly certain he wouldn't hurt anyone else who didn't deserve it—and she thought that when he had a chance to reason it through, he would come to the same conclusions.

What *really* bothered him was the nature of green magic. You coaxed it, you asked it, but you couldn't always force it to do exactly what you wanted—but he'd dealt with much worse than that. She was confident he would again; she would just have to be patient until he worked it out.

The prudent thing, she told herself, would be to leave him alone. He had a nasty temper when he was pushed.

Since prudence wasn't one of her attributes, she said, "Self-pity never accomplishes much, but sometimes it's nice to wallow in it for a while. Do hurry up though—I'm getting hungry." She tilted her head to indicate the sounds of people gathering on the other side of the curtain for their meal. "I'm tired of eating cold food."

Wolf closed both eyes. He stretched his neck to the left, then to the right. Only then did he open his eyes. Baleful lights glittered in their amber depths as he closed his hands ever so gently around her neck and pulled her forward until she had to tilt her chin up to look at him.

"Someday," he whispered, bending down until his lips were next to her ears, "you're going to step into the fire and find out that it really is hot."

"Burn me," she said in equally soft tones, and for a few moments he did—without a single spell.

When he released her, there was a measure of peace in his eyes. "Shall we go eat?"

She turned to go, and her eyes touched her father. Smile fading, Aralorn approached him and put her hand on his face.

"Got rid of the creepy crawly, but no luck yet, sir, on your entrapment," she murmured. "But tomorrow's another day."

Wolf's warm hand came down to rest on her shoulder. "Come."

SEVEN

———∞∞∞———

Wolf changed back into his four-footed form, then staggered. Aralorn put a hand on his shoulder to steady him, and he leaned against her with a sigh and an apologetic look.

"Sorry," he said.

"You need food," she replied, and pulled back the curtain, only to find that not only was the great hall filled with people dining, but every head was turned to her. By the intentness of their gazes, she figured that the guard told them all that she'd brought her uncle to look at the Lyon.

She bowed, and said, "We've made some progress, but the Lyon still sleeps."

She closed the curtain and set her own wards against casual interlopers since Wolf was in no condition to be working magic. By the time she was through, most of the diners had turned their attention back to their plates.

Aralorn snagged a clean trencher from a passing kitchen servant and sat at the nearest table, Wolf collapsing at her feet. She took one of her knives and cut a bit of this and that from the platters arrayed on the table and tossed a large piece of roasted goose breast at Wolf, who caught it easily and ate it with more haste than manners.

She took a hunk of bread from her trencher and put a piece of sliced meat on top of it. This she kept, placing the plate and its remaining contents on the floor for Wolf.

"There she is! I see her."

A loud voice drew her attention away from her meal as she saw two towheaded children running toward her.

"Aunt Aralorn. Hey, Aunt Aralorn, Father said you would tell us a story if we cornered you."

Putting their ages roughly at eight and five, Aralorn quickly came up with the identity of "Father." Falhart was the only one of her brothers old enough to have sired them.

"All right," she said, hiding her pleasure—as tired as she was, storytelling opportunities were not to be lost. "Tell Falhart you cornered me. I'll do some tale-telling in front of the fireplace after I'm finished eating."

The two scurried off in search of their father, and Aralorn finished the last of her bread. Wolf yawned as she picked the empty trencher off the floor and got to her feet.

"Come on, we'll take this to the kitchen and . . ." Her voice trailed off as she saw Irrenna making her way toward her.

It wasn't Irrenna that made her lose her train of thought, but the man who walked beside her. Flamboyantly clothed in amber and ruby, Lord Kisrah looked more like a court dandy than the holder of age-old power.

It was too soon for Irrenna's message to have reached him; he must have come for the Lyon's funeral.

Well, Aralorn thought, *if he didn't know who it was that he met in the ae'Magi's castle the night Geoffrey died, he will now.* Even if he wasn't involved with her father's collapse, he was not going to be friendly. If he was responsible for her father's condition . . . well, she wasn't always friendly either.

She let none of her worries appear on her face, nor did

she allow herself to hesitate as she approached them, dirty trencher in hand.

"You said that you weren't able to wake him?" asked Irrenna.

Kisrah, Aralorn noted warily, was intent, but not surprised at all at seeing her face in this hall. He had known who she was before coming here. He moved to the top of her suspects.

"That's right," said Aralorn. "My uncle agreed to come and look. He didn't know the spell that holds Father, but he was able to dispose of the baneshade—"

"Baneshade?" Kisrah broke in, frowning.

She nodded. "Apparently the one who did this has a whole arsenal of black arts—"

"*Black* arts?" he interrupted.

"You must not have looked in on him yet," she said. "Whoever laid the spell holding the Lyon used black magic. I'm not certain if you'd call the baneshade black magic precisely, but it attacked me the first time I worked magic in the room—the mage must have set it to guard my father. My uncle—my mother's brother, who is a shapechanger— is the one who identified it and rid us of it as well."

"My apologies," Irrenna broke in. "Allow me to present the Lady Aralorn, my husband's oldest daughter, to you, Lord Kisrah. Aralorn, this is Lord Kisrah, the ae'Magi. He came here as soon as he heard what happened to Henrick."

"It took me a while to connect Henrick's daughter with the Sianim mercenary the ae'Magi had me fetch for him," replied the Archmage, bowing over Aralorn's hand. "I suppose I had expected someone more like your sisters."

At her side, Wolf stiffened and stared at Kisrah with an interest that was definitely predatory. She took a firm grip on a handful of fur. She'd never told him of Kisrah's role in her capture and subsequent torture by the ae'Magi because she'd worried about his reaction.

"How did you make the connection?" asked Irrenna,

unaware of the coercive nature of Kisrah's "fetching" of Aralorn. "She has very little contact with us; she says she is afraid her work will draw us into jeopardy."

Sadness crept across his features, an odd contrast to the rose-colored wig he wore—like an emerald among a pile of glass jewels. "The council appointed me to investigate Geoffrey's death even before they called me to assume his role. I looked into the backgrounds of anyone who had anything to do with him in his last days. You"—he directed his speech to Aralorn—"provided me with a particularly odd puzzle and kept the investigation going much longer than it otherwise would have. It was especially difficult until I discovered that the Lyon's eldest daughter was of shapeshifter blood." He was almost as good with a significant pause as she herself was. After a moment, he turned back to Irrenna. "It was the Uriah that were his downfall. He was looking for a way to make them less harmful and lost control of the ones he had with him. There was not even a body left."

"It was an accident, then?" asked Irrenna. "I had heard that it was—though there were all of those rumors about his son."

"The council declared it an accident," confirmed Kisrah. "A tragedy for us all."

Aralorn noted how carefully he avoided saying that he believed the council's decision that his predecessor's death had been an accident. Surely he didn't—he'd *been* there.

"Would you care to look at my father? Or would you prefer to rest from your travels?" she asked.

Lord Kisrah turned back to her. "Perhaps I will eat first. After that, would you consider accompanying me to your father? I tried to open the wards when I arrived, but I couldn't get through."

It had been Kisrah, then, who'd tried the wards. Did he know Wolf's magic well enough to tell that he'd set the spells? *Stinking wards,* she thought. If she'd had the sense of a goose, she'd have set them herself in the first place.

". . . at first it might have been Nevyn's work, but I know his magic." He looked at her inquiringly, and Aralorn wondered what she'd missed while she was cursing herself.

"No, not Nevyn's, nor mine either—my mother's gift of magic is green magic. I can set wardings, of course, but the baneshade's presence called for a stronger magic. I did a favor for a wizard once, and he gave me an amulet . . ." Wizards were always giving tokens with spells on them, weren't they? At least in the stories she told they were. At her feet, Wolf moaned softly, so maybe she was wrong.

Kisrah's eyebrows raised in surprise. "An amulet? How odd. I've never heard of a warding set on an amulet. Do you have it with you?"

Yep, I was wrong.

Aralorn shook her head and boldly elaborated on her lie. "It wasn't that big a favor. The amulet itself was the main component of the spell—so it could only be activated once. I thought the baneshade warranted using it. But my uncle killed the creature, so it's safer now. I'll come with you to take them off."

He stared at her a moment, his pale blue eyes seeming blander than ever. But she had been a spy for ten years; she knew he saw only what she intended him to see. Innocently, she gazed back.

She was lying. He knew she was lying. He wasn't going to call her on it, though—which made her wonder what he was up to.

"I see," he said after a moment. "With the baneshade gone, did you look at the spell holding Henrick?"

She nodded. "I'm not an expert, though I can tell black magic. My uncle said that it feels as if there was more than one mage involved in the spelling."

"Black magic," he said softly, and she had the impression that it was the real man speaking and not his public face. For an instant, she saw both shame and fear in his eyes. Interesting.

"Why don't you get some food, Lord Kisrah," said Irrenna.

"That would be good," agreed Aralorn. She wanted to give Wolf time to recover a little before they went back to the bier room with Kisrah. "My brother sent a pair of his hellions to force me into telling a story or two, and I gave them my word of honor I would entertain them after I'd eaten."

Irrenna laughed. "You'll have to stay for it, Lord Kisrah. Aralorn is a first-rate storyteller."

"So I have heard," agreed the mage, smiling.

Aralorn sat cross-legged on the old bench near the fireplace where she'd spent many long winter hours telling stories. The children gathered around were different from the ones she remembered, but there was a large number of her original audience present, too. Falhart sat on the floor with the rest, a couple of toddlers on his lap. Correy leaned against a wall beside Irrenna and Kisrah, who stood with his food so that he could be close enough to hear.

"Now then," Aralorn said, "what kind of story would you like?"

"Something about the Wizard Wars," said one of the children instantly.

"Yes," said Gerem softly, as he approached the group from the shadows. "Tell us a story about the Wizard Wars."

Startled, Aralorn looked up to meet Gerem's eyes. They were no more welcoming than they had been earlier that day.

"Tell us," he continued, taking a seat on the floor and lifting one of the youngsters onto his lap, "the story of the Tear of Hornsmar, who died at the hands of the shapechangers in the mountains just north of here."

She was going to have to teach her brother some subtlety, but she could work with his suggestion. She needed a long story, to give Wolf as much time to recover as possible. One came to mind as if it had been waiting for her to recognize it.

"A story of the Wizard Wars, then, but the story of the Tear is overtold. I have instead a different tale for you. Listen well, for it contains a warning for your children's children's children."

Having caught their attention, Aralorn took a breath and sought the beginning of her tale. It took her a moment, for it wasn't one of the ones she told often.

"Long and long ago, a miller's son was born. At the time, this hardly seemed an auspicious or important event, for as long as there have been millers, they have been having children. It was not even an unusual occurrence for this miller, because he'd had three other sons and a daughter born in a similar fashion—but not a son like this. No one in the village had ever had a son like this." She saw a few smiles, and the hall quieted.

She continued, punctuating her story with extravagant gestures. "When Tam laughed, the flowers bloomed, and the chairs danced; when he cried, the earth shook, and fires sprang up with disconcerting suddenness. Concerned that the child would set fire to the mill itself and ruin his family, the miller took his problem to the village priest.

"In those days, the old gods still walked the earth, and their priests were able to work miracles at the gods' discretion, so the miller's action was probably the wisest one he could have taken.

"And so the boy was raised by the village priest, who became used to the fires and the earthquakes and quite approved of the blooming flowers. The miller was so relieved that when the temple burned down because of a toddler temper tantrum, he didn't even grumble about paying his share to rebuild it—and he grumbled about everything.

"Now, in those days, there was trouble brewing outside the village. Mages, as you all know, are temperamental at best, and at their worst . . ." Aralorn shuddered and was pleased to see several members of her audience shiver in sympathy. At her feet, Wolf made a soft noise that might have been laughter. Kisrah smiled, but in the dim light of the great hall, she couldn't tell if it was genuine or not.

"Kingdoms then were smaller even than Lambshold, and each and every king had a mage who worked for him. Usually, the most powerful mages worked only for themselves, for none of the small countries could afford to hire them for longer than it took to win a battle or two. The strongest mages of them all were the black mages, who worked magic with blood and death."

Gerem straightened, and said, "I never knew black magic was more powerful than the rest."

Aralorn nodded. "With black magic, the sorcerer has only to control the magic released; with other magics, he must gather the power as well. Collecting magic released in death takes nothing out of the mage . . . except a piece of his soul."

"You sound as if you've had personal experience," said Gerem challengingly.

Aralorn shook her head. "Not I."

When Gerem looked away from her, she continued the tale. "This balance of power had worked for centuries— until the coming of the great warrior, Fargus, and the discovery of gold in the mountains of Berronay." She rolled out the names with great ceremony, like the court crier, but added, much less formally, "No one knows, now, where Berronay or its mines were. No one knows much more about Fargus than his name. But it was his deeds that came close to destroying the world. For he ruled Berronay shortly after its rich mines were discovered and before anyone else knew how rich that discovery was. He amassed a great army with the intent of conquering the world—and he hired the fourteen most powerful mages in the world to ensure that he would do so.

"Tam's village was the smallest of three in the kingdom of Hallenvale—that's 'green valley' in the old tongue. It was located in the lush farmland in the rolling hills just northwest of the Great Swamp." Aralorn paused, sipping out of a pewter mug of water someone had snagged for her.

"But there isn't any farmland there," broke in a tawny-headed girl of ten or eleven summers.

"No," agreed Aralorn softly, pleased that the child had added to the drama of her story. "Not anymore. There's just an endless sea of black glass where the farmland used to be."

She paused and let them think about that for a little while. "As I said, Tam was raised in the small farming village by the priest. When the boy was twelve—the age of apprenticing—he was sent to the king's wizard for training. By the time he was eighteen, Tam was the most powerful wizard around—except for those using black magic."

Aralorn surveyed her audience. "There were a lot of black mages, though. Black magic was common then, and most people saw nothing wrong with it."

"Nothing?" asked Gerem.

"Nothing." Aralorn nodded. "Most of the mages used the blood and death of animals—if they used human deaths, they kept it quiet. If you kill a pig for eating, its death releases magic. Isn't it a waste if you take the animal's hindquarters and throw them in the midden? Why then is it not a waste to leave the magic of its death to dissipate unused?" She waited. "They thought so. But our Tam, you see, was different. He'd been raised by a priest of the springtime goddess—a goddess of life. Out of respect to her, he didn't sully himself with death."

Satisfied that she'd given them something to think about, she continued the story. "Fargus, with the wealth

of the gold mines of Berronay behind him, bade his mages
ease the way for his armies, and he took over land after
land. As each new country added to his wealth, he hired
more mages. Even the Great Swamp was no barrier to Fargus's mages, whose powers only grew as the number of the
dead and dying mounted.

"Now, Fargus was not the first warlord to conquer others
using the power of the black mages. A score of years earlier, the battles between Kenred the Younger and Agenhall
the Foolish had raged wildly until the backlash of magic
had sunk the whole country of Faen beneath the waves of
the sea. A hundred years before that, the ravages of the
Tear of Hornsmar destroyed the great forest of Idreth with
the magic of his sorceress mistress, Jandrethan." Aralorn
looked up and saw several members of her audience nodding at the familiar names. "But it was Fargus's war that
changed everything."

"Hallenvale," she went on, "came at last to Fargus's
notice, and he sent his magic-backed army to fight there.
But it was not an easy conquest. The king of Hallenvale was
a warrior and strategist without equal—called Firebird for
his temperament and the color of his hair. Ah, I see several
of you have heard of him. Hallenvale was a prosperous little country, as it had been ruled wisely for generations. The
Firebird used his wealth to gather together wizards of his
own, including Tam. The small unconquered countries all
around, knowing that if Hallenvale fell, their lands would
be next, aided him any way they could.

"A battle was fought on the Plains of Torrence. The armies
were equally matched: Thirty-two black mages fought for
Fargus, a hundred and seven wizards stood beneath the Firebird's banner—though these were mostly lesser mages."

She let her voice speed up and drop in pitch as she fed
them details of the fight. ". . . Spells were launched and
countered until magic permeated the very earth. After
three days, a pall hung over the plain, an unnaturally thick

fog, a fog so dense they could not see twenty paces through it. To the mages, whichever side they fought upon, the air was so heavy with magic that it took more power to force yet more magic into the area. *Fortunately*"—she let her tongue linger on the word and call it to her audience's attention—"there were so many dead and dying on the field that there was power enough to work more and greater magics.

"Tam, his power exhausted, was sent to the top of a nearby hill that he might get a better view of the battlefield. He did so. What he saw sent him galloping for the Firebird's personal mage, Nastriut."

"Wasn't the mage who escaped the sinking of Faen on a boat called *Nastriut*?" Falhart asked.

She nodded. "The very same. He was an old man by then, and tired from the battle. Tam coaxed him onto a horse and hauled him up to the top of the hill."

She sipped water and let the suspense build.

"Only a very great mage could have seen what Tam had, but Nastriut was one of the most powerful wizards of his generation. From the vantage point of the hill, Nastriut and Tam could see that the fog that had grown from the first day of the battle was not what either had thought. It was not a spell cast by one of Fargus's wizards or some side effect of the sheer volume of magic.

" 'Just before Faen fell into the sea,' Tam said, 'you saw a dark fog engulf the whole island.'

" 'There was magic so thick it hurt to breathe,' said Nastriut. 'Death, more death, and dreams of the power of blood. From the sea I saw it like a great hungry beast.' The old man shuddered and swallowed hard. 'Have you been dreaming of power, Tam? I have. Dreams of the power death brings and the lust that rises through my blood. It promises me youth that has not been my state for a century or more.'

" 'If I use black magic,' whispered Tam, 'my dreams tell

me that I can end all the fighting and go back to my home. Are you saying this thing is in my dreams?'

" 'Such dreams we all had before Faen died,' the old man said. 'I dreamed that we created this with the taint of death magic, but I had no proof. When this beast killed the island, it was half the size it is now. But it is the same, the same.' "

The great hall was deathly quiet, and Aralorn was able to drop her voice to a whisper that echoed—a trick of tone and architecture she'd discovered a long time ago.

"Tam could not have done it, but Nastriut's reputation was such that Fargus's mages left the battlefield to help. Over a hundred mages pooled their magic to create a desert of obsidian glass to contain the Dreamer their blood magic had brought into being. Nastriut died in the doing—and he was not alone. The rest of the wizards vowed never to use black magic again upon pain of death. To ensure that this promise was kept, they placed upon themselves a spell that allowed their magic to be controlled by one man—the first ae'Magi, Tam of Hallenvale."

"A pretty tale to cover the wizards' stupidity," said Gerem abruptly. "It was abuse of magic that created the glass desert, not some heroic effort to save the world."

Aralorn smiled at him. "I only tell the tale as it was told to me. You can judge it true or false if you wish. It won't change the results."

"The destruction of a dozen kingdoms," he said.

"You've been listening to your teachers." Aralorn smiled her approval. "But there were other results as well. The wizards were vulnerable, most of them trained to use magic in a way that was forbidden them. Now the people feared them and killed them wherever they found them. For generations, a mageborn child was killed as soon as it was recognized. Only in Reth or Southwood could wizards find sanctuary."

Aralorn surveyed her audience, child and adult alike.

"If you wonder if this story is true, ask the Archmage what the first words of the wizard's oath are, the oath every apprentice must make to his master since the ae'Magi was set over the mages at the end of the Wizard Wars."

"Ab earum satimon," said Kisrah. He frowned thoughtfully at Aralorn, then translated softly, "To protect our dreams. Where did you hear this story? I have never heard it before. I thought the glass desert was a mistake caused by a clash of magic gone wild and out of control."

"I told it to her," said Nevyn, stepping out from a doorway. "It's an old tale I heard somewhere—though Aralorn has improved upon it."

Aralorn nodded gravely in acknowledgment of the compliment as she rose from her seat. "I have heard several variations of the story since. Lord Kisrah, you wanted to see my father?"

"One more story, before you go?" asked Falhart. "Something less . . . dark, if you would? I don't know about anyone else, but I'd rather not spend the night trying to convince my children that there is nothing lurking in the shadows."

Aralorn glanced down at Wolf, who was lying on his side being patted by small hands, his eyes closed. It was unusually tolerant of him. In his human form, he avoided people's hands, other than her own, altogether. The wolf was less shy, but she wondered if he was really asleep. If so, a few minutes more could only help him.

She gave Falhart a challenging look. "No more comments about my height?"

He raised his right hand. "I swear."

She glanced at Kisrah.

"I can wait," he said.

Aralorn resumed her seat. "All right, let's see what I can come up with. Hmm. Yes."

She waited for it to quiet down, then began. "Not so very long ago, and not so far away, there lived a sorcerer's apprentice named Pudge. As you might expect from his name, he enjoyed nothing so much as a nice soft pudding, except perhaps a piece of cake. He especially liked it when the sorcerer's cook would try to cover up the fact that his cake had fallen by filling in the hole with sugary frosting this thick." Aralorn held up two fingers together and watched a smile cross the face of one of Falhart's brood at the thought of such a delicacy.

"Now, Pudge's master had several apprentices who teased him about his eating. They might have meant it kindly—but you and I know that doesn't matter. It got so that Pudge would take whatever sweet he happened to thieve from the kitchen and eat it in secret places where the others wouldn't find him.

"His favorite was a little cubby he'd found in the library. The passage was so small and insignificant that even if the sorcerer had remembered it, he would never have used it. It was, in fact, so narrow that only a child could squeeze though the long tunnel that led to a comfortably cozy ledge on the side of the sorcerer's castle several stories above the ground.

"As the months passed, and the cook's sugary treats took their toll, the passage grew tighter and tighter, until Pudge began to wonder if there wasn't some kind of shrinking spell laid upon it.

"'Perhaps,' he thought, 'perhaps, it once was a normal sort of hall and every day it gets smaller and smaller.'

"It was an idea he found pleasing, though he found no mention of such a spell in any of the books he was allowed to delve into. I might mention here that Pudge was quite an adept little sorcerer in his own right. Had he been of a different temperament, the other apprentices might have truly regretted their teasing.

"One bright and sunny morning, the cook made little cherry tarts, each just large enough to fit into one of Pudge's hands. Nobody makes a better thief than a boy— just ask the Traders, if you don't believe me. Nobody, that is, except a sorcerer. Pudge came out of the kitchen with twelve cherry tarts, and he scrambled to the library before the cook realized they were gone.

"He opened the passage and managed to squeeze in, though he had to push the pies, stored in a knapsack he used for such nefarious missions, ahead of him in order to fit. It was really only the thought of the cook's ire that made him fight and struggle through the passage. The cook was a man after Pudge's own heart, but he had a terrible temper and was best avoided for a while after a successful raid.

"At last, Pudge was safely through the passage and out on his ledge. He ate eleven of the tarts and shared the twelfth with a few passing birds. Then he decided it was time to go back." Aralorn paused.

"He couldn't get back," said a young boy seated near the back of the group.

"Why not?" asked Aralorn, raising her brows.

"Because he was too big!" chorused a series of voices (some of which were bass or baritone).

Aralorn smiled and nodded. "You're right, of course. It took several days before Pudge was thin enough to get back through the passage, and by that time, his master was getting really worried. Upon hearing of Pudge's adventures, the sorcerer taught Pudge a spell or two to help him get out of tight places." She waited for a moment to let the chuckles die down. "Over the years Pudge grew in both girth and power. You might know him better by his real name— Tenneten the Large, own mage to King Myr, current ruler of Reth." She stood up briskly and made a shooing motion. "All right, that's all for the night. Correy, if you could spare a moment?"

Correy approached her, with Kisrah somewhat behind him, as the children shuffled off to their respective parents.

"What did you need?" asked her brother.

"Hmm, well, you know that old vacant cottage where the hermit used to live? In the clearing, not too far from here?"

"The one Hart fell through the roof of when he was pretending he was a dragon?"

Surprised, she nodded. "That was well before your time."

"Some things become family legends," he replied. "Besides, the knowledge he gained reroofing the cottage came in useful when Father sent us to build a house for Ridane's priestess to live in."

"Ah," she said, wondering why her father was building houses for the death goddess's priestess. Guessing why he sent his sons to do it was easier—the Lyon liked to make certain his children knew as many skills as possible. He also liked to keep them humble. "Well, in any case, you need to send someone there to take care of a rather large carcass we left. It might attract some predators, and it's near some good winter pasture."

Correy nodded. "I saw that your wolf is missing some hide. Run into a bear?"

Aralorn coughed, glanced at Kisrah, who was listening in, and said, "Something of the sort, yes." There is nothing more disastrous than allowing your opponents to overestimate your abilities: Killing legendary monsters almost always led to that very thing.

"I'll see to it," he said. "Good night, Featherweight."

She reached way up and managed to ruffle his hair. "Good night, Blue-eyes."

Correy laughed and kissed her cheek.

"Good night, sir," he told Kisrah with a friendly nod.

Kisrah waited until Correy had gone. "Blue-eyes?" he asked.

If they'd been friends, she would have laughed; she satisfied herself with lifting an eyebrow instead. "Because they are not, of course."

He nodded seriously. "Of course. I compliment you on your storytelling."

She shrugged, rubbing her fingers into the soft fur

behind Wolf's ears. "It's a hobby of mine to collect odd tales. Some of them have even come in handy a time or two. Come, I'll take you to the bier room."

She set off across the great hall, which had largely emptied of people. She didn't look behind her, but she could hear the rustle of the Archmage's cloak and the click of Wolf's nails on the hard floor.

Before they reached the curtain, Kisrah stopped walking. Aralorn stopped and looked at him inquiringly.

"Do you think that the only reason black magic was abandoned was this beast in your story?"

"The Dreamer? I'm not certain that the Dreamer ever existed," replied Aralorn. "There's a less dramatic version of the story in which Tam himself creates the Dreamer in order to stop the general use of black magic. I am a green mage, my lord ae'Magi: I don't need to eat rotten meat to know that it is tainted. Blood magic . . . is as foul-smelling as a raw roast left out for a couple of days in the sun."

"Ah," said Kisrah. He frowned at her intently and changed the subject smoothly. "Did you kill the ae'Magi?"

"Geoffrey?" she asked, as if there had been a dozen Archmages killed in the last few years.

"Yes."

Aralorn folded her arms and leaned against the cold stone wall. Wolf settled at her feet with a sigh, though he kept a steady eye on Kisrah. The Archmage ignored him.

"The Uriah killed Geoffrey," she said softly. "Poor tormented creatures he, himself, created." Then she forced herself to relax and continue lightly. "At least that's what the mercenaries who were hired to clean up the castle reported."

"He had no trouble controlling them before," said Kisrah. "I've used the spells myself—they were neither difficult nor draining. And, Aralorn, despite what your friend, the wizard who gave you that *amulet*"—not one of her better stories, she admitted—"told you, Geoffrey didn't create the Uriah, just summoned them to do his bidding. I think that you have been misled."

She shrugged. She'd learned her lesson; she didn't argue with someone who might still be under the influence of the late ae'Magi's spells.

"You *were* there that night," he said. "I saw you."

"And if I say I killed him," asked Aralorn in a reasonable tone, "what then? You will kill me as well to even the score?"

"No," he said hoarsely. "My word of honor that I will not. Nor will I tell anyone else what you say to me. I believe I know who did the killing, but I need . . . I need to be certain."

Why? she thought to herself. *So you can justify the black magic used to hold my father as bait to trap Wolf?*

"How could I, a second-rate swordswoman and a third-rate green mage, do such a thing to the ae'Magi?" She indulged herself a bit more than was strictly safe, though she was careful that he would not hear the sarcasm in her voice. "Everyone knows how powerful a sorcerer he was— and a swordsman of the highest ability. Why would I want to kill him? He was the kindest, most tenderhearted—not to mention amusing—sorcerer I have ever met. His death was a great tragedy."

Second-rate swordswoman, but first-rate actress; Aralorn knew that Kisrah could only hear the sincerity in her voice. It was the sort of addlepated garbage everyone said about the last ae'Magi and meant in its absurd, simplistic whole—thanks to the ae'Magi's charisma spell, which lingered even now. If she hadn't accused Geoffrey of creating the Uriah, she thought, she might have persuaded Kisrah of her innocence in the Archmage's death.

Kisrah frowned at her. "You were there that night. Wielding a mage's staff . . ." He hesitated a bare instant, but obviously decided he might as well push all the way. "Wielding Cain's staff—it is very distinctive."

She wouldn't help him convict Wolf. Aralorn gave Kisrah a puzzled look. "I was there that night, but I don't recall any staff. I sometimes run messages for the Spymaster. When the Uriah started acting strangely, I left as soon as I could. I'm not a coward, but those things scare me. Look what they did to the ae'Magi."

Kisrah stared at her; she could almost taste his frustration. "The Uriah captured you for him. He had me translocate you to his castle. What did he want from you?"

Aralorn shrugged and modified her story without a pause. "A misunderstanding, I'm afraid. He thought that I had some knowledge of the whereabouts of King Myr. You remember that was about the time Myr, distraught over his parents' deaths, left without telling anyone where he had gone. It turns out that King Myr visited a healer, who lives quietly in the mountains near the king's summer residence." Without a qualm, she stuck to the official story. If it became widely known that Myr and the ae'Magi were enemies . . . it might confuse a lot of Myr's followers who were still under the influence of the previous ae'Magi. Perhaps time would solve that—perhaps not. "I actually did know where he was, but was told not to tell anyone—you know how the Spymaster is. The ac'Magi didn't intend any harm to him, obviously, but orders are orders. The ae'Magi eventually accepted that I couldn't tell him anything."

Storytelling did come in handy sometimes, Aralorn reflected. Take a grain of truth and embellish it with nonsense, and it was more believable than what had actually happened. It wasn't as if she really expected Kisrah to believe her anyway; she just wanted to keep him from deciding what had happened with any certainty.

Wolf whined, and it echoed weirdly in the stone-enclosed corridor. Maybe he was worried about how much storytelling she was doing this night. Probably he was right.

"Shall we go, Lord Kisrah? Or would you like to put

me to the question? I'm certain Father has some old thumb-screws around here somewhere."

The Archmage stared at her as if the intensity of his gaze alone would be enough to pick through the tale she'd woven. His expression was as far removed from the charming man of his public image as Wolf was from a sheep. The pink wig looked like the absurd camouflage it was. He looked very tired, she thought suddenly—as if he had spent more than one sleepless night lately.

"No doubt," he said tautly, "torture would get another answer out of you, equally plausible and equally false."

Aralorn smiled pleasantly at him; it wasn't difficult—few things gave her greater pleasure than frustrating someone else's attempt to gain information. "No doubt," she agreed congenially.

"Sometimes," he said with absolute conviction, "I wish there were a truth spell that really worked. Lead on, then, by all means," he said with a sigh, abruptly shifting back to the harmless dandy. "I would take a look at this spell that holds your father."

The guard had returned to his duty.

"Lord Kisrah is here to take a look at Father," she told him.

"Of course, Lady. Should I remain here, or would you like more privacy?"

Aralorn looked to the Archmage, who shrugged his indifference.

"Stay here," she said to the guard. "I'd rather not have any curious souls wander in while the ae'Magi is here."

"Yes, Lady." The guard smiled.

"The wardings are different," said Lord Kisrah, examining the curtains.

Aralorn shrugged and dispelled her wards. "It was a onetime warding amulet. These wards are mine."

He opened the curtain and passed through, murmuring

without looking at her. "The wardings were Cain's work—
I know it well. I've never heard of talismans of warding."

She was not so easily won from her chosen story. She
merely raised her eyebrow at him. "I had not heard of bane-
shades before today. Isn't it wonderful that we may learn
throughout our lifetimes. I assure you that the only ones
here when the wardings were drawn were my wolf and I.
You have your choice of mages." She gestured to Wolf,
who whined and wagged his tail gently. No human mage
could manage to stay in an animal form as long as Wolf had
tonight. That Cain ae'Magison was something other than
purely human was something his father had kept quiet.

Kisrah spared her a brief glare before continuing into
the room. She lit a magelight as she followed him in, but
he lit his own as well. Obviously, she thought with amusement, he didn't trust her. Smart man.

She tugged the curtain shut behind her, stopping just
inside the alcove, where she could see the sorcerer without
interfering with his magic.

Like Wolf, he placed a hand on her father's forehead and
made a gesture that looked somewhat similar. Watching
him closely, Aralorn saw the Archmage's full lips tighten
with some emotion or perhaps just the effort he put into the
spell. When he was done, he stepped back for a moment,
then began another spell.

At Aralorn's side, Wolf stiffened and took a swift step
forward, crouching slightly. Aralorn felt a swift rush of fear;
had she trusted too much to her knowledge of this man?

In spite of her suspicions, she really didn't believe he
would actually harm her father. His reputation aside, Aralorn had access to more rumors than a cat had kittens, and
she'd never heard a word to indicate he was dishonorable;
and *someone* had taken great care to keep from harming
her father. She knew too much about magic to make the
mistake of interrupting Kisrah, but she watched him narrowly and trusted Wolf to stop it if need be.

Whatever the spell the Archmage wrought, Aralorn could tell by the force of the magic gathering at his touch and the beads of sweat on his forehead that it was a powerful one. When he was through, Kisrah leaned against the bier for support.

"Cursed be," he swore softly, wiping his face with impatience. He turned to Aralorn, "Quickly, tell me the names of the magic-users who live within a day's ride of here."

"Human mages?"

"Yes."

Aralorn pursed her lips but could think of no reason to lie to him. "Nevyn, for one. I think Falhart's wife Jenna might be a hedgewitch—someone said something like that once—but you'd have to talk to them to be sure. I know she's the local midwife. Old Anasel retired to a cottage on the big farm over on the bluffs about a league to the south. I believe that he's senile now. That's it as far as I know—though there are probably a half dozen hedgewitches."

Kisrah shook his head. "Wouldn't be a hedgewitch. Anasel . . . Anasel might have been able to do it. I'll speak to Lady Irrenna about him. It is certainly not Nevyn. I know his work."

Aralorn tapped her fingers lightly on her thigh. Hedgewitches aside, Kisrah should have been able to answer the question about wizards for himself. He was, after all, the ae'Magi. All the trained human wizards, except for Wolf, were bound to him.

"Ask Irrenna about other mages as well—she might know something I don't, but after you do that, you might see if you can contact one of the Spymaster's wizards in Sianim. Tell them you're asking for me, and they won't charge you. If there is another wizard here, Ren will know."

Kisrah looked startled for a moment at her helpfulness, but he nodded warily. "I'll do that."

That night, comfortably ensconced in the bed, Aralorn watched as Wolf, in human form, scrubbed his face with a damp cloth.

"Wolf, what do you know about howlaas?"

He held the cloth and shook his head. "Something less than a story collector like you, I imagine."

She shrugged. "I was just wondering how long I'll be listening to the wind."

"Is it bothering you now?"

"Not as long as I stay away from windows."

"Give it a few days," he said finally. "If it doesn't stop soon, I'll see what I can find out."

She nodded. The thought that it might never fade was something she didn't want to dwell on. She came up with a change of topic.

"What was the second spell Lord Kisrah tried to work?" she asked. "The one you were worried about."

Wolf shrugged off his shirt and set it aside so he could wash more thoroughly. "I believe it was an attempt to unwork the spell holding your father."

Admiring the view, she said, "I thought that was what he was doing with his first spell?"

Wolf shook his head. "No. He was checking to make certain your father was still alive."

She thought about that, frowning. "Why did his second spell bother you?"

He wiped dry and took off his loose-fitting pants. "Because he didn't examine the spell before he tried to unwork it."

"Which means?"

"He knew what the spell was already."

She pulled back the cover from Wolf's side of the bed and patted it in invitation. "You think that Kisrah cast it?"

He joined her and spent a moment settling in. "Yes. I think that's exactly what it means."

"Then why couldn't he remove it?" she asked, scooting over until her head rested on his shoulder. "And why was he surprised by the baneshade's presence?"

"I think that another wizard has his hands in the brew. Remember, Kisrah asked about other wizards in the area."

Aralorn nodded. "So he can't release the spell until he finds the other mage?"

"Right."

"If he cast the spell with this other wizard, then why doesn't he know who it is?"

"Perhaps he set the spell in an amulet," said Wolf, grunting even before she poked him. "Seriously, I don't know."

"Nevyn," she said with a sigh. "It must have been Nevyn. I've heard that poor Anasel can hardly feed himself."

But Wolf shook his head. "If it was Nevyn, I'd expect that Kisrah would know it. Kisrah was telling the truth when he said it wasn't Nevyn—he's a terrible liar."

She wriggled her toe in the covers for a minute, then she twisted around and braced her chin on Wolf's chest. "So Kisrah decided that you and I had a hand in the former ae'Magi's death. In a fit of vengeance, he uses black magic on Father to draw me, and therefore you, into coming here, where he could exact vengeance. Then another wizard steps in to add his two bits' worth—I don't buy it."

"That's because you are trying to make whole cloth from unspun wool."

She grinned in the darkness. "You've been hanging around Lambshold too long. 'Sheepish' comments aside, I suppose, you're probably right. Do you have a better idea?"

"I have a suspicion, but I'll wait until I've had a little more time to think on it."

She yawned and shifted into a more comfortable position. "I think I'll sleep on it, too."

She really didn't expect to gain any insight while she lay dreaming, but it was several hours before morning when she awoke with her heart pounding.

"Wolf," she said urgently.

"Umpf," he said inelegantly.

She sat up, letting the chilly night air seep under the warm blankets. "I mean it, Wolf, wake up. I need your opinion."

"All right. I'm awake." He pulled the covers snug around his neck.

Almost hesitantly, she asked, "Did Kisrah look tired to you? I thought so, but I don't know him very well."

"Yes. There are a lot of people around here who haven't gotten enough sleep." Sleep-roughened as it was, his voice was almost difficult to understand.

Aralorn smoothed the covers as they lay over her lap, not at all certain her next question was important enough for the pain it would cause him. "When you saw her, the one time you saw her, did your mother have red hair?"

He withdrew instantly without moving at all.

"It's not an idle question," she told him. "I thought of something while I was telling stories tonight. I thought it was silly then, but now . . ."

"Yes," he said shortly, "she had red hair."

"Was it long or short?"

"Long," he bit out after a short pause. "Long and filthy. It smelled of excrement and death."

"Wolf," said Aralorn in a very small voice, looking at the bump her toes made under the quilts, "when you destroyed the tower, were you trying to kill yourself?"

She felt the bed move as he shifted his weight.

This question seemed to bother him less than the one about his mother. The biting tone was missing from his rough voice, and he sounded . . . intrigued. "Yes. Why do you ask?"

She ran her hands through her hair. "I'm not sure how

to tell you this without sounding like a madwoman. Just bear with me."

"Always." There was a bit of long-suffering in his tone.

She leaned back against him and smiled wryly. "Ever since you left this last time, I've been having nightmares. At first they weren't too different from the ones I had after you rescued me from the ae'Magi's dungeons, and I didn't think much more about them. About a week ago, they became more pointed."

She thought about them, trying to pick out the first that had been different. "The first set seemed to have a common theme. I dreamed that I was a child, looking for something I had lost—you. In another dream, I was back in the dungeon, blinded, and the ae'Magi asked me where you were—just as he did when he had me at the castle. It was so real I could feel the scratches on my arms and the congestion in my lungs. I've never had a dream that real."

She reached out a hand to rest on Wolf's arm for her own comfort. "I saw Talor again, and his twin. They were both Uriah this time, though Kai died before he could be changed."

She paused to steady her voice and wasn't too successful. "They asked me where you were."

"You think they were more than dreams?" She couldn't tell what he thought from his voice.

"I didn't at first, though I thought it was strange that in my dreams they never asked where 'Wolf' was—I don't think of you as 'Cain' very often. That's what my father asked me. He said, 'Don't tell me you've forgotten where you put Cain.'" She laughed softly, shaking her head. "As if you were a toy I'd misplaced." She grinned at him. "I thought that one was just worry because you'd left so abruptly."

She lost her smile. "That's where the color of your mother's hair comes in. The last dream, the one I had in the inn on the way here, was even odder than the others. At least they seemed to come from my experiences: This one wasn't about anything I'd ever seen."

"It concerned my mother?"

Aralorn nodded. "Partially, yes. It was more a series of dreams. They all concerned you—things you had done."

"What sorts of things?"

"Unpleasant ones. Like when your mother died. Someone who didn't know you as well as I do might have thought you didn't feel anything."

"I didn't."

Aralorn shot him a look of disbelief, remembering the boy's frozen face, then shook her head at him. "Right," she said dryly. "At any rate, that was the first part. In another, I was tied down, and you were going to kill me. But I knew there was something wrong, and I fought it. When I did, it . . . altered. I was watching again, and it was the ae'Magi who held the knife. He offered it to you, and you refused."

"I didn't always," commented Wolf softly—he had stiffened again.

Aralorn tightened her grip briefly on his arm. "I know. But you wouldn't smile while you killed—or talk either, for that matter. At any rate, the last part was when you destroyed the tower. What I saw at first presented you as a power-mad mage, but this time it was easier to shift the dream back to what really happened. I can picture you motivated by rage, hurt, or cold-blooded anger, but greed just doesn't fit."

"The story you told tonight made you think that something was sending you dreams like the Dreamer?" repeated Wolf carefully.

"It sounds even stupider when you say it than when I think it," she commented, but she slid back under the covers and huddled near his warmth just the same. How to explain the alien feel of the dreams without sounding even stupider? "I didn't know the color of your mother's hair, or that you were trying to destroy yourself with the tower. We are living in odd times." Times made odder by the last ae'Magi's foray into forbidden magics—she didn't need to say it. Wolf knew his father was in some part responsible for the changes taking place. "Dragons fly the Northland skies, and howlaas venture into Reth."

She continued without pause. "There has even been a resurgence in the followers of the old gods for the past several years. Look at the temple here. It's been centuries since there was a priest in residence, but there's one here now. The trappers have been decimated by nasty critters like the howlaa and other things that haven't been seen in generations. Is it so impossible that . . . that something else was awakened?"

Wolf broke in. "You mean that the black magic my father worked might have fed the Dreamer you told us about tonight?"

"Yes." She swallowed. "That howlaa today. It was sent, Wolf."

"Sent?" asked Wolf.

"Uhm." She nodded. "When I met its gaze, it spoke to me. Something evil sent it searching for us—it was meant to kill you." She hesitated, then continued. "Then there was the wind . . . Wolf, I believe that there is something evil here."

Silence lingered for a while as Wolf thought of what she'd said.

"Well," he said finally, "as long as we are throwing out odd theories, I have developed one of my own, just for you. It even has to do with dreaming."

"You didn't laugh at mine, so I won't laugh at yours," she promised.

"Right," he replied. "When it became obvious to me that Kisrah had worked the spell, I thought about just what it would have taken to persuade him to do so. I could only think of one thing—and tonight I realized that it was even possible. Let me tell you a little something you may not have known about human magic."

"That doesn't limit the topic much," she quipped.

He ruffled her hair. "Quiet, little mouse, and listen. Human mages have different talents; one of them—though it is very rare—is a form of farseeing. The mage's spirit leaves his body and can travel over vast distances in a matter of moments. In that state, he can speak to others in their dreams or merely watch them. Usually, they are invisible in that form—but occasionally they can be seen as a ghostly mist."

"All right," agreed Aralorn. "I think I've heard of that. It's called spirit travel or something of the sort—but I thought it was rare."

"Like shapeshifters," agreed Wolf.

"Your point," she acquiesced, grinning a little in the darkness of the chilly old castle room. "So you think that maybe my dreams might be coming from a human mage? Someone deliberately trying to get information from me?"

"My father could do it," said Wolf softly. "I heard him talking about it once with another wizard. They were discussing another mage, I think. I don't know which one. He said, 'Of course I'm certain he's a dreamwalker. I have some talent in that direction myself.' I think he used his talent to influence his rise to power—by speaking to the other mages as they slept." He hesitated a moment, then added, "I remember, because I marked a rune on my staff that kept him from doing the same to me as soon as I overheard him."

Aralorn tightened her arms around him, wondering how he was still sane after all his father had done to him. He squeezed her in return—to comfort her, she thought—and continued to speak without a pause.

"If the body of a dreamwalker is killed while the spirit is outside, the spirit remains alive for a time. He probably would not be able to work magic as a spirit, but he can persuade others to act on his behalf."

"A ghost?" she asked.

He grunted. "No. Ghosts are . . . bits of memory trapped in place. A spirit is—it's too late at night for lessons in magic theory, my Lady. Let me get back to the subject at hand. It is possible that my father managed to leave his body before the Uriah killed him. In that state, he could have visited Kisrah—as well as the other mage who appears to have had his hands in the pie—and persuaded them to act in his stead."

"You think the only reason Kisrah would use black magic . . ."

"Was if my father asked him to do so," said Wolf. "Yes."

"To use Father as bait for us."

"Perhaps."

Aralorn stiffened at his cautious tone, which usually meant things had gone from bad to worse. "What do you mean?"

"My father wanted to live forever, Lady. Do you think that he would be content with mere vengeance?"

"You think he's trying to use Father's body?"

"Your father can't work magic; but your father is connected intimately with three mages. Attack him with magic, and my father has a whole selection to choose among."

"He would prefer yours since you are the most powerful of the three." Aralorn shivered and settled closer. "I think I prefer the Dreamer."

"Perhaps," suggested Wolf mildly, "we'll be lucky, and it is only Kisrah trying to kill me."

She snickered into his shoulder. "Not everyone would look at that as lucky."

"Not everyone is looking at our list of alternatives."

"True." She yawned.

They fell silent, and she thought Wolf had drifted off to sleep. She patted him gently.

Her uncle had said that Wolf had a death wish.

She'd known that he had a tendency to be reckless, thought that it was something they shared. In her dreams (and she was convinced that the memories of Wolf's experiences were true dreams, however they'd been sent), she'd seen that he'd expected death when he'd destroyed the tower. He'd hoped for death. Apparently, he still did.

She took in a deep breath of his familiar scent and held it to her heart. She would not lose him.

"Tomorrow, I think we might visit the priestess of the death goddess," she said. He *had* been asleep, because her voice jerked him awake. "If there's a ghost or a Dreamer out there, the death goddess ought to know—don't you think?"

"Could be," Wolf muttered groggily. "Go to sleep, Aralorn."

EIGHT

"I hadn't expected this to become an expedition," muttered Aralorn softly to Sheen as she rocked back and forth with his exuberant stride. He was feeling frisky after his rest, and his steps were animated and quick. Wolf, gliding soundlessly beside the gray warhorse, gave her a sardonic look before turning his attention to the snowy path.

She shook her head, and said in a tone meant to carry to her escort, "It's not as if Lambshold is riddled with outlaws. Even if it were, I am fully capable of taking care of myself."

"See, Correy," boomed Falhart from behind her and somewhat to the left, "I told you she'd like to have some company."

"She's been gone a long time. She's probably forgotten where the temple is," said Correy solemnly, behind her and to the right. "Dead howlaas aside, an itty-bitty runt like her needs her big brothers to protect her."

Aralorn spun Sheen around on his hocks with enough speed to leave the stallion snorting and looking for the enemy. If she'd known what an overprotective streak the howlaa was going to stir up, she would never have let Correy know it was there. Let his stupid sheep get eaten by wolves. Protection she might have to put up with while she was here, but . . .

She pointed accusingly at Correy. "You promised no more jokes about my size."

"Or lack thereof," added Falhart smugly.

"No," said Correy. "Falhart is the one who promised. Besides, I just commented on *our* size, right, Gerem? Just because your thirteen-year-old brother is a hand and a half taller than you doesn't mean you're small. We just happen to be taller than most people."

"Especially itty-bitty runts like you," added Falhart helpfully.

She shook her head at the three of them. Hart had come because he wanted to get out and ride. Correy, she thought, had come out of an honest desire to protect her. Gerem, she strongly suspected, had come to save her hulking brothers from their nasty, shapeshifting sister, itty-bitty runt or not.

"Men," she snorted with mock disgust.

She pivoted Sheen until he faced their original direction and sent him off racing across the sun-sparkled snow, smiling when her brothers called out in protest at her head start as they picked up the race.

———

Ridane's temple was a large structure nestled in an isolated valley. Aralorn remembered the "new" temple as a ruin heavily overgrown with ivy, but even under the snow, she could see that was no longer the case. Someone had been doing quite a lot of work, and the result was elegant and impressive. The snug little house built unobtrusively on one side was a new addition to the site as well.

Correy pointed to it. "When Father heard there was a priestess at the temple, he rode here by himself to talk with her. When he got back, he sent me out with a score of workmen to build her a house to live in."

Falhart grinned at Aralorn. "Correy's been really helpful around here. He took several days to clear the ivy and a week to scrub the lichen off the stone. He even got the old well working again."

Before Correy could reply, a cheery "Who comes?" rang out from the cottage, and the door opened to reveal a woman bundled in a wool cloak dyed cherry red. She shut the door behind her and came out to greet them.

"My lords! And isn't it a cold day to be out visiting, I'm thinking." The priestess, for she could be no other, was close enough for Aralorn to see that her face matched the promise of her voice. A warm smile lit eyes the color of dark-stained oak, and it was aimed particularly at Correy.

Correy jumped lightly off his horse and took one of her hands in his, bringing it to his lips. "Any day with you in it, Lady, is as warm as midsummer's eve."

Hmm, thought Aralorn. *Maybe Correy didn't come to protect me after all.*

Falhart shook his head as he dismounted also. In tones of apologetic despair, he addressed the priestess. "Smooth-tongued demon, isn't he? I'm sorry, Tilda. It's my fault. I taught him all I knew."

"That took the better part of supper," confided Correy without releasing the priestess's hand. "And only that long because he was eating most of the time. It's amazing the man ever managed to get married in the first place."

Aralorn slipped off Sheen and dropped his reins to the ground.

"It's obvious that he wasn't teaching you manners," Aralorn muttered in a voice loud enough for everyone to hear, "or you would have introduced me by now."

"Forgive me, O Small-but-Sharp-Tongued-One," said Falhart, taking Aralorn's hand gallantly. "I have neglected my duties as older brother. Tilda, allow me to present my sister Aralorn. Aralorn, this is Tilda, priestess of the death goddess."

"The shapeshifter," murmured Tilda thoughtfully.

"The mercenary," Aralorn murmured back.

They exchanged cheerful grins. Then the priestess turned to Gerem, standing quietly beside his mount.

"Gerem," said the priestess, "well come. I haven't seen you since last summer."

Aralorn watched Gerem's face closely, but apparently Nevyn had no objection to the death goddess, for Gerem's smile was genuine, lighting his eyes as it touched his lips. "I'm sorry, Lady, but Correy made us stay home so he could have you to himself."

"To what do I owe this visit? Would you like to come in?" Tilda gestured to her house.

Correy shook his head. "Today's an official visit to the priestess, I'm afraid. Aralorn thinks Ridane might be able to shed some light on the matter with Father."

The priestess lost none of her warmth but nodded understandingly. "I was not surprised when I was told he was not dead—Ridane had said nothing of his death to me. I don't know if She knows any more than you do, but you may certainly ask. Would you go into the temple? I will meet you inside."

Aralorn followed her brothers to the main entrance of the temple. Correy started to open the rough-hewn, obviously temporary door, then hesitated.

"Aralorn, I think it might be best if you leave your wolf outside," he said.

"The wolf is one of the death goddess's creatures," said Gerem unexpectedly. "I doubt the goddess will object— though her priestess might."

Wolf settled the matter by slipping through the narrow opening and into the temple.

Aralorn shrugged. "I suspect this temple has been infested by everything from rats to cows over the last hundred years. One animal more or less will make little difference."

Correy shook his head but opened the door farther and allowed the rest of them to pass. As Aralorn moved by him, he caught her arm.

"Don't be fooled by Tilda's friendliness. The death goddess has a very real presence here. Be careful how far you choose to push Her."

Aralorn patted him gently on the top of his head—she had to stand on her toes to do it. "Go teach Lord Kisrah how to cast a light spell, baby brother. I'm not as uncivilized as it sometimes appears."

Brushing by him, she walked into the entrance hall. It was not very impressive as such things go. Although it was large enough for twoscore people to stand without feeling crowded, there was still a multitude of evidence of the temple's long spell of neglect. High above, the vaulted ceiling showed white plaster and gaping holes where frescoed wolves and owls once frolicked. The floor had been pulled up and the usable flagstone piled to one side. On the other side, several large and crudely made benches lined the wall.

Though there was no sign of a fire, the room was remarkably warm. When the men began to toss their cloaks and gloves on the benches, Aralorn did the same.

As she dropped her gloves on top of her cloak, the creak of door hinges drew her attention to the far end of the room. The doors set in the wall were neither makeshift nor temporary; only years produced such a fine patina in bronze. They swung slowly open with a ponderousness in keeping with their hoary age.

Dressed in robes of black and red, Tilda stepped through the doorway onto the narrow platform set between the doors and the three stairs down to where Aralorn and her brothers waited. They approached the priestess with varying degrees of wariness, reverence, and enthusiasm.

When Correy stopped several feet from the stairs, the rest of them did as well, leaving the priestess above them.

"You are come to ask about the Lyon." The priestess's voice had lost the hills accent and the warmth. Her earthy beauty was in no way faded, but it seemed out of place.

Aralorn thought it wasn't Tilda speaking at all. A shiver ran through her. She could never have stood for such a thing; the last ae'Magi had come close to controlling her thoughts. Even as part of her shuddered in distaste, she felt a flash of awe—and satisfaction. This priestess was a priestess in truth; even her small store of green magic told her that much. She might really be able to help the Lyon.

"My father lies with the seeming of death," said Correy, when no one else spoke. "Can you free him?"

She seemed to consider it a moment, and Aralorn held her breath. Finally, the priestess shook her head. "No. There are limits on the things that I control. This is no death curse, though he may die of it, and I can do little but speed his death. That I will not do without reason."

"How long—" Aralorn's voice cracked, and she had to try again. "How long before he dies of the magic?"

"A fortnight more will the spell hold stable. Until that time, he comes not unto me."

"Two weeks," said Aralorn softly to herself.

"As I said," replied the priestess.

"Do you know of the Dreamer?" asked Aralorn, drawing surprised looks from her brothers.

The priestess turned her head to the side, considering.

"The creature that sleeps in the glass desert," Aralorn clarified further.

"Ah," said the priestess. "Yes . . . I had forgotten that name . . ."

"Has it awakened?"

The priestess hesitated. "I would not know of it, unless it killed—and that was not its way. It incited others to do its killing."

Falhart spoke for the first time. "Do you know anything about the farm that was burned to the ground?"

"Yes. Death visited there and was caught to pay the price of the Lyon's sleep."

"You mean," said Gerem, with a tension that was strong enough to attract Aralorn's interest, "something was killed there. That death was used in the magic that ensorcelled my father."

The priestess nodded. "As I said."

"Is Geoffrey ae'Magi dead, or does his spirit attend the living?" asked Aralorn.

"He is dead," said Tilda. "But in the way of such men, much of him lives on in the hearts of those who loved him."

She swayed alarmingly. Disregarding his wariness for the goddess in concern for the woman, Correy jumped up the short flight of stairs and wrapped an arm around her waist.

"Here, now," he said, helping her sit on the floor.

"Did you get the answers you needed?" she asked. "She left without warning me. Usually, I can tell when She's ready to leave, and I can give notice of the last question. Otherwise, you are left with the most important thing unanswered."

"It was fine," said Aralorn thoughtfully. She would rather have had a simple yes or no to her last question, but she hadn't really expected as much help as they'd gotten. Usually priests and priestesses were much less forthcoming and a lot more obscure when they did tell you something.

"Aralorn"—Tilda got to her feet and shook out her robes briskly, obviously putting off whatever weakness the goddess's visit had left her with—"I wonder if you would mind speaking with me in private for a bit."

Since Aralorn had been debating how to phrase the same request, she nodded immediately. "Of course." Last night she'd thought of another thing that Ridane could help her with.

Tilda walked down the stairs and, with a shooing motion, said, "Go along now and wait for us in the cottage. There are some fresh scones on the table, help yourselves."

Aralorn's brothers left without a protest. As he turned to close the door behind them, Gerem shot a calculating look at Aralorn. When she smiled and waved, he frowned and pulled the door shut with a bang that reverberated in the large, mostly empty room.

"He doesn't trust me," commented Aralorn, shaking her head.

"With Nevyn around, you're lucky anyone does," said Tilda in reply.

"For someone who lives several hours from the hold, you know an awful lot about my family." Aralorn rubbed the itchy place behind Wolf's ears.

The death goddess's priestess grinned companionably and answered Aralorn's observation. "My news travels fast—Correy's new horse has a rare turn of speed."

Aralorn returned her smile. "You wanted to talk to me about something?"

"Hmm." Tilda looked down and tapped her foot. "The goddess told me to ask you if you would change shape for me."

Of all the things she could have asked, that was something Aralorn had not expected.

"Why?"

"You are a shapeshifter," Tilda said. "A few weeks ago, I saw an animal that had no business being in the woods. A shapeshifter was the only explanation I could come up with, though, other than the fact that there hasn't been a report of a howlaa around here for generations, the animal didn't seem unnatural. I asked Ridane if I'd be able to tell the difference between a shapeshifter and a natural animal; She told me to ask you." The priestess smiled. "Since you hadn't been here in a long time, I did wonder. When you came here today, She reminded me again to ask you."

"There was a howlaa," said Aralorn. "It was killed yesterday, not far from the keep. But I don't see any reason to refuse to change in front of you: a favor for a favor."

"What is it you need of me?" asked Tilda warily.

Aralorn threaded her fingers through the hair on Wolf's neck and cleared her throat. "I have this friend who needs to get married."

Tilda's jaw dropped for a moment. "No one's ever asked me that before."

Not surprising, thought Aralorn. There hadn't been a priestess of Ridane here for generations, and even when there had been, few people chose to be married in Her temple. Marriage bonds set by the goddess of death had odd consequences: Two people so bound could not live if one died.

Aralorn was counting on three things: that no one would see the marriage lines written in Tilda's recording book and use them to trace Cain ae'Magison to Aralorn and her wolf; that Wolf and his unbalanced education wouldn't know about the quirk of Ridane's marriages; and that, afterward, when she told him, he'd want her life more than his own death.

"You can perform a marriage ceremony?" Aralorn asked.

"Yes," Tilda said slowly. "I know the rites."

Aralorn inclined her head formally. "Thank you."

She turned to Wolf, who had been staring at her incredulously since she'd begun speaking.

"Well?" she said.

He glanced at Tilda for a moment, then swung his yellow gaze back to Aralorn.

Evidently deciding that Aralorn had already spoiled any chance to maintain his secrecy, he asked, "Why?"

Because I don't want to lose you, she thought. That sounded right to her, so she said, "Because I don't want to lose you, not ever. I love you."

Her declaration seemed to mean something to him

though he'd heard it before. He stood so still that she could barely see him breathe.

"It is too dangerous," he said finally. "Someone will see the records."

His voice was so sterile she could read nothing from it. A good sign, she thought. If he'd known what the marriage would mean, he'd have refused her outright. "Too dangerous" was no refusal, and he knew her too well to think that it was.

"Who would ask a temple of the death goddess for a record of marriage lines?" asked Aralorn reasonably. "And an avatar of a goddess surely won't be caught up in the residue of your father's spells." She turned to Tilda, who was watching them with some fascination. "Would you agree to keep this marriage secret?"

Slowly, she nodded. "Barring that it violates any request of Ridane, yes."

"I know you, Aralorn," Wolf said in a low growl. "You do not fight in the regular forces because you don't like the ties that bind such folk to each other. You work alone, and prefer it. You have many people who like you and some people you like, but no one who is truly a friend. You protect yourself with a shield of friendliness and humor."

"I have friends," she said, taken aback by his assessment; it had come from nowhere—and she thought he was wrong. She wasn't the loner; he was.

"No," Wolf said. "Whom did you tell when you came here?"

"I left a note for the Mouse."

"Work," he said. "You believed your father had died, and you told no one. What did the note to Ren say? That you'd been called home on family business? Did you tell him the Lyon was dead or leave it for his other spies?"

He was right. How odd, she thought, to see yourself through someone else's view and discover a stranger.

"You fight to have no bonds to anyone," he continued, an odd hesitation in his rough voice. "You don't even come to visit your family because you fear the pain of those ties. But you would tie yourself to me anyway. Because you love me."

She felt stripped naked and bewildered. "Yes," she said, when he seemed to be waiting for some response.

"If you wish to marry me," he said, "I am most honored."

Tilda cleared her throat awkwardly. "Uhm. I'm not actually certain that I can marry someone to a wolf."

Aralorn gathered her tattered defenses together and managed a grin. "I agree. Wolf?"

Wolf could no more have resisted putting on a show for the priestess than a child could resist a sweet.

Black mist swirled up to engulf him until he was merely a darker shadow in the blackness. Gradually, the mist rose to the height of a man before falling away to reveal Wolf's human shape, complete with his usual silver mask.

Aralorn turned to Tilda, who had recovered from her initial surprise, and indicated Wolf. "May I introduce you to Cain, son of Geoffrey ae'Magi. But I call him Wolf, for obvious reasons."

"Cain the Black," whispered Tilda, horrified. She drew a sign in the air that glowed silver and green.

Wolf shook his head in disgust. "You can hardly think, whatever tales you have heard, that I would attack a priestess in her own temple. Not the brightest of moves."

"Don't mind him," offered Aralorn. "He always responds to other people's fear this way—not that the fear is always unwarranted, mind you, but, generally speaking, he's harmless enough."

"You want me to wed you to Cain the Black?" asked Tilda, sounding like she'd had one too many shocks.

"Look," said Aralorn, stifling her impatience. "I'm not asking *you* to marry him. Do this for me . . . ask the goddess what She thinks of Wolf . . . Cain. Then decide what you would do."

Tilda spared Wolf another wary glance. "I'll do that. Wait a moment."

She sat on the middle stair and bowed her head—without removing the sign she'd drawn. It hung in the air, powered by human magic rather than anything of the goddess's. Tilda was mageborn. Aralorn wondered if she should add the priestess's name to the list of mages Kisrah had requested.

"You've taken quite a risk," murmured Wolf in a voice that went no farther than Aralorn's ears. "What if the goddess decides I am so tainted by my early deeds that I should die to pay for them?"

Aralorn shook her head, not bothering to lower her voice. "I know my stories. The goddess has always had a weakness for rogues and reprobates—just like me."

"You're right," agreed Tilda quietly, visibly calmer. Her sign faded quickly, without a motion on Tilda's part. "She likes you—very much. If you would like to stand before me, the goddess of death will bind you tighter than the threads of life."

"Take off the mask, please," Aralorn asked him.

He slanted a glance at the priestess and flicked his fingers toward his face. The mask disappeared and left his face bare of scars. Aralorn touched his cheek.

The priestess stood on the middle step, and Wolf took Aralorn's hand formally on his forearm. They faced Tilda together: Aralorn in her riding leathers, doubtless, she thought, smelling of horses; Wolf in his customary sartorial splendor, not a hair out of place.

"Who stands before me?" asked Tilda formally.

"Wolf of Sianim, who once was Cain ae'Magison."

"Aralorn of Sianim, once of Lambshold."

"To what purpose would you come?"

"To wed." They answered together.

"For all things to come, either good or evil? Desiring no other mate?"

"Yes," said Wolf.

"Yes," agreed Aralorn.

Tilda took out a small copper knife and pricked her thumb so that a drop of blood formed. She pressed it to the hollow of Aralorn's throat, then to Wolf's.

"Life to life entwined as the goddess wills, so be it. Kiss now, and by this shall the deed be sealed."

Wolf bent and touched his lips to Aralorn's.

"Done!" The priestess's word rang with a power that had nothing to do with magic.

"It shall be recorded," said Tilda, "that Wolf of Sianim married Aralorn of Sianim on this date before Tilda, priestess of Ridane."

"Thank you." Wolf bowed his head.

From her perch on the stairs, Tilda leaned forward and kissed the top of his head. "We wish you nothing but the best."

Wolf drew back, startled at the gesture. He started to say something, but shook his head instead. Without a word or an excess bit of magic, he shifted to his lupine form.

Aralorn looked at the priestess with full approval. "Now, do you still want me to shift for you?"

Tilda shook her head with a sigh. "It's not necessary. I had no idea that he was anything other than a wolf."

Aralorn laughed. "Neither did my uncle the shapeshifter— and we can usually tell our kind. Hold a moment." She knew her change wasn't as graceful or impressive as Wolf's, but it was swift. She chose the icelynx because she'd been working on it and because someday she might have to spend some time at the temple: She didn't want Tilda to be looking too hard at strange mice.

She arched her back to rid herself of the final tingles of the change. The shadows held fewer secrets in this form, but there were fewer colors as well. Staring at the priestess's face, Aralorn could see a hint of satisfaction in Tilda's eyes.

No, Aralorn thought, *this should be a fair exchange of favors.* She lay down on the floor and began tentatively to hide herself within the icelynx's instincts. She was better with the mouse—and it was less dangerous that way, but she trusted that Wolf would stop her if she lost control of her creation. When she had done what she could to disguise herself, she waited for ten heartbeats, then allowed herself to reemerge.

Hiding so deeply always left her with a headache to remind her why she seldom went to such extremes. She stood up, shook herself briskly, then shifted back to human form.

"Well," asked Aralorn, rubbing her arms briskly, "could you tell I was not the real thing?"

Tilda took a deep breath and loosened her shoulders with a rolling motion. "When you first changed, yes, but for a moment while you lay still, no."

"I think then you should be all right. Most of the shapeshifters don't care to get that deep into their creations," said Aralorn. "There's always the chance that the shaper might get lost in his shape."

"Thank you," said Tilda. "I found that to be most . . . enlightening."

Me, too, thought Aralorn, who had learned that a cleric mage was going to be harder to get her mouse shape past than human mages were—but not impossible.

———

Correy edged his horse even with Sheen, but waited until Aralorn made eye contact before speaking. "We only have two weeks to break this spell."

Aralorn nodded. "I think it's time to really talk with the ae'Magi. I may know some things he doesn't. Perhaps together we might think of something."

"Why did you ask the question about the Dreamer?" queried Gerem, pushing forward until he was on Falhart's off side. "It is just a story."

Though her other brothers rode coursers, bred for speed and ease of gait, Gerem's horse, like Sheen, was bred for war. Younger than Sheen, with a rich sorrel coat, there was something in the horse's carriage that reminded Aralorn strongly of her own stallion. His nostrils were flared, and his crest bowed, though Gerem rode with a light hand— Sheen did the same when she was upset.

There was something about the deliberately casual tone combined with his horse's agitation that planted an odd thought in her head. She sat back, and Sheen halted abruptly, forcing the men to stop also for politeness's sake. Gerem appeared surprised at her reaction to his question, but she didn't allow that to speed her tongue. *Thirteen,* she thought, *Gerem is thirteen.*

"How," she said finally, "have you been sleeping at night lately? Have you been having bad dreams?"

A muscle twitched in his cheek. "And if I have?"

"Are they dreams of our father?" she speculated softly. "Perhaps you dreamed of his death before he actually fell?"

Gerem paled.

"Aralorn," said Falhart sharply, "pick on someone up to your fighting weight. Anyone can have seemings."

"Not seemings," said Aralorn firmly, not removing her eyes from Gerem's face. "They felt like reality, didn't they?"

Without warning, Gerem slipped his feet out of his stirrups and dropped to the ground. He made it into the bushes before they all heard the sounds of his being violently ill.

Guilt caused Aralorn more than a twinge of discomfort as she dismounted as well.

Gerem reappeared looking, if anything, paler than before. "I thought it was a dream," he said hollowly. "It had to have been—I don't know anything about magic or how it works. But I dreamed of lighting a fire and making a great magic. It burned until I thought the flesh was coming off my hands. I thought it was a dream, but when I awoke, the farm had been torched, and there were ashes on my boots. I . . . think"—he stopped and swallowed heavily, then said it all in a rush—"I think I must have put the spell on Father."

"Nonsense," said Falhart bracingly.

"Don't be an idiot," snapped Correy.

"I think you might be right," murmured Aralorn thoughtfully if unkindly. Then she continued quickly. "No, now don't look at me like that. It certainly wasn't his fault if he did. You asked me why I inquired about the Dreamer. This is the kind of thing it was supposed to be able to do. It seduced its victims into doing what it wanted, either by promising them something they wanted or by making them think they were doing something else." She looked at their solemn faces. "It is said that the Tear of Hornsmar had a dream one night. A serpent attacked him in his bed. When he awoke, he turned to tell his mistress, Jandrethan, of his nightmare—which was still vivid in his mind. He found that she had been beheaded by his own sword, which he still clutched in his right hand."

"But the Dreamer is just a story," said Gerem. "Like—like—dragons."

"Ah," said Aralorn, swinging lightly back into the saddle. "But so are shapeshifters, my lad. And I am living proof that sometimes the stories have facts behind them." She crossed her arms over the saddlebow and shook her head at him, but when she spoke, her voice was gentle. "Don't take it to heart so, Gerem. Like enough there was nothing you could have done about it anyway."

Though he remounted, Correy made no move to push on. "We have two weeks before Father dies. Kisrah will try his best . . . but there has to be something we can do. Aralorn, do you know any sorcerers who might be of help?

If it is black magic that holds Father, perhaps a mage who has worked with such things can help."

"You do know that it is a death sentence for any mage who admits to working such magic," commented Aralorn without glancing at Wolf.

"Yes." Correy hesitated. "I spoke with Lord Kisrah before we left this morning. He told me to ask you . . . He said that he thought you might know Geoffrey ae'Magi's son, Cain."

"He thought what?" asked Aralorn, as she damned the Archmage for voicing his suspicions out loud. If it became common knowledge she knew Wolf, they were in deep trouble.

"He thought you might know Cain the Black," repeated Correy obligingly. "It is well-known that Cain worked with the darker aspects of magic, as Lord Kisrah has not. He suggested that we might be well-advised to call upon someone with more experience in these matters."

"Been keeping bad company, little sister?" asked Falhart in deceptively gentle tones.

"Never worse than now," she agreed lightly. Sheen snorted, impatient with the long stop, and she patted him on the neck, giving herself some time to pick her reply. "I have been communicating with someone who knows something about the dark arts. He assures me that he is doing all that he can."

"Who—"

"Well enough," said Correy, over the top of Gerem's impatient question. "That's all that we can ask."

"Is it?" asked Gerem hotly. "I've been having other dreams too, dreams of Geoffrey ae'Magi's son. Isn't it in the least suspicious that the only mage known to work the black magic of old happens to associate with our sister when such magic strikes the Lyon of Lambshold? Doesn't that bother anyone but me?"

Abruptly, Aralorn kneed Sheen, and the warhorse

jumped forward until she could turn him to face Gerem with only inches between them, tapping the stallion's neck when he nipped at the sorrel's rump. "Yes, plague it, it does. And worries me as well, if you want to know the truth of the matter. Only one man knew that . . . Cain and I know each other—and as far as I know, he died before he could tell anyone." *I hope he's dead,* thought Aralorn. *I hope so.* "If he's not dead, then we have a greater evil to face than some storytime creature."

She drew in a deep breath, and the war stallion shifted beneath her—every muscle ready to fight at her command. "Plague it," she said.

She took Sheen a safe distance from the other horses and tried to get a handle on her temper. "I'm sorry for that," she said finally. "I know that we are all under a great deal of strain. It absolutely was not Cain who ensorcelled Father. He does not work with black magic any longer."

"The ae'Magi," said Correy in hushed tones. "That's the evil man you're talking about. He just died a couple of months ago."

"Don't be an ass, Correy," said Falhart with a laugh. "He was the kindest of men . . . warmhearted and generous to a fault."

Correy started to say something further when Aralorn caught his eye and shook her head strongly at him.

"You're right, Falhart," she said quietly. "He was a most unusual man."

"A man of sterling character," said Gerem. *Unlike you,* he meant. "I never met him, but I never heard anyone say a word against him."

"Never," agreed Aralorn solemnly.

"Never," said Correy on an indrawn breath. "Not once. No complaints—everyone loved him."

"Absolutely," said Falhart seriously.

"I wonder," said Correy thoughtfully, to no one in

particular, "where his son picked up all the knowledge of black magic."

Aralorn smiled at him approvingly before sending Sheen down the trail to Lambshold.

———————

She took her time grooming Sheen, as did Correy his own horse. Falhart and Gerem left for their own business, and as soon as they were gone, Correy turned his horse out into its run and leaned against the wall near where Aralorn was running a soft cloth over Sheen's dappled hindquarters.

"Tell me about the last ae'Magi," he said, kneeling to pet Wolf.

Before she answered, she glanced casually around the stables, but there were no grooms around near enough to overhear. "Why do you ask?"

"Because you're right. I've never heard anyone say a word against him. That's just not natural." With a last pat, he stood up. "I met him several times at court, and I liked him very much. I never talked to him—but I had this feeling he was a wonderful person even though I didn't know him at all. It didn't even strike me as odd until I thought about it today. And Hart . . ."

"Yes?" asked Aralorn with a smile.

"He *despises* courtiers of any type—except those of us related to him by blood. He only tolerates Myr because the king is a wonderful swordsman. There is this as well: Falhart makes an exception for you and his wife, but he really doesn't like magic. He prefers things he can face with his broadsword or quarterstaff. That attitude tends to carry over to sorcerers. Oh, he's not as bad as say, Nevyn, about it—but, I've never heard him approve of any of them. Yet he considers the last ae'Magi a paragon among men? Hart has never mentioned anything in particular that Geoffrey did to inspire the kind of enthusiasm he showed today."

"Geoffrey," said Aralorn quietly, "was a Darranian. Did you know that?"

"No," said Correy, with the same disbelief she had felt the first time she'd heard it.

"It twisted him, I think. You've seen what being a Darranian wizard did to Nevyn. Nevyn pretends he is not a mage; Geoffrey had to be the greatest. So he looked farther for his power than a less driven man might have."

Wolf growled at her.

She smiled at him. "All right, so perhaps he was just evil." Turning back to Correy, she said, "It doesn't matter why he was the way he was, only that he was a black mage such as the world has not seen since the Wizard Wars."

"The ae'Magi was a black mage? Why didn't someone notice?" asked Correy.

"Hmm." Aralorn began brushing Sheen again. "One of the first things we all learn about magic is that a mage cannot take over a man's mind, that free will is stronger. That may be true of green magic, like mine, and all other forms of human magic—but it is not true of black magic. I saw the ae'Magi whip the skin off a man's back while the man begged for more. The ae'Magi created a spell that made everyone his adoring slave. It protected him and gave him easy access to his victims. As he amassed more power, he extended the spell. Even now, his magic hasn't faded entirely—as you saw with Falhart."

"Why aren't you or I afflicted?"

She shook her head. "About you, I don't know for certain. Some people seemed a little immune to it, though most of them were mageborn. You have a priestess of Ridane for a lover, and that might help. Or it could simply be the fading of the spell."

"So your shapeshifter blood protected you?"

She nodded. "Yes." She hesitated, but decided the more people with as much information as was safe, the more likely it was that someone would figure out how to save the Lyon. "I suspect it might also have had something to do with my close association with another mage."

"His son."

She shrugged, then nodded.

"You said that you're afraid Geoffrey is not dead?"

"All that was found in the ae'Magi's castle were bits and pieces of Uriah leavings. It was impossible to know for certain that the ae'Magi's remains were there. The bindings between the Archmage and the other sorcerers were broken, and the wizard's council assumed that meant Geoffrey was dead. But who can say for certain?"

"If he was not killed," said Correy slowly, "would he have any reason to look for you?"

Aralorn nodded. "He wanted to conquer death, and he thought he could do it through his son. He knows I am . . . a friend of his son—I, Aralorn of Lambshold, not just of Sianim. He might also have a touch of vengeance in his motivation. We—ah—had something to do with his untimely demise."

Correy gave her a small smile. "If he's not dead, it would be his *almost* demise."

"Point to you," she agreed.

"You think he is responsible for what happened to Father," said Correy slowly. "That he set Father up as bait, knowing you would go to Cain for help."

"I think that if he were alive, that is what he would do, yes."

"Do you think he is alive?"

"No." She sighed, rolling her shoulders to relieve the strain of reaching Sheen's back. Short people should have short horses. "I hope not."

"Kisrah knew," said Correy slowly. "He knows about you. Did the last ae'Magi tell him?"

"I don't know," she said. "Probably. Or he scryed it somehow."

"Was it Kisrah who ensorcelled Father?" he asked.

"I think . . . I think it was Kisrah and Gerem. I think someone used both of them to set a trap that neither was responsible for." That sounded right and fit with Kisrah's actions.

"Someone like Geoffrey ae'Magi."

She nodded. "He's not the only possibility." But he was—unless a legendary, possibly fictitious, creature had begun to stir again. Unfortunately, the ae'Magi's surviving a Uriah attack without use of his magic was more likely than the emergence of a creature who'd been trapped under a sea of glass for ten centuries.

"Have you really asked for Cain's help?" asked Correy. "Knowing it could be a trap set for him?" He hesitated. "Knowing what he is?"

She decided that defending Wolf to her brother could be put off for another time, so she simply said, "He's doing what he can."

She set the cloth down on a rough bench, took up a comb, and began to work on Sheen's tail. The stallion jerked his tail irritably, twitching it halfway out of her hand before resigning himself to his fate with a sigh.

Aralorn had been going back through the information she'd given her brother and regretted some of it.

"Correy, for your own safety, don't talk to anyone about the ae'Magi. His spell is waning, but it is by no means gone—most especially in connection with people he associated closely with, like Lord Kisrah. And I would appreciate it if you would try to keep Hart and Gerem from bandying Cain's name about, for my safety. There are any number of mages who would like to have something to use against him, someone he cares about—like me."

"You care about him, too," said Correy.

"Yes," she agreed without looking at Wolf. "I do."

"I will try to keep the others quiet," Correy promised. He patted her on the shoulder and walked down the wide aisle between stalls. As he left, the wind, which had been still all day, flitted through the open stable doors in a ragged gust.

Death is coming . . . Death and madness dreaming . . .

"Aralorn," said Wolf sharply, coming to his feet.

She shivered, and, knowing he couldn't hear the screaming shrieks, gave him a half smile. "I'm all right. It's just the wind. Wolf, do you still think that talking to Kisrah is a good idea?"

"I don't know that we have any other option," he replied. "If he can tell me what spell was used to bind your father, I may be able to unweave it. It's obvious Gerem, if he's had any training at all, barely knows how to call a light spell; he couldn't tell me what he did even if you could persuade him to talk to me. Kisrah will know what his part in the spell was. Otherwise, two weeks doesn't give me a lot of time to prowl through old books for an answer. Whether Kisrah knew it before your father was ensorcelled or not, he obviously knows that I am involved with you. Talking with him won't make matters any worse."

"You don't think that he's the impetus behind this?"

"He could be," he said. "But he has information we need—and now that I'm rested, I can handle Kisrah if he tries anything."

"Then I'll go look for him as soon as I finish with Sheen," she said, and went back to work.

Grooming was soothing and required just enough thought that she could distract herself from the worry that the Lyon would gradually fade into death no matter what they could do, and that the possibility the ae'Magi (and no other man held that title in her heart of hearts for all that it now belonged to Kisrah) was still alive lingered. Most of all, she could allow the work to keep her from the confession she was beginning to dread more than all the other evils the future could hold: How was she going to tell Wolf that she'd married him to keep him alive? It had seemed a good idea at the time. However, she'd had a chance to think it over. Would he see it as another betrayal?

Sheen stamped and snorted, and Aralorn coaxed her hands to soften the strokes of the comb.

"Shh," she said. "Be easy."

NINE

⟨∞∞∞⟩

It wasn't as hard to find Kisrah as she had thought it might be. He was seated on a bench in the main hall, talking to Irrenna.

"Truthfully, I don't know what can be done, Irrenna. I have to find the wizard who initiated the spell—and it's no one I've ever dealt with before." He yawned.

"We kept you up half the night with our problems," said Irrenna apologetically.

He took her hand and kissed it. "Not at all, Lady. I have been having troubled dreams lately. Perhaps I'll go up and rest."

His words stopped Aralorn where she was, and an icy chill crept over her.

Aralorn had been sleeping just fine. Her own dreams had stopped when Wolf had come back to guard her sleep.

She'd been assuming that the dreaming had stopped because the one giving all of them dreams had either given up on her, changed his mind, or been kept out by some stray effect of Wolf's power. What if it was something simpler than that? What if the dream sender was detectable in some way? Maybe he had stopped because he was worried Wolf would notice what he was doing.

Perhaps, she thought, perhaps it might be better to watch what happened when Kisrah was asleep before she spoke to him. She turned on her heels and left before anyone saw her.

"Why aren't we chasing down Kisrah?" asked Wolf mildly.

She glanced around hurriedly, though she knew Wolf wouldn't have said anything if anyone could have overheard.

"Tomorrow," she said. "We'll talk tomorrow. I want to go spend some time with Father."

———

Aralorn crouched on the rosewood wardrobe behind a green vase in the room Kisrah had been given. She'd spent most of the day avoiding the Archmage. She didn't want to talk to him until after she'd done a little bit of spying.

When she told Wolf what she planned, he'd paid her the compliment of not arguing: Or at least he restrained himself to a few pithy comments about certain people's rashness leading them into hot water. She'd left him to stew in her room, wolves being somewhat more unexpected guests than mice were. And, although he'd tried other shapes, the only one he could hold on to reliably was the wolf. If she didn't see anything in Kisrah's room, then she and Wolf could hide Wolf from her brother Gerem while he slept. Not even Wolf could conceal himself from the Archmage with magic.

She still hadn't told him what she'd done by marrying him. She didn't fear his anger—but she found that the thought of hurting him was painful. She'd have to do it soon, though. The whole thing would be worse than useless if he managed to get himself killed before she told him that his death would mean hers, too: There was one more reason than the obvious one that people didn't lightly ask Ridane's priests to officiate in weddings.

Her hiding place wasn't ideal. It gave her a clear view of the bed while leaving her well concealed behind the vase, but there was nothing else to hide behind. If Kisrah saw her, she would be forced to run in the open.

The distance wouldn't have been a problem if he hadn't been a mage. Wizards had rather abrupt methods of dealing with mice, methods that could leave her no time to run.

It was as Aralorn's vivid imagination came up with unusual and painful ways in which a wizard could dispose of a mouse that Kisrah came into the room. And, of course, if she managed to get herself killed—Wolf would die, too. The irony of that situation didn't escape her. She sat very still in the shadow of the vase, not even allowing her itchy whiskers to twitch.

Kisrah seemed to be taking longer to get to bed than he needed to: tidying up the already painfully neat room, refolding an extra quilt at the end of his bed, and messing around in the wardrobe. As if, thought Aralorn hopefully as she cowered behind her vase, he was dreading facing his dreams.

Without his public mask, he looked even more tired than he had earlier. In the harsh illumination of the light spell he'd summoned rather than lighting the candles, he looked ten years older than he was.

"Gods, what a mess," he said tiredly. As he was staring at the perfectly tidy bed when he spoke, Aralorn assumed he wasn't talking about the room.

He stared at the bed a moment longer, then ran a hand through his artfully styled hair. With a sigh, he stripped out of his flamboyant clothes, leaving on only a pair of purple cotton half trousers.

Clothing in hand, he approached Aralorn's chosen hiding

place. The wardrobe swayed slightly as he opened the doors and hung his garments, and Aralorn wished that it were summer so there would at least have been some flowers in the vase to offer more cover. A taller wardrobe would have been nice, one that didn't leave the top level with Kisrah's gaze. She didn't so much as twitch a whisker until he turned away.

A fire had been lit shortly after Aralorn had arrived in the room, and some of the winter dampness that plagued old stone buildings had left the air. Kisrah pulled a chair near the fireplace in front of the merry flames.

She gave a relieved sigh and tried not to stare at him; some people, most of the mageborn, could feel it when they were the center of attention. He gazed deeply into the rose-and-orange light of the burning pine and never turned his head toward the vase with the mouse settled behind it.

In spite of her precarious position, the warmth of the fire had Aralorn half-asleep herself before Kisrah finally pulled back the bedclothes, climbed between the muslin sheets, and put out his magelight. She shook herself gingerly, careful that her claws made no sound on the polished wood.

The lack of Kisrah's magelight was no handicap to her rodent eyes—the dying embers of the fire provided more than enough light to see with. The rhythms of Kisrah's breathing slipped slowly into sleep. Aralorn waited intently.

She couldn't have pinpointed exactly what first alerted her to the second presence in the room. It could have been a slight sound or the fur on her back ruffling as if a chill wind had blown into the room, though the air remained still and comfortable.

She took her eyes from the bed in time to see a pale mist settle before the fire. Slowly, it condensed into a familiar form. The voice was so soft she wouldn't have heard it if she hadn't been so close . . . perhaps she wouldn't have heard it

if she hadn't met the howlaa. It felt like that, sounds heard
without her ears.

*You were not to come here, Kisrah. Someone will con-
nect you with the deed, then where will you be?* Aralorn
trembled with utter terror as she watched Wolf's presum-
ably dead father. His lips did not move, though she heard
his voice clearly.

*What have you done, my old friend? You said the spell
was for Cain, to hold him without harm.* It was Kisrah
who spoke. She dared a glance at the bed, but Kisrah lay
unmoving; to all appearances he was sleeping deeply.

*And who would have used it on him? I was the most
powerful mage in the world, and he destroyed me. Which of
my friends should I have sent against him? You would have
done it had I asked—but you would not have succeeded.*
Geoffrey's voice was soft. *Should I have let him kill you,
too? I did what I had to. This way, no one is harmed.*

There was a short pause, then Kisrah said, *Why black
magic? And why bring others into it, to blacken their souls
as well?*

*If it were not black, any mage could unwork the spell.
As for the others—*Geoffrey's voice softened with understanding—*did you not try and unwork the spell? If it had
been only one, anyone could have freed the Lyon. The time
is not yet met for him to awaken. Have patience, all will
be well.*

Aralorn tried to make herself even smaller without
moving so much as a hair. She very much would rather that
neither of the participants in this bizarre conversation realized that there was a mouse listening to every word.

*The Lyon will die if something is not done soon. She has
no intention of bringing Cain into this, or she would have
done it long since. No good can come of this, Geoffrey.
Evil begets only evil. The magic that I, and whatever other
poor benighted fools you chose to aid you wrought here, is
evil. I should not have done it.*

Geoffrey's voice was harsh. *You think my son is so stupid that you could snare him any other way? I searched for him fruitlessly for years without catching him—because I could not find the right bait. Now I have it. Don't fret yourself, he's here with her. Cain's mother was a shapeshifter. She gave him the ability to use green magic, something I failed to recognize until it was too late because of his talent with human magic. The mixture proved volatile—too volatile for his sanity. At least I hope he is insane . . . that is easier to accept than flesh of my flesh being so given to evil.*

Geoffrey paused as if putting aside an old grief. Aralorn's face twisted into a snarl, an expression that sat oddly on the mouse's face as she traded terror for rage at last. She put aside all thoughts of an ancient evil, satisfied that her enemy was Geoffrey ae'Magi. She and Wolf must have failed. *This is Geoffrey ae'Magi. He twists and manipulates with a skill I might envy if he did not use it as he does.*

Kisrah did not respond, and at last the phantom continued. *Don't be so impatient. I told you he would come. He might even be here already. I've seen him take the shape of animals before. Have you looked closely at Aralorn's wolf?*

With those words, Geoffrey's form dissolved. As it left the room, Lord Kisrah drew in a deep breath that was more of a gasp and sat up, clutching his head and grimacing in pain. He got up slowly, like an old man, and stirred the coals in the fire before setting a log in the grate. It was a very long time before he went back to sleep, and Aralorn didn't move until he did.

A very cautious mouse crept out of the room at last, shivering and wary.

———

Wolf, in human form and wearing his mask, opened the door and let Aralorn into her room before she had a chance to knock. Startled, she looked quickly around to make certain there was no one to see him before stepping through the door and pushing it closed behind her.

"What's wrong?" he asked after a brief look at her face. "What frightened you?"

She stepped closer to him and pressed against his warm chest. She felt him stiffen momentarily, as he still did at unexpected touches, then he relaxed and pulled her more tightly to him. She took a deep breath, feeling her panic abate.

She stepped back to see his face.

"Thanks, I needed that." She hesitated. "I saw . . . Wolf, it was your father. I was watching Kisrah sleep when your father materialized in the room."

He didn't appear surprised, just tugged her closer again and bent to rest his head on top of hers as she told him the whole of what she had seen.

"He has to be dead," she whispered. "He has to be, but I swear to you this was him."

"Are you certain it was he?"

An illusion? Aralorn examined her memory. Illusionists could not create an actual double any more than a shape-shifter could take on the appearance of a specific person. There were too many fine details to be missed—a mole behind the earlobe, the slant of a smile, the swing of a walk.

"Not unless it was created by an illusion master who knew your father very well," she said finally. "Every nuance of speech or expression was Geoffrey's." She frowned. "Though he didn't really speak. I would say that it was mindspeaking, but I've never been able to send or receive by mind. I understood everything he said—*they* said— quite clearly."

"Dreamspeaking is different," replied Wolf. "If Kisrah was asleep, probably it was a dreamspeaker—which was one of my father's odder talents."

"Dreamspeaking as in dreamwalking?" asked Aralorn.

"It can be part of the same gift. Did my father have a scent?"

"What do you mean?" she asked, shocked at the inane . . . Wait, not such an inane question after all. "Allyn's toadflax, I never thought of that. I don't remember . . ." A mouse's sense of smell was not as good as a wolf's, but it was better than a human's.

"Father had a scent that he always wore: cloves and—"

"—cinnamon," she broke in. "I remember. I would have noticed that. I don't think he had any scent at all."

"Dreamwalker then," said Wolf. She couldn't tell what he thought about it. "Though it's a rare talent, my father was not the only dreamspeaker among the wizards. Whatever you saw was not a real person but a similitude. Any dreamwalker who knew my father well could produce it."

"So it isn't your father," she said with a rush of relief.

"I didn't say that." Wolf sighed and tightened his hold. "Dreamwalking is one of the two or three things that wizards are supposed to be able to do for a while after they die."

"There are a lot of dead wizards around?" Aralorn asked.

Wolf shrugged. "I've never seen any. There are stories, but no one really believes them." He hesitated. "It's just that if any wizard would come back from the dead, it would be my father."

"So this is either your father or another wizard who knows a lot about your father."

"If Kisrah were a little better at self-deception," said Wolf, loosening his hold, "it could even have been him. I never heard that dreamwalking was one of his abilities, but most of the great mages have several."

"Kisrah thought your father was a good man," she returned.

"My father's magic was powerful enough to reach Sianim," he said. "Certainly he'd have put stronger spells on any wizard close enough to smell black magic. On his own,

Kisrah is pretty observant: He'd know if he was causing my father's appearances in his dreams."

"I was hoping for the Dreamer." Aralorn stepped away and began undressing.

"You just think the Dreamer would make a better story," he said.

She frowned at him. "What's the use of going to all this work if you can't brag about it when you're through? If it is your father, we have to be quiet about it." She took a step nearer to him, then said suspiciously, "If I didn't know you better, I would say that you're cheerful. You are never cheerful around the subject of your father."

"My father isn't a cheery topic," he said. "But whether we are dealing with him, some other wizard, or a creature out of one of your stories is something that can wait. I think I have a solution to our more immediate problem. I've been doing some thinking while you were gone, and I've remembered a few things. If we can get Kisrah and Gerem's cooperation, I think I can break the spell on your father."

She stilled. "Are you sure?"

"My dear Lady, nothing's certain in this life, but it should work."

"What about the possibility of Geoffrey's attacking you?"

"*If* Kisrah and Gerem are willing to cooperate, it shouldn't be a problem."

He sounded very certain, but so had Geoffrey.

"Kisrah's not very happy with what's been done to my father, or his own part in it," she said. "But convincing him that Geoffrey is . . . was . . . is—*Plague it!*—that Geoffrey *was-and-is* not a good man won't be easy."

"Hmm," Wolf said. "I think I might have an idea or two on that score."

He was, she noticed, dividing their problem into two: save her father and deal with his. That he believed her father's ensorcellment was solvable was beyond good. She could feel herself relax into belief in his ability. That he was ignoring his father was less good. She worried that it was less confidence in his own skills than it was indifference to danger to his life. It was time to let him know what she had done.

"Wolf," she said, "I—"

"I know," he said with a wicked smile glinting in his eyes. "We've done enough work for now." The smile left his eyes, and his hands traced her face.

"I've never had a family before," he said in wonder. "Not really. It feels so strange to belong to you and have you belong to me."

She looked up at him and opened her lips, but she couldn't do it. Couldn't tell him that she'd married him to force him to take care of himself, not when it obviously meant so much more to him than that. Come to think of it, it meant a lot more than that to her as well. It was just that . . . Wolf had belonged to her for a long time in a way that tied them far more than any goddess could.

She reached up and tugged at his mask, and he let it fall into her hands.

"Don't hide from me," she said.

Dropping the cold silver false face on the floor, she pulled his head down so she could kiss him fully.

————

Wolf held her while she slept, and smiled. His wife was a manipulative minx; but then, he'd known that for a long time. The difference between her and his father was that she manipulated people for their own good—or at least what she perceived to be the greater good. He wondered when she'd break down and tell him.

How could she think that he wouldn't know what she'd done? As soon as the priestess placed the blood-bond between them, he'd realized what it was, had known what

Aralorn had tried to do. He was not a well-trained mage in most areas, but black magic he knew well. A blood-bond was well within his area of expertise.

He sent a caress through the tie the death goddess had placed between them, and Aralorn sighed, shifting against him.

He could sever it when he needed to. He'd tell her that after she managed to confess her deed—he couldn't resist the urge to tease her a little and teach her a lesson about trying to manipulate him as she did the rest of the world.

"If you had known how to find me, you would have come to me when you were told your father had died," he said softly, and, remembering her face when he'd shown up at Lambshold, he knew it was true. How odd that someone loved *him*. That *Aralorn* loved him.

He pulled her closer and relished the light feeling that had come over him, softening the edge of the inner core of rage that was always with him. He was happy, he thought with some surprise.

If she thought so much of him, it might be worth the risk of the potential for disaster that clung to him through his magic. Maybe—he kissed the top of her head—maybe they could discover a way to control his magic rather than destroy it with his death.

———

Aralorn awoke early and began planning what was best to do. She didn't know if Kisrah would take his nighttime visitor's information at face value or if he could tell that Wolf was Cain by some arcane human magic. Wolf said that he needed Kisrah's help. There was a chance that Kisrah would attack Wolf the first time he saw him. She couldn't risk it. She needed to talk to the Archmage first.

She liked Kisrah, but if he reacted badly, she would kill him before he got a chance at Wolf—if she could. She certainly would hate to do something like that in front of witnesses. So she needed a meeting without Wolf and outside of Lambshold.

Aralorn sat up and waited for Wolf to awaken. She wiggled a little. Nothing. She stared at him. Nothing. She reached her hands toward his side.

He rolled over and caught them. "If you tickle me this early in the morning, I'll see to it that you regret it."

She laughed. "How long have you been awake?"

"Long enough," he growled, completing his roll.

———————

Sometime later, he said, "Now, what was so important that you woke your husband up before the birds?"

He liked that word, she'd noticed, liked being her husband and the formalization of their bonds to each other. Given how hard he'd tried to keep a distance from her from the beginning of their association, she found it unexpectedly touching.

"Wasn't this enough?" she asked, trying for a sultry tone. It wasn't a role that she'd ever tried as a spy.

He bit one of her fingers gently. "Yes. So let us go back to sleep."

She bit him back, harder.

"Ouch," he said obligingly, but without any real emphasis, so she didn't feel that she had to apologize.

"That's what you get for trying to be funny. We need to go talk to Kisrah."

Wolf grunted, then said, "So, what have you plotted for the poor man?"

Aralorn decided to overlook his attitude. "We'll need to be careful—don't you snort at me; I can be cautious when I have to be. I think I will take him on a ride along the trail to Ridane's temple. Whoever visited him last night told him that you were Cain. I think that until I get a chance to talk to Kisrah, you need to stay out of sight."

"Ah," he said. "You meant *I* need to be cautious."

She grinned. "You're the one under the death sentence. Is Kisrah still under the influence of Geoffrey's charisma spell?"

"Probably," he replied. "If I were my father, I certainly would take no chances as far as Kisrah or any other high-ranking mage was concerned."

"Can you break it?"

She felt him shrug. "I don't know, but that was my thought as well. *If* my father is truly dead and can work no more magic, and if he chose to ensure that Kisrah never be a problem as I believe he would have—I might be able to."

"It would be easier to get his cooperation if he didn't attack me every time I said something nasty about his predecessor—and I don't know how else to proceed."

"I'll do what I can," he promised.

———

Aralorn finally found Kisrah in the bier room with her father. He'd arisen earlier than she'd expected, and she'd missed him at breakfast. A few questions to scattered servants had sent her to her father's bier.

He looked up at the sound the curtain made as she entered and watched her with a hooded glance from his seat on one of the tables meant for gifts and flowers. He looked a bit like a gaudy bouquet in a combination of mauve and emerald that offended even Aralorn's indifferent sense of style, but the bright array made the little room less somber.

"Lady Aralorn," he said, acknowledging her entrance after he'd returned her stare for several seconds.

She bent and kissed her father's slack face, taking a moment to reassure herself that he still lived, before turning back to the Archmage. "I visited the death goddess's temple yesterday," she said without preamble.

"I know," said Kisrah. "Correy told me."

She toyed with the front of the Lyon's shirt, straightening it carefully where it had been pulled askew. Finished, she turned to the Archmage. "I owe you my apologies, sir. I have been rude. I know that you have come to help my father, and I'm sorry to be so secretive. My only excuse is that the last few days have been nerve-racking at best, and I've been a spy for long enough that questions make me nervous."

"You sought me out to apologize?" asked the Archmage with a touch of wariness.

Although she noted that he hadn't accepted her apology, Aralorn smiled and shook her head. "Not primarily, though it needed to be done. There are things that we should speak of, but outside of the keep walls. Would you ride with me?"

Kisrah gazed at the stone floor. "Where is your wolf? I was under the impression that he went everywhere with you."

She pursed her lips thoughtfully and added a little bait. "That's one of the things I need to speak with you about."

The Archmage leaned back against the wall. When he spoke, it seemed off the topic of discussion. "I fought a campaign against the Darranians with your father once, did you know?"

"Yes," she answered.

"Battles are odd things," he said in musing tones. "Sometimes it seems as if you do nothing but hack and slash; at other times it seems as if you do nothing at all for weeks at a time. During the former, you learn a lot about your comrades by their actions; during the latter, you learn about them from their speech."

His gaze rested on the Lyon's quiet figure. "Your father is ferocious, tireless, and absolutely honorable. But more than that, he is cunning, always thinking—especially in the thick of battle, when everyone else is lost in bloodlust. He taught me a lot about how to judge men, to choose leaders and followers. He knew every man in our group and used them according to their strengths, and he tried to know as much about the men we fought as he did our own." He reached out and touched the Lyon's still face. "I

learned to love him as much as I ever did my own father—
as I expect every man to fight under him felt."

While he spoke, Aralorn half sat, half leaned against
the bier. When he paused to make sure she was listening,
she nodded.

"While we waited for battle, we talked, your father and I.
He told me something of you. He told me you'd fought
with him against brigands here at Lambshold and said he'd
rather have had you beside him than any three men. He'd
have brought you to fight by his side as he did Falhart if
it hadn't been for his lady wife. He said you were clever,
devious, and deadly—said you could outthink and outride
any man he had with him, including himself."

"You have a reason for all this praise, I trust," said Aralorn.

Kisrah nodded, and a sudden grin lit his face. "Absolutely. First, let me say that I do not accept your apology,
as I'm certain that you intended every frustrating minute
of our last meeting—and enjoyed it as well. Devious and
manipulative, your father said."

He sobered, and Aralorn thought it might be sadness
that crossed his face. "But—despite what I have been told,
having the father you do, you could not be without honor
and decency. I hope that a productive talk might shed some
light on a few things. I think that I, too, have some things to
tell you that it were better to talk of outside these walls." He
paused, and continued softly. "You might bring your wolf."

Aralorn nodded. "I'm sure Wolf will join us at some
point in our journey. Father's got enough animals around
here that you shouldn't have a problem finding a mount:
I assume by the speed of your arrival that you chose to
translocate yourself—"

She didn't know why she'd brought that up until she
realized she was watching his face for guilt. There was
none, of course; he hadn't realized what Geoffrey had done
to her after Kisrah had used his magic to transport her into
the ae'Magi's care.

Instead, Kisrah nodded, with a faint grimace of distaste. "Not my favorite spell, but it was important that I get here as soon as possible.

"You're a braver man than I am," murmured Aralorn. "I'll meet you in the stables. Ask Falhart if you need help finding warm clothing."

———————

Aralorn had intended to take him only a short distance before stopping to talk, but she hadn't counted on the wind. It kicked up when they were just out of sight of the keep.

The voices screamed through her ears: screams that brought visions of Geoffrey's dungeons and dying children, the cries of the Uriah—shambling, rotting things that had once been human but now only hungered. Sheen picked up on her agitation and began snorting and dancing in the snow, mouthing his bit uncertainly as he waited for an ambush to leap from the nearest bush.

Hoping that the wind would settle down, she kept going. At this rate, they'd be at the temple before she could talk. She tried to ignore the wind for as long as she could, but at last she tucked the reins under her knees and tugged a woolen scarf from around her neck and wrapped it tightly around her ears.

"Are you all right?" asked Kisrah.

"I seem to have developed a bit of a problem with the wind," she said truthfully: She tried to limit her lies when she could, especially when she was talking to wizards.

"Earache?" said Kisrah with some sympathy.

"I'm looking for someplace less windy," she told him. "I hadn't planned on riding all the way to the goddess's temple for a little private conversation."

He smiled. "I could do with a little exercise anyway. But if you can find a sheltered place I might be able to do something about the wind."

She frowned at him. "You human mages," she said.

"Always so ready to impose your will where it doesn't belong. There's a small valley not too far from here; we'll be free from the wind without any magic at all."

He looked startled for a moment. "I've never been referred to in quite those terms. Do you not think of yourself as human, then?"

She smiled tightly, her tension owing more to the wind than any irritation with him. "No. But I won't use the terms my shapeshifter cousins use for mageborn who use unformed magic. They aren't flattering. Human will have to do."

As she'd thought it might, the steep sides of the valley—well, gully, really—provided some relief from the wind. Aralorn stopped Sheen and cautiously removed the scarf from her ears. The roar had died to a dull whisper she could safely ignore.

"Why don't you start, as you still owe me for your rudeness yesterday?" said Kisrah after he'd stopped and turned his horse so he faced her directly.

"All right," agreed Aralorn readily. "How much do you know about charismatic spells?"

"What?" he asked in some surprise, but he answered her question without waiting for her to repeat herself. "I've never heard of one that was not black magic."

"Yes," said Wolf from behind them, "they are. Of the blackest kind."

Aralorn turned to frown at Wolf. He was supposed to wait until she'd made certain that Kisrah wouldn't attack him on sight. She supposed that it said something about Kisrah's state of mind that he did not.

Wolf was in human form, clothed as always in black—an affectation Aralorn was determined to change. It wasn't that he didn't look good in it, just that it was a bit morbid at times. The silver mask was nowhere evident, and the magic-scarred face looked worse than usual in the bright winter sunlight.

"Cain," said Kisrah softly, as if he hadn't really believed what the specter had told him.

Wolf bowed shallowly without letting his eyes drop from the Archmage's. "Lord Kisrah."

"You are here to tell me the importance of . . . these charismatic spells, I assume?"

Wolf shook his head. "I wouldn't have mentioned them myself, but as Aralorn has seen fit to do so, I will explain—better yet, I'll cast one." He made an economical motion with his hand.

Aralorn sucked in a breath at his recklessness. She would have thought the battle with his father would have cured him of seeking battle with another powerful mage. Couldn't he have just told Kisrah how the spell worked?

Kisrah looked white and strained, but he gestured with equal rapidity—a counterspell, thought Aralorn—or rather a breaking spell of some sort, because it wasn't possible to directly counter an unknown spell.

"Here," said Wolf softly. "I'll give you more magic to work with."

Aralorn didn't see anything happen, but a moment later Kisrah swore and pulled a thick gold-and-ruby ring off his finger, tossing it into the snow. It must have been quite warm, as it fell quickly through to the ground, then melted a fair-sized hole around it that exposed the yellowed grass beneath.

For Aralorn's benefit, Wolf said, "He just broke the charisma spells—both of them."

Aralorn looked at the ring, seeing the magic imbued in it. "Both of them?"

"Mine and my father's."

Kisrah nodded, looking stunned as he stared at the ring. "Geoffrey gave me that ring. I can't believe I didn't see that it was runescribed. Why would he do that?"

"My father," observed Wolf, his hoarse voice sounding

even dryer than usual, "was very good at making people overlook things when he chose."

"The ring was runescribed?" asked Aralorn. She put her hands on her hips and glared at Wolf. "So mages do use rings and amulets for spells."

"*Not* for warding spells," said Wolf repressively. "The runes are too complex to fit on an amulet—at least a warding that would keep out much more than errant mice."

"Ensorcelled," said the Archmage, ignoring their by-play. "A charm spell, indeed, but to what purpose?"

"What indeed?" said Wolf.

"The ae'Magi spread his charisma spell over a fair bit of territory before he met his untimely end," said Aralorn. "Why do you think everyone loved him so? Even people who'd barely heard of him."

Kisrah stared at her.

"Who would ever think that the reason there were so few children in the villages around the ae'Magi's castle was because the ae'Magi was killing them for the power he could get from untrained mages?" she said.

"He . . ." Kisrah's voice trailed off, then became firmer. "He wouldn't do that. He couldn't. A rune set in a ring—maybe. But I felt the power you had to use, Cain. No one could keep a spell like that running for long over more than a few people."

"No one worries about charisma spells," agreed Wolf. "They require too much power to be of use, and the control of the ae'Magi bars black magic anyway. Unless, of course, you are the ae'Magi and are perfectly willing to turn elsewhere for your power. There are a lot of spells that require too much power without death magic, sex magic, or, at the very least, blood, aren't there? Some spells that haven't been worked since the Wizard Wars."

Kisrah flinched.

"He gave you such a spell to work, didn't he?" asked

Aralorn softly. "He gave you the proof, himself, that he knew . . . that he knows black magic."

She wasn't going to tell Kisrah that they weren't sure that it was Geoffrey who had been visiting his dreams.

The Archmage looked up sharply.

"I've had a few dreams, too," she said. "Dreams of blood and magic."

"Yes." His voice crackled like the ice under the horses' hooves. "I set up part of the spell that holds the Lyon, plague take you both. I had to use black magic to do it."

"Why?" asked Wolf.

"Shortly after Geoffrey disappeared, before anyone knew what might have happened to him, I awoke one night, and there he was, standing beside my bed. I was overjoyed at first, thinking that he was found—but then he told me he was one of the dreamwalking dead. He told me that you and your"—he glanced at Aralorn and changed the word he was going to use—"that you and Aralorn had killed him."

"Did he tell you how it was done?" asked Aralorn. Had Kisrah been given true dreams or false?

"He said that you used one of the Smith's weapons to destroy his magic and left him in the castle, which was full of Uriah, without defense." Kisrah paused. "He asked me why I hadn't helped him." The wizard took in a deep breath, but his voice was unsteady when he continued. "I was there that night. I woke alone in the bedchamber with the body of the woman"—he glanced at Aralorn, his eyes hot with remembered fury—"the woman you killed with Cain's staff. It was nigh on a quarter of an hour later when I felt Geoffrey's grip on the Master Spells break. I could have saved him had I acted sooner."

The Archmage's voice was taut with sorrow and rage. He was lost in his habitual opinion of Geoffrey ae'Magi, forgetting for the moment that he'd had any doubts about Geoffrey's virtue.

"Better that you didn't," said Aralorn, hoping to jolt him out of the remnant of the spell's effect before he goaded himself into attacking them. It didn't work.

Kisrah's eyes flashed with anger. "He was my friend, and you killed him." He turned abruptly toward Wolf, his horse snorting at the sudden jerk on its bit. "I know you, Cain, I know what you have done. I've seen the color of the magic you wield, and it stinks of evil. Should I take your word about his character?"

"Yet you worked black magic for Geoffrey ac'Magi yourself, didn't you?" said Aralorn coldly, provoked by Kisrah's verbal strike at Wolf. "Just as Cain did. Was it a goat you killed or a hen? Do you think that you are the purer for not having touched human blood? You know, of course, that Cain has done that, and you suspect he's done more. You suspect that he's killed, raped, tortured, and maimed. But don't feel too superior—if we can't break this spell within the next two weeks, my father will die. He will die because of your decision to play with black magic, because Geoffrey's ghost taught you how to use death to gain power, more power than you might have had without resorting to black magic. When you wanted revenge, it was easy to overcome the scruples of a lifetime, wasn't it? And you are a grown man who was taught right from wrong by people who loved you; not—"

"Enough, Aralorn," Wolf broke in gently.

She bit back the words that might have wounded Wolf more than they hurt Kisrah. "Sorry," she said.

"No," said Kisrah, mistakenly believing her apology was to him. "You're right. About what I have done, and why." He looked at Wolf. "That doesn't mean that what *you* have done is right, only that I am guilty of similar actions."

Wolf shrugged when it became apparent that Kisrah was not going to speak further. "I have used no black magic since I left him; if you look, you will not find its touch on me. What I have done, I am responsible for—but for no more than that. As for accepting our word on the ae'Magi's intentions, don't be a fool." Wolf bent down and picked up the ruby ring. "My father gave this to you. You know the spell it contained as well as I do—you broke it yourself. Why would my father need such a thing unless he was as we say?"

"I would be a fool," said Kisrah softly, ignoring the ring Wolf held for him, "if, having found my judgment questionable once, I leap without thought a second time. Give me time to think over what we have talked about. I knew Geoffrey for most of my life. He was more than just a mentor to me." He flexed his hands on the reins. "The girl Aralorn killed the night you destroyed Geoffrey—her name was Amethyst, and she was not yet twenty years old."

"Do you remember"—Wolf's rasp was so low that Aralorn could barely hear it over the wind—"that thing you came upon in the dungeons?"

Kisrah shivered, but Aralorn thought it might have been from the cold; they had been standing for a while.

"Yes," said the Archmage. "I couldn't sleep. It was dark, and I heard someone moving around in the cells, so I called a magelight and looked inside."

He swallowed heavily at the memory of what he'd seen. "The next thing I remember is you standing in front of me and my face hurt where you slapped me. 'Screams only agitate it,' you said. 'It can't get out.'"

Kisrah's lips twitched in something that might have been a faint smile. "Then you said, 'It doesn't like to eat sorcerers anyway—especially those without half the sense of a cooped chicken.'"

Wolf said, "Two days before, that thing had been my father's whore. I believe she was fifteen. A peasant, of course, and so of little account except for her beauty. Father liked beautiful things. He also liked to experiment. He showed you some of them. I believe you referred to them as my father's 'unfortunate hobbies.'"

A myriad of expressions flittered across Kisrah's face. Anger, disbelief . . . then dawning horror.

"The night I met you in the ae'Magi's castle," said Aralorn quietly, "after you were unconscious, the girl you'd slept with sprouted fangs and claws. I suppose I could have just left rather than killing her: She was far more interested in eating you than me."

Kisrah didn't say anything.

Aralorn spread her hands to show they were empty, the universal sign of truce. "If you want to ride by yourself a bit—the horse knows the way back to the keep. We can leave you."

Kisrah hesitated, then nodded. "If you would, please. That might be best."

"Well?" asked Aralorn.

Wolf, who'd shifted in front of Kisrah into his four-footed form for travel, shook his head. "I don't know. It depends upon which he loves best, my father or the truth."

He put on a brief burst of speed that precluded talk. Like Kisrah, she thought, he wanted a moment to himself.

The wind had picked up again as they'd ridden back onto less sheltered ground. It was not enough to send her shrieking for cover, but it was a near thing. It spoke to her in a hundred whispers that touched her ears with bits and scraps of information directly out of her imagination.

"Wolf?" she asked, when the sound grew too much.

"Ump?"

"Wizards have their specialties, right? Like the farseer who works for Ren."

"Ump."

A conversation takes two people, one of whom says something other than "Ump." She thought about letting him be. His past was a sensitive topic, and she and Kisrah, between them, had all but beaten him over the head with it. The wind carried the sobs of a young child, bringing with the sound a hopeless loneliness that chilled her to the bone in an echo of her dreams of Wolf's childhood. She tried again. She remembered a story about the gaze of the howlaa driving a man mad; too bad she hadn't recalled that before she looked into its eyes.

"What is Kisrah's specialty?"

"By the time a mage becomes a master, he has more than one area of expertise."

"You knew him before that," she persisted. "What was his field?"

"Moving things."

"Like translocation?" asked Aralorn.

"Yes." Wolf sighed heavily and slowed. "But he worked more with objects and delicate things—like picking locks or unbuckling saddle girths."

"No wonder Father likes him," she observed, relieved that he'd decided to talk. "Saddle girths and horseshoes have lost as many battles as courage and skill have won. What was Nevyn's specialty?"

"Nevyn?" said Wolf. "I don't know that I remember. By the time he got to Kisrah, he was in pretty rough shape— and the two of them didn't really spend a lot of time with my father, in any case. He is fortunate he went to Kisrah; if he'd come to my father, he'd have been a babbling idiot for the rest of his life—I thought at the time that it looked like it might go either way." His voice reflected the indifference he'd felt at the time, showing Aralorn how badly he'd closed down because she'd reminded him of what he'd once been.

"I hadn't realized it had been so bad for him." Aralorn pulled her scarf from the pocket she'd stashed it in and wrapped it around her ears. This conversation hadn't helped either of them as much as she'd hoped it would. It hadn't distracted her from the voices, nor had it restored

Wolf's mood. "I guess he was lucky to come out of all that with only a few quirks about shapeshifters."

The wind swayed the larger branches now and sent odd bits of snow to swirl in place.

"Come on," said Wolf. "See if that old fleatrap can move out a little; no sense wasting what's left of the day playing in the snow."

TEN

Aralorn was slipping choice bits of mutton to Wolf when Falhart came up behind her.

"If Irrenna catches you feeding that wolf at the table, she's likely to banish him outside," he said.

She shook her head, holding down another piece. "As long as we're discreet, she'll leave him in peace. She doesn't want a hungry wolf roaming the castle. He'll just go into the kitchens to be fed—and there she'll be, without a spit boy. It might take the cook several days to replace whomever he ate, not to mention the fuss."

Falhart gave Wolf a wary glance, then began to laugh. "Scourge on you, Aralorn, if you didn't have me believing it. Which brings me to my mission. I have a half dozen youngsters and a few not so young who've been approaching me all dinner to see if you would give us another story."

"An audience," said Aralorn, scraping the last of her dinner onto a small bit of bread and popping it into her mouth. "See, Wolf, *some* people appreciate me."

He didn't seem to hear her, lost in thought as he'd been since they'd gotten back. If she could take back what she'd said to Kisrah, she would have—not that Kisrah didn't need to hear it. She would have bitten her tongue off, leaving Kisrah believing his version of Geoffrey ae'Magi the rest of his life, rather than hurt Wolf.

Despite his apparent disinterest, Wolf trailed her as she left to greet her audience and made himself comfortable at her feet.

Kisrah was not there, though she knew he'd returned from their ride. She didn't see Gerem, either, but Freya and Nevyn were seated on a bench against the wall, just close enough to hear.

She chose her story primarily for Wolf, something light and happy that should appeal to the rest of her audience as well. As laughter warmed the room better than any winter fire, Wolf rested his head on her lap with a sigh.

When Aralorn awoke the following morning, she found a red-tailed hawk perched on the back of a chair near the fireplace, preening its feathers. Wolf was gone.

"For a man who was worried about showing himself among humans, you certainly are volunteering your time generously," she said severely.

The hawk fluttered his feathers noisily into place. "He said you'd probably be grumpy when you woke up. I can't say I approve of your choice of mates, niece."

"Your own choice being superior," she said.

The hawk bobbed its head and squawked with laughter, and the chair rocked dangerously beneath him. "True, true," Halven chortled as he settled back down.

"Wolf told you we were married?" asked Aralorn.

"Yes, child," said the hawk. "And he asked me to tell you to amuse yourself. He's off to find the ae'Magi."

"Did he say which one?" Aralorn stretched. It had taken Wolf a long time to get to sleep last night even though she'd done her best to tire him.

"Which one?" Her uncle cocked his head at her. "There is only one ae'Magi."

Aralorn pursed her lips. "We're not certain that's true." She told Halven the things that Wolf had told her about his father and the dreams that she, Gerem, and Kisrah had experienced. After a brief hesitation, she told him of Wolf's relationship to Geoffrey ae'Magi and exactly how the last ae'Magi had died. She didn't easily give up information—except when that information might be vital. She had a feeling that they might need help before this was over, and her uncle would be a lot of help if he so chose.

Halven made an odd little sound that Aralorn couldn't decipher, but the incredulity in his voice when he spoke was clear enough. "So you think that a *human* mage who is dead is walking in the dreams of a shapeshifter and the newest human Archmage, and they are not able to stop it? The dead have very little power over the living unless the living grant that power to them. I can think of a half dozen more likely things—including the return of the Dreamer."

"I was able to take control of my dreams," said Aralorn. "And Kisrah loved Geoffrey and welcomed him. I don't think Gerem has any defenses against magical attacks." Someone—Nevyn—should have seen to it that Gerem had started training a long time ago.

She looked away from the hawk as she worked out some things she'd never put together before. "The dreams I was given were true dreams, Uncle. At first, whoever sent them to me had tried to alter them, but I was able to see through to the true memories. The dreams concerned things that only the ae'Magi and Wolf knew about."

"How do you know Wolf didn't send the dreams?"

"It was *not* Wolf," she said.

"Where was he when your father was enspelled?" Her

uncle's voice was somber. "If his father was a dreamwalker, can you say for certain he is not? He wouldn't necessarily even know he was doing it. You've seen how his magic escapes him."

Aralorn snorted. "If you knew Wolf, you would understand just how stupid it is to accuse him."

She tried to think how to put into words something that was so clear to her that it was almost instinctive. "First, he would never involve other wizards in his spellcasting. He doesn't trust anyone except maybe me that much. He would never—*not ever*—voluntarily share as much of his past as I saw in that dream. I knew him for years before he would admit to being anything but a wolf."

"I think that it is a better possibility than a dead wizard," said Halven. "Humans just don't interact with the natural world well enough to do anything after they are dead."

Aralorn digested that comment for a minute. "You mean shapeshifters do?"

The hawk gave its version of a laugh. "Not to worry. Most people who die don't linger to torment the living."

"The only other explanation that we've come up with is that the Dreamer has awakened," she told him.

Halven made a derisive sound.

"Do you have another explanation?" she asked.

"What about another dreamwalking wizard? A living dreamwalker might be able to do what you have described," he said.

"I'm told it's a rare talent," said Aralorn.

"Not rarer than a dead human mage who is making everyone tap to his tune," said Halven. "Have you figured out why someone decided to attack the Lyon?"

She shrugged. "As we discussed earlier, it is probably to get me here. There are any number of people after Wolf, and some of them know that where I go, Wolf is not far behind."

"To get Wolf here and do what?" asked Halven. "What do they want?"

She frowned at him. "To kill him."

"You don't know that," Halven said. "Maybe they only need you."

She laughed ruefully. "I don't die easily. And other than as bait for Wolf, I can't think of a reason any wizard would want me."

"If they kill you, they kill him," he reminded her.

"Only since day before yesterday," she said. "And how did you know about that?"

"After I objected to finding my niece in a man's bed, Wolf told me Ridane's priestess married you."

"You couldn't care less if I was sleeping with the sheep," she said tartly.

"He didn't know that. You didn't invite me to the wedding."

"I didn't know for certain that I was going to go through with it until we were there. I had to do something," she told him, trying to stem the defensive tone that wanted to ease into her words. She'd known that she was making him more vulnerable—she was certainly more easily killed than he. But her reasoning still stood. "You said he had a death wish, and I believe you."

"So you tricked him into the death goddess's binding?" asked her uncle. There was, she thought, a certain admiration in his tone. "That's the reason for your sudden marriage. He'll take more care of himself now."

"Uhm," she said. "I haven't told him about the side effect of being married by Ridane."

"He doesn't know?"

"He wasn't raised next to Ridane's temple," she answered. "She's not worshipped many places anymore. The gods have been quiet for a long time."

Two beady eyes stared at her unblinkingly. "What good is marrying him going to do if he doesn't know that his death will kill you also? You've undercut the very reason for the marriage."

She started to defend herself, but a slow smile caught her unexpectedly. "Not really."

The marriage itself, she thought, had accomplished what she had sought to enforce with the bond the priestess had set between them. From the awed tone in Wolf's voice when she'd asked him if he'd marry her to last night when, after they'd retired to this room, he'd brought his pain to her and allowed her to help him forget. She was still a little stiff from the methods they'd employed.

Her uncle waited for a moment, and when she didn't continue, he said, "Just make sure you don't die before you tell him."

She grinned. "I'll try to keep that from happening." She threw back the bedcovers, restless with prebattle nerves. She knew how to deal with those. "Rather than wait around for Wolf, I'm going to visit Falhart and persuade him to fight with me. You're welcome to come if you'd like."

———

She found Falhart, finally, in the accounting room, slaving over the books. As she walked into the little room, she heard him swear, and he began to scratch out what he'd written.

"Why don't you find someone who likes those things?" asked Aralorn with a certain amount of fellow feeling. Give her a scroll of stories or a five-volume history, and she'd devour them, but account books were a whole different kettle of fish. Somewhere in the volumes stacked neatly against the walls was a large number of accounting sheets in her own poorly scribed hand.

Falhart looked up and scraped the hair from his eyes. "No one, but no one, likes to keep the accounts. Father, Correy, and I switch off, and this is my month." He eyed the hawk on her shoulder, nodded at it, then focused on the pair of staves she carried in one hand.

She grinned. "Want to play, big brother? Bet you a copper I can take you two times out of three."

"Make it a silver, and I'll do it," he said, pushing back his chair. "But I get to use my staff."

She shook her head at him. "Your staff is fine, but someone has given you an inflated idea of what they pay us mercenaries, Hart. I'll go three coppers and not a bit more."

"Three coppers isn't enough to make it worth my time," he said.

"I guess you'll just have to stay here and do the books then," replied Aralorn with a commiserating pat on his arm. "Come on, Halven, let's see who else we can find."

"All right, all right, three coppers it is," grumbled Falhart, then he brightened. "Maybe I can find someone else to lay a bet with."

Aralorn examined his bearlike form and shook her head as she started for the training grounds. "And who are you going to find who will bet on a woman against a brute like you?"

"You did," he pointed out.

"Yes, but I've fought you before."

They faced off in the old practice ground. It was cold, and the sand was packed hard, though the snow had been swept away. Once they started fighting, the cold wouldn't matter. Aralorn wielded one of her staves while Falhart held a quarterstaff half again as large and twice as thick as hers. Halven had opted for a better perch on the corner of the stable roof.

"You're sure you don't want to use a quarterstaff as well?" Falhart asked, watching her warily.

"Only a brute like you gains an advantage wielding a tree," she replied. "It's all right, though; you'll need all the advantages you can find, big brother."

Falhart laughed and tossed his staff lightly in the air. "You may have learned something in the past ten years,

Featherweight. But so have I. What are the rules for this bout?"

"Three points," said Aralorn. "Any hit between the shoulders and waist is good. Arms, head, and below the waist doesn't count."

"Right," said Falhart, and he struck.

His swing had more speed than a man of his size had any right to have. Aralorn stepped respectfully out of its path and tapped him gently on the temple.

"Zap," she murmured as she darted away, "you're dead."

"No point," grunted Falhart, sweeping at her knees.

Rather than avoiding the sweep, Aralorn stepped lightly on the center of the quarterstaff between his hands and vaulted over his back. She touched her staff to his back twice in rapid succession before he had time to turn, and quickly bounced away.

"Two points," called one of the onlookers in a gleeful voice.

She didn't get away free though; as she jumped back, one end of his staff caught her in the diaphragm.

"Oof." Though the blow was light, Aralorn expelled a breath of air unexpectedly.

Falhart backed away quickly, clearly worried. "Are you all right?"

She shot him a mock-disgusted look. "I said 'oaf,' you ox. You're going to lose this round if you treat me like your little sister."

"Just like to make certain my prey is feeling all right before I destroy it." Falhart gave her a gentle smile as he circled her warily. "It's more sporting that way. My point."

Aralorn shook her head. "Poor babbling fool, I think I must have hit his head harder than I meant to."

The two combatants exchanged merry grins before they went at it again. Falhart gained another point with a feint that he pulled back after she thought he was committed to the blow past the point he could alter it. In revenge she stuck her staff between his legs and toppled him to the ground.

"'Ware, down it comes," she deadpanned in the carrying cry of an axeman felling a tree.

He caught her in the ribs as he came rolling to his feet. "Too busy being funny, Featherweight. Lost you the game."

She shook her head in mock despair. "Beaten by a man . . . I'll never live it down."

Falhart patted her gently. "Poor little girl—oof."

Aralorn removed her elbow from his midsection. "Don't patronize me after you've beaten me. Losing puts me in a foul temper."

"I'll remember that," said Lord Kisrah cordially, stepping onto the training grounds, Wolf at his heels. "Lady, if you would walk with me a bit? In private?"

She'd barely had a chance to warm up and had been planning on a few more rounds with Falhart before she was done. But she preferred the real battle to sparring bouts.

"Certainly, Lord Kisrah. I will leave the scene of my defeat, and my opponent can go back to accounts."

The triumphant look faded from Falhart's face. "Thanks for the reminder—but remember, you owe me three coppers." He waited until she started fumbling with her purse, then he said, "Double or nothing this time tomorrow?"

He was planning something; she could hear it in his voice. "Five coppers altogether. No more," she said.

"You've got it, Featherweight." He gave in much too easily. He was planning some mischief or other.

She frowned at him, and he grinned unrepentantly. "I'd better get back to the accounts," he said, and took his leave.

Kisrah extended his arm, and Aralorn set her staves against the stable wall before shaking her head at him. "You don't want to touch me right now," she said, pulling on her overtunic, sweater, and cape. "Save good manners for when I'm not sweaty."

He gave a half bow, sending the long ribbons in his hair

a-fluttering as he let his arm fall gracefully to his side. "As you wish, Lady Aralorn."

"We could go to the gardens," she suggested, trailing her fingers over Wolf's ears.

Kisrah and Wolf fell in step on either side of her as she led the way to Irrenna's pride and joy.

In the summer, the gardens were beautiful, but the winter left nothing more than frost-covered barren branches and gray stalks pressing up through the snow. The walks were swept, though, so they didn't have to wade through the drifts.

"I know it's chilly," apologized Aralorn, "but no one much comes here in the winter."

He raised an eyebrow. "So why didn't we come here yesterday instead of riding out in the cold?"

"Because now you know who Wolf is," she said. "I was worried how you would react. A body is much easier to hide outside the keep walls."

He stopped walking. "I'd laugh if I didn't think you were serious."

"Maybe a bit," she said. "Come, let's move while we talk; it'll keep us warm." She was aware without actually looking at him that her uncle had followed them and was making lazy circles around them.

"Did you see Falhart's face?" asked Wolf. "He thinks you threw the fight."

"What do you think?" she asked blandly.

"I think you got cocky and lost."

"You know me so well," she admitted.

Kisrah gave Wolf a baffled frown. "Are you sure you're Cain?"

Wolf tilted his head considering, then said, "I am."

They walked for a while between sleeping flower beds. Aralorn turned her sweaty face into the cold air and paced beside the Archmage and felt grateful that there was no wind this morning.

"I have thought upon yesterday's conversation," Kisrah said finally. "In the end, there is only one answer. Black magic is evil. Good never breeds from evil—and I can see no good in this in any case. But I cannot remove the spell. If you are able to do so, I'll help in any way I can. I know that Nevyn is one of the mages who added to the spell, but there is another."

"We know the other," said Aralorn. "My brother Gerem."

"Gerem?"

"Sometimes magic ability doesn't show until adolescence," commented Wolf, answering Kisrah's surprise.

"But Nevyn would have seen it," said Kisrah. "He would have told me."

Aralorn pursed her lips, and said, "Nevyn is very fond of my brother. Do you think that he would encourage anyone he cared for to go through the same abuse he suffered?"

"That's a very serious charge," observed Kisrah softly. "Untrained wizards are a danger to themselves and everyone around them."

"So are trained wizards," said Aralorn. Before the wizards she strolled with could comment, she continued blandly. "My brother cast a spell in his sleep. He didn't have a chance to resist. My understanding, from the stories I've heard, is that a formal apprenticing would have protected him from such use."

"Yes," agreed Kisrah. "There are not many mages who can control the minds of others in such a fashion, anyway—even with black magic at their call. But given that the consequences of such control are dire, precautions are always taken. Apprentices are safeguarded."

"You'll have problems with my brother," predicted Aralorn. "Nevyn is convinced that magic, any magic, is evil. I think he's managed to persuade my brother. Most especially, shapeshifters are abominations."

"Magic isn't evil," said Kisrah.

"All Darranians believe magic is evil," said Aralorn.

"Geoffrey ae'Magi believed that and embraced it. Nevyn believes it, and he's trying his best to protect my brother. We need Gerem's cooperation to save my father. We need you to get Nevyn to ask him to help."

"I can get Nevyn to help," agreed Kisrah, a bit more optimistically than Aralorn felt was warranted, but maybe he knew Nevyn better than she. "Shall we meet tonight in the bier room?"

Wolf shook his head. "This kind of black magic doesn't require the night. You all will be more comfortable in the daylight."

"Black magic?" questioned Kisrah sharply. "It shouldn't be necessary to unwork the spell with black magic."

"This spell was set with blood and death by three wizards. It will require sacrifice to unwork," Wolf said.

"I thought that black magic couldn't be worked in the day," said Aralorn.

"It can be worked anytime," answered Kisrah.

"Sometimes it works better at night," corrected Wolf. In the shadows of the hedge, his pale golden eyes glittered with light reflected from the snow on the ground. The harsh macabre voice somehow made the barren garden something strange and frightening. "Terror can add power to a spell, and fear is easier to inspire in the night."

Aralorn noticed that Kisrah's even pace had faltered. Wolf only did things like this when he was in a particularly dark mood. She hoped that it was nothing more than talking about black magic that had brought it on and not something about unworking the spell to free the Lyon.

She hid her worry, and said dryly, "You sound like a ghoul, Wolf." Her words cut through the mood Wolf had established, and the garden was merely a collection of plants awaiting spring again. "Is there something you haven't told me about yourself?"

He flattened his ears in mock irritation, and said direly, "Much. But if the thought of my late sire's ghost has failed to touch your undeveloped sense of prudence, nothing I have done will accomplish that either."

Aralorn watched Kisrah's expression out of the corner of her eye and was satisfied when humor replaced the unease that had been in his face earlier. The gods knew that Wolf was not a soothing man to associate with, but there was no need to worry Kisrah at this point.

"Tomorrow morning, then?" said Kisrah. "At first dawn?"

Aralorn nodded. "Tomorrow."

"Kisrah," said Wolf. "What did you kill to work your spell?"

"A Uriah," he said uncomfortably. "I had intended to use my own blood—it should have been enough. I was working the spell in the basement workroom when a passageway door opened, and the Uriah came stumbling in. It must have escaped the Sianim mercenaries who took care of cleaning up the Uriah Geoffrey left scattered about. I killed it, and the spell slipped my control and used the creature's death instead of my blood."

"Ah," said Wolf. "Thank you."

Kisrah nodded and turned on his heel with every sign of a man escaping.

"Uriah," said the hawk after Kisrah was gone, settling on the top of a trellis that bore the thorny gray vines of a climbing rose. "Human sacrifice. Aralorn, I begin to believe what you told me this morning. Maybe I have been underestimating human mages." He stared coldly down at Wolf.

"How did you know what the Uriah are?" asked Aralorn.

"Human mages are very good at warping things unnaturally," said Halven. "Any shapeshifter looking at a Uriah can see the true nature that human magic has perverted. Only a human mage could be so blind as to not understand his own work. Why didn't you tell him that he'd made your task more difficult?"

"I would rather the secret of their making die with my

father," Wolf said. "I do not expect that Kisrah would be anything but repelled—but he might tell others or write it down for someone to discover."

"Ah," said Halven. "Sometimes it is a good thing that human mages are so blind, and some knowledge is best lost. But Kisrah's ignorance has caused you trouble." Halven sighed. "I had better help you control your magic, Nephew. So much of your magics require balance—of which Kisrah has some, you have little, Gerem has none, and Nevyn has less than that."

"He's in worse shape than I am?" asked Wolf, sounding surprised, but Aralorn thought it was more because Halven named him nephew than her uncle's assessment of Nevyn.

Halven laughed. "Nevyn has been broken and badly mended. Your spirit is strong as an oak, wolf-wizard. It may be a bit battered, but as long as you don't misdirect it, you'll be fine." He cocked his head at Aralorn. "There is something different since your marriage. You may be right."

"She's right about what?" asked Wolf.

"You keep out of this, Uncle," snapped Aralorn. "Wolf, can we talk of this later?"

She could have sworn that there was laughter in Wolf's eyes, but it was gone almost before she saw it. She couldn't think of anything they'd said that he would find funny.

"If you'd like," Wolf said.

"I can't do anything about the nature of the sacrifice," said Halven. "I can't do anything about Nevyn. But I think I can help you with your magic problem. Aralorn, haven't you taught him to center?"

"*I* can't center," she said, exasperated. "Just how do you expect me to teach someone else? Besides, centering is more of an exercise in . . ." Her voice trailed off as she realized what she was going to say.

"Control." Her uncle's voice was smug. "We need someplace warm and private."

"We can work in my room," suggested Aralorn. "That would allow us some privacy and warmth as well."

"I'll meet you there," said the hawk, taking flight.

"Wolf," said Aralorn, once they were alone.

"Yes?"

"You haven't worked black magic since you left your father's home, have you?"

"No."

Aralorn tilted her face into the sun, though she felt no warmth on her skin. "I don't know a lot about human magic, but I do know that good seldom comes from evil. I don't want you to hurt yourself to save my father."

"Aralorn," said Wolf, "you worry too much. I have worked such magic before."

"And chose not to do it again, until now." She turned a rock over with the toe of her boot and kicked it into the snow.

"This is not your doing, Lady. It is my father's work."

"Would you work black magic if it were not my father?" she asked.

"Would he be ensorcelled if he weren't your father?" he returned. "We'd best not keep your uncle waiting. I'll be all right, Aralorn."

Wolf is the only expert I have, thought Aralorn. *If he says there will be no harm in it for him . . .* He'd never tell her if there was.

Frowning unhappily, she started back for the castle, with Wolf padding by her side.

———

Aralorn lay on the bare floor of her room and reconsidered calling her room warm—without the rugs to cover it, the floor was icy. Halven was taking Wolf through some basic meditation exercises, things she'd learned the first summer she'd spent with him.

In honor of the lesson, her uncle had taken on the shape of a venerable old man, with a rounded face and belly—someone to inspire confidence, she supposed.

Wolf, to Aralorn's surprise, had left the mask off. Halven had already seen the scars, of course—but Wolf used the mask as much for a shield as he did to cover his scars.

"Now, stop that," her uncle admonished Wolf, in tones Aralorn would bet tomorrow's winnings against Falhart that no one had used on Wolf in a very long time, if ever. "I don't want you to do anything to the wood—just feel it. See the growth patterns, the years where water was hard to come by and the years where it was abundant. Feel the difference between the old oak of the original floor and the plank of maple that someone used to replace an old board—yes, that's the one. Let yourself feel how much easier magic slides through the oak than it does through the maple. Aralorn, an exercise does no good unless you do it."

"Yes, sir." She grinned, obediently losing herself in the pitted surface of the wooden floorboards.

There was almost a sensuous pleasure in working with the wood. Oak had a sparkle to it that always made her feel as if she ought to glow with joy while she worked with it. Not that she could do much more with it than look. A few shapes, some basic spells, and a little inventive lock picking—that was about as far as her command of magic went. That didn't mean that she couldn't enjoy it for its own sake.

"Now that you know the wood beneath you, children, I want you to concentrate on yourselves. Feel the texture of the floor against your skin, the fabric that separates you from the support of the wood. Ideally, of course, there would be no fabric, but I understand that you humans are sensitive about exposing your bodies. As I discovered in training Aralorn, the distraction of the clothing is less by far than the distraction of not wearing any at all."

"Not to mention it's warmer this way," murmured Aralorn, her eyes still closed.

"Enough, child. I am the teacher here. You will merely listen and absorb my wisdom."

"Of course. I shiver at your feet in humble awe at the—"

"Kessenih"—he interrupted—"would be happy to take over the training of you; I believe that she offered to do it the last summer you came to us."

Kessenih, as Aralorn recalled, had wanted to peel the skin from her feet and make her walk back to Lambshold— who'd have thought she'd have gotten so upset over a chicken egg in her shoe?

"Yes, sir. Sorry, sir."

Halven had changed, she thought. He'd always been cold to her, though he'd sponsored her training. After a moment she decided it could be that she, herself, had changed. As a child, she'd always been too much in awe of Halven to tease him. She'd never been able to relax around him, but now . . . everything crystallized, like a wooden puzzle that suddenly slid into shape.

It felt odd seeing herself in the way she had always been able to look into wood, to feel her heart beat and *know* why it did. Like an outsider, she could see into the fears and petty angers, touch the bond that tied her to her mate.

"I've *got* it . . ." It startled her so much that she sat up and lost it again, but she laughed anyway.

"So you did," said Halven, sounding pleasantly surprised. "See if you can explain it to Wolf. Sometimes two talk better than one."

"What did you find?" asked Wolf.

"My center," she said, sounding as shocked, as elated as she felt. "I've always been able to sense it well enough that I can use magic, but it was never clear. Like being in a boat and knowing that there's water under me, but not being in the lake myself."

"So this time you fell in?" Wolf sounded amused.

Aralorn grinned at him. "And the water was superb, thank you."

"You," said Halven to Wolf, "have no sense of center at all, that I can see. Without centering, it is impossible to be grounded—to be aware of yourself and your surroundings at a level where it is safe to work green magic. If we can get you there, then having your magic run amok should no longer be a problem."

He ran a hand down his beard. "For human magic, this is not necessary—you control the magic with your thinking self. Like working a logic problem, with just a touch of artistry to give it form. Green magic is just the opposite. Your . . . emotions, your *needs*, generate the magic with just a touch of conscious control. Aralorn has been working half-blind for most of her life, and *you* are wiggling puppet strings without knowing which string is connected to which puppet." He looked pleased with his analogy, savoring it for a moment before turning back to Aralorn. "You found it once—do it again."

It took her a while before she could do it reliably, but once she had it, Halven went back to work on Wolf.

———

If it had been difficult for Aralorn to relax into her center, it was nightmarish for Wolf. Control had been his bulwark for most of his life, a defense against the things he had done and what was done to him. Unless he could give it up, he would never be able to control his magic: a paradox he understood in his head, but not in his heart, where it mattered.

It made for a long afternoon. By the end of it, he was sweating, Halven was sweating, and Aralorn was exhausted, but Wolf came out of it with a better sense of self, if not precisely his center. An achievement that left Halven nodding grudgingly.

"At least," he said, helping Wolf to his feet, "you know

that there are strings on your fingers now. If you don't know what they do, you can elect not to tug on them." He sounded almost as tired as he looked.

"Thank you," said Wolf.

Halven smiled slyly. "Couldn't do less for my sister's daughter's mate, now could I?" He slid from old man to bird shape. "I expect you to keep her in line."

"How?" asked Wolf, amused.

Halven let out a bark of laughter. "Don't know. I've never seen it done. Open the shutters now, and I leave you children to your rest."

———

"Well," Aralorn said after Halven had left, "I don't know about you, but I'm hungry."

Wolf gave her what might have been a wolfish smile without his scars, looking more relaxed than she'd ever seen him. "I could eat a sheep."

"You think so?" she said thoughtfully, pulling on her boots. "I'm not so sure; the local shepherds are awfully quick with their arrows."

He laughed, changing gracefully into wolf shape.

———

Most of the family was already eating when they made it to the great hall. Aralorn slipped into her old place between Falhart and Correy. Nevyn, sitting directly across from her, pointedly didn't look up when she sat down. Freya shrugged apologetically once and otherwise ignored her husband's distress.

". . . when I came out of the village smithy, there was my meek and ladylike wife screaming at the top of her lungs." Falhart stopped to eat a bite of food, giving Aralorn a quick view of his wife on his other side with her head bowed and a flush creeping up her cheekbones.

"I thought something was wrong and was charging

to the rescue when I realized what she was saying." He cleared his throat and raised his bass rumble to a squeaky soprano. "Three geese, I tell you! I need three. I don't want four or two—I need three. I don't care if they are mated pairs. I am going to eat them, not breed them!" Falhart laughed.

Aralorn was too tired to join in the usual family chatter and picked at her food. The familiar scents and voices, some deeper now than they had been, were soothing.

She let her eyes trail across her siblings with the magic she'd been working all day. She'd occasionally been able to use her magic to look deeply into a person, but never for more than a moment or two.

It was an odd experience, her senses interpreting what her magic told her sometimes as color—Falhart radiated a rich brown that warmed those around him. Irrenna was musical chimes, clear and beautiful. Even though he sat at the far end of the table, Aralorn could feel Gerem's magic flickering eagerly, vibrating on her skin like the wings of a moth. One of the little children, a toddler, had it, too. She'd have to remember to tell her father . . . She turned abruptly and caught Nevyn staring at her.

Wide-eyed, she saw what Halven had meant when he'd said that Nevyn was broken and poorly mended. She had no experience to interpret what she saw, but it was like looking at a tree split by lightning. As the thought occurred to her, that's what she saw, as if an illusionist had superimposed the image over Nevyn's human form. One side of the tree struggled to recover, but the branches were gnarled, and the leaves were edged with an unhealthy gray. The other side was black and burnt.

Nevyn pulled his eyes away, but that didn't release Aralorn from the vision. Sharp teeth closed on her hand, and she dropped her eyes to see Wolf beneath the table, glowing like lightning. Dazed, she blinked her eyes rapidly, only to see the bright wolf imposed on her eyelids.

Wolf growled, and Aralorn took in a deep breath and set her magic aside.

"You are quiet tonight," said Correy in her ear. "Have you found out anything more about Father?"

His tone was conversational, so he hadn't noticed her doing anything unusual.

"Enough to be hopeful," she said, striving for a normal tone.

"Do you know who might have done it?" asked Freya.

Warily, Aralorn looked at her, but she saw only the face that Freya had always shown her.

Aralorn shrugged and, because she was thinking about what had just happened rather than paying attention to the conversation, she said more than she should have. "I think so, but he is dead now—so knowing who he is doesn't do us much good."

"Who?" asked Irrenna from the head of the table, her voice sharp.

Aralorn put down her knife and fork. "No one it would be healthy to accuse at this point. When I'm more certain of my facts, I'll tell you. I promise."

Irrenna looked at her narrowly for a moment, then nodded. "I'll hold you to your promise."

ELEVEN

~~~~~~⧖⧖⧖~~~~~~

The castle was quiet in the early-morning hour they'd chosen for their meeting. She and Wolf got to the bier room before dawn, more because she was too nervous to sleep longer than anything else. The guards had gotten used to her coming and going at odd hours, though this morning's portal defender had given an odd look to the hen she'd stolen from the kitchen coop.

Wolf told her that he might need it if he decided to break the spell right then. Wolf hadn't had to catch the blasted thing, of course.

She paced restlessly in the little room, taking a twisted path around the bier and the woven chicken basket, stopping now and again to touch her father.

Wolf lay with his nose tucked between his forepaws, watching her pace. "They'll be here soon enough. Stop that."

"Sorry"—she sat on her heels next to him and leaned against the wall—"I'm just anxious."

"More anxious than the hen," he commented shortly, "and with less reason, too."

As if to emphasize his point, the hen clucked contentedly in its nest of hay. Aralorn stuck a sore finger in her mouth—the chicken had been upset when she grabbed it. "Nasty critter, anyhow."

"Who's a nasty critter?" asked Gerem suspiciously, pulling the curtain aside so he could enter.

"The hen," said Aralorn, pointing at the villain with her chin.

Gerem peered at the battered crate. "What'd you bring a hen here for? Mother's going to pitch a fit!"

"To free your Father," replied Wolf.

Gerem came as close to jumping out of his skin as anyone Aralorn had ever seen. Three shades whiter than he'd been when he came in, he stared at Wolf.

"I see Kisrah informed him completely," murmured Wolf sarcastically, wagging his tail gently as he returned the stare. "How much do you want to bet we get to inform him what method we're using as well."

"We needed him here," warned Aralorn. "I don't think that we can complain how it was done." She stood up and turned to her brother. "Gerem, I'd like to introduce you to my—to my Wolf. At one point in time, he went by the name of Cain—son of Geoffrey ae'Magi. I'd suggest you be polite to him; at present, he appears to be the best chance we have of resurrecting Father."

"The old ae'Magi's son is a shapechanger?"

Aralorn blinked at him. One of the things her brother didn't know, apparently, was Cain ae'Magison's reputation. She supposed that made a certain amount of sense. Gerem had been a young boy when Cain dropped out of public view.

"Sometimes," agreed Aralorn. "I find it a good thing that he takes after his mother's side of the family."

"Dead?" asked Wolf. "Of course, Father's dead as well."

She rolled her eyes at him. "Do you *have* to go out of your way to intimidate everyone? Wouldn't it be nice if we could all work together this morning?"

"Ah," said Kisrah, entering the room rather languidly.

He had to duck around the curtain to make certain it didn't bend the pale pink feather that was set jauntily into his elaborate hairstyle. Wearing a three-foot-long feather was not something *Aralorn* would have done in his place; but then, she wouldn't have worn pink with scarlet and emerald either. The brass bells on the heels of his shoes were nice, though—if impractical.

"I thought I would be the first one here. I see you brought the chicken. Marvelous. I thought I might have to do it."

"We ought to make you do it," said Wolf thoughtfully, "if only to see what the chickens would do when they heard those bells."

"Unkind," admonished Kisrah. "To intimate that I would risk scuffing these boots chasing chickens—what do you think I studied magic for, dear man?"

"They are joking," said Aralorn, watching Gerem's face. There were some benefits to Kisrah's three-foot-long feather—it was hard to be frightened in the presence of such a creation.

Unexpectedly, Gerem grinned. "I'd place bets on Lord Kisrah. Nevyn told me about the time you chased a pick-pocket into the heart of the infamous slums of Hathendoe and came back unscathed. A chicken should be child's play."

"Stole my best gloves," agreed Kisrah solemnly. "Purple with green spots, just the color and shape of spring peas."

Gerem laughed but stopped when he saw Kisrah's mournful face.

"Don't worry about hurting his feelings," rumbled Wolf. "He knows what the rest of the world thinks about his clothes."

Reassurance was not exactly Wolf's strong point, so Aralorn was pleasantly surprised that he'd gone out of his way to smooth the waters.

The Archmage grinned, looking Gerem's age despite

his wrinkles. "Faugh, Cain, you ruined it. He would have begged my pardon in another moment."

"I like the bells," commented Aralorn, leaning a shoulder against the wall. "Perhaps I'll get myself a pair."

Kisrah looked superior. "Spies don't wear bells."

She snorted. "Fat lot you know about spies. I was in your household for three months, and you never even knew my name."

He frowned, staring at her intently. "The maidservant . . . Lura—"

"Not even close." She shook her head mournfully.

"She's a shapeshifter," said Gerem. "She wouldn't look like herself."

"Even if you did manage to guess what part she played, she'd never admit it," added Wolf, coming to his feet.

He took on human form, leaving off the mask and the scars—for Gerem's sake, Aralorn thought. She glanced at her brother, who was looking nervous again. Yes, she was definitely going to have to do something about the black clothing. It was hard to look intimidating in . . . say, yellow. She grinned at the thought of Wolf dressed in yellow, with a bow to hold his hair back in its queue.

Kisrah drew in his breath at seeing Geoffrey's face on Wolf.

"You need to wear a different color," she said out loud, to distract both Wolf and Kisrah from something neither cared to think about. "Black is so . . . so—"

"Conservative," chided Kisrah, recovering from his initial shock.

Gerem looked from Kisrah in pink, red, and green to Aralorn in her muddy-colored tunic and trousers, then advised dryly, "Keep the black."

Wolf, bless his soul, smiled—a small smile that bore little resemblance to the charm of his father's. "I intend to."

The curtain rattled again, and Nevyn shut it carefully behind him. He surveyed the room, his eyes stopping on Wolf.

"Cain," he said, in a tone that was more of an acknowledgment than a greeting.

At his entrance, Wolf had gone still, almost, thought Aralorn, apprehensive.

"Nevyn."

"It's been a long time. I—I—I had forgotten how much you look like him." The stutter irritated Nevyn, and he stiffened further.

Rather than make things worse, as was his general reaction to people who feared him, Wolf merely nodded. "Shall we begin?"

"Yes," agreed Kisrah. "We're all here now." He looked around, and for lack of a better place, he pulled himself up on the bier to sit beside the Lyon. "What do you need from us?"

"I need to know what you have wrought," said Wolf. "So I can unmake it."

"Then I'll tell my part first." The ae'Magi wiggled his feet, and the bells chimed softly in response.

"Tell us all of it," suggested Aralorn. "Not just the spell—not everyone here knows what has been going on. I suspect that Gerem, for one, has no idea what happened to him, and we still only have guesses about who is responsible for this mess."

"The whole story?" asked Kisrah. "There are parts that should remain secret."

"Everyone here knows how my father died, or should," said Wolf. "We might as well tell our version, too—after you are through with your story, Kisrah."

"Very well, then," agreed the ae'Magi. "I'm no storyteller, but I'll tell you as much as I remember. Shortly after Geoffrey—the ae'Magi—died . . . I had a dream."

Aralorn saw Gerem stiffen, like a good hound on a scent: Gerem had dreamed, too.

Kisrah continued. "Geoffrey came to me as I slept and sat upon the end of my bed—just as he used to.

" 'My friend,' he said. 'I have nowhere else to turn. I need your magic to come to my touch.'

"This surprised me greatly, for he was the greatest mage I ever saw.

" 'A spell?' I asked. 'Can't you work it yourself?'

"He shook his head chidingly, and said, with that grin he used when I was being particularly obstinate, 'Dead men cannot use magic, child.'

"I woke up, sweating like a frightened horse, but there was nothing in my room that hadn't been there when I went to sleep. I thought at first that it had simply been a dream. But I'd forgotten what Geoffrey was."

"A dreamwalker," said Nevyn softly.

Kisrah nodded. "Exactly." He looked at Gerem. "Do you know what dreamwalking is?"

"Yes," replied Gerem. "Nevyn does it."

Nevyn is a dreamwalker? thought Aralorn.

"Right," agreed Kisrah. "There are a number of mages who can dreamwalk at the most basic level—fardreaming, it's called. While fardreaming, a mage can send his spirit outside his body, usually no farther than a mile or two. Dreamwalking, though, is much more powerful and unusual. Nevyn and Geoffrey are the only living mages I've heard of who can send their spirits anywhere they want to. Generally speaking, a dreamwalker cannot affect the physical world—like moving chairs or tables. I say 'generally' because one or two of the better dreamwalkers were said to have tossed a chair or two."

"Or a knife," added Wolf dryly.

Kisrah nodded. "I stand corrected. A dreamwalker also cannot work magic in his spirit form. What he *can* do is look and listen without people suspecting they are being watched. And, though he can't talk in a normal manner, he can communicate in a fashion called dreamspeaking."

"Like a mindspeaker?" asked Gerem.

Kisrah nodded, "Only better. It takes one mindspeaker to hear another. A dreamspeaker can make himself heard by anyone he wants."

Aralorn thought about the conversation she'd overheard and wondered if the dreamwalker who'd been Geoffrey had known that she was there listening.

"Anyone?" asked Gerem. "I thought that when a wizard becomes an apprentice, his dreams are protected by the Master Spells."

"That's right," said Kisrah, though his mouth tightened just a little. "Smart lad. Yes, the Master Spells protect young wizards to a certain extent. There are other ways to ward yourself, too. It is possible for a dreamwalker to manipulate an unprotected person through dreams. Un-ethical, but there you are. But dreamspeaking isn't any more manipulative than normal speech."

Yes, thought Aralorn, watching Gerem as relief touched his face. *No need to feel so guilty. You were not protected from the dreamwalker's manipulations.* Kisrah and Nevyn had known what they were doing.

Aloud, she asked, "Is magic necessary for dreamwalk-ing, or are there dreamwalkers who are not mages?"

"Dreamwalking is a magic talent, like transporting things or illusions. Geoffrey said"—Kisrah hesitated—"if a dreamwalker's body is killed while he is walking, his spirit can remain behind. Like a ghost, but with the full consciousness of the living person. He told me that the second time he came. And then he told me how he died." Kisrah looked at Wolf, who looked back without any expression at all.

"He told me that you came back because you'd heard that he was looking for you, and you were tired of it. He said that you argued about your use of black magic. He finally tried to use the Master Spells to limit your ability to work magic." Without dropping his gaze from Wolf's,

Kisrah said, "That's one of the ways that an ae'Magi can control rogue wizards, Gerem—as a last resort."

He seemed to be waiting for a response from Wolf, but after a fruitless pause, Kisrah continued. "In any case, he said he underestimated your power and the strength that black magic had given you; the spell was reversed. There came a point when you could have stopped it. He said you held the power for long enough to say something ironic— I've forgotten exactly what—and then you killed him."

He believes it, thought Aralorn, *at least at this moment.*

"As a point of fact," said Aralorn mildly, "it didn't happen like that. I was there. Wolf did not kill Geoffrey; nor did I." She started to tell them more about the last ae'Magi but caught the subtle shake of Wolf's head in the corner of her eye. He was right. She had to be careful not to trigger whatever was left of the charisma spells. "He was killed by the Uriah."

Kisrah stared at her, but she didn't drop her gaze.

"Only the ae'Magi, Wolf, and I were there the night he died," she continued mildly. "If your visitor was Geoffrey, then he put my father in danger—without Wolf's cooperation, you three would not be able to remove the ensorcell- ment from my father. You have the word of a goddess that if it is not removed soon, the Lyon will die. Your dream- walker asked you to work black magic upon an innocent man—is this something a good man would do? If it was not Geoffrey, then he doesn't know what happened any more than you do."

Kisrah rubbed his eyes. "At any rate, Geoffrey's story is the one I believed when he asked me to work some magic for him. It was supposed to be for you, Cain. It would not kill you, just hold you for the wizard's council's justice. I agreed. He told me that he needed me to find a secret room in his bedroom. So I found the room and the sword he'd hidden there. With his directions fresh in my mind,

I inscribed on the sword the rune he told me. Runes are not my strong point, and the one he used was unfamiliar and complex. It required all of my concentration to get it right. Just as I finished the last line, something grabbed my shoulder."

He took a deep breath. "There was a Uriah standing just behind me, reflex took over, and I beheaded it with the sword—only then did magic pour into the rune I'd just finished." Kisrah closed his eyes. "I didn't know it needed blood magic. I don't think I did. At the time, I told myself it was an accident that turned the spell black. I wanted to destroy the sword, offered to spell something else for him—anything else."

The Archmage sighed. "He said that the sword was the only sure bait, that perhaps the black magic would work in our favor. Even the Master Spells had failed to hold Cain; maybe it would take black magic to counter black magic. Geoffrey was always good at getting his own way by fair means or foul." He paused, as if surprised by what he'd said. "By the time I realized that he'd intended to use black magic all along, I was already resigned to it. Maybe I'd have done it for him anyway."

"Did Geoffrey tell you to send the sword here, or did you suggest it?" asked Aralorn. When the Archmage had died, he knew that she and Wolf were together—but she was certain that he hadn't made the connection between her and Lambshold. She took great care that most people didn't know.

"Geoffrey," he said. "The night after I brought the sword back with me, he told me he wanted me to send it to Nevyn. He told me that Nevyn's sister by marriage was Cain's lover. I sent the sword. Only afterward did I begin to question what I had done."

The hen clucked in its crate, reminding everyone in the room (except perhaps for Gerem and Nevyn, who Aralorn was not certain knew what they'd been planning) that black magic was needed to release the Lyon. Aralorn looked at the bird thoughtfully for a moment.

"Perhaps a more noble motive might have allowed me to shut my eyes longer to what I had done." Kisrah smiled grimly at Wolf. "I didn't work the spell to capture Cain and save the world from dark magic—I worked it for revenge. I hated you for taking my friend from me. I knew that the end result of Geoffrey's plan was your death."

"I would have expected no less," agreed Wolf softly. "I know what he was to you. What was the rune he had you draw?"

From an inner pocket, Kisrah produced a sheet of paper with two neat drawings he gave to Wolf. Since drawing the rune itself would activate it, rune patterns were split into two drawings that, when laid one over the other, formed the rune. Aralorn had never been able to put the patterns together in her head without getting a headache, but Wolf nodded, as if it made sense to him.

"What did he have you add to it?" he asked Nevyn.

Nevyn had taken a seat on the floor where he could lean against the wall, as far from where Wolf stood as he could get. He had listened to Kisrah's story with his eyes closed; dark shadows and lines of weariness touched his face. At Wolf's question, he dug into the pouch attached to his belt and mutely handed him two sheets of paper.

Wolf took them and held them up separately, frowning. "Where did you place it? On the blade as well?"

Nevyn nodded. "Farther down on the blade, near the point."

"Another binding spell of some sort," said Kisrah after a moment of staring over Wolf's shoulder. "Had you seen it before, Nevyn?"

He shook his head. "No."

"Cain?"

Wolf shook his head as well, but slowly. "Not exactly, no."

"Did he ask you to kill anything?" asked Kisrah.

"No," said Nevyn. "But what I did was worse." He turned slightly to address everyone. "I knew that the spell was intended for the Lyon and that he was to be the bait that drew Aralorn and . . . Cain here." His voice grew quieter. "I—I—I suggested it to him. Aralorn hadn't come here for ten years. When he asked me what would make her return, I told him that I thought the only thing that would work was if someone died—if Henrick died."

He looked at Wolf, and his voice became guttural. "So he put a spell on the Lyon that only you could break. Black magic, he said, so that Kisrah would not know how to unwork the spell. I told him that you might not come, might not expose yourself for someone you didn't know. So he decided to see if we could trap Aralorn in it as well. I called the baneshade here and set it to extend the spell to Aralorn."

"Do you know what he intended to do to Wolf—sorry, Cain—once he was here?" asked Aralorn, interested in what Geoffrey had told Nevyn. "After all, here he is . . . and no one has moved against him."

Nevyn shrugged. "Kisrah was to come upon Cain working black magic, and then he'd have to face justice at the ae'Magi's hands."

Kisrah's bells rang as he started in surprise. "My dear Nevyn, I don't think I have the power to constrain or kill Cain—you haven't seen what he can do."

"After unworking the spell on the Lyon, he would be in no shape to resist you." He sat forward suddenly, a bitter twist to his mouth. "You can rot, Cain, for all I care. But Henrick has been more of a father to me than my own ever thought of being, and *I* helped to trap him. Any magic that binds a person as tightly as he is bound will be tricky to unwork at best. It has become increasingly obvious that Geoffrey doesn't care if Henrick lives or dies—but *I* do. If I can help you, I will—if you die in the process, so much the better."

"All right," said Wolf, and Aralorn eyed him sharply.

"What did you do with the sword after you worked the spell?" asked Kisrah.

Nevyn drew in a breath. "I gave it to Henrick the day he was enspelled; I met him at the stables as he was leaving to inspect the burnt-out croft. I told him a messenger brought it from Aralorn." He lowered his eyes. "Henrick gave me his old campaign sword, told me to put it in the armory, and carried the one I'd given him."

With a casualness that spoke of more practice than Aralorn had suspected, he gestured with both hands, and a sword appeared on the floor in front of them. "This sword. You see why we knew that he would carry this one."

It wasn't a ceremonial sword, nor was it ornate. But even Aralorn, who was admittedly not the best of sword judges, could see the care that had gone into its making. The pommel was wood, soft finished—nothing spectacular, but high quality nonetheless. It was the blade that attested to the care that had gone into the sword's making. Countless folds of a repeating pattern marked the blade: a masterwork of a talented swordsmith.

Wolf knelt and ran a hand over it without touching. "There's no magic to it now other than the power of a sharp blade." He smiled. "It belonged to my father's predecessor. I suspect that means it is yours now, Kisrah."

"No," said the Archmage, sounding revolted. "If there's no more harm in it, then it should be the Lyon's, assuming you can fix this. He's paid enough for it."

Once he'd called the blade, Nevyn had ignored it completely. Rising to his feet, he walked around Wolf to the bier.

"He'll hate me when he knows what I have done." Nevyn stared at the Lyon's body.

"No," said Aralorn gently. "He never expected any of his children to be perfect. Tell him what you have told us; he'll understand. He liked Geoffrey, too."

Nevyn shook his head.

"My turn," said Gerem, flushing when his voice cracked.

"Your turn," agreed Aralorn.

"I've been having strange dreams for a long time. Nightmares mostly." He swallowed heavily. "I don't really know where to start."

They waited patiently, giving him a chance to get his thoughts in order.

Finally, he looked at Aralorn. "I don't know what life here was like when you were a child, but to me it always seemed as if I was lost in a crowd. I'm clumsy with a blade and have no interest in hunting some poor fox or wolf. The only thing I *can* do is ride, but in this family even Freya and Lin do that well. The week . . . the week that Father was ensorcelled, he talked to me once—and *that* was to ask me if I had any clothes that fit." Self-consciously, he pulled a sleeve down so it briefly covered the bones in his wrist before sliding back up.

"One night I dreamed that I saddled my horse and rode up to the old croft. There was a rabbit hiding under a bush that I killed with an arrow. Something happened then . . . when it died I felt a rush of power that filled me until I could hold no more. I walked the fence line of the croft, chanting as the rabbit's blood dripped to the ground."

There was a grim factuality to his story that Aralorn could not help but approve. To a boy who disliked hunting, the realization of what he had done must be sickening.

"When I was through, I dipped my finger into the rabbit's death wound, and I was thinking of Father, on how much this would impress him, how proud he would be to have a son who was a mage. I made a mark on the corner post of the fence."

"What did the mark look like?" asked Wolf.

"Two half circles, one above the other—connected bottom to top."

Wolf frowned. "Open to the left or right or one each way?"

"To the left."

Wolf closed his eyes as if it allowed him to better visualize the spell.

Still looking at the drawings, he asked, "You said you were chanting. Do you remember what you said?"

Gerem frowned. "No. It was in Rethian, though, because I knew what I was saying at the time. I remember thinking that it was strange. I remember that it rhymed." He was silent for a moment. "Something about feeding, I think. Death, magic, and dreaming, but that's all I can remember."

"And then you burned the croft," said Wolf.

Gerem nodded. "They said later there were animals in the barn." He sounded sick.

"Be glad there weren't people," commented Aralorn.

"Thanks," he said sourly, but with a touch of humor. "Now I can have nightmares about that every night, too."

"You thought this was a dream?" asked Kisrah.

Gerem nodded. "Until we received news of the burning of the croft. Even then I didn't really believe I'd been the one to burn the croft until Father collapsed." He paused and looked at Aralorn. "I am *really* glad he isn't dead. After he was brought back to the keep, I took out my hunting knife—there was dried blood on the blade just beneath the handle where my cleaning cloth might have missed."

"Gerem," said Kisrah, "of all of us here, you hold the least guilt. Without the protection of the spells binding master to apprentice, a dreamwalker of Geoffrey's caliber could make you do anything he wanted you to. You are no more guilty of killing that rabbit, burning the animals in the barn, or entrapping the Lyon than a sword is guilty of the wounds it opens."

Aralorn could have kissed him.

Gerem's lips twitched up just a little. "You're saying that I was just a hatchet that happened to be in the right place at the right time."

The Archmage smiled and nodded. "After we free your father, I'll speak to him about setting up a real apprenticeship." He turned to Nevyn. "I'll make certain he doesn't have your experiences, Nevyn. You should have told—" He stopped when Nevyn flinched and shook his head. "It doesn't matter now."

Wolf folded the drawings and put them into a pouch he carried on his belt.

"Do you know enough to release him?" asked Aralorn.

Wolf hesitated. "I will only get one chance at this. I'd like to think about it a little more. I know where Father kept his favorite spell books: Let me take a day or so to look through them before I try this."

"In my library," said Kisrah dryly.

"Not exactly," said Wolf. "Remind me sometime to show you some of the secrets you ought to know about the ae'Magi's castle. In the meantime, I need to look a few things up."

"That sounds like a good idea to me," said Kisrah. "Do you need any help?"

Wolf shook his head. "No. There are only two rune books he used—it wasn't Father's forte either."

Kisrah bit his lip. "May I talk to you in private before you go, Cain?"

Wolf raised one eyebrow in surprise. "Certainly." He took Aralorn's hand and raised it to his lips. "I'll be back this evening."

She smiled and kissed his cheek. "Fine."

He turned back to the Archmage. "Shall we walk?"

———

Kisrah led the way to the frozen gardens, making no attempt to talk until they were out in the cold.

"Cain, the Master Spells are missing—or rather half of them are."

"What?" Shock broke through Wolf's preoccupation with the spell he would have to perform in order to free Aralorn's father.

"Haven't you noticed?"

Wolf shook his head, still feeling disbelief—the Master Spells held the fabric of wizardry together. "They haven't had any effect on me for a long time."

"Without the spells, the position of ae'Magi is no more than a courtesy title. I have no way of controlling a rogue wizard, no way of detecting black magic unless I am in the proximity of whoever is working it. When I found them in Geoffrey's library, the pages that contained the ae'Magi's half of the rune spells were missing."

Ah, thought Wolf, as he said, "I don't know where they are."

"I believe you," said Kisrah, leaving Wolf feeling odd—as if he'd braced himself for an attack that hadn't come. "You had no motive to take them. If anyone could have controlled you with them, Geoffrey would have done so a long time ago. Do you know where he would have hidden them?"

"The only time that I saw them, they were in the ae'Magi's grimoire in the vault in the library."

"They are no longer there. If you find them—"

"I'll bring them to you. It's not rogue wizards that bother me; it's what will happen if everyone realizes you no longer control them."

"Witch hunts," agreed Kisrah grimly.

Wolf nodded. "I'll look out for them, but don't be surprised if I don't find them. Father wasn't the only wizard who dabbled in the black arts—I know there were at least two others. It would be worth their lives to keep them from you."

Kisrah swore heatedly. "I hadn't thought of that. Who are they?"

Wolf shrugged. "I don't know their names, and they kept their faces hidden. Do you still have the other half of the spells?"

Kisrah nodded. "We hid them as soon as it was clear that something had happened to Geoffrey's."

"I'll look," promised Wolf again, then turned away from the ae'Magi.

"Cain," Kisrah said.

"Yes?"

"Thank you."

Wolf swept him a low bow before heading briskly out of the gardens. He would look, but he suspected the spells were long gone, maybe destroyed. Not entirely a bad thing, he decided after a while. Geoffrey ae'Magi could not have been the only ae'Magi who used them for other than their intended purposes, otherwise there wouldn't be so many black grimoires left after ten centuries.

He had a library to visit with more urgent business. More than he needed his father's books, he needed a quiet place.

———

Aralorn waited until Gerem and Nevyn followed the other mages out the door before turning to the chicken in the crate.

"Coming out, Halven?" she asked.

The hen let out a startled squawk.

She pulled the lid off the crate and shook her head. "Don't give me that. If you wanted to remain anonymous, you could have made your clucks less pointed. Otherwise, I'd never have thought to check to see if the chicken was really a chicken. I never have been able to switch from one sex to the other."

The hen jumped to the top of the crate and landed on the floor as her uncle—this time in the form of a tall red-headed man wearing the clothes of one of the Trader Clans.

"Having you around makes spying much more interesting," he said, sounding pleased.

"What would you have done if he'd been ready to unwork the spell and tried to sacrifice you?" she asked.

He grinned. "I wouldn't have let him slit my throat, but I was pretty sure that he'd want to consider the spells for a while."

"Be that as it may, I for one am glad you're here. How much do you know about human magic?"

Halven raised his eyebrows. "Less than Wolf, I imagine."

"He's busy—and I'm not certain that it's something I want to discuss with him right now. Just how powerful would a dreamwalker have to be in order to control a howlaa?"

"Ah, dreamwalking is not just a human talent, and I do know a little something about it." He scratched his chin. "Howlaas are magical creatures, much more difficult to influence than a half-fledged boy like Gerem. Dreamwalking is more common among us than among the humans, but we don't tend to be nearly as powerful. I know two dreamwalkers; only one of them can dreamspeak. We don't even have stories of dreamwalkers who can influence others the way Gerem was, except for the—what was it you called it? Ah yes, the Dreamer."

"Now you've heard the whole story of the spell on the Lyon. Do you still think that a dead dreamwalker couldn't do this?"

"Maybe one could," he said. "Kisrah and Nevyn's part, yes. I am less certain of whoever held your brother in thrall—I'd think that would take a fair bit of power. The howlaa? I just don't see how a dead man would have the power to do that. But I haven't talked to any dead dreamwalkers to be certain of it."

"Maybe," she said thoughtfully, "I should go talk to someone who knows more about dead people."

The wind was gusty as Aralorn took the path to the temple, but it didn't bother her as much today. Perhaps her lessons on centering helped her to block the voices more effectively, or else the ability was fading with time. She rather hoped for the latter.

The temple doors stood open, so she rode directly there, dismounted, and left Sheen standing outside.

"Tilda?" she called softly. The room appeared deserted, though by no means empty. In spite of the open door, it was warm inside, but there was no sign of a fire. She shivered and backed out of the temple, closing the doors carefully behind her.

Leading Sheen toward the little cottage, she told him, "I don't know why that should unnerve me when I run around with wizards and shapechangers, but it does."

There was a hitching post in front of the cottage, and Aralorn dropped Sheen's reins beside it.

"Be good," she said, and patted him on the shoulder before taking the shoveled path to the door of the cottage.

"Enter," bade a cheerful voice when she knocked. "I'm in the kitchen, baking."

Sure enough, when Aralorn opened the door, the smell of warm yeast billowed out.

"It's me, Aralorn." She followed the smell to find Tilda up to her elbows in bread dough. "I see I caught you working."

Tilda laughed. "Shh. Don't tell. A priestess is supposed to stand around and look mysterious."

"That's all right, I generally get plenty of mysterious. Speaking of which, the temple door was opened. I shut it before I came here."

Tilda smiled. "Well then, we both welcome you here."

"Thank you," said Aralorn with what aplomb she'd

managed to develop running around with Wolf. "I came because I need to ask you a few questions."

"Me or the priestess?"

Aralorn shrugged. "Whichever one can answer my questions. Geoffrey ae'Magi is dead, right?"

"Yes," Tilda answered without hesitation. "Ridane sometimes tells me when significant people die."

Aralorn let out a harsh breath of relief. She'd been pretty sure of it, but hearing it was better. She could deal with him dead—it was the living Geoffrey who had scared the courage out of her. "A great many people, including the current ae'Magi, are convinced that his spirit is dreamwalking around Lambshold. Is that possible?"

"Dreamwalking?" Tilda stopped kneading her bread and looked thoughtful. "I don't know." She closed her eyes and took in a deep breath.

Something stirred in the air. It wasn't magic, but it was like enough to it that Aralorn could feel it drift through her and wrap itself about the priestess.

When Tilda opened her eyes, the pupil filled her iris, making her eyes appear almost black. "No," she said. "There are a few ghosts in the area, old things for the most part. But nothing strong enough to influence the living."

Aralorn nodded slowly. "That's what I needed to know. Thank you." She turned to go.

"Wait," said the priestess. "There is something . . ."

"Yes?"

Tilda stared at her bread for a moment before looking up. She was pale as milk, and her pupils were contracted as if she stood in the noonday sun rather than in a cozy but rather dim cottage. "If you are not very careful and very clever, there will be several more deaths soon."

"I am always clever," responded Aralorn, with more humor than she felt. "Careful, we may have to work around." Tilda still looked upset, so Aralorn added, "I know that there is danger. It should not take me long to discover what has been happening these last few weeks. Once I know that—I'll know what can be done."

"Ridane says that the web is spun, and one person at Lambshold will die no matter what you do."

Aralorn had not dealt with gods much, but she was a firm believer in writing her own future. She was not about to let Ridane decide the fate of her family and friends. "I'll do what I can. Thank you, Tilda. You've helped a great deal."

Nevyn, she thought as she mounted Sheen. *It is Nevyn.*

The stallion snorted and sidled and generally kept her attention until they were well on their way back to Lambshold. As she'd listened to Gerem's story, she had known it wasn't Geoffrey. If Geoffrey had known that there was a mage of Gerem's potential, untrained, at Lambshold, he would have moved mountains to get to him—untrained mages gave him so much more power than trained mages. So Geoffrey hadn't known about Gerem before he died. And, as a dead man seeking revenge, he would not have used Gerem to do his work—he'd have used Anasel. Surely a doddering old man who had been a great mage would have been a better target. But Nevyn avoided Anasel as he avoided most of the mageborn if he could. If he needed two other mages to help him, it would be Kisrah and Gerem. But Nevyn would never hurt her father.

One of Aralorn's greatest talents as a spy, other than being able to turn into a mouse, was her ability to take a few bits of knowledge and knit them into a whole story.

Kisrah told her that Nevyn was a dreamwalker.

Kisrah had long been a favorite of the ae'Magi's and spent a lot of time at the ae'Magi's castle.

Nevyn, who'd already suffered from being a mageborn Darranian, had been first apprenticed to a wizard who had abused him. That wizard, though powerful, had a bad enough reputation that the ae'Magi had never associated with him willingly.

Those were the facts she had. It was enough for an experienced storyteller to work out the probabilities.

She saw in her head that boy, wary and nervous, taken by his new master to the ae'Magi's castle. Abused children try to protect themselves any way they can. They hide, they try to please their abuser, they use their magic. Santik had not been a dreamwalker; certainly his apprentice would have used his talent to spy upon him to try to stay safe. Perhaps dreamwalking to watch his master had already been a habit when he'd gone into Kisrah's care.

Kisrah would certainly have taken his new apprentice to the ae'Magi to see if Geoffrey had suggestions on how to handle the boy. Like Kisrah himself, Nevyn had had the promise of power, and Geoffrey would never have let such a wizard in his presence without ensuring that he, too, was caught up in the charisma spell. Maybe Nevyn had a ring like Kisrah's or some other bit of jewelry, given to him by the ae'Magi.

She wondered how long it had been before Nevyn, dreamwalking, had first spied upon the ae'Magi. Because once he had been abused, he certainly would have had trouble believing in the goodness of those assigned to his care. Spying on Kisrah would have caused him no harm. But the ae'Magi . . . Even Kisrah, an adult, had been torn by the discrepancy between how he felt about Geoffrey because of the charisma spell and what he witnessed at the ae'Magi's castle. And Kisrah hadn't seen half of it. Wolf had—and Aralorn would have bet that Nevyn had as well.

Ah, gods, she thought. *The poor boy.*

Sheen guided himself for a bit while she dropped her reins to wipe at her eyes. He shook his head when she drew the reins taut again.

That first time, she thought, *how old was Nevyn the first time? What did he see?*

She'd seen Geoffrey kill children, had seen a man she knew in the face of a shambling Uriah, had seen a woman who turned into a flesh-eating thing—and she'd only been around the last ae'Magi for weeks, not years. Wolf had experienced worse—and so, she was certain, had Nevyn. All the while he'd been defenseless, caught up by the ae'Magi's spell that bound him to think that the Archmage was the best, most wonderful of good men.

Each thread of the story flowed worse than the last.

Spying on the ae'Magi would have allowed Nevyn access to black magic. Geoffrey was a dreamwalker, too. Had he known that Nevyn was spying?

Of course he had, she thought. How could he not? Geoffrey had been as powerful as only a black mage who was also the Archmage could be. Had he compared them, Wolf and Nevyn, as he taught them both things children should never have to know? Nausea curled in her belly. It would have given him great pleasure to have them both, she thought, one boy who fought him and one who had already been taught to please an abusive master and now had one he was forced to love.

Nevyn would have been fully under the influence of the ae'Magi's magic. *Knowing* that the ae'Magi was wonderful and seeing the horrors he committed. What had that done to Nevyn?

"Aralorn!" bellowed Falhart from the stable door as she rode up. "You missed our date."

"Date?" she raised her eyebrows.

"Rematch, double or nothing—don't you remember?"

"Ah," she said. "I wasn't certain you'd let me have another match since you won the first. Luck can't be with you all the time."

"Luck, she says!" He appealed to the interested spectators

who'd begun gathering in the courtyard at his first bellow. Then he turned back to Aralorn. "Skill it was, and right well you know it, small one."

"Big people have farther to fall," she retorted. "Let me get my staves, and I'll meet you there." She'd tire her body, then see if she could piece together some way to save her father, Nevyn, and Wolf. Because, with Nevyn as the enemy, Wolf was still at risk.

TWELVE

Falhart was waiting for Aralorn when she got to the practice grounds. He'd stripped down to his trousers, which was gutsy of him, if not too smart. A leather shirt was fair protection against bruises—and the cold for that matter.

Shirtless, he appeared even larger than he did clothed, and if that flesh was tinged blue from the weather, it didn't detract from the whole. From the looks of him, he trained as hard as any new recruit, for there wasn't a spare bit of flesh anywhere.

If she'd been the kind of person who was easily intimidated, she'd have been getting nervous. As it was, she looked around but didn't see his wife or any other reason for the display—though there was a fair-sized crowd beginning to gather.

Aralorn generally preferred to keep as much clothing on as possible when fighting someone who didn't know her; the less anyone saw of her muscles, the more they underrated her abilities—not that she expected Falhart to underestimate her. Perhaps he fought stripped down to intimidate his opponent. If she were as large as he, she might try that tack, but she wouldn't expect it to be too effective against a small woman who was used to fighting musclebound men.

"Let you win once, and you get visions of invulnerability," she mourned, gesturing toward his discarded clothing. "Just think of the bruises you'll carry tomorrow."

"You talk pretty big for a little thing who got beaten soundly yesterday," he returned, working his big staff in a pattern that made it blur and sing.

His weapon was impressive: He was using his war staff rather than the practice one he'd had yesterday. It was half a foot taller than he was and as big around as he could comfortably hold—Aralorn doubted she could close her hand around it. It was stained almost black and shod with polished steel that caught the light as he made it dance. She shook her head at him—there were easier ways to warm up.

Watching the gathering crowd, Aralorn grinned at the looks of awe her brother was receiving from the young men. Obviously, he didn't put on a display like this every day.

In comparison, she knew that she made a pitiful showing. She'd picked the same single staff she'd fought with yesterday: Her staff looked like a child's toy in comparison to Falhart's. She set it aside as she warmed up, stretching her muscles but not using them appreciably.

She could hear active betting in the crowd, which meant that someone expected her to win, which surprised her given Hart's show of force.

"Got those five coppers handy?" she asked, as a way of announcing she was ready to fight. "I don't accept credit."

"I've got them," said Correy, pushing his way to the fore of the crowd and stepping over the low barrier that defined the ring. "Can't even buy a night's stay in a decent inn for that, Aralorn. Are you sure you don't want to up the bet?"

She shook her head. "I never bet more than ten—and then only if it is a bet I'm certain to win. Any more than that, and I might miss it. I'm just a poor mercenary, not heir to a landed noble like some people I know. And, Correy, anyone who spends five coppers for a night at the inn better be paying for more than room and board, or else he's getting rooked. Falhart, are you through wasting your strength yet?"

He looked at Correy, who nodded.

Which was odd—unless she tied it in with Falhart's bare chest and the active betting. "It's not kind to sucker people who can't afford it, Correy," she said softly.

"I'm not taking more than they can afford—Father pays his men well." He turned his back to the crowd so he wouldn't be overheard. "Besides, Hart's not throwing the fight. He just told me that he'd be surprised if you let him win twice in a row."

"He owes me a gold for fighting without my shirt," murmured Hart. "I get that win or lose."

Aralorn grinned at him, "Does your wife know you take your shirt off for money?"

"Just don't tell Irrenna," he pleaded—only half joking.

"Oh-ho," she crowed. "This sounds like blackmail material."

Hart rolled his eyes, "Can we get on with this? It's blasted cold out here."

Aralorn straightened and shook her shoulders out. "Fine. I'll add a little black to your blue skin."

Correy stepped out of the ring, leaving it to the combatants.

The secret of fighting against a man using a tree was never to be where he thought you were going to be. Her staff could turn his, but if she was stupid enough to try to block his directly, it would snap.

For the first few minutes, they fought silently, trying to take each other by surprise before it turned into an endurance contest. Falhart had to move more bulk around than Aralorn, but she had to move hers faster because of the length of his reach, so they were both breathing heavily when they backed off.

"There's a story I once heard," she said, pacing around the ring without taking her eye off him, "about a thief-taker who worked for the king of Southwood several generations back. His name was Anslow."

"Never heard of him," grunted Falhart, moving at her in a rush. She dove under his blow, tucked her stick neatly between his knees, and twisted. He fell to the ground, rolling, and she jumped lightly back out of his reach. "Don't try that move on me again," he warned. "Twice is pushing it."

She shrugged, grinning. "Some moves bear repeating, if only for entertainment value. That's the trouble with your being so large—it's too much fun to watch you fall."

They circled warily for a moment. Without the protection of a shirt, Falhart was more cautious than he'd been the day before. "Why don't you continue with your story?"

Aralorn nodded, walking backward as he stalked her. "Anslow solved crimes that had stumped many before him, winning a reputation as the best of his kind. There are stories of cases he solved with nothing but a bit of thread or a single footprint."

Falhart closed, taking a swing at her middle. Aralorn didn't even pause in her story as she avoided the blow. "He was a legend in his own time, and lawbreakers walked in fear of his shadow. But there was one criminal who did not fear him."

"Stay put, you runt," he snapped, as she dodged past him, catching him a glancing hit on his ribs.

"Point," she crowed. "This criminal was a killer who chose women for victims."

"I can see his—*point*," muttered Falhart as he caught her squarely in the back, knocking the breath out of her.

Chivalrously, he stepped back and waited for her to breathe again. It took her a moment before she came to her feet.

"Allyn's toadflax, Hart, that's going to hurt tomorrow."

He grinned, showing not the least hint of remorse. "That's the point of the whole thing."

"Right," she said dryly, though she couldn't help smiling.

This was *fun*. She hadn't been able to really cut loose since her last good sparring partner had been killed. If you didn't trust the skills of your opponent, you couldn't use your best moves against him unless you wanted to kill him. With a wild yell, she launched an attack designed to do nothing more than tire Falhart out.

"You were telling me about the thief-taker," he said, matching her blow for blow and adding a few moves of his own to show her she wasn't in control of the fight.

"Ah," she said, slipping nimbly out of the path of his quarterstaff. "So I was. The killer took his prey only once a year, on the first day of spring. He laid his victims out in some public place in the dark of the night. As the years passed, the killer taunted Anslow, sending him notes and clues that did the thief-taker no good."

While he was extended in a thrust that she'd turned aside, she slipped the end of her staff sideways and hit him squarely in the breastbone, where it left a bruise to match the one on his ribs. "Two."

He growled and circled. She stuck her tongue out at him; he made a face.

"The night before the killer would take his fifteenth victim," she continued, "Anslow took every note the killer had sent him and set them before him, trying to find a pattern. He thought it was someone he knew, for the notes contained a few private references—things that only Anslow should have known."

She broke off speaking, for Falhart moved in with a barrage of blows that required all of her concentration to counter. At last, he managed to hit her staff directly, snapping it in two. The blow continued more gently, but she came out of the encounter with sore ribs.

"Two," he said.

She snapped in with the remnants of the staff and poked him in the belly—gently. "Three—my match."

There were loud groans from the audience as they sorted out who owed what to whom. Falhart grinned and leaned on his staff.

"So, tell me the rest of the story," he said, breathing heavily.

She sat down briefly on the ground, but the cold drove her to her feet. "About Anslow? Where was I?"

"He had the notes from the killer in front of him."

"Ah, yes. Those notes. He set them out on his desk, oldest to newest. He had noticed early on that the killer's handwriting bore a strong resemblance to his own—but it was the last letter he stared at. The killer's hand had developed a tremor; the letters were no longer formed with a smooth, dark flow of ink. Just recently, Anslow had noticed that his hands shook when he wrote. He himself was the killer."

She touched the broken end of one of the sections of her staff in the dirt and dragged it back and forth gently in random patterns.

Falhart frowned. "How could he be the killer and not know it?"

Aralorn contemplated her broken staff as if it might hold the secrets of the universe. "There is a rare illness of the spirit in which a person can become two separate beings occupying the same body. There is a shadow that forms, watching everything the primary person does, knowing what he knows—but the real person may have no knowledge of what the shadow does when he controls the body." She flipped the piece into the air and caught it.

"Strange," observed Falhart, shaking his head.

Correy came up to them and took Aralorn's hand in his, turned her palm upright, and placed six copper coins in it, talking to Falhart all the while. "Thanks for the tip, Hart. I got ten-to-one odds. It was only six to one before they had a chance to compare your manly figure with the midget here—you can put your shirt back on now."

————————

Wolf stared at the rows of books in his shelves, caressing the bindings gently. He didn't pull any out—that could wait. He knew which ones held the information he needed. But he already knew what the spell would cost, had known, really, since Kisrah had told him that he'd killed a Uriah to set his spell, though he'd held out some hope until he'd heard everything that had been put into the binding magic holding the Lyon. He had known that his father had at last succeeded in destroying him.

A human had died to power the spell created by three mages. A human death was needed to unmake it. A Uriah counted as a person, ensorcelled and altered though he was— he had been a man once. If Kisrah had known the nature of the Uriah, he would have known such a sacrifice was necessary. He might have told Aralorn, then she would believe it was her decision to make. Wolf knew that it was his, and he had made it as soon as he realized what would be needed.

How ironic that when he finally decided that he might actually deserve to live, he discovered that he was going to have to die. How had his father known that he would love Aralorn enough to sacrifice himself for her? Except that it wasn't really for her, he realized, though that was part of it.

He touched the backs of a half dozen of his favorite books, not rare grimoires but heroes' tales. It was his father who had caused this, and only Geoffrey ae'Magi's son could put an end to his father's evil once and for all—if Cain ae'Magison could stiffen his will to it.

He had always come to his books for the strength he needed to resist his father. So he had come here, to his collection of books that rested deep in the heart of a mountain in the Northlands, to find the strength to do the right thing.

He walked on through the rows of books, pausing here and there to set one straight until he reached his worktable. Not bothering with the chairs, he sat on the table itself, right next to the pair of books he'd retrieved from the ae'Magi's castle. He touched a splatter of ink, remembering days not long past that he and Aralorn had worked there, searching through the books for just the right spell. He remembered the ink that stained her hand and the table as she scratched out notes in handwriting that was just short of illegible.

He remembered bringing her from his father's dungeons more dead than alive, laying her still form on the couch, worrying that what he'd done for her wouldn't be enough—that she would die and leave him alone again.

He remembered and wept where there was no one to see.

———

Aralorn fretted through dinner. Her theory was a fishing net with holes a sailing ship could get through.

She knew the story about Anslow was true. She'd had it from Ren the Mouse, who'd been a personal friend of the thief-taker. Was she wrong in thinking that the odd vision she'd had of Nevyn as a tree split down the middle meant he had no idea of what his darker half had done?

For that matter, why was she certain it was Nevyn? Kisrah might have depths she'd never seen. Why couldn't he be the one who was dreamwalking? It was he who said that Geoffrey and Nevyn were the only ones who could dreamwalk. He might have lied. Maybe he and Nevyn were in it together.

Aralorn stared at the ceiling. Matters that had seemed so clear riding back from Ridane's temple now seemed muddled. She really did not have enough evidence to know who was behind the Lyon's bespelling—only that it was not Geoffrey.

"Aralorn, are you all right?" asked Irrenna.

Aralorn glanced up and realized that everyone was

looking at her—obviously she'd missed something. Or maybe she'd been staring at the pickled eel on the flat of her knife for too long.

"Yes, sorry," she answered. "Just tired."

She set the black stuff back on her plate. Snake she could take or leave, but freshwater eel was beyond horrible—especially pickled. She vowed not to let herself get so distracted at mealtime again if the results could be so hazardous.

"I was asking you when you needed to be back at Sianim," said Irrenna.

"Uhm." She smiled. "I didn't exactly take a formal leave of absence. Just left them a note. If they need me, they know where to find me."

She would tell Wolf that she knew that it wasn't Geoffrey, so he could take what precautions he could. When her father was back on his feet, they'd figure out the rest.

———

Wolf came back while she was getting ready for bed, surprising her by teleporting himself right into the room. She knew that he preferred to find somewhere private because the first few moments after he translocated, he was disoriented. He looked pale, but she thought it might just be the result of the spell.

"Any luck?" she asked.

"I have what I need," he responded, swaying slightly where he stood.

He closed his eyes, and she ran to offer a supportive arm.

"Sorry," he said. "Just dizzy."

She was near enough to him to smell the familiar scent of the cave. "My nose tells me you've been to the Northlands. I thought you were going to check your father's library."

"My dear Aralorn," he said, without opening his eyes, "a fair portion of my father's library is in the cave."

She laughed and hugged him, tucking her head against him in a manner that had become familiar.

"Did you find what you needed?" she asked.

"Yes," he said, tightening his arms until she squeaked.

"I figured out something, too," she said.

"Oh?" He nuzzled at her neck, scratching her a little with the faint roughness of beard that was new-grown since that morning.

"Wolf, stop that—it tickles. It isn't your father."

"How did you come to that conclusion?"

He switched his attentions to her ear, and she shivered at the effect of his warm breath against her sensitive skin.

"He would—Wolf . . ." She couldn't speak for a moment.

"Hmm?"

"I asked Ridane's priestess. She says he's dead and not influencing anyone here."

He stilled, then kissed the top of her head. "Smart."

"Always," she said smugly.

"I love you," he said.

"Of course you do," she said, to make him laugh— which it did. "I love you, too. Now you can kiss me."

He bent down to her ear again, and whispered, "How long were you going to take before you told me that the priestess bound us together unto death?"

Now it was her turn to still. She felt guilty for half a breath, then she realized what his words really meant.

"How long have you known? Plague take you, Wolf."

She tried to take a step away, but he held her too tightly. His breath seemed to be behaving oddly—then she realized he was laughing. She hit him—not hard enough to hurt, just enough to express her displeasure.

"Aralorn, Aralorn," he tried to croon between laughs and pretending her halfhearted blows were hurting him. "Did you think I wouldn't feel it when the priestess set a blood-bond between us? I am a black mage, my love. I understand about blood-bonds—and I can break them if I wish."

"This one was set by a goddess," she informed him.

"Maybe she could set a bond between us I could not break," he told her. "But this one I could. If I wanted to."

He lifted her off the floor to allow himself better access to her mouth—as well as various and sundry other sensitive areas. Aralorn caught her breath and braced her hands on his shoulders.

"I know you love me," he told her, the laughter dying from his eyes.

She found herself blinking back tears as she heard how profoundly that knowledge had affected him.

"I know you love me, too," she said, before her mouth was occupied by things other than speech.

———

Afterward, he slept. Snuggled tightly against him, Aralorn closed her eyes and wished she didn't have to ask him to use the dark arts. He had tried to kill himself once rather than use them, but for her he would take the part he had been given. She didn't know that she was worth it.

No good comes from black magic, Kisrah had said. Ridane's priestess had told her that someone would die before long. Aralorn shivered and shifted closer to Wolf as if she could protect him by her presence.

It hadn't been said, but the assumption Wolf had led them all to was that he would remove the spell tomorrow. Surely that would give the dreamwalker something to fret about.

Maybe he'd be walking again tonight.

She decided the best place to keep watch would be in Nevyn's room. It might already be too late, but there was still a fair portion of the night left—and it had been about this time that she'd seen "Geoffrey" talking to Kisrah.

She started to slide out of bed.

"Aralorn?" Wolf sounded sleepy.

"I'm going spying for a couple of hours," she said quietly,

though he was already awake. She should have known that she couldn't sneak out on him. "I have a few questions to clean up, and this might be my only chance to do it."

He cupped her face in the darkness and pulled her until she rested her forehead on his for a moment. "All right," he said. "Be careful."

She tilted her face until her lips met his. "I will."

She dressed in the dark, not bothering with shoes. Though, after a brief moment of thought, she grabbed her sword to go along with her knives. If she ended up facing an enraged sorcerer, she'd just as soon have Ambris's help as not.

In the darkness, Wolf said softly, "I love you."

Aralorn looked back, but the bed was too shadowed. She could distinguish nothing more than the shape of him in it. "I love you, too. See you in a few hours."

"Yes," he said.

He waited in the darkness and counted slowly to a hundred before getting to his feet. He dressed with care. He'd done many hard things in his life; in some ways this was not the worst. At least this time it was clearly the best answer for everyone.

He wished that he could postpone it, but he was unlikely to get another such opportunity soon. He'd been cudgeling his brain for a way to keep her away from him for long enough. Trust Aralorn to make things easy for him. He took his knife from his belt and tested it lightly against the ball of his thumb. A drop of dark liquid ran down the edge of his hand, and he licked it clean.

———

Aralorn was making her way up the stairs when a soft sound alerted her to someone else's presence. She froze where she was, searching the darkness above her for any hint of movement. At last she saw a flash of lighter color where the minimal light touched the railing to the right of the stairway.

She darted up the stairs, blessing the stone under her feet for its silence—it was far more difficult to sneak up a wooden stairway. If she had been in a hall, she would have found a dark corner to hide in, but the stairway was too narrow for that. The best that she could hope for was to meet them at the top of the stairs.

She told herself that there was no reason to feel nervous about meeting someone walking the halls here, but she had been a spy for too long. Her instincts kept her on edge.

As she rounded the last stair, she came face-to-face with Gerem. He couldn't have heard her, but he gave no evidence of surprise.

"Gerem?" she asked.

He frowned at her, but vaguely, as if he were concentrating on something else. "What are you doing here?" he asked, but without real interest.

"I was just going to ask you that." There was something wrong with him, she thought. His words were soft and slurred as if he'd been drinking, though she smelled no alcohol when she leaned closer to him.

"Death walks here tonight," he said, not at all dramatically, rather as if he were talking about grooming his horse.

An ice-cold chill swept up her spine, as much from his tone as from what he said. "Gerem, why don't I take you to your room. Wouldn't you like to go back to sleep?"

He nodded slowly. "I have to sleep."

He took a step forward, forcing Aralorn down a step from the landing, giving him as much of an advantage in height as Falhart had over her.

Gently she took his arm and tried to turn him, stepping up as she did so. It was a move she often used on stubborn pack animals that refused to go where she wanted them; turning worked much better than pushing or pulling. "Your room is this way, brother mine. You can sleep there."

He shook his head earnestly. "You don't understand. I *have* to go to the stables."

"The stables? What's in the stables?"

He stopped tugging against her hold and bent down until his face was level with hers. "I killed Father," he whispered.

"Stuff and nonsense, Gerem. Father is not dead." She looked around for the nearest source of help. This wasn't near anyone's sleeping chambers—those were a floor above them. No one would hear her . . . But then she remembered that Irrenna had given Kisrah the Lyon's library to sleep in.

"Kisrah!" she shouted, hoping her voice would penetrate the thick oak door.

"Let me go. I don't want to hurt you."

"No more do I," she muttered.

Gerem pulled a knife with a slow and awkward movement. Once he had it out, he held it as if he didn't know what to do with it now that it was in his hand.

Misled by that and by his earlier claim of clumsiness, Aralorn tried a simple grab to relieve him of the weapon. She should have realized that the Lyon wouldn't let any of his sons go without training. As smoothly as he must have done it a hundred times in practice, he caught her hand in his free one and used leverage to twist her around until her back was against him, her arms caught firmly by his off hand, and the cool edge of his knife laid against her throat.

Without the knife, she'd have gotten out of it easily enough—a former thief of the Trader Clans had taught her a number of interesting tricks—but the knife made any movement on her part highly stupid. Half-grown though he was, he was still stronger and bigger than she was—and better trained than she'd thought. She didn't want him to grow to adulthood knowing that he'd killed his sister, so she remained very still.

"What are you going to do in the stables, Gerem?" she asked as unaggressively as possible. *Give him some time to break the hold the dreamwalker has woven,* she thought. *Keep him talking.*

"Sleep." His arms relaxed a shade but not enough.

"Why do you need to sleep in the stables?" She kept her voice in big-sister-to-little-brother tones, not frightened-victim-with-knife-at-throat. If you reminded someone you were at their mercy too often, they just might decide to kill you and get it over with.

He tightened his grip. "I *killed* Father. Don't you under-stand?"

Abruptly, he twisted, thrusting her at someone who'd been approaching from behind. She knocked the man flat and heard Gerem running down the stairs.

She swore like any guttersnipe and leapt to her feet, not-ing only peripherally that it was Kisrah she'd landed on.

Though instincts would have sent her tearing off after Gerem, she took the time to change. The goose would be faster gliding down the stairs than the icelynx would be since the stone offered no grip to claws.

"What the—" croaked Kisrah as he sat up in time to witness the last part of the change.

"After him," she said, and took flight.

By now, Gerem was already down the stairs. He didn't bother with the more polite methods of getting to the sta-bles but threw the bolts on the shutters of a window and jumped through.

He's going to break a leg doing that, thought Aralorn. The window might be waist high inside the keep, but it was better than half a story higher on the outside. Closing her wings, she darted through the open window after him.

Hurry, said the wind's unwelcome voice. *Death is waiting.*

Let it wait, then, she thought.

She'd overshot Gerem and was close to the stables before she could turn around. Goose wings were meant for great sweeping turns, not falcon-quick maneuvering. Espe-cially a domestic goose that had to work far too hard to fly. She started to turn back when she saw the howlaa.

It waited in front of the stables in the moonlit courtyard, the wind carrying its scent away from the sensitive noses of the horses in the stables. She thought about how unexpectedly the last howlaa had come upon her and wondered if it could control the wind and keep its scent from prey.

The dead one's mate, said the wind, as clearly as if someone were whispering into her ears. *Dream-called and hungry for blood.*

Closer, she could see differences between this one and the one she'd killed before. Its mane was longer and darker, with red as well as yellow tints. Its eyes, though, were the same, crystal so deep she could drown in its depths.

Spelled, she thought. It had magic to compel its victims to meet its eyes. It wasn't just stupidity on her part that had let her be caught by the first howlaa.

Called by the howlaa, she let herself get too close. Only when it moved was she able to break the hold of its eyes. It rose to its hind legs with lethal swiftness and struck. Aralorn tucked her wings and dove to the ground, avoiding the crushing blow by a margin so slim as to be nonexistent.

The wind laughed alternately in thunderous then high tones that hurt her ears. *Wind-touched,* it said. *Howlaa bait. How could you think to approach it unnoticed?*

Gerem ran into the courtyard. He dropped his knife and looked at the howlaa. It returned his look, freezing him where he stood. Ignoring Aralorn, it took a step forward, then cried out in the chilling, whining tones she'd heard before.

———

Alone, so alone without the harmonies its mate provided. She wanted to find the one who brought them to this cursed place and rip his mind away, but the caller was too strong and could not be disobeyed. This child must die first.

Aralorn launched herself from the ground, changing in midflight to her own human form. When she dropped, she landed on the howlaa, much as she had its mate—and this time she had Ambris instead of her knives.

But the howlaa dropped as soon as Aralorn touched her, rolling agilely on the cold ground, making Aralorn scramble to get off it in time without coming within reach of the creature's talons. She wasn't wholly successful.

Blood poured down her arm as she backed away rapidly, and she'd lost Ambris; the sword lay on the ground behind the howlaa. It was easily within Gerem's reach, but her brother hadn't moved since he'd come to the courtyard. The howlaa stood between Aralorn and her brother—between Aralorn and the sword.

Well, she thought wryly, at least she had its attention. Without a weapon, she wasn't going to hold its attention long—not unless it was hungry. But—there was help in the stables. She gave a long, shrill whistle as she backed up one slow step, then another.

She was grateful for every second she'd shaved off the time it took to change to icelynx form, for as soon as the howlaa realized what she was doing, it charged.

Aralorn's vision was still trying to adjust to the difference between human and cat when the howlaa was upon her. She barely managed to avoid the howlaa's swipe by running underneath it and out the other side. This put her on the right side of the howlaa to retrieve her sword if she wanted to take human form. She hesitated and decided not to risk changing again. It was just possible that the icelynx would have a better chance than a human bearing a sword. As soon as the thought occurred to her, she changed.

She shook her head and tried to ignore the lingering itches and tingles the shift had left her. Tension caused her to yowl irritably at her bulky foe—between its noise and hers, they were going to have the entire keep out here soon. Not that it would be a bad thing to have a few more people to help with the howlaa.

She and the wind demon paced back and forth, Aralorn

keeping between the howlaa and its intended prey. That the howlaa didn't just attack was a hopeful sign. She hadn't been absolutely certain that howlaas were vulnerable to the poison of an icelynx bite, but the larger animal's caution gave her hope. She was careful to avoid looking the howlaa in the eye, watching instead for the slight tensing of muscles that would presage a charge.

She had no illusions about her chances for survival. *Thank the gods,* she thought, *that Wolf can break Ridane's bond if I happen to get my stupid self killed.*

Kisrah, who must have taken a safer route through a door, entered the courtyard wearing only a pair of light-colored sleeping pants. When he saw the howlaa, he stopped.

"Aralorn. Which one are you?" he asked urgently.

The sound of his voice seemed to release Gerem from the howlaa's hold, but instead of running, he took two steps forward.

Sensing Aralorn's distraction, the howlaa chose that moment to close. It mewled as it ran, somehow a much more chilling sound than the roar of a bear or lion. Aralorn was forced to engage to keep it away from the two unarmed men.

She tried to leap on the howlaa's back again, but her weakened shoulder betrayed her, and she stumbled at the last minute, rolling frantically under the beast. She thought later that the stumble had saved her life, for the great jaws just missed closing on her back.

Instead, the howlaa caught her with its paw instead, but it hadn't had room to put much force behind the blow. It hurt, though, landing right on top of the bruises Falhart had left on her back that afternoon. The blow, relatively light as it was, sent her rolling farther under the howlaa.

While the howlaa scrambled to back away, where its size and power better offset her speed, Aralorn used her claws on the icy ground to gain her feet, then launched herself at the nearest vulnerable place she could find. Her fangs sank through the heavy coat that protected its ribs and into the howlaa's side.

The howlaa shook itself wildly, trying to dislodge her, but it only succeeded in driving her teeth in deeper. Aralorn felt the throbbing of the glands beneath her eyeteeth as they pumped poison deep into the howlaa's flesh. Unfortunately, it was too far from any major artery to kill swiftly.

The howlaa was almost as fast as the icelynx, and ten times its weight; it was only luck that had allowed her to last this long against it.

Even as the thought crossed her mind, the howlaa dropped to its side, crushing her beneath it. The weight of the howlaa kept her from breathing properly, and she grew dizzy with lack of air. A dull thud sounded in Aralorn's ears, and the howlaa's body heaved at the same time.

With a shriek of rage, the howlaa came to its feet, but it didn't move as swiftly as it had before—neither did Aralorn, for that matter. The wind demon's cry was answered with a stallion's high-pitched scream as Sheen, called by Aralorn's whistle, attacked the howlaa again, teeth bared and front feet flying. Relentless and fearless, the stallion drove the creature away from Aralorn.

On her feet again, Aralorn ran—or rather, hobbled—for her sword. She was glad that she'd been working with Halven, because she wasn't altogether certain she could have shifted back to human form in the shape she was in without the extra potency that being better centered gave her. She'd done all the damage the lynx could manage; her right arm was too weak to maintain a four-footed attack. She hadn't had time to take a close look at the damage the howlaa had done to her shoulder, and battle heat kept her from noticing the pain—but, considering the speed with which she had lost strength, she was afraid that it was worse than she had thought.

Exhaustion washed over her in waves as she completed

her fourth shift. She noticed, almost absently, that Kisrah was struggling with Gerem and that there were other people in the stableyard now. She took Ambris in her good left hand and turned back to the fight.

A normal horse wouldn't have stood a chance against such an opponent, but Sheen was war-trained and iron shod. His winter shoes were rough-bottomed like a file for better grip on ice and snow, and the damage they inflicted when propelled by a ton of battle-maddened stallion was not inconsiderable. He was canny, too, taking care to avoid the front end of the howlaa when he could.

Aralorn found the energy somewhere to run, keeping clear of Sheen's line of attack. The horse sported a dark slash down his ribs, but in the darkness she couldn't see how bad it was. Squealing, he spun and kicked with his hind legs, but missed because the howlaa collapsed abruptly. Both Aralorn and Sheen drew to a halt, watching the creature warily. Its ribs rose once, twice, then stopped.

The icelynx's poison, thought Aralorn in relief, allowing her sword tip to drop.

"It's all right, Sheen," she crooned to the snorting stallion, knowing her voice would calm him faster than anything else. "It's dead now."

THIRTEEN

———❦———

Wolf stood just inside the curtain of the bier room and wove a thin layer of darkness so that a casual observer would not see the light around the edges of the heavy fabric and realize that there was someone in the room with the Lyon. Green magic rose to his desire, if not his call, and the spell thickened with other magics to conceal his presence.

Wolf waited, but when the lingering magic dissipated and did not return, he took on human form, called his staff, and used it to light the room. He walked to the Lyon and ran his fingers lightly over the still face.

Aralorn had always laughed about how little she resembled the rest of the family, but Wolf could see the strong line of her jaw and the arrangement of her features in her father's face. Take away the coloring and the size difference, and it was easy to tell that the Lyon was her sire. His skin was cool under Wolf's touch.

"This is your last night of rest, my lord," Wolf murmured aloud. "I hope your dreaming was pleasant."

He took off his belt pouch and emptied the contents,

mostly chalks, ink, and quills, on the bier next to the Lyon. It would take some time to set the spells that would undo the Lyon's binding.

———————

Aralorn walked around the howlaa's body, murmuring a soft reassurance to her stallion. After a long moment, Sheen lost his battle stance and nuzzled her hard enough to knock her back several steps. She examined the cuts in his side and sighed with relief. They were shallow, and the bleeding was already slowing. He wouldn't be carrying a saddle for several days, but she thought if the cuts were cleaned and doctored, that would be the worst of it.

Aralorn was torn between the dictates of a lifetime of training—tend to your horse first—and the knowledge that Gerem was still in danger. She compromised by turning Sheen into a small empty pen beside the stables and promising him better care as soon as she was done.

The wind had shifted direction, bringing the scent of the dead howlaa through the stables. Horses thumped and whinnied, bringing grooms running to stand gawking over the body of the howlaa.

Aralorn avoided them all and hurried to where Kisrah had Gerem pinned, picking up Ambris along the way and sheathing her.

"He's been trying for his knife," said Kisrah, as soon as she was within conversation range. "Seeing how anxious he was to go for the howlaa, I thought the knife might be an equally bad idea."

"Can you hold him for a bit more?" she asked. "I'll go for Nevyn."

Kisrah looked relieved. "Good thought. Nevyn's a dreamwalker. He will know how to help your brother. I'll enlist one of the stableboys—who seem to be finally figuring out something is going on out here—and take him up to

Nevyn's rooms if you'll go ahead of us and tell him what to expect."

"Right," said Aralorn, not bothering to address Kisrah's assumption that Nevyn was the cure rather than the cause for Gerem's condition. Kisrah had, by saving her brother, provided her satisfactory proof that he wasn't involved any deeper than he had claimed. Gerem would be safe with Kisrah.

She left them there, pushing herself to run though her shoulder protested the pounding gait. She had to go the long way around on her own human feet; she couldn't jump back through the window in human form, and she wasn't up to any more shapeshifting for a while.

As she had hoped, Kisrah had come out the nearest side door—one that was usually kept bolted, so at least she didn't have to run halfway around the keep. She heard a few people stirring, awakened by the commotion by the stable, but she didn't see anyone as she came upon the door to her rooms.

She should stop and get Wolf for backup. She stopped before the door and put a hand on it. Wolf could handle Nevyn if Aralorn couldn't persuade him with her words.

Unfortunately, she was under no illusion about what Wolf would do to anyone who tried to hurt her. If she gave him some time to cool down, to understand—if there was something to understand—then he would act as reason dictated. But in the heat of the initial discovery . . . it was safer for everyone if she went at this alone.

She took her hand off the door and continued on.

Nevyn and Freya had rooms a floor above the hall where she'd found Gerem. Aralorn didn't bother to knock as she walked in.

The first thing she saw was Freya sleeping soundly on the bed, her peaceful features revealed by the flickering light of the fireplace.

The sound of the door opening hadn't disturbed Nevyn either: He was waiting for her in a chair on the opposite side of the fireplace from the bed. The firelight illuminated one side of his face clearly, while the other lay in shadows.

"I thought you might come," he said softly. Then, seeing her glance at her sleeping sister, he said, "Don't worry, she's sleeping until morning."

The sound of his voice sent a chill of unease coursing through her veins. Nevyn spoke Rethian with a thick Darranian accent she'd never heard him use.

"Let Gerem go, Nevyn," she said.

"You aren't beautiful," he said, as if she had never spoken at all. "What magic do you work that holds a man to you like that? Ten years, and the thought of seeing you was more important than punishing *him* for killing Geoffrey. Geoffrey, who was my teacher, my creator—giving me life and understanding when Nevyn would have seen me dead."

"Punishing Wolf?" she asked.

He nodded jerkily. Even in the dimly lit room, Aralorn could see the flush that swept up his cheeks as he abruptly leaned forward, every muscle in his body tightening. His voice, in stark contrast to his posture, was soft and slow. "How could you take up with *him*? We waited and waited for you to come home. Then Geoffrey died, and I found out you'd taken his killer as your lover."

"How did you find out?" she asked.

Nevyn took a deep breath in through his nose. "Geoffrey told me when he told me that Cain killed him. Cain is evil, don't you understand?"

He could have found out about her relationship with Cain while he was dreamwalking, she thought.

"Cain did not kill Geoffrey," Aralorn told him. "What he knows about black magic, Geoffrey taught him—as he taught you."

Nevyn shook his head. "No. Geoffrey was *good*. He helped me. It was Cain . . . in the night while Nevyn slept.

I saw—I saw it all. Night after night, he called me to perform for me and to teach me . . . I showed you it all, I gave
you dreams so that you would know what he was. What I
did." His voice dropped to a whisper. "What he forced me
to do."

"I don't remember," she said. "I only dreamed of Wolf."
But after she said it, she wondered if it was really true. The
story, Nevyn's story, had come to her so completely while
she was riding back from Ridane's temple—could she have
come up with it from some half-remembered dreams?

"You only kept dreams of *him*," said Nevyn, his voice
dark and ugly. "You're just a shapeshifting, magic-tainted
whore. I've told him and told him, but he loves you. *Loves*
you when he hates his magic, hates *me* because he can't
quit using his magic, can't give me up altogether."

He laughed slyly. "But you ruined it the first time he saw
the two of you together. It took him a long time to realize
that your wolf was Cain—but then, Nevyn was always a
little slow."

"You *are* Nevyn," she said, but he ignored her.

"He sent the howlaa then, on impulse. Then he worried
and worried until it was killed. Stupid sod forgot that he
needs Cain to free the Lyon. If the Lyon is harmed, he'll
never believe it wasn't his fault."

"You knew enough about black magic to set the spell,"
she said, changing the subject, because it didn't seem helpful to try to argue with this shade of Nevyn about Nevyn's
guilt or innocence. "Why can't you unwork it yourself?"

"If he'd succeeded in killing Cain, I could *tell* Nevyn
enough about it to work the spell—but he'd never be able
to do it. No stomach for it, I'm afraid. Kisrah might do it,
but he doesn't love the Lyon enough." He sounded both
amused and exasperated.

"Why try to kill Gerem?" asked Aralorn.

"The spell needs a human death," he said. "Gerem is
already tainted by magic, and I needed someone whom

Nevyn could see dead. I couldn't leave the choice to Cain. But I don't need Gerem anymore." As he spoke the last word, he came up out of the chair and struck with the sword that he'd held in the shadows.

She saw his intention in his face an instant before he moved, so she threw herself backward, and his blade missed.

Swords, she thought as she stumbled to catch her balance. *Plague it, why does it always have to be swords?* She dodged another slice as she pulled Ambris.

It was obvious from the first blow who the better swordsman was, and it wasn't Aralorn. He had been good when she left, and he obviously hadn't quit practicing. He might even give Wolf a run for his money. She caught the edge of his blade on Ambris and let it slide off.

Even if she'd been able to use her good arm, she wouldn't have stood a chance. Even if she'd been an excellent swordswoman, she would have had a problem: She was using Ambris. She didn't want to hurt Nevyn at all—she certainly didn't want to steal his magic. She wasn't certain that was what would happen—Nevyn wasn't trying for godhood as Geoffrey had been. But that was the trouble with ancient artifacts—no one really knew what they did.

There was a game she knew, one her uncle taught her, called *Taefil Ma Deogh*, Steal the Dragon. Strategy and skill were necessary, but it was deviousness that determined who won and who lost. The last time Aralorn stayed with her mother's people, she had beaten her uncle eight times out of ten.

Devious, she thought, parrying furiously. *Do the unexpected.*

She turned and ran—out the door, down the hall to the nearest empty room, and through the doorway. The room was dark, which suited Aralorn just fine. She slid Ambris into a tall, narrow vase, where she wouldn't be immediately obvious.

Nevyn's sprinting footsteps were almost at the door as she gathered herself together for another shapechange. She was too weak, too many changes with too little rest between.

Gasping a little, she centered herself and tried again. Pain seared her from toes to fingertips, but as his form appeared in the doorway, she slipped into the shape of a mouse. She huddled just behind the door as he came into the room, called a magelight, and looked briefly around. She waited until he left, then scampered out the door and back to his bedroom.

———

Wolf finished the last of the painstakingly drawn ink lines on the Lyon's face. When he was through, he looked over all of his work carefully, for he wouldn't get a second chance. Satisfied that all was in order, he took out his knife. He should sever the bond he shared with Aralorn before he started, but the chances were too great that she'd find him before he was done. He had to wait until the last moment.

He slid the sharp blade sideways across one wrist. Touching the tip of a fresh quill pen into the dark liquid that pooled in his wound, he began painstakingly retracing the inked lines with blood.

———

In Nevyn's room, Aralorn shifted once more to human shape, shaking and shuddering when she was done. If she survived this night, it would be days before she could do so much as light a candle with magic.

She could hear him searching for her, quick footsteps, doors opening quietly. Her heart settled; the sweat dried; and, after a few moments, the pain of overusing her magic receded except for a nagging headache.

She found a likely ambush spot, just inside his door. She was counting on him to believe she would have gone for help rather than come back to face him on her own.

He neared the door, making no attempt at stealth, and Aralorn breathed as silently as she could. He walked in confidently; his first glance fell to the bed. That was all the opening she needed.

With a war cry designed to make him start, she leapt to his back and wrapped one arm around his neck and grabbed the elbow of her opposite arm. This locked the bones of her forearms against the arteries that carried blood to his brain. The mercenaries called it a "nighty-night," and, if she could hold it for a count of fifteen, Nevyn should drop unconscious. The first five counts would be the telling ground because after that, he would get weaker fast. Surprise counted for two, then he slammed her against the edge of the door.

She held on, ignoring the pain for the moment, though she knew that she was going to have a vertical bruise to go with the horizontal one Falhart had given her with his quarterstaff. The second time Nevyn slammed her back, it hurt worse because he managed to catch her howlaa-wounded shoulder on the door, so she bit his ear to distract him. He tried to twist away and stumbled, which would have been all right except that it gave him an idea that she would rather he not have thought of.

He threw himself backward on the floor, and the air left her lungs with a faint hint of protest.

Twelve, she thought.

He managed to bring his shoulders up and smash her head onto the floor.

Fourteen, plague it, go to sleep.

He repeated his previous move with such success that Aralorn was starting to feel woozy herself. Luckily, it was the last one he made.

Lying under him, she waited to catch her breath before sending Nevyn into a more lasting sleep with the dregs of her magic. She'd never have been able to do it with him awake.

Should have just hit him over the head, she thought when she was finished, and touched her bottom lip gently with her tongue to inspect that damage he'd wrought with the back of his head, *so there's a chance I'd have killed him. I could have lived with that.*

"Aralorn?"

Nevyn's body blocked her view of the door, but she knew Kisrah's voice.

"I suspect she's under him somewhere, but she's small enough that it might take us a while to find her," observed Gerem a bit shakily.

"Ha-ha," she said coldly. "Never tease a person who knows enough about you for blackmail."

"Never get grumpy with someone you need to help drag bodies off you," replied her brother, sounding somewhat calmer after ascertaining that Nevyn was still alive. "What have you done to Nevyn—and why hasn't Freya woken up?"

"Sleep spell—not mine. I did Nevyn, though," she replied, then allowed a touch of whine to her voice. "Want to lever Nevyn off before we have a long conversation? I need to find Wolf and see if he can get a message to my uncle and get him here before Nevyn wakes up. It might also be nice to breathe."

"Aralorn?" asked a third voice, right on cue. "You were looking for me?"

Kisrah and Gerem between them managed to drag poor Nevyn off to the side.

"I should have known that you couldn't resist sticking around when things were about to get interesting, Uncle," said Aralorn, sitting up gingerly: Her head hurt, her back hurt, and her shoulder felt as if she'd been clawed by a howlaa and beaten against the door a couple of times.

"Actually," he replied, "I was looking for you. I've talked to a few of our elders, and they say that there is no way a dead dreamwalker could do the kinds of things you think Geoffrey ae'Magi has done. I stopped by your room first, but no one was there, so I came here instead."

"It wasn't Geoffrey; it was Nevyn," said Aralorn.

"Nevyn?" asked Gerem, sounding hostile. "Nevyn would never hurt Father."

"Who are you?" asked Kisrah.

"Kisrah, meet my uncle Halven—he's a shapeshifter who's been trying to help. Uncle Halven, this is Kisrah, the current ae'Magi." Introductions done, she continued without taking a breath. "Nevyn has a problem," she said, then stopped. There had to be a way to explain without sounding like a madwoman. Her weak sleep spell wasn't going to keep him under much longer. She had to make them believe her before he awoke.

"Nevyn is ill," said Kisrah, kneeling beside Aralorn. He patted the sleeping man's shoulder gently. "If I'd thought that he would have harmed anyone but himself, I never would have sent him here. He was half-mad when we took him from Santik. I'd hoped he'd settle down with me, but he was too damaged. I thought that this was the perfect place for him; he's seemed happy since he came here."

"Part of him is," said Aralorn. "But there is a part of him that is not."

"There is an unusual separation of his spirit," observed her uncle.

"I think that the part of him that dreamwalks has separated itself almost completely," Aralorn said. "He was talking about himself as if he were two different people."

"I've heard that green mages are great healers," said Kisrah diffidently. "Is there anything that you can do to help him?"

He'd taken the right tone; Halven preened before the respect in the Archmage's voice. "Since I can see the damage, I might be able to do something," he said. Graciously, he half bowed to Aralorn. "I think you're right. It's the dreamwalking part of him that has split off from his spirit.

What is broken can be mended together again—as long as the cause for the break is gone."

"Santik is dead, and so is Geoffrey," said Aralorn in answer.

She got to her feet and backed away so that Halven and Kisrah could have free access to Nevyn.

It was over, she thought. Nevyn had been certain that Wolf could free her father. But as his words came back to her, the relief she'd been feeling stopped.

"Human death," she said.

The two mages were involved in their discussion over Nevyn, but Gerem said, "What?"

Halven had said Wolf hadn't been in her room.

"Gods," she said. And she'd been so grateful there were no more secrets between them while she was fighting the howlaa because after her probable demise, Wolf would know exactly how she had felt about him. She could see now how careful he'd been to clear up any misunderstanding that might lie between them, any regrets or doubts that she might have.

If Nevyn knew that it would take a human sacrifice, Wolf did as well.

"Aralorn?" Gerem touched her arm. "What is it?"

Wolf knew, and, like Nevyn, he'd chosen a sacrifice. If Nevyn had realized just who Wolf had picked, he wouldn't have tried to kill Gerem.

"He told me three times," she said softly. "He said he loved me, three times."

"Aralorn?" asked Gerem again.

She didn't bother to answer but bolted out the door and sprinted down the hall. She took the stairs in leaping strides, ignoring the danger of falling, ignoring the pain in her shoulder, which throbbed in time with her steps.

The great hall was dark, and there was no sign of light behind the alcove curtain, but Aralorn felt the richness of magic at work.

She threw back the curtains and stepped into the darkness, only then feeling the wrongness of the power. It slid across her skin like thick, filthy oil. A moment later, the full effect of the tainted magic hit her as strongly as any fear spell she'd ever felt, leaving her unable to take a step forward for the sheer terror of what lay ahead.

It didn't feel like a fear spell, though, so she had no antidote for its effects. Perhaps it was a side effect of the magic Wolf was working. As she hesitated in the darkness, fighting the urge to turn tail and run, she could feel the surge of power, and the corruption of the magic grew stronger.

"Deathsgate and back, Wolf," she said, managing to put one foot in front of the other once, then again, until she stood on the far side of the darkness. "I warned you."

He stood behind her father, who was covered with markings. Wolf's scarred face was almost as masklike as the silver one. He touched the side of the Lyon's face with the first finger of each hand as his macabre voice chanted words in a language she'd never heard. His staff, balanced upright on the claws on its base, glowed radiantly from just behind his right shoulder. Lights and shadows fought for his face so it was unevenly illuminated.

The scent of blood and herbs was neither unpleasant nor pleasurable. It was much hotter than it should have been in a stone room in the winter, and the heat and strong scent combined to make her almost dizzy.

He hadn't noticed her come in, but she wasn't surprised. The worst thing a human wizard can do is lose control of a spell, so most of them had incredible powers of concentration—she would have expected no less of Wolf.

Relief swept her briefly at the sight of him still standing, breaking the hold of terror. Her thoughts clear for the first time since she entered the room, she saw the runes that covered the bier and the floor around it. Runes in herbs and chalk and char, but too many of them were drawn in blood.

She looked up swiftly to note how pale his skin was

where it was not scarred, and she knew where the blood had come from. His voice rose hoarsely, and the magic surged as he called; it was so strong, her skin tingled, and so foul, she wanted to vomit.

Wolf pulled his hands away from her father, and she saw the dark wound on his wrist. The slowness of the bleeding told its own story, though Wolf should have been unconscious before he lost so much blood. Or dead.

"*No!* Plague take you, Wolf!" she said, and ran, ignoring the runes she destroyed on her way, ignoring the knowledge that by breaking his concentration, she could destroy herself and her father as well.

She broke his focus, and he looked up. For a moment, she had a clear view of his scarred face, then the light from his staff went out. She caught him as he fell—as they fell—cushioning his head against her. She grabbed his sticky wrist and wrapped her hand around it, sealing the wound with her own flesh, but his skin was colder than it should be in a room this warm.

In her heightened state, she could feel the wild magic he'd called reach for him, could feel his life fading. She had no time for panic; instead, she drew in a deep, calming breath and centered herself . . .

———————

Kisrah watched Gerem follow Aralorn out of the room. He'd overheard enough to have a pretty good idea of where they were going—especially since, once he looked for it, he could feel magic taking shape somewhere in the keep.

Kisrah wasn't certain that it wouldn't be better if Wolf didn't survive. No matter that Kisrah was virtually convinced that Aralorn was right to claim that Geoffrey was a villain. It did not take away the fact that Wolf knew black magic and carried its taint. By Wolf's own admission, the Master Spells had not allowed Geoffrey to control him—and even if they had, the Master Spells were gone.

If he followed her, he would be forced to choose—to help Wolf or to kill him; so he chose to stay with Nevyn while Aralorn's uncle tried to heal him.

"This damage had been mostly scarred over once," the shapechanger said, finally looking up from Nevyn. "And only recently torn asunder. Violently."

"Can you heal him?"

But Halven was looking around the room. "Where is Aralorn?"

"Rescuing Wolf," Kisrah said.

Halven gave him a sharp glance but turned back to Nevyn. "I can mend the surface," he said. "That ought to give Nevyn control over his dreamwalking self—probably return him to where he was before this most recent damage. True healing of such an old hurt will take a very long time, but it can be done."

"If he'll let you try," said Kisrah. "He's stubborn, and his life has not made him fond of magic."

Halven's eyes grew cold. "After the damage he's done here, he'll accept my healing, or I'll kill him myself. Henrick is a friend of mine."

"Nevyn is my friend," said Kisrah in warning.

The shapeshifter's mouth turned up, but his eyes did not warm. "Let me do what I can for him now, then. You go help Aralorn—there's something going on in the bier room. Can you feel it?"

Caught, Kisrah hesitated. "Yes."

"Go," said Halven. "This will be easier without you here."

But not easier for me, Kisrah thought. He would have to choose.

Halven waited for the door to swing shut behind the Archmage before turning again to his patient. The quiet was helpful but not necessary. Once he knew what had to be done, it was not difficult: A spirit was not meant to be divided. All he had to do was provide the magic to assist the weaving.

It did not take long before it was done as well as magic could make it. Only time would completely heal the rift. When he was finished, he waved his hand, and Nevyn's eyelids fluttered.

Nevyn opened his eyes.

"Welcome back, sir," said Halven, not unkindly. "I think we may have much to discuss."

Nevyn rolled to a sitting position and buried his face in both hands. "It was me," he said. "It was me all along."

———

Aralorn held Wolf's wrist tightly in one hand, sealing the wound, though she feared it was too late. With her free hand, she touched the artery in his neck. For a horrible moment, she thought that he had no pulse, but then she felt the faint beat beneath her fingertips.

He'd been holding to consciousness with magic, she thought. When she'd distracted him, he'd lost control of the power sustaining him and fainted.

They should both be dead. She'd broken the cardinal rule of magic and interrupted Wolf. His spell should have turned this corner of Lambshold into a melted slag like the tower in the ae'Magi's castle.

It had not.

She was so weary. If she'd been a human mage, she would have had to watch Wolf die. But there was so much power in the room that the warmth of it strengthened her.

Most of the power was in the spell that awaited some missing component to act: Wolf's death. Aralorn could feel the magic coerced and caged into some shape of Wolf's devising, but it was human born, and she could not touch it. But flickering around the spell like a candle flame in the wind was other power, a latticework of green magic that held the spell at bay: Wolf's magic protecting her still.

Someone came into the room, and a last vestige of caution made her look up for an instant and see Gerem stagger through the spell of darkness and silence that covered the curtain to the bier room. In that moment of inattention, when she strayed from her center, Ridane's bond stretched tight.

Aralorn cried out at the pain and drove her fingers into Wolf's shoulder and wounded wrist.

"Don't you leave me, you bastard." She gritted out the words, and called his green magic to her.

Even though she was careful to leave enough magic to hold Wolf's spell, power flooded her, filling her veins with icy fire and making it difficult to breathe. She couldn't tell where the pain was coming from now, from the too-great magic that had answered her call or from the death goddess's binding that stretched taut and thin between them.

She had no idea what she was doing.

She bowed down and pressed her forehead against his too-cool flesh. She fed him magic at first, but it flowed through him and back into her without leaving any virtue behind. It was his magic, and he'd called it to save her, not himself.

She growled deep in her throat. "Not yet," she said. "I'll not lose you to your own stubbornness."

She took the magic and twisted it until it was attached to her, then thrust it back into him like a needle pulling her life force through him.

"Wolf," she murmured, touching his unresponsive lips, "don't you die on me."

She could feel that his pulse had steadied with the force she'd added, but she could feel, too, that it wasn't going to be enough. Remembering how she had touched her father's life, she began singing to aid her work. She hadn't consciously chosen the song, and was almost amused when she realized it was a rather lewd drinking song—so be it. If anyone knew how to fight off the cold thought of death, it was a bunch of drunken mercenaries.

The music soon soothed her into a trance that allowed her to seep into the pattern of Wolf's death. With more need than skill, she followed Wolf's spirit where it lingered, held by thin traces of life.

Recklessly, she threw energy to his fading spirit, to anchor him to his body, using his own magic to do it. She found the bond the death goddess had drawn between them and gripped it like a rope to pull him to her, only to find it gripped in return as Wolf, free from reason and memory, helped her at last.

She came out of her trance slowly, gradually becoming aware of Wolf's head in her lap, the unusual warmth of the stones beneath her, and the wild, surging magic that filled the room.

"Crap," she said. She'd called upon too much magic and released the power that had been bound in Wolf's spell.

She swung her gaze around to look for the reason that the walls were still standing. Kisrah stood before the darkness that was the entrance to the room. His feet were braced and his arms held wide. Gerem stood just behind him, gripping his shoulder with one hand in a position that even Aralorn recognized as "feeding."

"Wolf?" she said, shaking him with her good arm. "Wolf, wake up."

"Good idea," muttered Kisrah, "We're not going to be able to hold this back much longer."

Aralorn took the hint and quit being so gentle. *"Wolf,"* she barked with force enough to please a drill sergeant. "You've got to wake up, love. We need you."

He stirred this time and opened his eyes, frowning at her in puzzlement. He started to speak, and his eyes widened as his senses told him what was going on.

"Gods," he growled, sitting up a little too abruptly.

She caught him before he could fall back and held him while he closed his eyes against the dizzying weakness of extreme blood loss. Since his weight hit her bad arm with a certain amount of force, she was feeling a bit dizzy herself.

"What did you think you were doing?" he rasped. "You know better than to interrupt a spell in progress."

"Hmm," she agreed. "Deathsgate and back, remember? You shouldn't have tried this."

"Excuse me," interrupted Kisrah politely, though his voice sounded a little strained. "Not to break in on a personal moment or anything, but do you suppose you could give me a little advice, Wolf?"

"Hmm," said Wolf. "I suppose 'run' won't work?"

Kisrah laughed, which was a mistake.

Power lit the room with a faint red haze, and the temperature went from warm to hot in an instant. Aralorn felt the surge in magic so strong that it hurt. The smell of scorching cloth filled the room, and the stones gave off an odd grumbling noise. Sweat gathered on Kisrah's face, and Gerem was looking almost as drained as Kisrah.

"Your magic held it in check while you were unconscious," said Aralorn urgently. "Green magic, Wolf. Can you call it again?"

In answer, green magic slid over her skin in a caress, then spilled over the imminent spell like oil over boiling water. Gently, it worked its way between the spell and Kisrah's magic.

Wolf vibrated in her arms, shaking with the control that it took not to fight for domination over the green magic.

"What in the name of . . ." murmured Kisrah, relaxing his stance. "I've never seen anything like this."

"Green magic," replied Wolf in a strained voice. "It scares me, too. But I *think* it will work."

" 'Think'?"

Wolf's scarred lips writhed into a semblance of a smile. "Would you rather I said 'hope'?"

As Wolf took up the reins of the magic, Kisrah relaxed and ran his hands through his hair, leaving it an untidy mess. Actually, thought Aralorn with exhaustion-born whimsy, he looked quite different from his usual self, his lemon-colored sleeping trousers setting off pale skin stretched over a swordsman's muscles, his feet bare.

"Now what do we do?" he asked.

"Well," said Wolf, "at this stage the spell can't be banished, for it has already been given a taste of that which was promised. Can you feel the hunger? So what we do is bring it into completion." He turned to Aralorn, who was already shaking her head, but she was too weak to do anything more. "I love you, dear heart. If you love me as well, you'll allow me this. Someone must die tonight—I won't allow my father to kill again and not do something about it."

He held her gaze with his own until tears slid down her cheeks.

"Ridane said someone had to die," said Aralorn. "This is what she meant, wasn't it? The nature of the spell laid on Father is such that either he dies, or someone else does. I didn't bring you back for this, Wolf."

His eyes warmed, and he touched her face. "If you hadn't brought me back, my love, Ridane's bond would have taken you with me. I should have severed it before I started the spell—I waited too late. I didn't want to lose you."

He dropped his hands, leaving her cold and alone. "This was laid upon your father because of me; should he die for my sins?"

"Not your sins," returned Aralorn heatedly. "Your father's sins."

"No," said Nevyn from the doorway. "My sins."

The darkness that had blocked the door was gone, banished by Nevyn, or perhaps her uncle, who stood behind him. Nevyn's face was grim and pale.

"I have allowed myself to be used," he said. "I allowed

Geoffrey to twist my thoughts until I have become what my father thought I was."

He stepped forward until he stood before Wolf, facing him. "I thought that it was you who was corrupt, who needed destroying—instead, I find that you are willing to sacrifice yourself for a man you barely know. Evil corrupted me; it has tempered you."

He turned to Aralorn and crouched in front of her.

"Sister," he said softly, so quietly that she knew that no one else in the room heard exactly what he said. "Story-Spinner, weave a good one for Freya when she wakes— that she will honor the father of the child she carries, for its sake."

Exhaustion made Aralorn's thoughts slow. She was preoccupied with keeping Wolf alive, and it made her slow.

When Nevyn surged to his feet, and told Wolf, "Use this," she finally caught on. "Nevyn, *wait*." But it was already too late.

Nevyn called upon his magic and was engulfed in flames so hot that his flesh melted from his bones like water.

"Wolf?" said Aralorn in a voice she hardly recognized, so thickened was it from grief. But there was a real possibility, given Wolf's reluctance to use black magic, that he would refuse Nevyn's sacrifice.

But it was Kisrah who said, "Don't let him die in vain, Wolf."

———

Wolf hesitated, torn between the horror of using yet another person's death to fuel his magic and the desires of the man who had given his life for his convictions.

"Please," whispered Aralorn, tears of grief sliding down her face.

He dropped his knife and lifted his arms, drawing the power of Nevyn's death to him. He waited for the filth to settle on his soul, but the death magic rested quietly within his grasp, as if a dead man's blessing had the ability to wipe clean the foul work to which Wolf had been put.

The respite was brief, for as he willed it, the hold that had kept the spell in abeyance began to fade slowly, allowing Wolf to take control of one part before releasing another. No benediction could wash away the evil of the black art that comprised the spell, and Wolf shook under the force of it even as he threaded death magic through it in completion.

The spell pulsed wildly for a moment before concentrating upon the still form of the Lyon, then, as swiftly as the flight of a hawk, it was gone, leaving the room reeking with the stench of evil.

Wolf dropped to his knees.

Aralorn slid across the floor to the small mess of charred bones, where Kisrah and Gerem already knelt.

"What is happening? Who is that man?"

Aralorn looked up to see Irrenna standing in the entranceway, clad only in her nightrobes. The lady's gaze traveled around the room, pausing at the silent form of her husband before halting on Aralorn's tear-streaked face.

"There is a dead howlaa by the stables," Irrenna said. "We were trying to find out how it got there when there was a terrible noise, as if the stones of the keep were shifting."

"Oh, Mother," croaked Aralorn, as Correy and Falhart, who must have been drawn by the same sound, came into the room as well. "Irrenna," she tried again. "Nevyn saved Father, but he died in the doing of it."

"The Lyon's waking now," said Kisrah.

Gerem jumped up and ran to the bier. Kisrah lingered a moment. He murmured something that Aralorn couldn't hear and conjured a white rose, which he set just inside the charred area. Then he, too, left the dead for the living.

Irrenna froze for an instant before she, Falhart, and Correy all ran to the Lyon's side.

Bound by weakness and inclination, Aralorn stayed by

Nevyn's remains. She touched the blackened skull gently, as if a stronger touch would have hurt him. "Rest in peace, Nevyn."

A cold nose touched her hand, and she turned to Wolf, who wore his wolf form once more.

His golden eyes were dim with sorrow, and Aralorn drew him close, pressing her face into Wolf's shoulder. "I know," she said. "I know."

FINIS

Far to the east, the Dreamer stirred. It had been for naught—all the manipulation, all the work, and its own tool had betrayed it.

It had known the dreamwalker was not stable, but it had not expected him to choose to die so that the Lyon would live. By that choice, he had rendered the magic useless for the Dreamer to feed upon. Cain's death would not have been useless, for the Archmage's son had been used by the Dreamer before; not even the purity of Cain's willing self-sacrifice would have stopped the Dreamer from feeding.

It would sleep now, but its sleep would not be as long, or as deep. It would not have to wait another millennium for a corrupt Archmage to awaken it. When Geoffrey ae'Magi had died, it had seen to it that the Master Spells would not be used again.

The Dreamer stirred, then settled beneath the weight of the ancient bindings. It would wait.

Aralorn examined the healing cut on Sheen's side. It looked as if it had been healing a week rather than three days; she was going to have to talk to the stablemaster and find out what he used for ointment.

She wouldn't need it for her shoulder. Halven had taken care of the cuts left by the howlaa's claws, though it still ached a bit when she overworked her arm. She heard someone enter the stables and stuck her head over Sheen's door.

"You're leaving today." Her father moved a little stiffly, but otherwise showed little sign of any aftereffects of the spell.

Aralorn smiled. "Yes, sir, as soon as Kisrah comes back with my wolf. They went hunting with the boys—I include Falhart in that category."

He reached up and rubbed Sheen's forehead. "I understand you've been making quite a reputation for yourself."

"Me or the horse?"

He grinned. "You."

She raised her eyebrows, and said, "Let's just say that having a shapeshifter for a spy, whether they know it or not, hasn't hurt Sianim any."

"I've missed you," he said softly.

"I've missed you, too. I'll be back, though. If you let me know, I'll come after Freya's babe is born."

The Lyon's hand stilled on the horse's forehead. "I wish Nevyn would be alive to see it. They waited so long for this child."

She nodded. She'd told him the truth about Nevyn, knowing that he would not judge his son-in-law for it.

Freya deserved the truth as well, if she wanted it. Aralorn had left that for her father to decide. Freya hadn't spoken to her since she'd awakened to the news that her husband was dead. Maybe she already knew at least part of what had been going on.

"This friend of yours, the one Nevyn was after when he set the spell on me. He is safe?"

"I think so," she said. "With Geoffrey well and truly dead, no one but Kisrah and the family know that I was ever involved with him."

Neither Gerem nor Kisrah had challenged the story she'd told Irrenna and repeated often since—that the last ae'Magi hadn't been the man he'd appeared to be. He'd made an attempt on King Myr's life, and, in response, she and his son had moved against him. They had thought he died, a victim of the Uriah—but he was a dreamwalker, and survived long enough to set up his son's death. It had been Nevyn, she explained, who had figured out how to break the spell, but in doing so, had brought about his own death. Nevyn deserved to be a hero—and Geoffrey, who had hurt Nevyn so badly, deserved whatever blame fell to him.

With Kisrah's corroborating testimony regarding the character of the previous ae'Magi, almost everyone seemed to accept the tale. Aralorn suspected that Kisrah had done something to the hold the previous ae'Magi's spells had continued to have—because no one challenged him or seemed unnaturally sure of Geoffrey's goodness.

The Lyon rubbed his beard. "I knew Geoffrey, but I met Cain a time or two as well—when he was younger than Gerem by a few years."

"I didn't know that."

"Up until that point, I'd been favorably impressed by the ae'Magi. I was curious about his son though, mostly because of the stories that were circulating about him even then."

"What did you think of him when you met him?" she asked, curious.

"He . . . Something that Correy said leads me to believe that the relationship that you have with Cain is somewhat more than friendship."

She smiled slowly. "You might say that, yes."

"Then bring him with you the next time you come down—tell him he doesn't have to come and go mysteriously as he did this time. Irrenna and I would be pleased to have him as a guest."

Her smile widened, and tears threatened as she slipped out the door, so she could give him a hug. "I love you, Da."

No matter what her father said, it still wasn't safe for too many people to know where the Archmage's infamous son was, but she'd tell Wolf what her father said. It would matter to him.

He bent down, and whispered, "Especially if one of you teaches my cook how to make those little cakes that you had at the king's coronation. I know you were playing cook, so the nasty-looking guard must have been Cain."

Her mouth dropped open, and she took two steps back and kinked her neck so she could look him in the eyes. "How did you know?"

He shook his head. "I'm not really certain, to tell you the truth. But I've always been able to tell who you are, no matter what shape you wear."

———

"You didn't tell him we were married," Wolf said with neutrality he didn't feel as he paced by Sheen's side. Had she been ashamed of him?

She shook her head. "He'd have been hurt that he missed the ceremony," she told him. "We can do it up properly later, when it won't be tied up with Nevyn's deal, don't you think? You have his approval, though, if that helps."

That bewildered him. How could he approve of Cain, the ae'Magi's despised son, for his daughter? "He doesn't know me."

"He's met you," she told him. "He knows what you did here and why. That was apparently enough for him—oh, and he really wants to know how you made those little cakes you fixed for Myr's coronation."

Wolf stopped. Sheen halted beside him, and Aralorn waited with unusual (for her) patience for him to speak. He didn't know what to say.

"You married me so I would not seek death for fear of causing yours," he said.

She got that mysterious smile that usually meant she knew more than she should about something, but all she said was "Yes."

He didn't know why that bothered him so much. And if he couldn't explain it to himself, how could he explain it to her?

She took pity on him eventually.

"Wolf," she said. "Married is wonderful, married is lovely. But I loved you before that, and you were mine before that. Only you for me—only me for you. That's how it was before our marriage." The smile fell away and left her pale and determined. "That's how it was when I found you in that pit trap all those years ago—I knew as soon as I first saw your eyes. But then, I've known all my life what love is. It took you, who had nothing to compare it to, rather longer to figure it out, to understand what is between us. But even when you did not understand or recognize it— it was always love."

Sheen sighed and shifted his weight, but Aralorn didn't turn her attention from Wolf as he took her words and warmed himself on them.

"Yes," he said, and started out for the inn where they would spend the night. "Yes. That is how it is."

She rode beside him, and he didn't need to turn his head to know that she was there.

The revised and updated debut novel from the
#1 *New York Times* bestselling author
of the Mercy Thompson series

PATRICIA BRIGGS

MASQUES

After an upbringing of proper behavior and oppressive
expectations, Aralorn fled her noble birthright for a life
of adventure as a mercenary spy. Her latest mission
involves gathering intelligence on the increasingly powerful sorcerer Geoffrey ae'Magi. But in a war against a
foe armed with the power of illusion, how will she know
who the true enemy is—or where he will strike next?

penguin.com

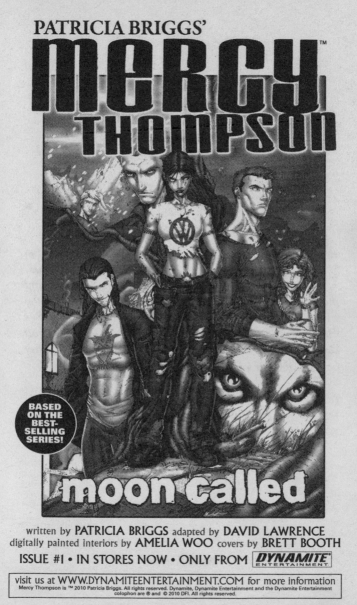